PUFFIN BOOKS

PERCY JACKSON AND THE LIGHTNING THIEF

Praise for the Percy Jackson series:

'A fantastic blend of myth and modern. Rick Riordan takes the reader back to the stories we love, then shakes the cobwebs out of them' – Eoin Colfer, author of *Artemis Fowl*

'It's *Buffy* meets *Artemis Fowl*. Thumbs up' – *Sunday Times*

'This is the stuff of legends' – *Guardian*

'Cool, mad and very funny!' – *Flipside*

'Riordan delivers puns, jokes and subtle wit, alongside a gripping storyline' – *Sunday Telegraph*

'Sure to become a classic' – *Sunday Express*

'Unputdownable' – *Irish Times*

PERCY JACKSON

AND THE
LIGHTNING
THIEF

RICK
RIORDAN

PUFFIN

To Haley, who heard the story first

PUFFIN BOOKS

UK | USA | Canada | Ireland | Australia
India | New Zealand | South Africa

Puffin Books is part of the Penguin Random House group of companies
whose addresses can be found at global.penguinrandomhouse.com.

puffinbooks.com

First published in the USA by Hyperion Books for Children 2005
Published in Great Britain by Puffin Books 2005
This edition published 2013

002

Percy Jackson and the Sea of Monsters: first published in the USA by
Hyperion Books for Children and in Great Britain by Puffin Books 2006

Text copyright © Rick Riordan, 2005, 2006

The moral right of the author has been asserted
All rights reserved

Set in Centaur MT
Printed in Great Britain by Clays Ltd, St Ives plc

A CIP catalogue record for this book is available from the British Library

ISBN: 978-0-141-34680-9

www.greenpenguin.co.uk

ACKNOWLEDGEMENTS

Without the assistance of numerous valiant helpers, I would have been slain by monsters many times over as I endeavoured to bring this story to print. Thanks to my elder son, Haley Michael, who heard the story first; my younger son, Patrick John, who at the age of six is the levelheaded one in the family; and my wife, Becky, who puts up with my many long hours at Camp Half-Blood. Thanks also to my cadre of middle-school beta-testers: Travis Stoll, clever and quick as Hermes; C. C. Kellogg, beloved as Athena; Allison Bauer, clear-eyed as Artemis the Huntress; and Mrs Margaret Floyd, the wise and kindly seer of middle-school English. My appreciation also to Professor Egbert J. Bakker, classicist extraordinaire; Nancy Gallt, agent *summa cum laude*; Jonathan Burnham, Jennifer Besser, and Sarah Hughes for believing in Percy.

CONTENTS

I I ACCIDENTALLY VAPORIZE MY PRE-ALGEBRA TEACHER

Look, I didn't want to be a half-blood.

If you're reading this because you think you might be one, my advice is: close this book right now. Believe whatever lie your mom or dad told you about your birth, and try to lead a normal life.

Being a half-blood is dangerous. It's scary. Most of the time, it gets you killed in painful, nasty ways.

If you're a normal kid, reading this because you think it's fiction, great. Read on. I envy you for being able to believe that none of this ever happened.

But if you recognize yourself in these pages – if you feel something stirring inside – stop reading immediately. You might be one of us. And once you know that, it's only a matter of time before *they* sense it too, and they'll come for you.

Don't say I didn't warn you.

My name is Percy Jackson.

I'm twelve years old. Until a few months ago, I was a boarding student at Yancy Academy, a private school for troubled kids in upstate New York.

Am I a troubled kid?

Yeah. You could say that.

I could start at any point in my short miserable life to prove it, but things really started going bad last May, when our sixth-grade class took a field trip to Manhattan — twenty-eight mental-case kids and two teachers on a yellow school bus, heading to the Metropolitan Museum of Art to look at ancient Greek and Roman stuff.

I know — it sounds like torture. Most Yancy field trips were.

But Mr Brunner, our Latin teacher, was leading this trip, so I had hopes.

Mr Brunner was this middle-aged guy in a motorized wheelchair. He had thinning hair and a scruffy beard and a frayed tweed jacket, which always smelled like coffee. You wouldn't think he'd be cool, but he told stories and jokes and let us play games in class. He also had this awesome collection of Roman armour and weapons, so he was the only teacher whose class didn't put me to sleep.

I hoped the trip would be okay. At least, I hoped that for once I wouldn't get in trouble.

Boy, was I wrong.

See, bad things happen to me on field trips. Like at my fifth-grade school, when we went to the Saratoga battlefield, I had this accident with a Revolutionary War cannon. I wasn't aiming for the school bus, but of course I got expelled anyway. And before that, at my fourth-grade school, when we took a behind-the-scenes tour of the Marine World shark pool, I sort of hit the wrong lever on the catwalk and our class took an unplanned swim. And the time before that . . . Well, you get the idea.

This trip, I was determined to be good.

All the way into the city, I put up with Nancy Bobofit, the freckly red-headed kleptomaniac girl, hitting my best friend, Grover, in the back of the head with chunks of peanut butter-and-ketchup sandwich.

Grover was an easy target. He was scrawny. He cried when he got frustrated. He must've been held back several grades, because he was the only sixth grader with acne and the start of a wispy beard on his chin. On top of all that, he was crippled. He had a note excusing him from PE for the rest of his life because he had some kind of muscular disease in his legs. He walked funny, like every step hurt him, but don't let that fool you. You should've seen him run when it was enchilada day in the cafeteria.

Anyway, Nancy Bobofit was throwing wads of sandwich that stuck in his curly brown hair, and she knew I couldn't do anything back to her because I was already on probation. The headmaster had threatened me with death-by-in-school-suspension if anything bad, embarrassing, or even mildly entertaining happened on this trip.

'I'm going to kill her,' I mumbled.

Grover tried to calm me down. 'It's okay. I like peanut butter.'

He dodged another piece of Nancy's lunch.

'That's it.' I started to get up, but Grover pulled me back to my seat.

'You're already on probation,' he reminded me. 'You know who'll get blamed if anything happens.'

Looking back on it, I wish I'd decked Nancy Bobofit

right then and there. In-school suspension would've been nothing compared to the mess I was about to get myself into.

Mr Brunner led the museum tour.

He rode up front in his wheelchair, guiding us through the big echoey galleries, past marble statues and glass cases full of really old black-and-orange pottery.

It blew my mind that this stuff had survived for two thousand, three thousand years.

He gathered us around a four-metre-tall stone column with a big sphinx on the top, and started telling us how it was a grave marker, a *stele*, for a girl about our age. He told us about the carvings on the sides. I was trying to listen to what he had to say, because it was kind of interesting, but everybody around me was talking, and every time I told them to shut up, the other teacher chaperone, Mrs Dodds, would give me the evil eye.

Mrs Dodds was this little maths teacher from Georgia who always wore a black leather jacket, even though she was fifty years old. She looked mean enough to ride a Harley right into your locker. She had come to Yancy halfway through the year, when our last maths teacher had a nervous breakdown.

From her first day, Mrs Dodds loved Nancy Bobofit and figured I was devil spawn. She would point her crooked finger at me and say, 'Now, honey,' real sweet, and I knew I was going to get after-school detention for a month.

One time, after she'd made me erase answers out of old maths workbooks until midnight, I told Grover I didn't think Mrs Dodds was human. He looked at me real serious and said, 'You're absolutely right.'

Mr Brunner kept talking about Greek funeral art.

Finally, Nancy Bobofit snickered something about the naked guy on the *stele*, and I turned around and said, 'Will you *shut up?*'

It came out louder than I meant it to.

The whole group laughed. Mr Brunner stopped his story.

'Mr Jackson,' he said, 'did you have a comment?'

My face was totally red. I said, 'No, sir.'

Mr Brunner pointed to one of the pictures on the *stele*. 'Perhaps you'll tell us what this picture represents?'

I looked at the carving, and felt a flush of relief, because I actually recognized it. 'That's Kronos eating his kids, right?'

'Yes,' Mr Brunner said, obviously not satisfied. 'And he did this because . . .'

'Well . . .' I racked my brain to remember. 'Kronos was the king god, and —'

'God?' Mr Brunner asked.

'Titan,' I corrected myself. 'And . . . he didn't trust his kids, who were the gods. So, um, Kronos ate them, right? But his wife hid baby Zeus, and gave Kronos a rock to eat instead. And later, when Zeus grew up, he tricked his dad, Kronos, into barfing up his brothers and sisters —'

'Eeew!' said one of the girls behind me.

'— and so there was this big fight between the gods and the Titans,' I continued, 'and the gods won.'

Some snickers from the group.

Behind me, Nancy Bobofit mumbled to a friend, 'Like we're going to use this in real life. Like it's going to say on our job applications, "Please explain why Kronos ate his kids".'

'And why, Mr Jackson,' Brunner said, 'to paraphrase Miss Bobofit's excellent question, does this matter in real life?'

'Busted,' Grover muttered.

'Shut up,' Nancy hissed, her face even brighter red than her hair.

At least Nancy got in trouble, too. Mr Brunner was the only one who ever caught her saying anything wrong. He had radar ears.

I thought about his question, and shrugged. 'I don't know, sir.'

'I see.' Mr Brunner looked disappointed. 'Well, half credit, Mr Jackson. Zeus did indeed feed Kronos a mixture of mustard and wine, which made him disgorge his other five children, who, of course, being immortal gods, had been living and growing up completely undigested in the Titan's stomach. The gods defeated their father, sliced him to pieces with his own scythe, and scattered his remains in Tartarus, the darkest part of the Underworld. On that happy note, it's time for lunch. Mrs Dodds, would you lead us back outside?'

The class drifted off, the girls holding their stomachs, the guys pushing each other around and acting like doofuses.

Grover and I were about to follow when Mr Brunner said, 'Mr Jackson.'

I knew that was coming.

I told Grover to keep going. Then I turned towards Mr Brunner. 'Sir?'

Mr Brunner had this look that wouldn't let you go – intense brown eyes that could've been a thousand years old and had seen everything.

'You must learn the answer to my question,' Mr Brunner told me.

'About the Titans?'

'About real life. And how your studies apply to it.'

'Oh.'

'What you learn from me,' he said, 'is vitally important. I expect you to treat it as such. I will accept only the best from you, Percy Jackson.'

I wanted to get angry, this guy pushed me so hard.

I mean, sure, it was kind of cool on tournament days, when he dressed up in a suit of Roman armour and shouted: 'What ho!' and challenged us, sword-point against chalk, to run to the board and name every Greek and Roman person who had ever lived, and their mother, and what god they worshipped. But Mr Brunner expected me to be as good as everybody else, despite the fact I have dyslexia and attention deficit disorder and I had never made above a C- in my life. No – he didn't expect me to be *as good*; he expected me to be *better*. And I just couldn't learn all those names and facts, much less spell them correctly.

I mumbled something about trying harder, while Mr

Brunner took one long sad look at the *stele*, like he'd been at this girl's funeral.

He told me to go outside and eat my lunch.

The class gathered on the front steps of the museum, where we could watch the foot traffic along Fifth Avenue.

Overhead, a huge storm was brewing, with clouds blacker than I'd ever seen over the city. I figured maybe it was global warming or something, because the weather all across New York state had been weird since Christmas. We'd had massive snow storms, flooding, wildfires from lightning strikes. I wouldn't have been surprised if this was a hurricane blowing in.

Nobody else seemed to notice. Some of the guys were pelting pigeons with Lunchables crackers. Nancy Bobofit was trying to pickpocket something from a lady's bag, and, of course, Mrs Dodds wasn't seeing a thing.

Grover and I sat on the edge of the fountain, away from the others. We thought that maybe if we did that, everybody wouldn't know we were from *that* school – the school for loser freaks who couldn't make it elsewhere.

'Detention?' Grover asked.

'Nah,' I said. 'Not from Brunner. I just wish he'd lay off me sometimes. I mean – I'm not a genius.'

Grover didn't say anything for a while. Then, when I thought he was going to give me some deep philosophical comment to make me feel better, he said, 'Can I have your apple?'

I didn't have much of an appetite, so I let him take it.

I watched the stream of cabs going down Fifth Avenue, and thought about my mom's apartment, only a little ways uptown from where we sat. I hadn't seen her since Christmas. I wanted so bad to jump in a taxi and head home. She'd hug me and be glad to see me, but she'd be disappointed, too. She'd send me right back to Yancy, remind me that I had to try harder, even if this was my sixth school in six years and I was probably going to be kicked out again. I wouldn't be able to stand that sad look she'd give me.

Mr Brunner parked his wheelchair at the base of the handicapped ramp. He ate celery while he read a paperback novel. A red umbrella stuck up from the back of his chair, making it look like a motorized café table.

I was about to unwrap my sandwich when Nancy Bobofit appeared in front of me with her ugly friends – I guess she'd gotten tired of stealing from the tourists – and dumped her half-eaten lunch in Grover's lap.

'Oops.' She grinned at me with her crooked teeth. Her freckles were orange, as if somebody had spray-painted her face with liquid Cheetos.

I tried to stay cool. The school counsellor had told me a million times, 'Count to ten, get control of your temper.' But I was so mad my mind went blank. A wave roared in my ears.

I don't remember touching her, but the next thing I knew, Nancy was sitting on her butt in the fountain, screaming, 'Percy pushed me!'

Mrs Dodds materialized next to us.

Some of the kids were whispering: 'Did you see –'

'– the water –'

'– like it grabbed her –'

I didn't know what they were talking about. All I knew was that I was in trouble again.

As soon as Mrs Dodds was sure poor little Nancy was okay, promising to get her a new shirt at the museum gift shop, etc., etc., Mrs Dodds turned on me. There was a triumphant fire in her eyes, as if I'd done something she'd been waiting for all semester. 'Now, honey –'

'I know,' I grumbled. 'A month erasing textbooks.'

That wasn't the right thing to say.

'Come with me,' Mrs Dodds said.

'Wait!' Grover yelped. 'It was me. *I* pushed her.'

I stared at him, stunned. I couldn't believe he was trying to cover for me. Mrs Dodds scared Grover to death.

She glared at him so hard his whiskery chin trembled.

'I don't think so, Mr Underwood,' she said.

'But –'

'You – *will* – stay – here.'

Grover looked at me desperately.

'It's okay, man,' I told him. 'Thanks for trying.'

'Honey,' Mrs Dodds barked at me. '*Now.*'

Nancy Bobofit smirked.

I gave her my deluxe I'll-kill-you-later stare. I then turned to face Mrs Dodds, but she wasn't there. She was standing at the museum entrance, way at the top of the steps, gesturing impatiently at me to come on.

How'd she get there so fast?

I have moments like that a lot, when my brain falls asleep or something, and the next thing I know I've missed something, as if a puzzle piece fell out of the universe and left me staring at the blank place behind it. The school counsellor told me this was part of the ADHD, my brain misinterpreting things.

I wasn't so sure.

I went after Mrs Dodds.

Halfway up the steps, I glanced back at Grover. He was looking pale, cutting his eyes between me and Mr Brunner, like he wanted Mr Brunner to notice what was going on, but Mr Brunner was absorbed in his novel.

I looked back up. Mrs Dodds had disappeared again. She was now inside the building, at the end of the entrance hall.

Okay, I thought. She's going to make me buy a new shirt for Nancy at the gift shop.

But apparently that wasn't the plan.

I followed her deeper into the museum. When I finally caught up to her, we were back in the Greek and Roman section.

Except for us, the gallery was empty.

Mrs Dodds stood with her arms crossed in front of a big marble frieze of the Greek gods. She was making this weird noise in her throat, like growling.

Even without the noise, I would've been nervous. It's weird being alone with a teacher, especially Mrs Dodds. Something about the way she looked at the frieze, as if she wanted to pulverize it . . .

'You've been giving us problems, honey,' she said.

I did the safe thing. I said, 'Yes, ma'am.'

She tugged on the cuffs of her leather jacket. 'Did you really think you would get away with it?'

The look in her eyes was beyond mad. It was evil.

She's a teacher, I thought nervously. It's not like she's going to hurt me.

I said, 'I'll – I'll try harder, ma'am.'

Thunder shook the building.

'We are not fools, Percy Jackson,' Mrs Dodds said. 'It was only a matter of time before we found you out. Confess, and you will suffer less pain.'

I didn't know what she was talking about.

All I could think of was that the teachers must've found the illegal stash of candy I'd been selling out of my dorm room. Or maybe they'd realized I got my essay on *Tom Sawyer* from the Internet without ever reading the book and now they were going to take away my grade. Or worse, they were going to make me read the book.

'Well?' she demanded.

'Ma'am, I don't . . .'

'Your time is up,' she hissed. Then the weirdest thing happened. Her eyes began to glow like barbecue coals. Her fingers stretched, turning into talons. Her jacket melted into large, leathery wings. She wasn't human. She was a shrivelled hag with bat wings and claws and a mouth full of yellow fangs, and she was about to slice me to ribbons.

Then things got even stranger.

Mr Brunner, who'd been out in front of the museum a

minute before, wheeled his chair into the doorway of the gallery, holding a pen in his hand.

'What ho, Percy!' he shouted, and tossed the pen through the air.

Mrs Dodds lunged at me.

With a yelp, I dodged and felt talons slash the air next to my ear. I snatched the ballpoint pen out of the air, but when it hit my hand, it wasn't a pen any more. It was a sword – Mr Brunner's bronze sword, which he always used on tournament day.

Mrs Dodds spun towards me with a murderous look in her eyes.

My knees were jelly. My hands were shaking so bad I almost dropped the sword.

She snarled, 'Die, honey!'

And she flew straight at me.

Absolute terror ran through my body. I did the only thing that came naturally: I swung the sword.

The metal blade hit her shoulder and passed clean through her body as if she were made of water. *Hisss!*

Mrs Dodds was a sand castle in a power fan. She exploded into yellow powder, vaporized on the spot, leaving nothing but the smell of sulphur and a dying screech and a chill of evil in the air, as if those two glowing red eyes were still watching me.

I was alone.

There was a ballpoint pen in my hand.

Mr Brunner wasn't there. Nobody was there but me.

My hands were still trembling. My lunch must've

been contaminated with magic mushrooms or something.

Had I imagined the whole thing?

I went back outside.

It had started to rain.

Grover was sitting by the fountain, a museum map tented over his head. Nancy Bobofit was still standing there, soaked from her swim in the fountain, grumbling to her ugly friends. When she saw me, she said, 'I hope Mrs Kerr whipped your butt.'

I said, 'Who?'

'Our *teacher*. Duh!'

I blinked. We had no teacher named Mrs Kerr. I asked Nancy what she was talking about.

She just rolled her eyes and turned away.

I asked Grover where Mrs Dodds was.

He said, 'Who?'

But he paused first, and he wouldn't look at me, so I thought he was messing with me.

'Not funny, man,' I told him. 'This is serious.'

Thunder boomed overhead.

I saw Mr Brunner sitting under his red umbrella, reading his book, as if he'd never moved.

I went over to him.

He looked up, a little distracted. 'Ah, that would be my pen. Please bring your own writing utensil in the future, Mr Jackson.'

I handed it over. I hadn't even realized I was still holding it.

'Sir,' I said, 'where's Mrs Dodds?'

He stared at me blankly. 'Who?'

'The other chaperone. Mrs Dodds. The pre-algebra teacher.'

He frowned and sat forward, looking mildly concerned. 'Percy, there is no Mrs Dodds on this trip. As far as I know, there has never been a Mrs Dodds at Yancy Academy. Are you feeling all right?'

2 ⚡ THREE OLD LADIES KNIT THE SOCKS OF DEATH

I was used to the occasional weird experience, but usually they were over quickly. This twenty-four/seven hallucination was more than I could handle. For the rest of the school year, the entire campus seemed to be playing some kind of trick on me. The students acted as if they were completely and totally convinced that Mrs Kerr – a perky blonde woman whom I'd never seen in my life until she got on our bus at the end of the field trip – had been our pre-algebra teacher since Christmas.

Every so often I would spring a Mrs Dodds reference on somebody, just to see if I could trip them up, but they would stare at me like I was psycho.

It got so I almost believed them – Mrs Dodds had never existed.

Almost.

But Grover couldn't fool me. When I mentioned the name Dodds to him, he would hesitate, then claim she didn't exist. But I knew he was lying.

Something was going on. Something *had* happened at the museum.

I didn't have much time to think about it during the days, but at night, visions of Mrs Dodds with talons and leathery wings would wake me up in a cold sweat.

The freak weather continued, which didn't help my mood. One night, a thunderstorm blew out the windows in my dorm room. A few days later, the biggest tornado ever spotted in the Hudson Valley touched down only fifty miles from Yancy Academy. One of the current events we studied in social studies class was the unusual number of small planes that had gone down in sudden squalls in the Atlantic that year.

I started feeling cranky and irritable most of the time. My grades slipped from Ds to Fs. I got into more fights with Nancy Bobofit and her friends. I was sent out into the hallway in almost every class.

Finally, when our English teacher, Mr Nicoll, asked me for the millionth time why I was too lazy to study for spelling tests, I snapped. I called him an old sot. I wasn't even sure what it meant, but it sounded good.

The headmaster sent my mom a letter the following week, making it official: I would not be invited back next year to Yancy Academy.

Fine, I told myself. Just fine.

I was homesick.

I wanted to be with my mom in our little apartment on the Upper East Side, even if I had to go to public school and put up with my obnoxious stepfather and his stupid poker parties.

And yet . . . there were things I'd miss at Yancy. The view of the woods out my dorm window, the Hudson River in the distance, the smell of pine trees. I'd miss Grover, who'd been a good friend, even if he was a little strange. I worried how he'd survive next year without me.

I'd miss Latin class, too – Mr Brunner's crazy tournament days and his faith that I could do well.

As exam week got closer, Latin was the only test I studied for. I hadn't forgotten what Mr Brunner had told me about this subject being life-and-death for me. I wasn't sure why, but I'd started to believe him.

The evening before my final, I got so frustrated I threw the *Cambridge Guide to Greek Mythology* across my dorm room. Words had started swimming off the page, circling my head, the letters doing one-eighties as if they were riding skateboards. There was no way I was going to remember the difference between Chiron and Charon, or Polydictes and Polydeuces. And conjugating those Latin verbs? Forget it.

I paced the room, feeling like ants were crawling around inside my shirt.

I remembered Mr Brunner's serious expression, his thousand-year-old eyes. *I will accept only the best from you, Percy Jackson.*

I took a deep breath. I picked up the mythology book.

I'd never asked a teacher for help before. Maybe if I talked to Mr Brunner, he could give me some pointers. At least I could apologize for the big fat 'F' I was about to score on his exam. I didn't want to leave Yancy Academy with him thinking I hadn't tried.

I walked downstairs to the faculty offices. Most of them were dark and empty, but Mr Brunner's door was ajar, light from his window stretching across the hallway floor.

I was three steps from the door handle when I heard voices inside the office. Mr Brunner asked a question. A voice that was definitely Grover's said, '. . . worried about Percy, sir.'

I froze.

I'm not usually an eavesdropper, but I dare you to try not listening if you hear your best friend talking about you to an adult.

I inched closer.

'. . . alone this summer,' Grover was saying. 'I mean, a Kindly One in the *school*! Now that we know for sure, and *they* know too –'

'We would only make matters worse by rushing him,' Mr Brunner said. 'We need the boy to mature more.'

'But he may not have time. The summer solstice deadline –'

'Will have to be resolved without him, Grover. Let him enjoy his ignorance while he still can.'

'Sir, he *saw* her . . .'

'His imagination,' Mr Brunner insisted. 'The Mist over the students and staff will be enough to convince him of that.'

'Sir, I . . . I can't fail in my duties again.' Grover's voice was choked with emotion. 'You know what that would mean.'

'You haven't failed, Grover,' Mr Brunner said kindly. 'I should have seen her for what she was. Now let's just worry about keeping Percy alive until next autumn –'

The mythology book dropped out of my hand and hit the floor with a thud.

Mr Brunner went silent.

My heart hammering, I picked up the book and backed down the hall.

A shadow slid across the lighted glass of Brunner's office door, the shadow of something much taller than my wheelchair-bound teacher, holding something that looked suspiciously like an archer's bow.

I opened the nearest door and slipped inside.

A few seconds later I heard a slow *clop-clop-clop*, like muffled wood blocks, then a sound like an animal snuffling right outside my door. A large dark shape paused in front of the glass, then moved on.

A bead of sweat trickled down my neck.

Somewhere in the hallway, Mr Brunner spoke. 'Nothing,' he murmured. 'My nerves haven't been right since the winter solstice.'

'Mine neither,' Grover said. 'But I could have sworn . . .'

'Go back to the dorm,' Mr Brunner told him. 'You've got a long day of exams tomorrow.'

'Don't remind me.'

The lights went out in Mr Brunner's office.

I waited in the dark for what seemed like forever.

Finally, I slipped out into the hallway and made my way back up to the dorm.

Grover was lying on his bed, studying his Latin exam notes like he'd been there all night.

'Hey,' he said, bleary-eyed. 'You going to be ready for this test?'

I didn't answer.

'You look awful.' He frowned. 'Is everything okay?'

'Just . . . tired.'

I turned so he couldn't read my expression, and started getting ready for bed.

I didn't understand what I'd heard downstairs. I wanted to believe I'd imagined the whole thing.

But one thing was clear: Grover and Mr Brunner were talking about me behind my back. They thought I was in some kind of danger.

The next afternoon, as I was leaving the three-hour Latin exam, my eyes swimming with all the Greek and Roman names I'd misspelled, Mr Brunner called me back inside.

For a moment, I was worried he'd found out about my eavesdropping the night before, but that didn't seem to be the problem.

'Percy,' he said. 'Don't be discouraged about leaving Yancy. It's . . . it's for the best.'

His tone was kind, but the words still embarrassed me. Even though he was speaking quietly, the other kids finishing the test could hear. Nancy Bobofit smirked at me and made sarcastic little kissing motions with her lips.

I mumbled, 'Okay, sir.'

'I mean . . .' Mr Brunner wheeled his chair back and forth, like he wasn't sure what to say. 'This isn't the right place for you. It was only a matter of time.'

My eyes stung.

Here was my favourite teacher, in front of the class, telling me I couldn't handle it. After saying he believed in me all year, now he was telling me I was destined to get kicked out.

'Right,' I said, trembling.

'No, no,' Mr Brunner said. 'Oh, confound it all. What I'm trying to say ... you're not normal, Percy. That's nothing to be –'

'Thanks,' I blurted. 'Thanks a lot, sir, for reminding me.'

'Percy –'

But I was already gone.

On the last day of the term, I shoved my clothes into my suitcase.

The other guys were joking around, talking about their vacation plans. One of them was going on a hiking trip to Switzerland. Another was cruising the Caribbean for a month. They were juvenile delinquents, like me, but they were *rich* juvenile delinquents. Their daddies were executives, or ambassadors, or celebrities. I was a nobody, from a family of nobodies.

They asked me what I'd be doing this summer and I told them I was going back to the city.

What I didn't tell them was that I'd have to get a summer job walking dogs or selling magazine subscriptions, and spend my free time worrying about where I'd go to school in the autumn.

'Oh,' one of the guys said. 'That's cool.'

They went back to their conversation as if I'd never existed.

The only person I dreaded saying goodbye to was Grover but, as it turned out, I didn't have to. He'd booked a ticket to Manhattan on the same Greyhound as I had, so there we were, together again, heading into the city.

During the whole bus ride, Grover kept glancing nervously down the aisle, watching the other passengers. It occurred to me that he'd always acted nervous and fidgety when we left Yancy, as if he expected something bad to happen. Before, I'd always assumed he was worried about getting teased. But there was nobody to tease him on the Greyhound.

Finally I couldn't stand it any more.

I said, 'Looking for Kindly Ones?'

Grover nearly jumped out of his seat. 'Wha — what do you mean?'

I confessed about eavesdropping on him and Mr Brunner the night before the exam.

Grover's eye twitched. 'How much did you hear?'

'Oh . . . not much. What's the summer-solstice deadline?'

He winced. 'Look, Percy . . . I was just worried for you, see? I mean, hallucinating about demon maths teachers . . .'

'Grover —'

'And I was telling Mr Brunner that maybe you were overstressed or something, because there was no such person as Mrs Dodds, and . . .'

'Grover, you're a really, really bad liar.'

His ears turned pink.

From his shirt pocket, he fished out a grubby business card. 'Just take this, okay? In case you need me this summer.'

The card was in fancy script, which was murder on my dyslexic eyes, but I finally made out something like:

Grover Underwood, Keeper
Half-Blood Hill
Long Island, New York
(800)009-0009

'What's Half –'

'Don't say it aloud!' he yelped. 'That's my, um . . . summer address.'

My heart sank. Grover had a summer home. I'd never considered that his family might be as rich as the others at Yancy.

'Okay,' I said glumly. 'So, like, if I want to come visit your mansion.'

He nodded. 'Or . . . or if you need me.'

'Why would I need you?'

It came out harsher than I meant it too.

Grover blushed right down to his Adam's apple. 'Look, Percy, the truth is, I – I kind of have to protect you.'

I stared at him.

All year long, I'd gotten in fights keeping bullies away from him. I'd lost sleep worrying that he'd get beaten up next year without me. And here he was acting like he was the one who defended *me*.

'Grover,' I said, 'what exactly are you protecting me from?'

There was a huge grinding noise under our feet. Black smoke poured from the dashboard and the whole bus filled with a smell like rotten eggs. The driver cursed and limped the Greyhound over to the side of the highway.

After a few minutes clanking around in the engine compartment, the driver announced that we'd all have to get off. Grover and I filed outside with everybody else.

We were on a stretch of country road – no place you'd notice if you didn't break down there. On our side of the highway was nothing but maple trees and litter from passing cars. On the other side, across four lanes of asphalt shimmering with afternoon heat, was an old-fashioned fruit stand.

The stuff on sale looked really good: heaping boxes of blood-red cherries and apples, walnuts and apricots, jugs of cider in a claw-foot tub full of ice. There were no customers, just three old ladies sitting in rocking chairs in the shade of a maple tree, knitting the biggest pair of socks I'd ever seen.

I mean these socks were the size of sweaters, but they were clearly socks. The lady on the right knitted one of them. The lady on the left knitted the other. The lady in the middle held an enormous basket of electric-blue yarn.

All three women looked ancient, with pale faces wrinkled like fruit leather, silver hair tied back in white bandannas, bony arms sticking out of bleached cotton dresses.

The weirdest thing was, they seemed to be looking right at me.

I looked over at Grover to say something about this and saw that the blood had drained from his face. His nose was twitching.

'Grover?' I said. 'Hey, man —'

'Tell me they're not looking at you. They are. Aren't they?'

'Yeah. Weird, huh? You think those socks would fit me?'

'Not funny, Percy. Not funny at all.'

The old lady in the middle took out a huge pair of scissors — gold and silver, long-bladed, like shears. I heard Grover catch his breath.

'We're getting on the bus,' he told me. 'Come on.'

'What?' I said. 'It's a thousand degrees in there.'

'Come on!' He prised open the door and climbed inside, but I stayed back.

Across the road, the old ladies were still watching me. The middle one cut the yarn, and I swear I could hear that *snip* across four lanes of traffic. Her two friends balled up the electric-blue socks, leaving me wondering who they could possibly be for — Sasquatch or Godzilla.

At the rear of the bus, the driver wrenched a big chunk of smoking metal out of the engine compartment. The bus shuddered, and the engine roared back to life.

The passengers cheered.

'Darn right!' yelled the driver. He slapped the bus with his hat. 'Everybody back on board!'

Once we got going, I started feeling feverish, as if I'd caught the flu.

Grover didn't look much better. He was shivering and his teeth were chattering.

'Grover?'

'Yeah?'

'What are you not telling me?'

He dabbed his forehead with his shirt sleeve. 'Percy, what did you see back at the fruit stand?'

'You mean the old ladies? What is it about them, man? They're not like . . . Mrs Dodds, are they?'

His expression was hard to read, but I got the feeling that the fruit-stand ladies were something much, much worse than Mrs Dodds. He said, 'Just tell me what you saw.'

'The middle one took out her scissors, and she cut the yarn.'

He closed his eyes and made a gesture with his fingers that might've been crossing himself, but it wasn't. It was something else, something almost – older.

He said, 'You saw her snip the cord.'

'Yeah. So?' But even as I said it, I knew it was a big deal.

'This is not happening,' Grover mumbled. He started chewing at his thumb. 'I don't want this to be like the last time.'

'What last time?'

'Always sixth grade. They never get past sixth.'

'Grover,' I said, because he was really starting to scare me. 'What are you talking about?'

'Let me walk you home from the bus station. Promise me.'

This seemed like a strange request to me, but I promised he could.

'Is this like a superstition or something?' I asked.

No answer.

'Grover – that snipping of the yarn. Does that mean somebody is going to die?'

He looked at me mournfully, like he was already picking the kind of flowers I'd like best on my coffin.

3 GROVER UNEXPECTEDLY LOSES HIS TROUSERS

Confession time: I ditched Grover as soon as we got to the bus terminal.

I know, I know. It was rude. But Grover was freaking me out, looking at me like I was a dead man, muttering, 'Why does this always happen?' and, 'Why does it always have to be sixth grade?'

Whenever he got upset, Grover's bladder acted up, so I wasn't surprised when, as soon as we got off the bus, he made me promise to wait for him, then made a beeline for the restroom. Instead of waiting, I got my suitcase, slipped outside, and caught the first taxi uptown.

'East One Hundred and Fourth and First Avenue,' I told the driver.

A word about my mother, before you meet her.

Her name is Sally Jackson and she's the best person in the world, which just proves my theory that the best people have the rottenest luck. Her own parents died in a plane crash when she was five, and she was raised by an uncle who didn't care much about her. She wanted to be a novelist, so she spent high school working to save enough money for a college with a good creative-writing programme. Then her uncle got cancer, and she had to quit school in her senior year to take care of him. After he died, she was left with no money, no family and no diploma.

The only good break she ever got was meeting my dad.

I don't have any memories of him, just this sort of warm glow, maybe the barest trace of his smile. My mom doesn't like to talk about him because it makes her sad. She has no pictures.

See, they weren't married. She told me he was rich and important, and their relationship was a secret. Then one day, he set sail across the Atlantic on some important journey, and he never came back.

Lost at sea, my mom told me. Not dead. Lost at sea.

She worked odd jobs, took night classes to get her high school diploma, and raised me on her own. She never complained or got mad. Not even once. But I knew I wasn't an easy kid.

Finally, she married Gabe Ugliano, who was nice the first thirty seconds we knew him, then showed his true colours as a world-class jerk. When I was young, I nicknamed him Smelly Gabe. I'm sorry, but it's the truth. The guy reeked like mouldy garlic pizza wrapped in gym shorts.

Between the two of us, we made my mom's life pretty hard. The way Smelly Gabe treated her, the way he and I got along . . . well, when I came home is a good example.

I walked into our little apartment, hoping my mom would be home from work. Instead, Smelly Gabe was in the living room, playing poker with his buddies. The television was blaring. Crisps and beer cans were strewn all over the carpet.

Hardly looking up, he said around his cigar, 'So, you're home.'

'Where's my mom?'

'Working,' he said. 'You got any cash?'

That was it. No *Welcome back. Good to see you. How has your life been the last six months?*

Gabe had put on weight. He looked like a tuskless walrus in thrift-store clothes. He had about three hairs on his head, all combed over his bald scalp, as if that made him handsome or something.

He managed the Electronics Mega-Mart in Queens, but he stayed home most of the time. I don't know why he hadn't been fired long before. He just kept on collecting pay cheques, spending the money on cigars that made me nauseous, and on beer, of course. Always beer. Whenever I was home, he expected me to provide his gambling funds. He called that our 'guy secret'. Meaning, if I told my mom, he would punch my lights out.

'I don't have any cash,' I told him.

He raised a greasy eyebrow.

Gabe could sniff out money like a bloodhound, which was surprising, since his own smell should've covered up everything else.

'You took a taxi from the bus station,' he said. 'Probably paid with a twenty. Got six, seven bucks in change. Somebody expects to live under this roof, he ought to carry his own weight. Am I right, Eddie?'

Eddie, the superintendant of the apartment building, looked at me with a twinge of sympathy. 'Come on, Gabe,' he said. 'The kid just got here.'

'Am I *right*?' Gabe repeated.

Eddie scowled into his bowl of pretzels. The other two guys passed gas in harmony.

'Fine,' I said. I dug a wad of dollars out of my pocket and threw the money on the table. 'I hope you lose.'

'Your report card came, brain boy!' he shouted after me. 'I wouldn't act so snooty!'

I slammed the door to my room, which really wasn't my room. During school months, it was Gabe's 'study'. He didn't study anything in there except old car magazines, but he loved shoving my stuff in the closet, leaving his muddy boots on my windowsill, and doing his best to make the place smell like his nasty cologne and cigars and stale beer.

I dropped my suitcase on the bed. Home sweet home.

Gabe's smell was almost worse than the nightmares about Mrs Dodds, or the sound of that old fruit lady's shears snipping the yarn.

But as soon as I thought that, my legs felt weak. I remembered Grover's look of panic – how he'd made me promise I wouldn't go home without him. A sudden chill rolled through me. I felt like someone – something – was looking for me right now, maybe pounding its way up the stairs, growing long, horrible talons.

Then I heard my mom's voice. 'Percy?'

She opened the bedroom door, and my fears melted.

My mother can make me feel good just by walking into

the room. Her eyes sparkle and change colour in the light. Her smile is as warm as a quilt. She's got a few grey streaks mixed in with her long brown hair, but I never think of her as old. When she looks at me, it's like she's seeing all the good things about me, none of the bad. I've never heard her raise her voice or say an unkind word to anyone, not even me or Gabe.

'Oh, Percy.' She hugged me tight. 'I can't believe it. You've grown since Christmas!'

Her red-white-and-blue Sweet on America uniform smelled like the best things in the world: chocolate, licorice, and all the other stuff she sold at the candy shop in Grand Central. She'd brought me a huge bag of 'free samples', the way she always did when I came home.

We sat together on the edge of the bed. While I attacked the blueberry sour strings, she ran her hand through my hair and demanded to know everything I hadn't put in my letters. She didn't mention anything about my getting expelled. She didn't seem to care about that. But was I okay? Was her little boy doing all right?

I told her she was smothering me, and to lay off and all that, but secretly, I was really, really glad to see her.

From the other room, Gabe yelled, 'Hey, Sally – how about some bean dip, huh?'

I gritted my teeth.

My mom is the nicest lady in the world. She should've been married to a millionaire, not to some jerk like Gabe.

For her sake, I tried to sound upbeat about my last days at Yancy Academy. I told her I wasn't too down about the expulsion. I'd lasted almost the whole year this time. I'd made some new friends. I'd done pretty well in Latin. And honestly, the fights hadn't been as bad as the headmaster said. I liked Yancy Academy. I really had. I put such a good spin on the year, I almost convinced myself. I started choking up, thinking about Grover and Mr Brunner. Even Nancy Bobofit suddenly didn't seem so bad.

Until that trip to the museum . . .

'What?' my mom asked. Her eyes tugged at my conscience, trying to pull out the secrets. 'Did something scare you?'

'No, Mom.'

I felt bad lying. I wanted to tell her about Mrs Dodds and the three old ladies with the yarn, but I thought it would sound stupid.

She pursed her lips. She knew I was holding back, but she didn't push me.

'I have a surprise for you,' she said. 'We're going to the beach.'

My eyes widened. 'Montauk?'

'Three nights – same cabin.'

'When?'

She smiled. 'As soon as I get changed.'

I couldn't believe it. My mom and I hadn't been to Montauk the last two summers, because Gabe said there wasn't enough money.

Gabe appeared in the doorway and growled, 'Bean dip, Sally? Didn't you hear me?'

I wanted to punch him, but I met my mom's eyes and I understood she was offering me a deal: be nice to Gabe for a little while. Just until she was ready to leave for Montauk. Then we would get out of here.

'I was on my way, honey,' she told Gabe. 'We were just talking about the trip.'

Gabe's eyes got small. 'The trip? You mean you were serious about that?'

'I knew it,' I muttered. 'He won't let us go.'

'Of course he will,' my mom said evenly. 'Your stepfather is just worried about money. That's all. Besides,' she added, 'Gabriel won't have to settle for bean dip. I'll make him enough seven-layer dip for the whole weekend. Guacamole. Sour cream. The works.'

Gabe softened a bit. 'So this money for your trip . . . it comes out of your clothes budget, right?'

'Yes, honey,' my mother said.

'And you won't take my car anywhere but there and back.'

'We'll be very careful.'

Gabe scratched his double chin. 'Maybe if you hurry with that seven-layer dip . . . And maybe if the kid apologizes for interrupting my poker game.'

Maybe if I kick you in your soft spot, I thought. And make you sing soprano for a week.

But my mom's eyes warned me not to make him mad.

Why did she put up with this guy? I wanted to scream. Why did she care what he thought?

'I'm sorry,' I muttered. 'I'm really sorry I interrupted your incredibly important poker game. Please go back to it right now.'

Gabe's eyes narrowed. His tiny brain was probably trying to detect sarcasm in my statement.

'Yeah, whatever,' he decided.

He went back to his game.

'Thank you, Percy,' my mom said. 'Once we get to Montauk, we'll talk more about . . . whatever you've forgotten to tell me, okay?'

For a moment, I thought I saw anxiety in her eyes – the same fear I'd seen in Grover during the bus ride – as if my mom too felt an odd chill in the air.

But then her smile returned, and I figured I must have been mistaken. She ruffled my hair and went to make Gabe his seven-layer dip.

An hour later we were ready to leave.

Gabe took a break from his poker game long enough to watch me lug my mom's bags to the car. He kept griping and groaning about losing her cooking – and more important, his '78 Camaro – for the whole weekend.

'Not a scratch on this car, brain boy,' he warned me as I loaded the last bag. 'Not one little scratch.'

Like I'd be the one driving. I was twelve. But that didn't matter to Gabe. If a seagull so much as pooped on his paint job, he'd find a way to blame me.

Watching him lumber back towards the apartment building, I got so mad I did something I can't explain. As Gabe reached the doorway, I made the hand gesture I'd seen Grover make on the bus, a sort of warding-off-evil gesture, a clawed hand over my heart, then a shoving movement towards Gabe. The screen door slammed shut so hard it whacked him in the butt and sent him flying up the staircase as if he'd been shot from a cannon. Maybe it was just the wind, or some freak accident with the hinges, but I didn't stay long enough to find out.

I got in the Camaro and told my mom to step on it.

Our rental cabin was on the south shore, way out at the tip of Long Island. It was a little pastel box with faded curtains, half sunken into the dunes. There was always sand in the sheets and spiders in the cabinets, and most of the time the sea was too cold to swim in.

I loved the place.

We'd been going there since I was a baby. My mom had been going even longer. She never exactly said, but I knew why the beach was special to her. It was the place where she'd met my dad.

As we got closer to Montauk, she seemed to grow younger, years of worry and work disappearing from her face. Her eyes turned the colour of the sea.

We got there at sunset, opened all the cabin's windows, and went through our usual cleaning routine. We walked on the beach, fed blue corn chips to the seagulls, and munched on blue jelly beans, blue saltwater taffy, and all the other free samples my mom had brought from work.

I guess I should explain the blue food.

See, Gabe had once told my mom there was no such thing. They had this fight, which seemed like a really small thing at the time. But ever since, my mom went out of her way to eat blue. She baked blue birthday cakes. She mixed blueberry smoothies. She bought blue-corn tortilla chips and brought home blue candy from the shop. This – along with keeping her maiden name, Jackson, rather than calling herself Mrs Ugliano – was proof that she wasn't totally suckered by Gabe. She did have a rebellious streak, like me.

When it got dark, we made a fire. We roasted hot dogs and marshmallows. Mom told me stories about when she was a kid, back before her parents died in the plane crash. She told me about the books she wanted to write someday, when she had enough money to quit the candy shop.

Eventually, I got up the nerve to ask about what was always on my mind whenever we came to Montauk – my father. Mom's eyes went all misty. I figured she would tell me the same things she always did, but I never got tired of hearing them.

'He was kind, Percy,' she said. 'Tall, handsome and powerful. But gentle, too. You have his black hair, you know, and his green eyes.'

Mom fished a blue jelly bean out of her candy bag. 'I wish he could see you, Percy. He would be so proud.'

I wondered how she could say that. What was so great about me? A dyslexic, hyperactive boy with a D+ report card, kicked out of school for the sixth time in six years.

'How old was I?' I asked. 'I mean . . . when he left?'

She watched the flames. 'He was only with me for one summer, Percy. Right here at this beach. This cabin.'

'But . . . he knew me as a baby.'

'No, honey. He knew I was expecting a baby, but he never saw you. He had to leave before you were born.'

I tried to square that with the fact that I seemed to remember . . . something about my father. A warm glow. A smile.

I had always assumed he knew me as a baby. My mom had never said it outright, but still, I'd felt it must be true. Now, to be told that he'd never even seen me . . .

I felt angry at my father. Maybe it was stupid, but I resented him for going on that ocean voyage, for not having the guts to marry my mom. He'd left us, and now we were stuck with Smelly Gabe.

'Are you going to send me away again?' I asked her. 'To another boarding school?'

She pulled a marshmallow from the fire.

'I don't know, honey.' Her voice was heavy. 'I think . . . I think we'll have to do something.'

'Because you don't want me around?' I regretted the words as soon as they were out.

My mom's eyes welled with tears. She took my hand, squeezed it tight. 'Oh, Percy, no. I – I *have* to, honey. For your own good. I have to send you away.'

Her words reminded me of what Mr Brunner had said – that it was best for me to leave Yancy.

'Because I'm not normal,' I said.

'You say that as if it's a bad thing, Percy. But you don't realize how important you are. I thought Yancy Academy would be far enough away. I thought you'd finally be safe.'

'Safe from what?'

She met my eyes, and a flood of memories came back to me – all the weird, scary things that had ever happened to me, some of which I'd tried to forget.

During third grade, a man in a black trench coat had stalked me on the playground. When the teachers threatened to call the police, he went away growling, but no one believed me when I told them that under his broad-brimmed hat, the man only had one eye, right in the middle of his head.

Before that – a really early memory. I was in pre school, and a teacher accidentally put me down for a nap in a cot that a snake had slithered into. My mom screamed when she came to pick me up and found me playing with a limp, scaly rope I'd somehow managed to strangle to death with my meaty toddler hands.

In every single school, something creepy had happened, something unsafe, and I was forced to move.

I knew I should tell my mom about the old ladies at the fruit stand, and Mrs Dodds at the art museum, about my weird hallucination that I had sliced my maths teacher into dust with a sword. But I couldn't make myself tell her. I had a strange feeling the news would end our trip to Montauk, and I didn't want that.

'I've tried to keep you as close to me as I could,' my mom said. 'They told me that was a mistake. But there's only one other option, Percy – the place your father wanted to send you. And I just . . . I just can't stand to do it.'

'My father wanted me to go to a special school?'

'Not a school,' she said softly. 'A summer camp.'

My head was spinning. Why would my dad – who

[40]

hadn't even stayed around long enough to see me born – talk to my mom about a summer camp? And if it was so important, why hadn't she ever mentioned it before?

'I'm sorry, Percy,' she said, seeing the look in my eyes. 'But I can't talk about it. I – I couldn't send you to that place. It might mean saying goodbye to you for good.'

'For good? But if it's only a summer camp . . .'

She turned towards the fire, and I knew from her expression that if I asked her any more questions she would start to cry.

That night I had a vivid dream.

It was storming on the beach, and two beautiful animals, a white horse and a golden eagle, were trying to kill each other at the edge of the surf. The eagle swooped down and slashed the horse's muzzle with its huge talons. The horse reared up and kicked at the eagle's wings. As they fought, the ground rumbled, and a monstrous voice chuckled somewhere beneath the earth, goading the animals to fight harder.

I ran towards them, knowing I had to stop them from killing each other, but I was running in slow motion. I knew I would be too late. I saw the eagle dive down, its beak aimed at the horse's wide eyes, and I screamed, *No!*

I woke with a start.

Outside, it really was storming, the kind of storm that cracks trees and blows down houses. There was no horse or eagle on the beach, just lightning making false daylight, and five-metre-high waves pounding the dunes like artillery.

With the next thunderclap, my mom woke. She sat up, eyes wide, and said, 'Hurricane.'

I knew that was crazy. Long Island never saw hurricanes this early in the summer. But the ocean seemed to have forgotten. Over the roar of the wind, I heard a distant bellow, an angry, tortured sound that made my hair stand on end.

Then a much closer noise, like mallets in the sand. A desperate voice – someone yelling, pounding on our cabin door.

My mother sprang out of bed in her nightgown and threw open the lock.

Grover stood framed in the doorway against a backdrop of pouring rain. But he wasn't . . . he wasn't exactly Grover.

'Searching all night,' he gasped. 'What were you thinking?'

My mother looked at me in terror – not scared of Grover, but of why he'd come.

'Percy,' she said, shouting to be heard over the rain. 'What happened at school? What didn't you tell me?'

I was frozen, looking at Grover. I couldn't understand what I was seeing.

'*O Zeu kai alloi theoi!*' he yelled. 'It's right behind me! Didn't you *tell* her?'

I was too shocked to register that he'd just cursed in Ancient Greek, and I'd understood him perfectly. I was too shocked to wonder how Grover had got here by himself in the middle of the night. Because Grover didn't have his trousers on – and where his legs should be . . . where his legs should be . . .

My mom looked at me sternly and talked in a tone she'd never used before: '*Percy.* Tell me *now!*'

I stammered something about the old ladies at the fruit stand, and Mrs Dodds, and my mom stared at me, her face deathly pale in the flashes of lightning.

She grabbed her purse, tossed me my rain jacket, and said, 'Get to the car. Both of you. *Go!*'

Grover ran for the Camaro – but he wasn't running, exactly. He was trotting, shaking his shaggy hindquarters, and suddenly his story about a muscular disorder in his legs made sense to me. I understood how he could run so fast and still limp when he walked.

Because where his feet should be, there were no feet. There were cloven hooves.

4 ⚡ MY MOTHER TEACHES ME BULLFIGHTING

We tore through the night along dark country roads. Wind slammed against the Camaro. Rain lashed the windshield. I didn't know how my mom could see anything, but she kept her foot on the gas.

Every time there was a flash of lightning, I looked at Grover sitting next to me in the backseat and I wondered if I'd gone insane, or if he was wearing some kind of shag-carpet trousers. But, no, the smell was one I remembered from kindergarten field trips to the petting zoo – lanolin, like from wool. The smell of a wet barnyard animal.

All I could think to say was, 'So, you and my mum . . . know each other?'

Grover's eyes flitted to the rearview mirror, though there were no cars behind us. 'Not exactly,' he said. 'I mean, we've never met in person. But she knew I was watching you.'

'Watching me?'

'Keeping tabs on you. Making sure you were okay. But I wasn't faking being your friend,' he added hastily. 'I *am* your friend.'

'Um . . . what *are* you, exactly?'

'That doesn't matter right now.'

'It doesn't matter? From the waist down, my best friend is a donkey —'

Grover let out a sharp, throaty '*Blaa-ha-ha!*'

I'd heard him make that sound before, but I'd always assumed it was a nervous laugh. Now I realized it was more of an irritated bleat.

'Goat!' he cried.

'What?'

'I'm a *goat* from the waist down.'

'You just said it didn't matter.'

'*Blaa-ha-ha!* There are satyrs who would trample you under hoof for such an insult!'

'Whoa. Wait. Satyrs. You mean like . . . Mr Brunner's myths?'

'Were those old ladies at the fruit stand a *myth*, Percy? Was Mrs Dodds a myth?'

'So you *admit* there was a Mrs Dodds!'

'Of course.'

'Then why —'

'The less you knew, the fewer monsters you'd attract,' Grover said, like that should be perfectly obvious. 'We put Mist over the humans' eyes. We hoped you'd think the Kindly One was a hallucination. But it was no good. You started to realize who you are.'

'Who I — wait a minute, what do you mean?'

The weird bellowing noise rose up again somewhere behind us, closer than before. Whatever was chasing us was still on our trail.

'Percy,' my mom said, 'there's too much to explain and not enough time. We have to get you to safety.'

'Safety from what? Who's after me?'

'Oh, nobody much,' Grover said, obviously still miffed about the donkey comment. 'Just the Lord of the Dead and a few of his blood-thirstiest minions.'

'Grover!'

'Sorry, Mrs Jackson. Could you drive faster, please?'

I tried to wrap my mind around what was happening, but I couldn't do it. I knew this wasn't a dream. I had no imagination. I could never dream up something this weird.

My mom made a hard left. We swerved onto a narrower road, racing past darkened farmhouses and wooded hills and PICK YOUR OWN STRAWBERRIES signs on white picket fences.

'Where are we going?' I asked.

'The summer camp I told you about.' My mother's voice was tight; she was trying for my sake not to be scared. 'The place your father wanted to send you.'

'The place you didn't want me to go.'

'Please, dear,' my mother begged. 'This is hard enough. Try to understand. You're in danger.'

'Because some old ladies cut yarn.'

'Those weren't old ladies,' Grover said. 'Those were the Fates. Do you know what it means — the fact they appeared in front of you? They only do that when you're about to . . . when someone's about to die.'

'Whoa. You said *"you"*.'

'No I didn't. I said *"someone"*.'

'You meant "you". As in me.'

'I meant you, like "someone". Not you, *you*.'

'Boys!' my mom said.

She pulled the wheel hard to the right, and I got a glimpse of a figure she'd swerved to avoid – a dark fluttering shape now lost behind us in the storm.

'What was that?' I asked.

'We're almost there,' my mother said, ignoring my question. 'Another mile. Please. Please. Please.'

I didn't know where *there* was, but I found myself leaning forward in the car, anticipating, wanting us to arrive.

Outside, nothing but rain and darkness – the kind of empty countryside you get way out on the tip of Long Island. I thought about Mrs Dodds and the moment when she'd changed into the thing with pointed teeth and leathery wings. My limbs went numb from delayed shock. She really *hadn't* been human. She'd meant to kill me.

Then I thought about Mr Brunner . . . and the sword he had thrown me. Before I could ask Grover about that, the hair rose on the back of my neck. There was a blinding flash, a jaw-rattling *boom!*, and our car exploded.

I remember feeling weightless, like I was being crushed, fried and hosed down all at the same time.

I peeled my forehead off the back of the driver's seat and said, 'Ow.'

'Percy!' my mom shouted.

'I'm okay. . . .'

I tried to shake off the daze. I wasn't dead. The car hadn't really exploded. We'd swerved into a ditch. Our driver's-side doors were wedged in the mud. The roof had cracked open like an eggshell and rain was pouring in.

Lightning. That was the only explanation. We'd been blasted right off the road. Next to me in the backseat was a big motionless lump. 'Grover!'

He was slumped over, blood trickling from the side of his mouth. I shook his furry hip, thinking, No! Even if you are half barnyard animal, you're my best friend and I don't want you to die!

Then he groaned, 'Food,' and I knew there was hope.

'Percy,' my mother said, 'we have to . . .' Her voice faltered.

I looked back. In a flash of lightning, through the mud-spattered rear windshield, I saw a figure lumbering towards us on the shoulder of the road. The sight of it made my skin crawl. It was a dark silhouette of a huge guy, like a football player. He seemed to be holding a blanket over his head. His top half was bulky and fuzzy. His upraised hands made it look like he had horns.

I swallowed hard. 'Who is –'

'Percy,' my mother said, deadly serious. 'Get out of the car.'

My mother threw herself against the driver's-side door. It was jammed shut in the mud. I tried mine. Stuck too. I looked up desperately at the hole in the roof. It might've been an exit, but the edges were sizzling and smoking.

'Climb out the passenger's side!' my mother told me. 'Percy – you have to run. Do you see that big tree?'

What?

Another flash of lightning, and through the smoking hole in the roof I saw the tree she meant: a huge, White House Christmas-tree-sized pine at the crest of the nearest hill.

'That's the property line,' my mom said. 'Get over that hill and you'll see a big farmhouse down in the valley. Run and don't look back. Yell for help. Don't stop until you reach the door.'

'Mom, you're coming, too.'

Her face was pale, her eyes as sad as when she looked at the ocean.

'No!' I shouted. 'You *are* coming with me. Help me carry Grover.'

'*Food!*' Grover moaned, a little louder.

The man with the blanket on his head kept coming towards us, making his grunting, snorting noises. As he got closer, I realized he *couldn't* be holding a blanket over his head, because his hands – huge meaty hands – were swinging at his sides. There was no blanket. Meaning the bulky, fuzzy mass that was too big to be his head . . . was his head. And the points that looked like horns . . .

'He doesn't want *us*,' my mother told me. 'He wants you. Besides, I can't cross the property line.'

'But . . .'

'We don't have time, Percy. Go. Please.'

I got mad, then – mad at my mother, at Grover the goat, at the thing with horns that was lumbering towards us slowly and deliberately like, like a bull.

I climbed across Grover and pushed the door open into the rain. 'We're going together. Come on, Mom.'

'I told you –'

'Mom! I am not leaving you. Help me with Grover.'

I didn't wait for her answer. I scrambled outside, dragging Grover from the car. He was surprisingly light, but I couldn't have carried him very far if my mom hadn't come to my aid.

Together, we draped Grover's arms over our shoulders and started stumbling uphill through wet waist-high grass.

Glancing back, I got my first clear look at the monster. He was seven feet tall, easy, his arms and legs like something from the cover of *Muscle Man* magazine – bulging biceps and triceps and a bunch of other 'ceps, all stuffed like baseballs under vein-webbed skin. He wore no clothes except under-wear – I mean, bright white Fruit-of-the-Looms, which would've been funny except for the top half of his body. Coarse brown hair started at about his bellybutton and got thicker as it reached his shoulders.

His neck was a mass of muscle and fur leading up to his enormous head, which had a snout as long as my arm, snotty nostrils with a gleaming brass ring, cruel black eyes, and horns – enormous black-and-white horns with points you just couldn't get from an electric sharpener.

I recognized the monster, all right. He had been in one of the first stories Mr Brunner told us. But he couldn't be real.

I blinked the rain out of my eyes. 'That's –'

'Pasiphae's son,' my mother said. 'I wish I'd known how badly they want to kill you.'

'But a he's a min –'

'Don't say his name,' she warned. 'Names have power.'

The pine tree was still way too far — a hundred metres uphill at least.

I glanced behind me again.

The bull-man hunched over our car, looking in the windows — or not looking, exactly. More like snuffling, nuzzling. I wasn't sure why he bothered, since we were only about fifteen metres away.

'Food?' Grover moaned.

'Shhh,' I told him. 'Mom, what's he doing? Doesn't he see us?'

'His sight and hearing are terrible,' she said. 'He goes by smell. But he'll figure out where we are soon enough.'

As if on cue, the bull-man bellowed in rage. He picked up Gabe's Camaro by the torn roof, the chassis creaking and groaning. He raised the car over his head and threw it down the road. It slammed into the wet asphalt and skidded in a shower of sparks for about half a mile before coming to a stop. The gas tank exploded.

Not a scratch, I remembered Gabe saying.

Oops.

'Percy,' my mom said. 'When he sees us, he'll charge. Wait until the last second, then jump out of the way — directly sideways. He can't change direction very well once he's charging. Do you understand?'

'How do you know all this?'

'I've been worried about an attack for a long time. I should have expected this. I was selfish, keeping you near me.'

'Keeping me near you? But —'

Another bellow of rage, and the bull-man started tromping uphill.

He'd smelled us.

The pine tree was only a few more metres, but the hill was getting steeper and slicker, and Grover wasn't getting any lighter.

The bull-man closed in. Another few seconds and he'd be on top of us.

My mother must've been exhausted, but she shouldered Grover. 'Go, Percy! Separate! Remember what I said.'

I didn't want to split up, but I had the feeling she was right — it was our only chance. I sprinted to the left, turned, and saw the creature bearing down on me. His black eyes glowed with hate. He reeked like rotten meat.

He lowered his head and charged, those razor-sharp horns aimed straight at my chest.

The fear in my stomach made me want to bolt, but that wouldn't work. I could never outrun this thing. So I held my ground, and at the last moment, I jumped to the side.

The bull-man stormed past like a freight train, then bellowed with frustration and turned, but not towards me this time, towards my mother, who was setting Grover down in the grass.

We'd reached the crest of the hill. Down the other side I could see a valley, just as my mother had said, and the lights of a farmhouse glowing yellow through the rain. But that was half a mile away. We'd never make it.

The bull-man grunted, pawing the ground. He kept

eyeing my mother, who was now retreating slowly downhill, back towards the road, trying to lead the monster away from Grover.

'Run, Percy!' she told me. 'I can't go any further. Run!'

But I just stood there, frozen in fear, as the monster charged her. She tried to sidestep, as she'd told me to do, but the monster had learned his lesson. His hand shot out and grabbed her by the neck as she tried to get away. He lifted her as she struggled, kicking and pummelling the air.

'Mom!'

She caught my eyes, managed to choke out one last word: 'Go!'

Then, with an angry roar, the monster closed his fists around my mother's neck, and she dissolved before my eyes, melting into light, a shimmering golden form, as if she were a holographic projection. A blinding flash, and she was simply . . . gone.

'No!'

Anger replaced my fear. Newfound strength burned in my limbs – the same rush of energy I'd got when Mrs Dodds grew talons.

The bull-man bore down on Grover, who lay helpless in the grass. The monster hunched over, snuffling my best friend, as if he were about to lift Grover up and make him dissolve too.

I couldn't allow that.

I stripped off my red rain jacket.

'HEY!' I screamed, waving the jacket, running to one side of the monster. 'Hey, stupid! Ground beef!'

'Raaaarrrrr!' The monster turned towards me, shaking his meaty fists.

I had an idea – a stupid idea, but better than no idea at all. I put my back to the big pine tree and waved my red jacket in front of the bull-man, thinking I'd jump out of the way at the last moment.

But it didn't happen like that.

The bull-man charged too fast, his arms out to grab me whichever way I tried to dodge.

Time slowed down.

My legs tensed. I couldn't jump sideways, so I leaped straight up, kicking off from the creature's head using it as a springboard, turning in midair, and landing on his neck.

How did I do that? I didn't have time to figure it out. A millisecond later, the monster's head slammed into the tree and the impact nearly knocked my teeth out.

The bull-man staggered around, trying to shake me. I locked my arms around his horns to keep from being thrown. Thunder and lightning were still going strong. The rain was in my eyes. The smell of rotten meat burned my nostrils.

The monster shook himself around and bucked like a rodeo bull. He should have just backed up into the tree and smashed me flat, but I was starting to realize that this thing had only one gear: forward.

Meanwhile, Grover started groaning in the grass. I wanted to yell at him to shut up, but the way I was getting tossed around, if I opened my mouth I'd bite my own tongue off.

'Food!' Grover moaned.

The bull-man wheeled towards him, pawed the ground again, and got ready to charge. I thought about how he had squeezed the life out of my mother, made her disappear in a flash of light, and rage filled me like high-octane fuel. I got both hands around one horn and I pulled backwards with all my might. The monster tensed, gave a surprised grunt, then – *snap!*

The bull-man screamed and flung me through the air. I landed flat on my back in the grass. My head smacked against a rock. When I sat up, my vision was blurry, but I had a horn in my hands, a ragged bone weapon the size of a knife.

The monster charged.

Without thinking, I rolled to one side and came up kneeling. As the monster barrelled past, I drove the broken horn straight into his side, right up under his furry rib cage.

The bull-man roared in agony. He flailed, clawing at his chest, then began to disintegrate – not like my mother, in a flash of golden light, but like crumbling sand, blown away in chunks by the wind, the same way Mrs Dodds had burst apart.

The monster was gone.

The rain had stopped. The storm still rumbled, but only in the distance. I smelled like livestock and my knees were shaking. My head felt like it was splitting open. I was weak and scared and trembling with grief. I'd just seen my mother vanish. I wanted to lie down and cry, but there was Grover, needing my help, so I managed to haul him up and stagger down into the valley, towards the lights of the farmhouse. I was crying, calling for my mother, but I held on to Grover – I wasn't going to let him go.

The last thing I remember is collapsing on a wooden porch, looking up at a ceiling fan circling above me, moths flying around a yellow light and the stern faces of a familiar-looking bearded man and a pretty girl, her blonde hair curled like Cinderella's. They both looked down at me, and the girl said, 'He's the one. He must be.'

'Silence, Annabeth,' the man said. 'He's still conscious. Bring him inside.'

5 ⚡ I PLAY PINOCHLE
WITH A HORSE

I had weird dreams full of barnyard animals. Most of them wanted to kill me. The rest wanted food.

I must've woken up several times, but what I heard and saw made no sense, so I just passed out again. I remember lying in a soft bed, being spoon-fed something that tasted like buttered popcorn, only it was pudding. The girl with curly blonde hair hovered over me, smirking as she scraped drips off my chin with the spoon.

When she saw my eyes open, she asked, 'What will happen at the summer solstice?'

I managed to croak, 'What?'

She looked around, as if afraid someone would overhear. 'What's going on? What was stolen? We've only got a few weeks!'

'I'm sorry,' I mumbled, 'I don't . . .'

Somebody knocked on the door, and the girl quickly filled my mouth with pudding.

The next time I woke up, the girl was gone.

A husky blond dude, like a surfer, stood in the corner of the bedroom keeping watch over me. He had blue eyes – at least a dozen of them – on his cheeks, his forehead, the backs of his hands.

* * *

When I finally came around for good, there was nothing weird about my surroundings, except that they were nicer than I was used to. I was sitting in a deck chair on a huge porch, gazing across a meadow at green hills in the distance. The breeze smelled like strawberries. There was a blanket over my legs, a pillow behind my neck. All that was great, but my mouth felt like a scorpion had been using it for a nest. My tongue was dry and nasty and every one of my teeth hurt.

On the table next to me was a tall drink. It looked like iced apple juice, with a green straw and a paper parasol stuck through a maraschino cherry.

My hand was so weak I almost dropped the glass once I got my fingers around it.

'Careful,' a familiar voice said.

Grover was leaning against the porch railing, looking like he hadn't slept in a week. Under one arm, he cradled a shoe box. He was wearing blue jeans, Converse hi-tops and a bright orange T-shirt that said CAMP HALF-BLOOD. Just plain old Grover. Not the goat boy.

So maybe I'd had a nightmare. Maybe my mom was okay. We were still on vacation, and we'd stopped here at this big house for some reason. And ...

'You saved my life,' Grover said. 'I ... well, the least I could do ... I went back to the hill. I thought you might want this.'

Reverently, he placed the shoe box in my lap.

Inside was a black-and-white bull's horn, the base jagged

from being broken off, the tip splattered with dried blood. It hadn't been a nightmare.

'The Minotaur,' I said.

'Um, Percy, it isn't a good idea –'

'That's what they call it in the Greek myths, isn't it?' I demanded. 'The Minotaur. Half man, half bull.'

Grover shifted uncomfortably. 'You've been out for two days. How much do you remember?'

'My mom. Is she really . . .'

He looked down.

I stared across the meadow. There were groves of trees, a winding stream, acres of strawberries spread out under the blue sky. The valley was surrounded by rolling hills, and the tallest one, directly in front of us, was the one with the huge pine tree on top. Even that looked beautiful in the sunlight.

My mother was gone. The whole world should be black and cold. Nothing should look beautiful.

'I'm sorry,' Grover sniffled. 'I'm a failure. I'm – I'm the worst satyr in the world.'

He moaned, stomping his foot so hard it came off. I mean, the Converse hi-top came off. The inside was filled with Styrofoam, except for a hoof-shaped hole.

'Oh, Styx!' he mumbled.

Thunder rolled across the clear sky.

As he struggled to get his hoof back in the fake foot, I thought, Well, that settles it.

Grover was a satyr. I was ready to bet that if I shaved his curly brown hair, I'd find tiny horns on his head. But I was too miserable to care that satyrs existed, or even Minotaurs.

All that meant was my mom really had been squeezed into nothingness, dissolved into yellow light.

I was alone. An orphan. I would have to live with . . . Smelly Gabe? No. That would never happen. I would live on the streets first. I would pretend I was seventeen and join the army. I'd do something.

Grover was still sniffling. The poor kid – poor goat, satyr, whatever – looked as if he expected to be hit.

I said, 'It wasn't your fault.'

'Yes, it was. I was supposed to *protect* you.'

'Did my mother ask you to protect me?'

'No. But that's my job. I'm a keeper. At least . . . I was.'

'But why . . .' I suddenly felt dizzy, my vision swimming.

'Don't strain yourself,' Grover said. 'Here.'

He helped me hold my glass and put the straw to my lips.

I recoiled at the taste, because I was expecting apple juice. It wasn't that at all. It was chocolate-chip cookies. Liquid cookies. And not just any cookies – my mom's homemade blue chocolate-chip cookies, buttery and hot, with the chips still melting. Drinking it, my whole body felt warm and good, full of energy. My grief didn't go away, but I felt as if my mom had just brushed her hand against my cheek, given me a cookie the way she used to when I was small, and told me everything was going to be okay.

Before I knew it, I'd drained the glass. I stared into it, sure I'd just had a warm drink, but the ice cubes hadn't even melted.

'Was it good?' Grover asked.

I nodded.

'What did it taste like?' He sounded so wistful, I felt guilty.

'Sorry,' I said. 'I should've let you taste.'

His eyes got wide. 'No! That's not what I meant. I just . . . wondered.'

'Chocolate-chip cookies,' I said. 'My mom's. Homemade.'

He sighed. 'And how do you feel?'

'Like I could throw Nancy Bobofit a hundred metres.'

'That's good,' he said. 'That's good. I don't think you should risk drinking any more of that stuff.'

'What do you mean?'

He took the empty glass from me gingerly, as if it were dynamite, and set it back on the table. 'Come on. Chiron and Mr D are waiting.'

The porch wrapped all the way around the farmhouse.

My legs felt wobbly trying to walk that far. Grover offered to carry the Minotaur horn, but I held on to it. I'd paid for that souvenir the hard way. I wasn't going to let it go.

As we came around the opposite end of the house, I caught my breath.

We must've been on the north shore of Long Island, because on this side of the house, the valley marched all the way up to Long Island Sound, which glittered about a mile in the distance. Between here and there, I simply couldn't process everything I was seeing. The landscape was

dotted with buildings that looked like ancient Greek architecture – an open-air pavilion, an amphitheatre, a circular
arena – except that they all looked brand new, their white
marble columns sparkling in the sun. In a nearby sandpit, a
dozen high school-age kids and satyrs played volleyball.
Canoes glided across a small lake. Kids in bright orange T-
shirts like Grover's were chasing each other around a cluster
of cabins nestled in the woods. Some shot targets at an
archery range. Others rode horses down a wooded trail, and,
unless I was hallucinating, some of their horses had wings.

Down at the end of the porch, two men sat across from
each other at a card table. The blonde-haired girl who'd
spoon-fed me popcorn-flavoured pudding was leaning on
the porch rail next to them.

The man facing me was small, but porky. He had a red
nose, big watery eyes and curly hair so black it was almost
purple. He looked like those paintings of baby angels –
what do you call them, hubbubs? No, cherubs. That's it. He
looked like a cherub who'd turned middle-aged in a trailer
park. He wore a tiger-pattern Hawaiian shirt, and he
would've fitted right in at one of Gabe's poker parties,
except I got the feeling this guy could've out-gambled even
my stepfather.

'That's Mr D,' Grover murmured to me. 'He's the camp
director. Be polite. The girl, that's Annabeth Chase. She's
just a camper, but she's been here longer than just about
anybody. And you already know Chiron . . .'

He pointed at the guy whose back was to me.

First, I realized he was sitting in the wheelchair. Then I

recognized the tweed jacket, the thinning brown hair, the scraggly beard.

'Mr Brunner!' I cried.

The Latin teacher turned and smiled at me. His eyes had that mischievous glint they sometimes got in class when he pulled a pop quiz and made all the multiple choice answers *B*.

'Ah, good, Percy,' he said. 'Now we have four for pinochle.'

He offered me a chair to the right of Mr D, who looked at me with bloodshot eyes and heaved a great sigh. 'Oh, I suppose I must say it. Welcome to Camp Half-Blood. There. Now don't expect me to be glad to see you.'

'Uh, thanks.' I scooted a little further away from him because, if there was one thing I had learned from living with Gabe, it was how to tell when an adult has been hitting the happy juice. If Mr D was a stranger to alcohol, I was a satyr.

'Annabeth?' Mr Brunner called to the blonde girl.

She came forward and Mr Brunner introduced us. 'This young lady nursed you back to health, Percy. Annabeth, my dear, why don't you go check on Percy's bunk? We'll be putting him in cabin eleven for now.'

Annabeth said, 'Sure, Chiron.'

She was probably my age, maybe a couple of centimetres taller, and a whole lot more athletic-looking. With her deep tan and her curly blonde hair, she was almost exactly what I thought a stereotypical California girl would look like, except her eyes ruined the image. They were a startling grey, like storm clouds; pretty, but intimidating, too, as if she were analysing the best way to take me down in a fight.

She glanced at the Minotaur horn in my hands, then back at me. I imagined she was going to say, *You killed a Minotaur!* or *Wow, you're so awesome!* or something like that.

Instead she said, 'You drool when you sleep.'

Then she sprinted off down the lawn, her blonde hair flying behind her.

'So,' I said, anxious to change the subject. 'You, uh, work here, Mr Brunner?'

'Not Mr Brunner,' the ex-Mr Brunner said. 'I'm afraid that was a pseudonym. You may call me Chiron.'

'Okay.' Totally confused, I looked at the director. 'And Mr D . . . does that stand for something?'

Mr D stopped shuffling the cards. He looked at me like I'd just belched loudly. 'Young man, names are powerful things. You don't just go around using them for no reason.'

'Oh. Right. Sorry.'

'I must say, Percy,' Chiron-Brunner broke in, 'I'm glad to see you alive. It's been a long time since I've made a house call to a potential camper. I'd hate to think I've wasted my time.'

'House call?'

'My year at Yancy Academy, to instruct you. We have satyrs at most schools, of course, keeping a lookout. But Grover alerted me as soon as he met you. He sensed you were something special, so I decided to come upstate. I convinced the other Latin teacher to . . . ah, take a leave of absence.'

I tried to remember the beginning of the school year. It seemed like so long ago, but I did have a fuzzy memory of there being another Latin teacher my first week at Yancy. Then, without explanation, he had disappeared and Mr Brunner had taken the class.

'You came to Yancy just to teach me?' I asked.

Chiron nodded. 'Honestly, I wasn't sure about you at first. We contacted your mother, let her know we were keeping an eye on you in case you were ready for Camp Half-Blood. But you still had so much to learn. Nevertheless, you made it here alive, and that's always the first test.'

'Grover,' Mr D said impatiently, 'are you playing or not?'

'Yes, sir!' Grover trembled as he took the fourth chair, though I didn't know why he should be so afraid of a pudgy little man in a tiger-print Hawaiian shirt.

'You *do* know how to play pinochle?' Mr D eyed me suspiciously.

'I'm afraid not,' I said.

'I'm afraid not, *sir*,' he said.

'Sir,' I repeated. I was liking the camp director less and less.

'Well,' he told me, 'it is, along with gladiator fighting and Pac-Man, one of the greatest games ever invented by humans. I would expect all *civilized* young men to know the rules.'

'I'm sure the boy can learn,' Chiron said.

'Please,' I said, 'what is this place? What am I doing here? Mr Brun – Chiron – why would you go to Yancy Academy just to teach me?'

Mr D snorted. 'I asked the same question.'

The camp director dealt the cards. Grover flinched every time one landed in his pile.

Chiron smiled at me sympathetically, the way he used to in Latin class, as if to let me know that no matter what my average was, *I* was his star student. He expected *me* to have the right answer.

'Percy,' he said. 'Did your mother tell you nothing?'

'She said . . .' I remembered her sad eyes, looking out over the sea. 'She told me she was afraid to send me here, even though my father had wanted her to. She said that once I was here, I probably couldn't leave. She wanted to keep me close to her.'

'Typical,' Mr D said. 'That's how they usually get killed. Young man, are you bidding or not?'

'What?' I asked.

He explained, impatiently, how you bid in pinochle, and so I did.

'I'm afraid there's too much to tell,' Chiron said. 'I'm afraid our usual orientation film won't be sufficient.'

'Orientation film?' I asked.

'No,' Chiron decided. 'Well, Percy. You know your friend Grover is a satyr. You know –' he pointed to the horn in the shoebox – 'that you have killed a Minotaur. No small feat, either, lad. What you may not know is that great powers are at work in your life. Gods – the forces you call the Greek gods – are very much alive.'

I stared at the others around the table.

I waited for somebody to yell, *Not!* But all I got was Mr D yelling, 'Oh, a royal marriage. Trick! Trick!' He cackled as he tallied up his points.

'Mr D,' Grover asked timidly, 'if you're not going to eat it, could I have your Diet Coke can?'

'Eh? Oh, all right.'

Grover bit a huge shard out of the empty aluminium can and chewed it mournfully.

'Wait,' I told Chiron. 'You're telling me there's such a thing as God.'

'Well, now,' Chiron said. 'God – capital *G*, God. That's a different matter altogether. We shan't deal with the metaphysical.'

'Metaphysical? But you were just talking about –'

'Ah, gods, plural, as in, great beings that control the forces of nature and human endeavours: the immortal gods of Olympus. That's a smaller matter.'

'Smaller!'

'Yes, quite. The gods we discussed in Latin class.'

'Zeus,' I said. 'Hera. Apollo. You mean them.'

And there it was again – distant thunder on a cloudless day.

'Young man,' said Mr D. 'I would really be less casual about throwing those names around, if I were you.'

'But they're stories,' I said. 'They're – myths, to explain

lightning and the seasons and stuff. They're what people believed before there was science.'

'Science!' Mr D scoffed. 'And tell me, Perseus Jackson —'

I flinched when he said my real name, which I never told anybody.

'— what will people think of your "science" two thousand years from now?' Mr D continued. 'Hmm? They will call it primitive mumbo jumbo. That's what. Oh, I love mortals — they have absolutely no sense of perspective. They think they've come so-o-o far. And have they, Chiron? Look at this boy and tell me.'

I wasn't liking Mr D much, but there was something about the way he called me mortal, as if . . . he wasn't. It was enough to put a lump in my throat, to suggest why Grover was dutifully minding his cards, chewing his soda can, and keeping his mouth shut.

'Percy,' Chiron said, 'you may choose to believe or not, but the fact is that *immortal* means immortal. Can you imagine that for a moment, never dying? Never fading? Existing, just as you are, for all time?'

I was about to answer, off the top of my head, that it sounded like a pretty good deal, but the tone of Chiron's voice made me hesitate.

'You mean, whether people believed in you or not,' I said.

'Exactly,' Chiron agreed. 'If you were a god, how would you like being called a myth, an old story to explain lightning? What if I told you, Perseus Jackson, that someday people would call *you* a myth, just created to explain how little boys can get over losing their mothers?'

My heart pounded. He was trying to make me angry for some reason, but I wasn't going to let him. I said, 'I wouldn't like it. But I don't believe in gods.'

'Oh, you'd better,' Mr D murmured. 'Before one of them incinerates you.'

Grover said, 'P-please, sir. He's just lost his mother. He's in shock.'

'A lucky thing, too,' Mr D grumbled, playing a card. 'Bad enough I'm confined to this miserable job, working with boys who don't even believe!'

He waved his hand and a goblet appeared on the table, as if the sunlight had bent, momentarily, and woven the air into glass. The goblet filled itself with red wine.

My jaw dropped, but Chiron hardly looked up.

'Mr D,' he warned, 'your restrictions.'

Mr D looked at the wine and feigned surprise.

'Dear me.' He looked at the sky and yelled, 'Old habits! Sorry!'

More thunder.

Mr D waved his hand again, and the wineglass changed into a fresh can of Diet Coke. He sighed unhappily, popped the top of the soda, and went back to his card game.

Chiron winked at me. 'Mr D offended his father a while back, took a fancy to a wood nymph who had been declared off-limits.'

'A wood nymph,' I repeated, still staring at the Diet Coke can like it was from outer space.

'Yes,' Mr D confessed. 'Father loves to punish me. The first time, Prohibition. Ghastly! Absolutely horrid ten years! The second time — well, she really was pretty, and I couldn't stay away — the second time, he sent me here. Half-Blood Hill. Summer camp for brats like you. "Be a better influence," he told me. "Work with youths rather than tearing them down." Ha! Absolutely unfair.'

Mr D sounded about six years old, like a pouting little kid.

'And . . .' I stammered, 'your father is . . .'

'*Di immortales*, Chiron,' Mr D said. 'I thought you taught this boy the basics. My father is Zeus, of course.'

I ran through D names from Greek mythology. Wine. The skin of a tiger. The satyrs that all seemed to work here. The way Grover cringed, as if Mr D were his master.

'You're Dionysus,' I said. 'The god of wine.'

Mr D rolled his eyes. 'What do they say, these days, Grover? Do the children say, "Well, duh!"?'

'Y-yes, Mr D.'

'Then, "Well, duh!" Percy Jackson. Did you think I was Aphrodite, perhaps?'

'You're a god.'

'Yes, child.'

'A god. You.'

He turned to look at me straight on, and I saw a kind of purplish fire in his eyes, a hint that this whiny, plump little man was only showing me the tiniest bit of his true nature. I saw visions of grape vines choking unbelievers to death, drunken warriors insane with battle lust, sailors screaming as their hands turned to flippers, their faces elongating into dolphin snouts. I knew that if I pushed him, Mr D would show me worse things. He would plant a disease in my brain that would leave me wearing a straitjacket in a rubber room for the rest of my life.

'Would you like to test me, child?' he said quietly.

'No. No, sir.'

The fire died a little. He turned back to his card game. 'I believe I win.'

'Not quite, Mr D,' Chiron said. He set down a straight, tallied the points, and said, 'The game goes to me.'

I thought Mr D was going to vaporize Chiron right out of his wheelchair, but he just sighed through his nose, as if he were used to being beaten by the Latin teacher. He got up, and Grover rose, too.

'I'm tired,' Mr D said. 'I believe I'll take a nap before the sing-along tonight. But first, Grover, we need to talk, *again*, about your less-than-perfect performance on this assignment.'

Grover's face beaded with sweat. 'Y-yes, sir.'

Mr D turned to me. 'Cabin eleven, Percy Jackson. And mind your manners.'

He swept into the farmhouse, Grover following miserably.

'Will Grover be okay?' I asked Chiron.

Chiron nodded, though he looked a bit troubled. 'Old Dionysus isn't really mad. He just hates his job. He's been . . . ah, grounded, I guess you would say, and he can't stand waiting another century before he's allowed to go back to Olympus.'

'Mount Olympus,' I said. 'You're telling me there really is a palace there?'

'Well now, there's Mount Olympus in Greece. And then there's the home of the gods, the convergence point of their powers, which did indeed used to be on Mount Olympus. It's still called Mount Olympus, out of respect to the old ways, but the palace moves, Percy, just as the gods do.'

'You mean the Greek gods are here? Like ... in *America*?'

'Well, certainly. The gods move with the heart of the West.'

'The what?'

'Come now, Percy. What you call "Western civilization". Do you think it's just an abstract concept? No, it's a living force. A collective consciousness that has burned bright for thousands of years. The gods are part of it. You might even say they are the source of it, or at least, they are tied so tightly to it that they couldn't possibly fade, not unless all of Western civilization were obliterated. The fire started in Greece. Then, as you well know – or as I hope you know, since you passed my course – the heart of the fire moved to Rome, and so did the gods. Oh, different names, perhaps – Jupiter for Zeus, Venus for Aphrodite, and so on – but the same forces, the same gods.'

'And then they died.'

'Died? No. Did the West die? The gods simply moved,

to Germany, to France, to Spain, for a while. Wherever the flame was brightest, the gods were there. They spent several centuries in England. All you need to do is look at the architecture. People do not forget the gods. Every place they've ruled, for the last three thousand years, you can see them in paintings, in statues, on the most important buildings. And yes, Percy, of course they are now in your United States. Look at your symbol, the eagle of Zeus. Look at the statue of Prometheus in Rockefeller Center, the Greek facades of your government buildings in Washington. I defy you to find any American city where the Olympians are not prominently displayed in multiple places. Like it or not – and believe me, plenty of people weren't very fond of Rome, either – America is now the heart of the flame. It is the great power of the West. And so Olympus is here. And we are here.'

It was all too much, especially the fact that *I* seemed to be included in Chiron's *we*, as if I were part of some club.

'Who are you, Chiron? Who . . . who am I?'

Chiron smiled. He shifted his weight as if he were going to get up out of his wheelchair, but I knew that was impossible. He was paralysed from the waist down.

'Who are you,' he mused. 'Well, that's the question we all want answered, isn't it? But for now, we should get you a bunk in cabin eleven. There will be new friends to meet. And plenty of time for lessons tomorrow. Besides, there will be toasted marshmallows at the campfire tonight, and I simply adore them.'

And then he did rise from his wheelchair. But there was

something odd about the way he did it. His blanket fell away from his legs, but the legs didn't move. His waist kept getting longer, rising above his belt. At first, I thought he was wearing very long, white velvet underwear, but as he kept rising out of the chair, taller than any man, I realized that the velvet underwear wasn't underwear; it was the front of an animal, muscle and sinew under coarse white fur. And the wheelchair wasn't a chair. It was some kind of container, an enormous box on wheels, and it must've been magic, because there's no way it could've held all of him. A leg came out, long and knobby-kneed, with a huge polished hoof. Then another front leg, then hindquarters, and then the box was empty, nothing but a metal shell with a couple of fake human legs attached.

I stared at the horse who had just sprung from the wheelchair: a huge white stallion. But where its neck should be was the upper body of my Latin teacher, smoothly grafted to the horse's trunk.

'What a relief,' the centaur said. 'I'd been cooped up in there so long, my fetlocks had fallen asleep. Now, come, Percy Jackson. Let's meet the other campers.'

6 ⚡ I BECOME SUPREME LORD OF THE BATHROOM

Once I got over the fact that my Latin teacher was a horse, we had a nice tour, though I was careful not to walk behind him. I'd done pooper-scooper patrol in the Macy's Thanksgiving Day Parade a few times, and, I'm sorry, I did not trust Chiron's back end the way I trusted his front.

We passed the volleyball pit. Several of the campers nudged each other. One pointed to the Minotaur horn I was carrying. Another said, 'That's *him*.'

Most of the campers were older than me. Their satyr friends were bigger than Grover, all of them trotting around in orange CAMP HALF-BLOOD T-shirts, with nothing else to cover their bare shaggy hindquarters. I wasn't normally shy, but the way they stared at me made me uncomfortable. I felt like they were expecting me to do a cartwheel or something.

I looked back at the farmhouse. It was a lot bigger than I'd realized – four storeys tall, sky blue with white trim, like an upmarket seaside resort. I was checking out the brass eagle weather vane on top when something caught my eye, a shadow in the uppermost window of the attic gable. Something had moved the curtain, just for a second, and I got the distinct impression I was being watched.

'What's up there?' I asked Chiron.

He looked where I was pointing, and his smile faded. 'Just the attic.'

'Somebody lives there?'

'No,' he said with finality. 'Not a single living thing.'

I got the feeling he was being truthful. But I was also sure something had moved that curtain.

'Come along, Percy,' Chiron said, his lighthearted tone now a little forced. 'Lots to see.'

We walked through the strawberry fields, where campers were picking bushels of berries while a satyr played a tune on a reed pipe.

Chiron told me the camp grew a nice crop for export to New York restaurants and Mount Olympus. 'It pays our expenses,' he explained. 'And the strawberries take almost no effort.'

He said Mr D had this effect on fruit-bearing plants: they just went crazy when he was around. It worked best with wine grapes, but Mr D was restricted from growing those, so they grew strawberries instead.

I watched the satyr playing his pipe. His music was causing lines of bugs to leave the strawberry patch in every direction, like refugees fleeing a fire. I wondered if Grover could work that kind of magic with music. I wondered if he was still inside the farmhouse, being lectured by Mr D.

'Grover won't get in too much trouble, will he?' I asked Chiron. 'I mean . . . he was a good protector. Really.'

Chiron sighed. He shed his tweed jacket and draped it over his horse's back like a saddle. 'Grover has big dreams,

Percy. Perhaps bigger than are reasonable. To reach his goal, he must first demonstrate great courage by succeeding as a keeper, finding a new camper and bringing him safely to Half-Blood Hill.'

'But he did that!'

'I might agree with you,' Chiron said. 'But it is not my place to judge. Dionysus and the Council of Cloven Elders must decide. I'm afraid they might not see this assignment as a success. After all, Grover lost you in New York. Then there's the unfortunate . . . ah . . . *fate* of your mother. And the fact that Grover was unconscious when you dragged him over the property line. The council might question whether this shows any courage on Grover's part.'

I wanted to protest. None of what had happened was Grover's fault. I also felt really, really guilty. If I hadn't given Grover the slip at the bus station, he might not have got in trouble.

'He'll get a second chance, won't he?'

Chiron winced. 'I'm afraid that *was* Grover's second chance, Percy. The council was not anxious to give him another, either, after what happened the first time, five years ago. Olympus knows, I advised him to wait longer before trying again. He's still so small for his age . . .'

'How old is he?'

'Oh, twenty-eight.'

'What! And he's in sixth grade?'

'Satyrs mature half as fast as humans, Percy. Grover has been the equivalent of a middle school student for the past six years.'

'That's horrible.'

'Quite,' Chiron agreed. 'At any rate, Grover is a late bloomer, even by satyr standards, and not yet very accomplished at woodland magic. Alas, he was anxious to pursue his dream. Perhaps now he will find some other career . . .'

'That's not fair,' I said. 'What happened the first time? Was it really so bad?'

Chiron looked away quickly. 'Let's move along, shall we?'

But I wasn't quite ready to let the subject drop. Something had occurred to me when Chiron talked about my mother's fate, as if he were intentionally avoiding the word *death*. The beginnings of an idea – a tiny, hopeful fire – started forming in my mind.

'Chiron,' I said. 'If the gods and Olympus and all that are real . . .'

'Yes, child?'

'Does that mean the Underworld is real, too?'

Chiron's expression darkened.

'Yes, child.' He paused, as if choosing his words carefully. 'There is a place where spirits go after death. But for now . . . until we know more . . . I would urge you to put that out of your mind.'

'What do you mean, "until we know more"?'

'Come, Percy. Let's see the woods.'

As we got closer, I realized how huge the forest was. It took up at least a quarter of the valley, with trees so tall and thick, you could imagine nobody had been in there since the Native Americans.

Chiron said, 'The woods are stocked, if you care to try your luck, but go armed.'

'Stocked with what?' I asked. 'Armed with what?'

'You'll see. Capture the flag is Friday night. Do you have your own sword and shield?'

'My own –'

'No,' Chiron said. 'I don't suppose you do. I think a size five will do. I'll visit the armoury later.'

I wanted to ask what kind of summer camp had an armoury, but there was too much else to think about, so the tour continued. We saw the archery range, the canoeing lake, the stables (which Chiron didn't seem to like very much), the javelin range, the sing-along amphitheatre, and the arena where Chiron said they held sword and spear fights.

'Sword and spear fights?' I asked.

'Cabin challenges and all that,' he explained. 'Not lethal. Usually. Oh, yes, and there's the mess hall.'

Chiron pointed to an outdoor pavilion framed in white Grecian columns on a hill overlooking the sea. There were a dozen stone picnic tables. No roof. No walls.

'What do you do when it rains?' I asked.

Chiron looked at me as if I'd gone a little weird. 'We still have to eat, don't we?' I decided to drop the subject.

Finally, he showed me the cabins. There were twelve of them, nestled in the woods by the lake. They were arranged in a U, with two at the base and five in a row on either side. And they were without doubt the most bizarre collection of buildings I'd ever seen.

Except for the fact that each had a large brass number above the door (odds on the left side, evens on the right), they looked absolutely nothing alike. Number nine had smokestacks like a tiny factory. Number four had tomato vines on the walls and a roof made out of real grass. Seven seemed to be made of solid gold, which gleamed so much in the sunlight it was almost impossible to look at. They all faced a commons area about the size of a soccer field, dotted with Greek statues, fountains, flower beds, and a couple of basketball hoops (which were more my speed).

In the centre of the field was a huge stone-lined firepit. Even though it was a warm afternoon, the hearth smouldered. A girl about nine years old was tending the flames, poking the coals with a stick.

The pair of cabins at the head of the field, numbers one and two, looked like his-and-hers mausoleums, big white marble boxes with heavy columns in front. Cabin one was the biggest and bulkiest of the twelve. Its polished bronze doors shimmered like a holograph, so that from different angles lightning bolts seemed to streak across them. Cabin two was more graceful somehow, with slimmer columns garlanded with pomegranates and flowers. The walls were carved with images of peacocks.

'Zeus and Hera?' I guessed.

'Correct,' Chiron said.

'Their cabins look empty.'

'Several of the cabins are. That's true. No one ever stays in one or two.'

Okay. So each cabin had a different god, like a mascot.

Twelve cabins for the twelve Olympians. But why would some be empty?

I stopped in front of the first cabin on the left, cabin three.

It wasn't high and mighty like cabin one, but long and low and solid. The outer walls were of rough grey stone studded with pieces of seashell and coral, as if the slabs had been hewn straight from the bottom of the ocean floor. I peeked inside the open doorway and Chiron said, 'Oh, I wouldn't do that!'

Before he could pull me back, I caught the salty scent of the interior, like the wind on the shore at Montauk. The interior walls glowed like abalone. There were six empty bunk beds with silk sheets turned down. But there was no sign anyone had ever slept there. The place felt so sad and lonely, I was glad when Chiron put his hand on my shoulder and said, 'Come along, Percy.'

Most of the other cabins were crowded with campers.

Number five was bright red – a real nasty paint job, as if the colour had been splashed on with buckets and fists. The roof was lined with barbed wire. A stuffed wild boar's head hung over the doorway, and its eyes seemed to follow me. Inside I could see a bunch of mean-looking kids, both girls and boys, arm wrestling and arguing with each other while rock music blared. The loudest was a girl maybe thirteen or fourteen. She wore a size XXXL Camp Half-Blood T-shirt under a camouflage jacket. She zeroed in on me and gave me an evil sneer. She reminded me of Nancy Bobofit, though the camper girl was much bigger and tougher looking, and her hair was long and stringy, and brown instead of red.

I kept walking, trying to stay clear of Chiron's hooves. 'We haven't seen any other centaurs,' I observed.

'No,' said Chiron sadly. 'My kinsmen are a wild and barbaric folk, I'm afraid. You might encounter them in the wilderness, or at major sporting events. But you won't see any here.'

'You said your name was Chiron. Are you really . . .'

He smiled down at me. '*The* Chiron from the stories? Trainer of Hercules and all that? Yes, Percy, I am.'

'But, shouldn't you be dead?'

Chiron paused, as if the question intrigued him. 'I honestly don't know about *should* be. The truth is, I *can't* be dead. You see, aeons ago the gods granted my wish. I could continue the work I loved. I could be a teacher of heroes as long as humanity needed me. I gained much from that wish . . . and I gave up much. But I'm still here, so I can only assume I'm still needed.'

I thought about being a teacher for three thousand years. It wouldn't have made my Top Ten Things to Wish For list.

'Doesn't it ever get boring?'

'No, no,' he said. 'Horribly depressing, at times, but never boring.'

'Why depressing?'

Chiron seemed to turn hard of hearing again.

'Oh, look,' he said. 'Annabeth is waiting for us.'

* * *

The blonde girl I'd met at the Big House was reading a book in front of the last cabin on the left, number eleven.

When we reached her, she looked me over critically, like she was still thinking about how much I drooled.

I tried to see what she was reading, but I couldn't make out the title. I thought my dyslexia was acting up. Then I realized the title wasn't even English. The letters looked Greek to me. I mean, literally Greek. There were pictures of temples and statues and different kinds of columns, like those in an architecture book.

'Annabeth,' Chiron said, 'I have masters' archery class at noon. Would you take Percy from here?'

'Yes, sir.'

'Cabin eleven,' Chiron told me, gesturing towards the doorway. 'Make yourself at home.'

Out of all the cabins, eleven looked the most like a regular old summer camp cabin, with the emphasis on *old*. The threshold was worn down, the brown paint peeling. Over the doorway was one of those doctor's symbols, a winged pole with two snakes wrapped around it. What did they call it . . . ? A caduceus.

Inside, it was packed with people, both boys and girls, way more than the number of bunk beds. Sleeping bags were spread all over on the floor. It looked like a gym where the Red Cross had set up an evacuation centre.

Chiron didn't go in. The door was too low for him. But when the campers saw him they all stood and bowed respectfully.

'Well, then,' Chiron said. 'Good luck, Percy. I'll see you at dinner.'

He galloped away towards the archery range.

I stood in the doorway, looking at the kids. They weren't bowing any more. They were staring at me, sizing me up. I knew this routine. I'd gone through it at enough schools.

'Well?' Annabeth prompted. 'Go on.'

So naturally I tripped coming in the door and made a total fool of myself. There were some snickers from the campers, but none of them said anything.

Annabeth announced, 'Percy Jackson, meet cabin eleven.'

'Regular or undetermined?' somebody asked.

I didn't know what to say, but Annabeth said, 'Undetermined.'

Everybody groaned.

A guy who was a little older than the rest came forward. 'Now, now, campers. That's what we're here for. Welcome, Percy. You can have that spot on the floor, right over there.'

The guy was about nineteen, and he looked pretty cool. He was tall and muscular, with short-cropped sandy hair and a friendly smile. He wore an orange tank top, cutoffs, sandals and a leather necklace with five different-coloured clay beads. The only thing unsettling about his appearance was a thick white scar that ran from just beneath his right eye to his jaw, like an old knife slash.

'This is Luke,' Annabeth said, and her voice sounded different somehow. I glanced over and could've sworn she was blushing. She saw me looking, and her expression hardened again. 'He's your counsellor for now.'

'For now?' I asked.

'You're undetermined,' Luke explained patiently. 'They don't know what cabin to put you in, so you're here. Cabin eleven takes all newcomers, all visitors. Naturally, we would. Hermes, our patron, is the god of travellers.'

I looked at the tiny section of floor they'd given me. I had nothing to put there to mark it as my own, no luggage, no clothes, no sleeping bag. Just the Minotaur's horn. I thought about setting that down, but then I remembered that Hermes was also the god of thieves.

I looked around at the campers' faces, some sullen and suspicious, some grinning stupidly, some eyeing me as if they were waiting for a chance to pick my pockets.

'How long will I be here?' I asked.

'Good question,' Luke said. 'Until you're determined.'

'How long will that take?'

The campers all laughed.

'Come on,' Annabeth told me. 'I'll show you the volleyball court.'

'I've already seen it.'

'Come on.'

She grabbed my wrist and dragged me outside. I could hear the kids of cabin eleven laughing behind me.

When we were a few metres away, Annabeth said, 'Jackson, you have to do better than that.'

'What?'

She rolled her eyes and mumbled under her breath, 'I can't believe I thought you were the one.'

'What's your problem?' I was getting angry now. 'All I know is, I kill some bull guy –'

'Don't talk like that!' Annabeth told me. 'You know how many kids at this camp wish they'd had your chance?'

'To get killed?'

'To fight the Minotaur! What do you think we train for?'

I shook my head. 'Look, if the thing I fought really was *the* Minotaur, the same one in the stories . . .'

'Yes.'

'Then there's only one.'

'Yes.'

'And he died, like, a gajillion years ago, right? Theseus killed him in the labyrinth. So . . .'

'Monsters don't die, Percy. They can be killed. But they don't die.'

'Oh, thanks. That clears it up.'

'They don't have souls, like you and me. You can dispel them for a while, maybe even for a whole lifetime if you're lucky. But they are primal forces. Chiron calls them archetypes. Eventually, they re-form.'

I thought about Mrs Dodds. 'You mean if I killed one, accidentally, with a sword –'

'The Fu . . . I mean, your maths teacher. That's right. She's still out there. You just made her very, very mad.'

'How did you know about Mrs Dodds?'

'You talk in your sleep.'

'You almost called her something. A Fury? They're Hades' torturers, right?'

Annabeth glanced nervously at the ground, as if she expected it to open up and swallow her. 'You shouldn't call them by name, even here. We call them the Kindly Ones, if we have to speak of them at all.'

'Look, is there anything we *can* say without it thundering?' I sounded whiny, even to myself, but right then I didn't care. 'Why do I have to stay in cabin eleven, anyway? Why is everybody so crowded together? There are plenty of empty bunks right over there.'

I pointed to the first few cabins, and Annabeth turned pale. 'You don't just choose a cabin, Percy. It depends on who your parents are. Or . . . your parent.'

She stared at me, waiting for me to get it.

'My mom is Sally Jackson,' I said. 'She works at the candy store in Grand Central Station. At least, she used to.'

'I'm sorry about your mom, Percy. But that's not what I mean. I'm talking about your other parent. Your dad.'

'He's dead. I never knew him.'

Annabeth sighed. Clearly, she'd had this conversation before with other kids. 'Your father's not dead, Percy.'

'How can you say that? You know him?'

'No, of course not.'

'Then how can you say —'

'Because I know *you*. You wouldn't be here if you weren't one of us.'

'You don't know anything about me.'

'No?' She raised an eyebrow. 'I bet you moved around

from school to school. I bet you were kicked out of a lot of them.'

'How –'

'Diagnosed with dyslexia. Probably ADHD, too.'

I tried to swallow my embarrassment. 'What does that have to do with anything?'

'Taken together, it's almost a sure sign. The letters float off the page when you read, right? That's because your mind is hardwired for ancient Greek. And the ADHD – you're impulsive, can't sit still in the classroom. That's your battlefield reflexes. In a real fight, they'd keep you alive. As for the attention problems, that's because you see too much, Percy, not too little. Your senses are better than a regular mortal's. Of course the teachers want you medicated. Most of them are monsters. They don't want you seeing them for what they are.'

'You sound like . . . you went through the same thing?'

'Most of the kids here did. If you weren't like us, you couldn't have survived the Minotaur, much less the ambrosia and nectar.'

'Ambrosia and nectar.'

'The food and drink we were giving you to make you better. That stuff would've killed a normal kid. It would've turned your blood to fire and your bones to sand and you'd be dead. Face it. You're a half-blood.'

A half-blood.

I was reeling with so many questions I didn't know where to start.

Then a husky voice yelled, 'Well! A newbie!'

I looked over. The big girl from the ugly red cabin was sauntering towards us. She had three other girls behind her, all big and ugly and mean-looking like her, all wearing camo jackets.

'Clarisse,' Annabeth sighed. 'Why don't you go polish your spear or something?'

'Sure, Miss Princess,' the big girl said. 'So I can run you through with it Friday night.'

'*Errete es korakas*,' Annabeth said, which I somehow understood was Greek for "Go to the crows", though I had a feeling it was a worse curse than it sounded. 'You don't stand a chance.'

'We'll pulverize you,' Clarisse said, but her eye twitched. Perhaps she wasn't sure she could follow through on the threat. She turned towards me. 'Who's this little runt?'

'Percy Jackson,' Annabeth said, 'meet Clarisse, Daughter of Ares.'

I blinked. 'Like . . . the war god?'

Clarisse sneered. 'You got a problem with that?'

'No,' I said, recovering my wits. 'It explains the bad smell.'

Clarisse growled. 'We got an initiation ceremony for newbies, Prissy.'

'Percy.'

'Whatever. Come on, I'll show you.'

'Clarisse –' Annabeth tried to say.

'Stay out of it, wise girl.'

Annabeth looked pained, but she did stay out of it, and

I didn't really want her help. I was the new kid. I had to earn my own rep.

I handed Annabeth my Minotaur horn and got ready to fight, but before I knew it, Clarisse had me by the neck and was dragging me towards a cinder-block building that I knew immediately was the bathroom.

I was kicking and punching. I'd been in plenty of fights before, but this big girl Clarisse had hands like iron. She dragged me into the girls' bathroom. There was a line of toilets on one side and a line of shower stalls down the other. It smelled just like any public bathroom, and I was thinking – as much as I *could* think with Clarisse ripping my hair out – that if this place belonged to the gods, they should've been able to afford classier toilets.

Clarisse's friends were all laughing, and I was trying to find the strength I'd used to fight the Minotaur, but it just wasn't there.

'Like he's "Big Three" material,' Clarisse said as she pushed me towards one of the toilets. 'Yeah, right. Minotaur probably fell over laughing, he was so stupid-looking.'

Her friends snickered.

Annabeth stood in the corner, watching through her fingers.

Clarisse bent me over on my knees and started pushing my head towards the toilet bowl. It reeked like rusted pipes and, well, like what goes into toilets. I strained to keep my head up. I was looking at the scummy water thinking, I will not go into that. I won't.

Then something happened. I felt a tug in the pit of my stomach. I heard the plumbing rumble, the pipes shudder. Clarisse's grip on my hair loosened. Water shot out of the toilet, making an arc straight over my head, and the next thing I knew, I was sprawled on the bathroom tiles with Clarisse screaming behind me.

I turned just as water blasted out of the toilet again, hitting Clarisse straight in the face so hard it pushed her down onto her butt. The water stayed on her like the spray from a fire hose, pushing her backwards into a shower stall.

She struggled, gasping, and her friends started coming towards her. But then the other toilets exploded, too, and six more streams of toilet water blasted them back. The showers acted up, too, and together all the fixtures sprayed the camouflage girls right out of the bathroom, spinning them around like pieces of garbage being washed away.

As soon as they were out the door, I felt the tug in my gut lessen, and the water shut off as quickly as it had started.

The entire bathroom was flooded. Annabeth hadn't been spared. She was dripping wet, but she hadn't been pushed out the door. She was standing in exactly the same place, staring at me in shock.

I looked down and realized I was sitting in the only dry spot in the whole room. There was a circle of dry floor around me. I didn't have one drop of water on my clothes. Nothing.

I stood up, my legs shaky.

Annabeth said, 'How did you . . .'

'I don't know.'

We walked to the door. Outside, Clarisse and her friends were sprawled in the mud, and a bunch of other campers had gathered around to gawk. Clarisse's hair was flattened across her face. Her camouflage jacket was sopping and she smelled like sewage. She gave me a look of absolute hatred. 'You are dead, new boy. You are totally dead.'

I probably should have let it go, but I said, 'You want to gargle with toilet water again, Clarisse? Close your mouth.'

Her friends had to hold her back. They dragged her towards cabin five, while the other campers made way to avoid her flailing feet.

Annabeth stared at me. I couldn't tell whether she was just grossed out or angry at me for dousing her.

'What?' I demanded. 'What are you thinking?'

'I'm thinking,' she said, 'that I want you on my team for capture the flag.'

7 ⚡ MY DINNER GOES UP IN SMOKE

Word of the bathroom incident spread immediately. Wherever I went, campers pointed at me and murmured something about toilet water. Or maybe they were just staring at Annabeth, who was still pretty much dripping wet.

She showed me a few more places: the metal shop (where kids were forging their own swords), the arts-and-crafts room (where satyrs were sandblasting a giant marble statue of a goat-man), and the climbing wall, which actually consisted of two facing walls that shook violently, dropped boulders, sprayed lava and clashed together if you didn't get to the top fast enough.

Finally we returned to the canoeing lake, where the trail led back to the cabins.

'I've got training to do,' Annabeth said flatly. 'Dinner's at seven thirty. Just follow your cabin to the mess hall.'

'Annabeth, I'm sorry about the toilets.'

'Whatever.'

'It wasn't my fault.'

She looked at me sceptically, and I realized it *was* my fault. I'd made water shoot out of the bathroom fixtures. I didn't understand how. But the toilets had responded to me. I had become one with the plumbing.

'You need to talk to the Oracle,' Annabeth said.

'Who?'

'Not who. What. The Oracle. I'll ask Chiron.'

I stared into the lake, wishing somebody would give me a straight answer for once.

I wasn't expecting anybody to be looking back at me from the bottom, so my heart skipped a beat when I noticed two teenage girls sitting cross-legged at the base of the pier, about five metres below. They wore blue jeans and shimmering green T-shirts, and their brown hair floated loose around their shoulders as minnows darted in and out. They smiled and waved as if I were a long-lost friend.

I didn't know what else to do. I waved back.

'Don't encourage them,' Annabeth warned. 'Naiads are terrible flirts.'

'Naiads,' I repeated, feeling completely overwhelmed. 'That's it. I want to go home now.'

Annabeth frowned. 'Don't you get it, Percy? You *are* home. This is the only safe place on earth for kids like us.'

'You mean, mentally disturbed kids?'

'I mean *not human*. Not totally human, anyway. Half-human.'

'Half-human and half-what?'

'I think you know.'

I didn't want to admit it, but I was afraid I did. I felt a tingling in my limbs, a sensation I sometimes felt when my mom talked about my dad.

'God,' I said. 'Half-god.'

Annabeth nodded. 'Your father isn't dead, Percy. He's one of the Olympians.'

'That's . . . crazy.'

'Is it? What's the most common thing gods did in the old stories? They ran around falling in love with humans and having kids with them. Do you think they've changed their habits in the last few millennia?'

'But those are just –' I almost said *myths* again. Then I remembered Chiron's warning that in two thousand years, *I* might be considered a myth. 'But if all the kids here are half-gods –'

'Demigods,' Annabeth said. 'That's the official term. Or half-bloods.'

'Then who's your dad?'

Her hands tightened around the pier railing. I got the feeling I'd just trespassed on a sensitive subject.

'My dad is a professor at West Point,' she said. 'I haven't seen him since I was very small. He teaches American history.'

'He's human.'

'What? You assume it has to be a male god who finds a human female attractive? How sexist is that?'

'Who's your mom, then?'

'Cabin six.'

'Meaning?'

Annabeth straightened. 'Athena. Goddess of wisdom and battle.'

Okay, I thought. Why not?

'And my dad?'

'Undetermined,' Annabeth said, 'like I told you before. Nobody knows.'

'Except my mother. She knew.'

'Maybe not, Percy. Gods don't always reveal their identities.'

'My dad would have. He loved her.'

Annabeth gave me a cautious look. She didn't want to burst my bubble. 'Maybe you're right. Maybe he'll send a sign. That's the only way to know for sure: your father has to send you a sign claiming you as his son. Sometimes it happens.'

'You mean sometimes it doesn't?'

Annabeth ran her palm along the rail. 'The gods are busy. They have a lot of kids and they don't always . . . Well, sometimes they don't care about us, Percy. They ignore us.'

I thought about some of the kids I'd seen in the Hermes cabin, teenagers who looked sullen and depressed, as if they were waiting for a call that would never come. I'd known kids like that at Yancy Academy, shuffled off to boarding school by rich parents who didn't have the time to deal with them. But gods should behave better.

'So I'm stuck here,' I said. 'That's it? For the rest of my life?'

'It depends,' Annabeth said. 'Some campers only stay the summer. If you're a child of Aphrodite or Demeter, you're probably not a real powerful force. The monsters might ignore you, so you can get by with a few months of summer training and live in the mortal world the rest of the year. But for some of us, it's too dangerous to leave. We're year-rounders. In the mortal world, we attract monsters. They sense us. They come to challenge us. Most of the time, they'll ignore us until we're old enough to cause trouble – about ten or eleven years old – but after that most demigods either make their way here, or they get killed off. A few manage to survive in the outside world and become famous. Believe me, if I told you the names, you'd know them. Some don't even realize they're demigods. But very, very few are like that.'

'So monsters can't get in here?'

Annabeth shook her head. 'Not unless they're intentionally stocked in the woods or specially summoned by somebody on the inside.'

'Why would anybody want to summon a monster?'

'Practice fights. Practical jokes.'

'Practical jokes?'

'The point is, the borders are sealed to keep mortals and monsters out. From the outside, mortals look into the valley and see nothing unusual, just a strawberry farm.'

'So . . . you're a year-rounder?'

Annabeth nodded. From under the collar of her T-shirt she pulled a leather necklace with five clay beads of different colours. It was just like Luke's, except Annabeth's also had a big gold ring strung on it, like a college ring.

'I've been here since I was seven,' she said. 'Every August, on the last day of summer session, you get a bead for surviving another year. I've been here longer than most of the counsellors, and they're all in college.'

'Why did you come so young?'

She twisted the ring on her necklace. 'None of your business.'

'Oh.' I stood there for a minute in uncomfortable silence. 'So . . . I could just walk out of here right now if I wanted to?'

'It would be suicide, but you could, with Mr D's or Chiron's permission. But they wouldn't give permission until the end of the summer session unless . . .'

'Unless?'

'You were granted a quest. But that hardly ever happens. The last time . . .'

Her voice trailed off. I could tell from her tone that the last time hadn't gone well.

'Back in the sick room,' I said, 'when you were feeding me that stuff –'

'Ambrosia.'

'Yeah. You asked me something about the summer solstice.'

Annabeth's shoulders tensed. 'So you *do* know something?'

'Well . . . no. Back at my old school, I overheard Grover and Chiron talking about it. Grover mentioned the summer solstice. He said something like we didn't have much time, because of the deadline. What did that mean?'

She clenched her fists. 'I wish I knew. Chiron and the satyrs, they know, but they won't tell me. Something is wrong in Olympus, something pretty major. Last time I was there, everything seemed so *normal.*'

'You've been to Olympus?'

'Some of us year-rounders – Luke and Clarisse and I and a few others – we took a field trip during winter solstice. That's when the gods have their big annual council.'

'But ... how did you get there?'

'The Long Island Railroad, of course. You get off at Penn Station. Empire State Building, special elevator to the six-hundredth floor.' She looked at me like she was sure I must know this already. 'You *are* a New Yorker, right?'

'Oh, sure.' As far as I knew, there were only a hundred and two floors in the Empire State Building, but I decided not to point that out.

'Right after we visited,' Annabeth continued, 'the weather got weird, as if the gods had started fighting. A couple of times since, I've overheard satyrs talking. The best I can figure out is that something important was stolen. And if it isn't returned by summer solstice, there's going to be trouble. When you came, I was hoping ... I mean – Athena can get along with just about anybody, except for Ares. And of course she's got the rivalry with Poseidon. But, I mean, aside from that, I thought we could work together. I thought you might know something.'

I shook my head. I wished I could help her, but I felt too hungry and tired and mentally overloaded to ask any more questions.

'I've got to get a quest,' Annabeth muttered to herself. 'I'm *not* too young. If they would just tell me the problem ...'

I could smell barbecue smoke coming from somewhere

nearby. Annabeth must've heard my stomach growl. She told me to go on, she'd catch me later. I left her on the pier, tracing her finger across the rail as if drawing a battle plan.

Back at cabin eleven, everybody was talking and horsing around, waiting for dinner. For the first time, I noticed that a lot of the campers had similar features: sharp noses, upturned eyebrows, mischievous smiles. They were the kind of kids that teachers would peg as troublemakers. Thankfully, nobody paid much attention to me as I walked over to my spot on the floor and plopped down with my Minotaur horn.

The counsellor, Luke, came over. He had the Hermes family resemblance, too. It was marred by that scar on his right cheek, but his smile was intact.

'Found you a sleeping bag,' he said. 'And here, I stole you some toiletries from the camp store.'

I couldn't tell if he was kidding about the stealing part. I said, 'Thanks.'

'No prob.' Luke sat next to me, pushed his back against the wall. 'Tough first day?'

'I don't belong here,' I said. 'I don't even believe in gods.'

'Yeah,' he said. 'That's how we all started. Once you start believing in them? It doesn't get any easier.'

The bitterness in his voice surprised me, because Luke seemed like a pretty easygoing guy. He looked like he could handle just about anything.

'So your dad is Hermes?' I asked.

He pulled a switchblade out of his back pocket, and for a second I thought he was going to gut me, but he just scraped the mud off the sole of his sandal. 'Yeah. Hermes.'

'The wing-footed messenger guy.'

'That's him. Messengers. Medicine. Travellers, merchants, thieves. Anybody who uses the roads. That's why you're here, enjoying cabin eleven's hospitality. Hermes isn't picky about who he sponsors.'

I figured Luke didn't mean to call me a nobody. He just had a lot on his mind.

'You ever meet your dad?' I asked.

'Once.'

I waited, thinking that if he wanted to tell me, he'd tell me. Apparently, he didn't. I wondered if the story had anything to do with how he got his scar.

Luke looked up and managed a smile. 'Don't worry about it, Percy. The campers here, they're mostly good people. After all, we're extended family, right? We take care of each other.'

He seemed to understand how lost I felt, and I was grateful for that, because an older guy like him – even if he was a counsellor – should've steered clear of an uncool middle-schooler like me. But Luke had welcomed me into the cabin. He'd even stolen me some toiletries, which was the nicest thing anybody had done for me all day.

I decided to ask him my last big question, the one that had been bothering me all afternoon. 'Clarisse, from Ares, was joking about me being "Big Three" material. Then

Annabeth . . . twice, she said I might be "the one". She said I should talk to the Oracle. What was that all about?'

Luke folded his knife. 'I hate prophecies.'

'What do you mean?'

His face twitched around the scar. 'Let's just say I messed things up for everybody else. The last two years, ever since my trip to the Garden of the Hesperides went sour, Chiron hasn't allowed any more quests. Annabeth's been dying to get out into the world. She pestered Chiron so much he finally told her he already knew her fate. He'd had a prophecy from the Oracle. He wouldn't tell her the whole thing, but he said Annabeth wasn't destined to go on a quest yet. She had to wait until . . . somebody special came to the camp.'

'Somebody special.'

'Don't worry about it, kid,' Luke said. 'Annabeth wants to think every new camper who comes through here is the omen she's been waiting for. Now, come on, it's dinnertime.'

The moment he said it, a horn blew in the distance. Somehow, I knew it was a conch shell, even though I'd never heard one before.

Luke yelled, 'Eleven, fall in!'

The whole cabin, about twenty of us, filed into the commons yard. We lined up in order of seniority, so of course I was dead last. Campers came from the other cabins, too, except for the three empty cabins at the end, and cabin eight, which had looked normal in the daytime, but was now starting to glow silver as the sun went down.

We marched up the hill to the mess hall pavilion. Satyrs joined us from the meadow. Naiads emerged from the canoeing lake. A few other girls came out of the woods — and when I say out of the woods, I mean *straight* out of the woods. I saw one girl, about nine or ten years old, melt from the side of a maple tree and come skipping up the hill.

In all, there were maybe a hundred campers, a few dozen satyrs, and a dozen assorted wood nymphs and naiads.

At the pavilion, torches blazed around the marble columns. A central fire burned in a bronze brazier the size of a bathtub. Each cabin had its own table, covered in white cloth trimmed in purple. Four of the tables were empty, but cabin eleven's was way overcrowded. I had to squeeze on to the edge of a bench with half my butt hanging off.

I saw Grover sitting at table twelve with Mr D, a few satyrs and a couple of plump blond boys who looked just like Mr D. Chiron stood to one side, the picnic table being way too small for a centaur.

Annabeth sat at table six with a bunch of serious-looking athletic kids, all with her grey eyes and honey-blonde hair.

Clarisse sat behind me at Ares's table. She'd apparently gotten over being hosed down, because she was laughing and belching right alongside her friends.

Finally, Chiron pounded his hoof against the marble floor of the pavilion, and everybody fell silent. He raised a glass. 'To the gods!'

Everybody else raised their glasses. 'To the gods!'

Wood nymphs came forward with platters of food:

grapes, apples, strawberries, cheese, fresh bread and yes, barbecue! My glass was empty, but Luke said, 'Speak to it. Whatever you want – non-alcoholic, of course.'

I said, 'Cherry Coke.'

The glass filled with sparkling caramel liquid.

Then I had an idea. '*Blue* Cherry Coke.'

The soda turned a violent shade of cobalt.

I took a cautious sip. Perfect.

I drank a toast to my mother.

She's not gone, I told myself. Not permanently, anyway. She's in the Underworld. And if that's a real place, then some day . . .

'Here you go, Percy,' Luke said, handing me a platter of smoked brisket.

I loaded my plate and was about to take a big bite when I noticed everybody getting up, carrying their plates towards the fire in the centre of the pavilion. I wondered if they were going for dessert or something.

'Come on,' Luke told me.

As I got closer, I saw that everyone was taking a portion of their meal and dropping it into the fire, the ripest strawberry, the juiciest slice of beef, the warmest, most buttery roll.

Luke murmured in my ear, 'Burnt offerings for the gods. They like the smell.'

'You're kidding.'

His look warned me not to take this lightly, but I couldn't help wondering why an immortal, all-powerful being would like the smell of burning food.

Luke approached the fire, bowed his head, and tossed in a cluster of fat red grapes. 'Hermes.'

I was next.

I wished I knew what god's name to say.

Finally, I made a silent plea. *Whoever you are, tell me. Please.*

I scraped a big slice of brisket into the flames.

When I caught a whiff of the smoke, I didn't gag.

It smelled nothing like burning food. It smelled of hot chocolate and fresh-baked brownies, hamburgers on the grill and wildflowers, and a hundred other good things that shouldn't have gone well together, but did. I could almost believe the gods could live off that smoke.

When everybody had returned to their seats and finished eating their meals, Chiron pounded his hoof again for our attention.

Mr D got up with a huge sigh. 'Yes, I suppose I'd better say hello to all you brats. Well, hello. Our activities director, Chiron, says the next capture the flag is Friday. Cabin five presently holds the laurels.'

A bunch of ugly cheering rose from the Ares table.

'Personally,' Mr D continued, 'I couldn't care less, but congratulations. Also, I should tell you that we have a new camper today. Peter Johnson.'

Chiron murmured something.

'Er, Percy Jackson,' Mr D corrected. 'That's right. Hurrah, and all that. Now run along to your silly campfire. Go on.'

Everybody cheered. We all headed down towards the

amphitheatre, where Apollo's cabin led a sing-along. We sang camp songs about the gods and ate toasted marshmallows and joked around, and the funny thing was, I didn't feel that anyone was staring at me any more. I felt that I was home.

Later in the evening, when the sparks from the campfire were curling into a starry sky, the conch horn blew again, and we all filed back to our cabins. I didn't realize how exhausted I was until I collapsed on my borrowed sleeping bag.

My fingers curled around the Minotaur horn. I thought about my mom, but I had good thoughts: her smile, the bedtime stories she would read me when I was a kid, the way she would tell me not to let the bedbugs bite.

When I closed my eyes, I fell asleep instantly.

That was my first day at Camp Half-Blood.

I wish I'd known how briefly I would get to enjoy my new home.

8 WE CAPTURE A FLAG

The next few days I settled into a routine that felt almost normal, if you don't count the fact that I was getting lessons from satyrs, nymphs and a centaur.

Each morning I took Ancient Greek from Annabeth, and we talked about the gods and goddesses in the present tense, which was kind of weird. I discovered Annabeth was right about my dyslexia: Ancient Greek wasn't that hard for me to read. At least, no harder than English. After a couple of mornings, I could stumble through a few lines of Homer without too much headache.

The rest of the day, I'd rotate through outdoor activities, looking for something I was good at. Chiron tried to teach me archery, but we found out pretty quick I wasn't any good with a bow and arrow. He didn't complain, even when he had to desnag a stray arrow out of his tail.

Foot racing? No good either. The wood-nymph instructors left me in the dust. They told me not to worry about it. They'd had centuries of practice running away from lovesick gods. But still, it was a little humiliating to be slower than a tree.

And wrestling? Forget it. Every time I got on the mat, Clarisse would pulverize me.

'There's more where that came from, punk,' she'd mumble in my ear.

The only thing I really excelled at was canoeing, and that wasn't the kind of heroic skill people expected to see from the kid who had beaten the Minotaur.

I knew the senior campers and counsellors were watching me, trying to decide who my dad was, but they weren't having an easy time of it. I wasn't as strong as the Ares kids, or as good at archery as the Apollo kids. I didn't have Hephaestus's skill with metalwork or – gods forbid – Dionysus's way with vine plants. Luke told me I might be a child of Hermes, a kind of jack-of-all-trades, master of none. But I got the feeling he was just trying to make me feel better. He really didn't know what to make of me either.

Despite all that, I liked camp. I got used to the morning fog over the beach, the smell of hot strawberry fields in the afternoon, even the weird noises of monsters in the woods at night. I would eat dinner with cabin eleven, scrape part of my meal into the fire, and try to feel some connection to my real dad. Nothing came. Just that warm feeling I'd always had, like the memory of his smile. I tried not to think too much about my mom, but I kept wondering: if gods and monsters were real, if all this magical stuff was possible, surely there was some way to save her, to bring her back . . .

I started to understand Luke's bitterness and how he seemed to resent his father, Hermes. So okay, maybe gods had important things to do. But couldn't they call once in a while, or thunder, or something? Dionysus could make Diet Coke appear out of thin air. Why couldn't my dad, whoever he was, make a phone appear?

Thursday afternoon, three days after I'd arrived at Camp Half-Blood, I had my first sword-fighting lesson. Everybody from cabin eleven gathered in the big circular arena, where Luke would be our instructor.

We started with basic stabbing and slashing, using some straw-stuffed dummies in Greek armour. I guess I did okay. At least, I understood what I was supposed to do and my reflexes were good.

The problem was, I couldn't find a blade that felt right in my hands. Either they were too heavy, or too light, or too long. Luke tried his best to fix me up, but he agreed that none of the practice blades seemed to work for me.

We moved on to duelling in pairs. Luke announced he would be my partner, since this was my first time.

'Good luck,' one of the campers told me. 'Luke's the best swordsman in the last three hundred years.'

'Maybe he'll go easy on me,' I said.

The camper snorted.

Luke showed me thrusts and parries and shield blocks the hard way. With every swipe, I got a little more battered and bruised. 'Keep your guard up, Percy,' he'd say, then whap me in the ribs with the flat of his blade. 'No, not that far up!' *Whap!* 'Lunge!' *Whap!* 'Now, back!' *Whap!*

By the time he called a break, I was soaked in sweat. Everybody swarmed the drinks cooler. Luke poured ice water on his head, which looked like such a good idea, I did the same.

Instantly, I felt better. Strength surged back into my arms. The sword didn't feel so awkward.

'Okay, everybody circle up!' Luke ordered. 'If Percy doesn't mind, I want to give you a little demo.'

Great, I thought. Let's all watch Percy get pounded.

The Hermes guys gathered around. They were suppressing smiles. I figured they'd been in my shoes before and couldn't wait to see how Luke used me for a punching bag. He told everybody he was going to demonstrate a disarming technique: how to twist the enemy's blade with the flat of your own sword so that he had no choice but to drop his weapon.

'This is difficult,' he stressed. 'I've had it used against me. No laughing at Percy, now. Most swordsmen have to work years to master this technique.'

He demonstrated the move on me in slow motion. Sure enough, the sword clattered out of my hand.

'Now in real time,' he said, after I'd retrieved my weapon. 'We keep sparring until one of us pulls it off. Ready, Percy?'

I nodded, and Luke came after me. Somehow, I kept him from getting a shot at the hilt of my sword. My senses opened up. I saw his attacks coming. I countered. I stepped forward and tried a thrust of my own. Luke deflected it easily, but I saw a change in his face. His eyes narrowed, and he started to press me with more force.

The sword grew heavy in my hand. The balance wasn't

right. I knew it was only a matter of seconds before Luke took me down, so I figured, What the heck?

I tried the disarming manoeuvre.

My blade hit the base of Luke's and I twisted, putting my whole weight into a downward thrust.

Clang.

Luke's sword rattled against the stones. The tip of my blade was a couple of centimetres from his undefended chest.

The other campers were silent.

I lowered my sword. 'Um, sorry.'

For a moment, Luke was too stunned to speak.

'Sorry?' His scarred face broke into a grin. 'By the gods, Percy, why are you sorry? Show me that again!'

I didn't want to. The short burst of manic energy had completely abandoned me. But Luke insisted.

This time, there was no contest. The moment our swords connected, Luke hit my hilt and sent my weapon skidding across the floor.

After a long pause, somebody in the audience said, 'Beginner's luck?'

Luke wiped the sweat off his brow. He appraised me with an entirely new interest. 'Maybe,' he said. 'But I wonder what Percy could do with a balanced sword. . . .'

Friday afternoon, I was sitting with Grover at the lake, resting from a near-death experience on the climbing wall. Grover had scampered to the top like a mountain goat, but the lava had almost got me. My shirt had smoking holes in it. The hairs had been singed off my forearms.

We sat on the pier, watching the naiads do underwater basket weaving, until I got up the nerve to ask Grover how his conversation had gone with Mr D.

His face turned a sickly shade of yellow.

'Fine,' he said. 'Just great.'

'So your career's still on track?'

He glanced at me nervously. 'Chiron t-told you I want a searcher's licence?'

'Well . . . no.' I had no idea what a searcher's licence was, but it didn't seem like the right time to ask. 'He just said you had big plans, you know . . . and that you needed credit for completing a keeper's assignment. So did you get it?'

Grover looked down at the naiads. 'Mr D suspended judgement. He said I hadn't failed or succeeded with you yet, so our fates were still tied together. If you got a quest and I went along to protect you, and we both came back alive, then maybe he'd consider the job complete.'

My spirits lifted. 'Well, that's not so bad, right?'

'Blaa-ha-ha! He might as well have transferred me to stable-cleaning duty. The chances of you getting a quest . . . and even if you did, why would you want *me* along?'

'Of course I'd want you along!'

Grover stared glumly into the water. 'Basket weaving . . . Must be nice to have a useful skill.'

I tried to reassure him that he had lots of talents, but that just made him look more miserable. We talked about canoeing and swordplay for a while, then debated the pros and cons of the different gods. Finally, I asked him about the four empty cabins.

'Number eight, the silver one, belongs to Artemis,' he said. 'She vowed to be a maiden forever. So of course, no kids. The cabin is, you know, honorary. If she didn't have one, she'd be mad.'

'Yeah, okay. But the other three, the ones at the end. Are those the Big Three?'

Grover tensed. We were getting close to a touchy subject. 'No. One of them, number two, is Hera's,' he said. 'That's another honorary thing. She's the goddess of marriage, so of course she wouldn't go around having affairs with mortals. That's her husband's job. When we say the Big Three, we mean the three powerful brothers, the sons of Kronos.'

'Zeus, Poseidon, Hades.'

'Right. You know. After the great battle with the Titans, they took over the world from their dad and drew lots to decide who got what.'

'Zeus got the sky,' I remembered. 'Poseidon the sea, Hades the Underworld.'

'Uh-huh.'

'But Hades doesn't have a cabin here.'

'No. He doesn't have a throne on Olympus, either. He sort of does his own thing down in the Underworld. If he did have a cabin here . . .' Grover shuddered. 'Well, it wouldn't be pleasant. Let's leave it at that.'

'But Zeus and Poseidon – they both had, like, a bazillion kids in the myths. Why are their cabins empty?'

Grover shifted his hooves uncomfortably. 'About sixty years ago, after World War II, the Big Three agreed they wouldn't sire any more heroes. Their children were just too powerful. They were affecting the course of human events too much, causing too much carnage. World War II, you know, that was basically a fight between the sons of Zeus and Poseidon on one side, and the sons of Hades on the other. The winning side, Zeus and Poseidon, made Hades swear an oath with them: no more affairs with mortal women. They all swore on the River Styx.'

Thunder boomed.

I said, 'That's the most serious oath you can make.'

Grover nodded.

'And the brothers kept their word – no kids?'

Grover's face darkened. 'Seventeen years ago, Zeus fell off the wagon. There was this TV starlet with a big fluffy eighties hairdo – he just couldn't help himself. When their child was born, a little girl named Thalia . . . well, the River Styx is serious about promises. Zeus himself got off easy because he's immortal, but he brought a terrible fate on his daughter.'

'But that isn't fair! It wasn't the little girl's fault.'

Grover hesitated. 'Percy, children of the Big Three have powers greater than other half-bloods. They have a strong aura, a scent that attracts monsters. When Hades found out about the girl, he wasn't too happy about Zeus breaking his oath. Hades let the worst monsters out of Tartarus to torment Thalia. A satyr was assigned to be her keeper when she was twelve, but there was nothing he could do. He tried to escort her here with a couple of other half-bloods she'd befriended. They almost made it. They got all the way to the top of that hill.'

He pointed across the valley, to the pine tree where I'd fought the Minotaur. 'All three Kindly Ones were after them, along with a hoard of hellhounds. They were about to be overrun when Thalia told her satyr to take the other two half-bloods to safety while she held off the monsters. She was wounded and tired, and she didn't want to live like a hunted animal. The satyr didn't want to leave her, but he couldn't change her mind, and he had to protect the others. So Thalia made her final stand alone, at the top of that hill. As she died, Zeus took pity on her. He turned her into that pine tree. Her spirit still helps protect the borders of the valley. That's why the hill is called Half-Blood Hill.'

I stared at the pine in the distance.

The story made me feel hollow, and guilty, too. A girl my age had sacrificed herself to save her friends. She had faced a whole army of monsters. Next to that, my victory over the Minotaur didn't seem like much. I wondered, if I'd acted differently, could I have saved my mother?

'Grover,' I said, 'have heroes really gone on quests to the Underworld?'

'Sometimes,' he said. 'Orpheus. Hercules. Houdini.'

'And have they ever returned somebody from the dead?'

'No. Never. Orpheus came close. . . . Percy, you're not seriously thinking –'

'No,' I lied. 'I was just wondering. So . . . a satyr is always assigned to guard a demigod?'

Grover studied me warily. I hadn't persuaded him that I'd really dropped the Underworld idea. 'Not always. We go undercover to a lot of schools. We try to sniff out the half-bloods who have the makings of great heroes. If we find one with a very strong aura, like a child of the Big Three, we alert Chiron. He tries to keep an eye on them, since they could cause really huge problems.'

'And you found me. Chiron said you thought I might be something special.'

Grover looked as if I'd just led him into a trap. 'I didn't . . . Oh, listen, don't think like that. If you *were* – you know – you'd never *ever* be allowed a quest, and I'd never get my licence. You're probably a child of Hermes. Or maybe even one of the minor gods, like Nemesis, the god of revenge. Don't worry, okay?'

I got the idea he was reassuring himself more than me.

That night after dinner, there was a lot more excitement than usual.

At last, it was time for capture the flag.

When the plates were cleared away, the conch horn sounded and we all stood at our tables.

Campers yelled and cheered as Annabeth and two of her siblings ran into the pavilion carrying a silk banner. It was about three metres long, glistening grey, with a painting of a barn owl above an olive tree. From the opposite side of the pavilion, Clarisse and her buddies ran in with another banner, of identical size, but gaudy red, painted with a bloody spear and a boar's head.

I turned to Luke and yelled over the noise, 'Those are the flags?'

'Yeah.'

'Ares and Athena always lead the teams?'

'Not always,' he said. 'But often.'

'So, if another cabin captures one, what do you do – repaint the flag?'

He grinned. 'You'll see. First we have to get one.'

'Whose side are we on?'

He gave me a sly look, as if he knew something I didn't. The scar on his face made him look almost evil in the torchlight. 'We've made a temporary alliance with Athena. Tonight, we get the flag from Ares. And *you* are going to help.'

The teams were announced. Athena had made an alliance with Apollo and Hermes, the two biggest cabins. Apparently, privileges had been traded – shower times, chore schedules, the best slots for activities – in order to win support.

Ares had allied themselves with everybody else: Dionysus, Demeter, Aphrodite and Hephaestus. From what I'd seen, Dionysus's kids were actually good athletes, but there were only two of them. Demeter's kids had the edge with nature skills and outdoor stuff, but they weren't very aggressive. Aphrodite's sons and daughters I wasn't too worried about. They mostly sat out every activity and checked their reflections in the lake and did their hair and gossiped. Hephaestus's kids weren't pretty, and there were only four of them, but they were big and burly from working in the metal shop all day. They might be a problem. That, of course, left Ares's cabin: a dozen of the biggest, ugliest, meanest kids on Long Island, or anywhere else on the planet.

Chiron hammered his hoof on the marble.

'Heroes!' he announced. 'You know the rules. The creek is the boundary line. The entire forest is fair game. All magic items are allowed. The banner must be prominently displayed, and have no more than two guards. Prisoners may be disarmed, but may not be bound or gagged. No killing or maiming is allowed. I will serve as referee and battlefield medic. Arm yourselves!'

He spread his hands, and the tables were suddenly covered with equipment: helmets, bronze swords, spears, oxhide shields coated in metal.

'Whoa,' I said. 'We're really supposed to use these?'

Luke looked at me as if I were crazy. 'Unless you want to get skewered by your friends in cabin five. Here – Chiron thought these would fit. You'll be on border patrol.'

My shield was the size of an NBA backboard, with a big caduceus in the middle. It weighed about a million pounds. I could have snowboarded on it fine, but I hoped nobody seriously expected me to run fast. My helmet, like all the helmets on Athena's side, had a blue horsehair plume on top. Ares and their allies had red plumes.

Annabeth yelled, 'Blue team, forward!'

We cheered and shook our swords and followed her down the path to the south woods. The red team yelled taunts at us as they headed off towards the north.

I managed to catch up with Annabeth without tripping over my equipment. 'Hey.'

She kept marching.

'So what's the plan?' I asked. 'Got any magic items you can loan me?'

Her hand drifted towards her pocket, as if she were afraid I'd stolen something.

'Just watch Clarisse's spear,' she said. 'You don't want that thing touching you. Otherwise, don't worry. We'll take the banner from Ares. Has Luke given you your job?'

'Border patrol, whatever that means.'

'It's easy. Stand by the creek, keep the reds away. Leave the rest to me. Athena always has a plan.'

She pushed ahead, leaving me in the dust.

'Okay,' I mumbled. 'Glad you wanted me on your team.'

It was a warm, sticky night. The woods were dark, with fireflies popping in and out of view. Annabeth stationed me next to a little creek that gurgled over some rocks, then she and the rest of the team scattered into the trees.

Standing there alone, with my big blue-feathered helmet and my huge shield, I felt like an idiot. The bronze sword, like all the swords I'd tried so far, seemed balanced wrong. The leather grip pulled on my hand like a bowling ball.

There was no way anybody would actually attack me, would they? I mean, Olympus had to have liability issues, right?

Far away, the conch horn blew. I heard whoops and yells in the woods, the clanking of metal, kids fighting. A blue-plumed ally from Apollo raced past me like a deer, leaped through the creek and disappeared into enemy territory.

Great, I thought. I'll miss all the fun, as usual.

Then I heard a sound that sent a chill up my spine, a low canine growl, somewhere close by.

I raised my shield instinctively; I had the feeling something was stalking me.

Then the growling stopped. I felt the presence retreating.

On the other side of the creek, the underbrush exploded. Five Ares warriors came yelling and screaming out of the dark.

'Cream the punk!' Clarisse screamed.

Her ugly pig eyes glared through the slits of her helmet. She brandished a two-metre spear, its barbed metal tip flickering with red light. Her siblings had only the standard-issue bronze swords – not that that made me feel any better.

They charged across the stream. There was no help in sight. I could run. Or I could defend myself against half the Ares cabin.

I managed to sidestep the first kid's swing, but these guys were not as stupid as Minotaurs. They surrounded me, and Clarisse thrust at me with her spear. My shield deflected the point, but I felt a painful tingling all over my body. My hair stood on end. My shield arm went numb, and the air burned.

Electricity. Her stupid spear was electric. I fell back.

Another Ares guy slammed me in the chest with the butt of his sword and I hit the dirt.

They could've kicked me into jelly, but they were too busy laughing.

'Give him a haircut,' Clarisse said. 'Grab his hair.'

I managed to get to my feet. I raised my sword, but Clarisse slammed it aside with her spear as sparks flew. Now both my arms felt numb.

'Oh, wow,' Clarisse said. 'I'm scared of this guy. Really scared.'

'The flag is that way,' I told her. I wanted to sound angry, but I was afraid it didn't come out that way.

'Yeah,' one of her siblings said. 'But see, we don't care about the flag. We care about a guy who made our cabin look stupid.'

'You do that without my help,' I told them. It probably wasn't the smartest thing to say.

Two of them came at me. I backed up towards the creek, tried to raise my shield, but Clarisse was too fast. Her spear stuck me straight in the ribs. If I hadn't been wearing an armoured breast plate, I would've been shish-kebabbed. As it was, the electric point just about shocked my teeth out of my mouth. One of her cabinmates slashed his sword across my arm, leaving a good-size cut.

Seeing my own blood made me dizzy, warm and cold at the same time.

'No maiming,' I managed to say.

'Oops,' the guy said. 'Guess I lost my dessert privilege.'

He pushed me into the creek and I landed with a splash. They all laughed. I figured as soon as they were through being amused, I would die. But then something happened. The water seemed to wake up my senses, as if I'd just had a bag of my mom's double-espresso jelly beans.

Clarisse and her cabinmates came into the creek to get me, but I stood to meet them. I knew what to do. I swung the flat of my sword against the first guy's head and knocked his helmet clean off. I hit him so hard I could see his eyes vibrating as he crumpled into the water.

Ugly Number Two and Ugly Number Three came at me. I slammed one in the face with my shield and used my sword to shear off the other guy's horsehair plume. Both of them backed up quick. Ugly Number Four didn't look really anxious to attack, but Clarisse kept coming, the point of her spear crackling with energy. As soon as she thrust, I caught the shaft between the edge of my shield and my sword, and I snapped it like a twig.

'Ah!' she screamed. 'You idiot! You corpse-breath worm!'

She probably would've said worse, but I smacked her between the eyes with my sword-butt and sent her stumbling backwards out of the creek.

Then I heard yelling, elated screams, and I saw Luke racing towards the boundary line with the red team's banner lifted high. He was flanked by a couple of Hermes guys covering his retreat and a few Apollos behind them, fighting off the Hephaestus kids. The Ares folks got up, and Clarisse muttered a dazed curse.

'A trick!' she shouted. 'It was a trick.'

They staggered after Luke, but it was too late. Everybody converged on the creek as Luke ran across into friendly territory. Our side exploded into cheers. The red banner shimmered and turned to silver. The boar and spear were replaced with a huge caduceus, the symbol of cabin eleven. Everybody on the blue team picked up Luke and started carrying him around on their shoulders. Chiron cantered out from the woods and blew the conch horn.

The game was over. We'd won.

I was about to join the celebration when Annabeth's voice, right next to me in the creek, said, 'Not bad, hero.'

I looked, but she wasn't there.

'Where the heck did you learn to fight like that?' she asked. The air shimmered, and she materialized, holding a Yankees baseball cap as if she'd just taken it off her head.

I felt myself getting angry. I wasn't even fazed by the fact that she'd just been invisible. 'You set me up,' I said. 'You put me here because you knew Clarisse would come after me, while you sent Luke around the flank. You had it all figured out.'

Annabeth shrugged. 'I told you. Athena always, always has a plan.'

'A plan to get me pulverized.'

'I came as fast as I could. I was about to jump in, but . . .' She shrugged. 'You didn't need help.'

Then she noticed my wounded arm. 'How did you do that?'

'Sword cut,' I said. 'What do you think?'

'No. It *was* a sword cut. Look at it.'

The blood was gone. Where the huge cut had been, there was a long white scratch, and even that was fading. As I watched, it turned into a small scar, and disappeared.

'I – I don't get it,' I said.

Annabeth was thinking hard. I could almost see the gears turning. She looked down at my feet, then at Clarisse's broken spear, and said, 'Step out of the water, Percy.'

'What –'

'Just do it.'

I came out of the creek and immediately felt bone tired. My arms started to go numb again. My adrenalin rush left me. I almost fell over, but Annabeth steadied me.

'Oh, Styx,' she cursed. 'This is *not* good. I didn't want . . . I assumed it would be Zeus. . . .'

Before I could ask what she meant, I heard that canine growl again, but much closer than before. A howl ripped through the forest.

The campers' cheering died instantly. Chiron shouted something in Ancient Greek, which I would realize, only later, I had understood perfectly: *'Stand ready! My bow!'*

Annabeth drew her sword.

There on the rocks just above us was a black hound the size of a rhino, with lava-red eyes and fangs like daggers.

It was looking straight at me.

Nobody moved except Annabeth, who yelled, 'Percy, run!'

She tried to step in front of me, but the hound was too fast. It leaped over her – an enormous shadow with teeth – and just as it hit me, as I stumbled backwards and felt its razor-sharp claws ripping through my armour, there was a cascade of thwacking sounds, like forty pieces of paper being ripped one after the other. From the hound's neck sprouted a cluster of arrows. The monster fell dead at my feet.

By some miracle, I was still alive. I didn't want to look underneath the ruins of my shredded armour. My chest felt warm and wet, and I knew I was badly cut. Another second, and the monster would've turned me into fifty kilograms of delicatessen meat.

Chiron trotted up next to us, a bow in his hand, his face grim.

'Di immortales,' Annabeth said. 'That's a hellhound from the Fields of Punishment. They don't . . . they're not supposed to . . .'

'Someone summoned it,' Chiron said. 'Someone inside the camp.'

Luke came over, the banner in his hand forgotten, his moment of glory gone.

Clarisse yelled, 'It's all Percy's fault! Percy summoned it!'

'Be quiet, child,' Chiron told her.

We watched the body of the hellhound melt into shadow, soaking into the ground until it disappeared.

'You're wounded,' Annabeth told me. 'Quick, Percy, get in the water.'

'I'm okay.'

'No, you're not,' she said. 'Chiron, watch this.'

I was too tired to argue. I stepped back into the creek, the whole camp gathering around me.

Instantly, I felt better. I could feel the cuts on my chest closing up. Some of the campers gasped.

'Look, I – I don't know why,' I said, trying to apologize. 'I'm sorry . . .'

But they weren't watching my wounds heal. They were staring at something above my head.

'Percy,' Annabeth said, pointing. 'Um . . .'

By the time I looked up, the sign was already fading, but I could still make out the hologram of green light, spinning and gleaming. A three-tipped spear: a trident.

'Your father,' Annabeth murmured. 'This is *really* not good.'

'It is determined,' Chiron announced.

All around me, campers started kneeling, even the Ares cabin, though they didn't look happy about it.

'My father?' I asked, completely bewildered.

'Poseidon,' said Chiron. 'Earthshaker, Stormbringer, Father of Horses. Hail, Perseus Jackson, Son of the Sea God.'

9 ⚡ I AM OFFERED
A QUEST

The next morning, Chiron moved me to cabin three.

I didn't have to share with anybody. I had plenty of room for all my stuff: the Minotaur horn, one set of spare clothes and a toiletry bag. I got to sit at my own dinner table, pick all my own activities, call 'lights out' whenever I felt like it and not listen to anybody else.

And I was absolutely miserable.

Just when I'd started to feel accepted, to feel I had a home in cabin eleven and I might be a normal kid – or as normal as you can be when you're a half-blood – I'd been separated out as if I had some rare disease.

Nobody mentioned the hellhound, but I got the feeling they were all talking about it behind my back. The attack had scared everybody. It sent two messages: one, that I was the son of the Sea God; and two, monsters would stop at nothing to kill me. They could even invade a camp that had always been considered safe.

The other campers steered clear of me as much as possible. Cabin eleven was too nervous to have sword class with me after what I'd done to the Ares folks in the woods, so my lessons with Luke became one-on-one. He pushed me harder than ever, and wasn't afraid to bruise me up in the process.

'You're going to need all the training you can get,' he promised, as we were working with swords and flaming torches. 'Now let's try that viper-beheading strike again. Fifty more repetitions.'

Annabeth still taught me Greek in the mornings, but she seemed distracted. Every time I said something, she scowled at me, as if I'd just poked her between the eyes.

After lessons, she would walk away muttering to herself: 'Quest . . . Poseidon? . . . Dirty rotten . . . Got to make a plan . . .'

Even Clarisse kept her distance, though her venomous looks made it clear she wanted to kill me for breaking her magic spear. I wished she would just yell or punch me or something. I'd rather get into fights every day than be ignored.

I knew somebody at camp resented me, because one night I came into my cabin and found a mortal newspaper dropped inside the doorway, a *New York Daily News*, opened to the Metro page. The article took me almost an hour to read, because the angrier I got, the more the words floated around on the page.

BOY AND MOTHER STILL MISSING AFTER FREAK CAR ACCIDENT

BY EILEEN SMYTHE

Sally Jackson and son Percy are still missing one week after their mysterious disappearance. The family's badly burned '78 Camaro was discovered last Saturday on a north Long Island road with the roof ripped off and the front axle broken. The car had flipped and skidded for several hundred metres before exploding.

Mother and son had gone for a weekend vacation to Montauk, but left hastily, under mysterious circumstances. Small traces of blood were found in the car and near the scene of the wreck, but there were no other signs of the missing Jacksons. Residents in the rural area reported seeing nothing unusual around the time of the accident.

Ms Jackson's husband, Gabe Ugliano, claims that his stepson, Percy Jackson, is a troubled child who has been kicked out of numerous boarding schools and has expressed violent tendencies in the past.

Police would not say whether son Percy is a suspect in his mother's disappearance, but they have not ruled out foul play. Below are recent pictures of Sally Jackson and Percy. Police urge anyone with information to call the following toll-free crime-stoppers hotline.

The phone number was circled in black marker.

I wadded up the paper and threw it away, then flopped down in my bunk bed in the middle of my empty cabin.

'Lights out,' I told myself miserably.

That night, I had my worst dream yet.

I was running along the beach in a storm. This time,

there was a city behind me. Not New York. The sprawl was different: buildings spread farther apart, palm trees and low hills in the distance.

About a hundred metres down the surf, two men were fighting. They looked like TV wrestlers, muscular, with beards and long hair. Both wore flowing Greek tunics, one trimmed in blue, the other in green. They grappled with each other, wrestled, kicked and head-butted, and every time they connected, lightning flashed, the sky grew darker, and the wind rose.

I had to stop them. I didn't know why. But the harder I ran, the more the wind blew me back, until I was running on the spot, my heels digging uselessly in the sand.

Over the roar of the storm, I could hear the blue-robed one yelling at the green-robed one, *Give it back! Give it back!* Like a kindergartner fighting over a toy.

The waves got bigger, crashing into the beach, spraying me with salt.

I yelled, *Stop it! Stop fighting!*

The ground shook. Laughter came from somewhere under the earth, and a voice so deep and evil it turned my blood to ice.

'Come down, little hero,' the voice crooned. 'Come down!'

The sand split beneath me, opening up a crevice straight down to the centre of the earth. My feet slipped, and darkness swallowed me.

I woke up, sure I was falling.

I was still in bed in cabin three. My body told me it was

morning, but it was dark outside, and thunder rolled across the hills. A storm was brewing. I hadn't dreamed that.

I heard a clopping sound at the door, a hoof knocking on the threshold.

'Come in.'

Grover trotted inside, looking worried. 'Mr D wants to see you.'

'Why?'

'He wants to kill . . . I mean, I'd better let him tell you.'

Nervously, I got dressed and followed, sure that I was in huge trouble.

For days, I'd been half expecting a summons to the Big House. Now that I was declared a son of Poseidon, one of the Big Three gods who weren't supposed to have kids, I figured it was a crime for me just to be alive. The other gods had probably been debating the best way to punish me for existing, and now Mr D was ready to deliver their verdict.

Over Long Island Sound, the sky looked like ink soup coming to a boil. A hazy curtain of rain was coming in our direction. I asked Grover if we needed an umbrella.

'No,' he said. 'It never rains here unless we want it to.'

I pointed at the storm. 'What the heck is that, then?'

He glanced uneasily at the sky. 'It'll pass around us. Bad weather always does.'

I realized he was right. In the week I'd been here, it had never even been overcast. The few rain clouds I'd seen had skirted right around the edges of the valley.

But this storm . . . this one was huge.

At the volleyball pit, the kids from Apollo's cabin were

playing a morning game against the satyrs. Dionysus's twins were walking around in the strawberry fields, making the plants grow. Everybody was going about their normal business, but they looked tense. They kept their eyes on the storm.

Grover and I walked up to the front porch of the Big House. Dionysus sat at the pinochle table in his tiger-striped Hawaiian shirt with his Diet Coke, just as he had on my first day. Chiron sat across the table in his fake wheelchair. They were playing against invisible opponents – two sets of cards hovering in the air.

'Well, well,' Mr D said without looking up. 'Our little celebrity.'

I waited.

'Come closer,' Mr D said. 'And don't expect me to kowtow to you, mortal, just because old Barnacle-Beard is your father.'

A net of lightning flashed across the clouds. Thunder shook the windows of the house.

'Blah, blah, blah,' Dionysus said.

Chiron feigned interest in his pinochle cards. Grover cowered by the railing, his hooves clopping back and forth.

'If I had my way,' Dionysus said, 'I would cause your molecules to erupt in flames. We'd sweep up the ashes and be done with a lot of trouble. But Chiron seems to feel this would be against my mission at this cursed camp: to keep you little brats safe from harm.'

'Spontaneous combustion *is* a form of harm, Mr D,' Chiron put in.

'Nonsense,' Dionysus said. 'Boy wouldn't feel a thing. Nevertheless, I've agreed to restrain myself. I'm thinking of turning you into a dolphin instead, sending you back to your father.'

'Mr D –' Chiron warned.

'Oh, all right,' Dionysus relented. 'There's one more option. But it's deadly foolishness.' Dionysus rose, and the invisible players' cards dropped to the table. 'I'm off to Olympus for the emergency meeting. If the boy is still here when I get back, I'll turn him into an Atlantic bottlenose. Do you understand? And Perseus Jackson, if you're at all smart, you'll see that's a much more sensible choice than what Chiron feels you must do.'

Dionysus picked up a playing card, twisted it, and it became a plastic rectangle. A credit card? No. A security pass.

He snapped his fingers.

The air seemed to fold and bend around him. He became a holograph, then a wind, then he was gone, leaving only the smell of fresh-pressed grapes lingering behind.

Chiron smiled at me, but he looked tired and strained. 'Sit, Percy, please. And Grover.'

We did.

Chiron laid his cards on the table, a winning hand he hadn't got to use.

'Tell me, Percy,' he said. 'What did you make of the hellhound?'

Just hearing the name made me shudder.

Chiron probably wanted me to say, *Heck, it was nothing. I eat hellhounds for breakfast.* But I didn't feel like lying.

'It scared me,' I said. 'If you hadn't shot it, I'd be dead.'

'You'll meet worse, Percy. Far worse, before you're done.'

'Done . . . with what?'

'Your quest, of course. Will you accept it?'

I glanced at Grover, who was crossing his fingers.

'Um, sir,' I said, 'you haven't told me what it is yet.'

Chiron grimaced. 'Well, that's the hard part, the details.'

Thunder rumbled across the valley. The storm clouds had now reached the edge of the beach. As far as I could see, the sky and the sea were boiling together.

'Poseidon and Zeus,' I said. 'They're fighting over something valuable . . . something that was stolen, aren't they?'

Chiron and Grover exchanged looks.

Chiron sat forward in his wheelchair. 'How did you know that?'

My face felt hot. I wished I hadn't opened my big mouth. 'The weather since Christmas has been weird, like the sea and the sky are fighting. Then I talked to Annabeth, and she'd overheard something about a theft. And . . . I've also been having these dreams.'

'I knew it,' Grover said.

'Hush, satyr,' Chiron ordered.

'But it is his quest!' Grover's eyes were bright with excitement. 'It must be!'

'Only the Oracle can determine.' Chiron stroked his

bristly beard. 'Nevertheless, Percy, you are correct. Your father and Zeus are having their worst quarrel in centuries. They are fighting over something valuable that was stolen. To be precise: a lightning bolt.'

I laughed nervously. 'A *what*?'

'Do not take this lightly,' Chiron warned. 'I'm not talking about some tinfoil-covered zigzag you'd see in a second-grade play. I'm talking about a two-foot-long cylinder of high-grade celestial bronze, capped on both ends with god-level explosives.'

'Oh.'

'Zeus's master bolt,' Chiron said, getting worked up now. 'The symbol of his power, from which all other lightning bolts are patterned. The first weapon made by the Cyclopes for the war against the Titans, the bolt that sheered the top off Mount Etna and hurled Kronos from his throne; the master bolt, which packs enough power to make mortal hydrogen bombs look like firecrackers.'

'And it's missing?'

'Stolen,' Chiron said.

'By who?'

'By *whom*,' Chiron corrected. Once a teacher, always a teacher. 'By you.'

My mouth fell open.

'At least' — Chiron held up a hand — 'that's what Zeus thinks. During the winter solstice, at the last council of the gods, Zeus and Poseidon had an argument. The usual nonsense: "Mother Rhea always liked you best," "Air disasters are more spectacular than sea disasters," et cetera.

Afterwards, Zeus realized his master bolt was missing, taken from the throne room under his very nose. He immediately blamed Poseidon. Now a god cannot usurp another god's symbol of power directly — that is forbidden by the most ancient of divine laws. But Zeus believes your father convinced a human hero to take it.'

'But I didn't —'

'Patience and listen, child,' Chiron said. 'Zeus has good reason to be suspicious. The forges of the Cyclopes are under the ocean, which gives Poseidon some influence over the makers of his brother's lightning. Zeus believes Poseidon has taken the master bolt, and is now secretly having the Cyclopes build an arsenal of illegal copies, which might be used to topple Zeus from his throne. The only thing Zeus wasn't sure about was which hero Poseidon used to steal the bolt. Now Poseidon has openly claimed you as his son. You were in New York over the winter holidays. You could easily have snuck into Olympus. Zeus believes he has found his thief.'

'But I've never even been to Olympus! Zeus is crazy!'

Chiron and Grover glanced nervously at the sky. The clouds didn't seem to be parting around us, as Grover had promised. They were rolling straight over our valley, sealing us in like a coffin lid.

'Er, Percy . . . ?' Grover said. 'We don't use the *c*-word to describe the Lord of the Sky.'

'Perhaps *paranoid*,' Chiron suggested. 'Then again, Poseidon has tried to unseat Zeus before. I believe that was question thirty-eight on your final exam . . .' He looked at me as if he actually expected me to remember question thirty-eight.

How could anyone accuse me of stealing a god's weapon? I couldn't even steal a slice of pizza from Gabe's poker party without getting busted. Chiron was waiting for an answer.

'Something about a golden net?' I guessed. 'Poseidon and Hera and a few other gods . . . they, like, trapped Zeus and wouldn't let him out until he promised to be a better ruler, right?'

'Correct,' Chiron said. 'And Zeus has never trusted Poseidon since. Of course, Poseidon denies stealing the master bolt. He took great offence at the accusation. The two have been arguing back and forth for months, threatening war. And now, you've come along – the proverbial last straw.'

'But I'm just a kid!'

'Percy,' Grover cut in, 'if you were Zeus, and you already thought your brother was plotting to overthrow you, then your brother suddenly admitted he had broken the sacred oath he took after World War II, that he's fathered a new mortal hero who might be used as a weapon against you . . . Wouldn't that put a twist in your toga?'

'But I didn't do anything. Poseidon – my dad – he didn't really have this master bolt stolen, did he?'

Chiron sighed. 'Most thinking observers would agree that thievery is not Poseidon's style. But the sea god is too proud to try convincing Zeus of that. Zeus has demanded that Poseidon return the bolt by the summer solstice. That's

June twenty-first, ten days from now. Poseidon wants an apology for being called a thief by the same date. I hoped that diplomacy might prevail, that Hera or Demeter or Hestia would make the two brothers see sense. But your arrival has inflamed Zeus's temper. Now neither god will back down. Unless someone intervenes, unless the master bolt is found and returned to Zeus before the solstice, there will be war. And do you know what a full-fledged war would look like, Percy?'

'Bad?' I guessed.

'Imagine the world in chaos. Nature at war with itself. Olympians forced to choose sides between Zeus and Poseidon. Destruction. Carnage. Millions dead. Western civilization turned into a battleground so big it will make the Trojan War look like a water-balloon fight.'

'Bad,' I repeated.

'And you, Percy Jackson, would be the first to feel Zeus's wrath.'

It started to rain. Volleyball players stopped their game and stared in stunned silence at the sky.

I had brought this storm to Half-Blood Hill. Zeus was punishing the whole camp because of me. I was furious.

'So I have to find the stupid bolt,' I said. 'And return it to Zeus.'

'What better peace offering,' Chiron said, 'than to have the son of Poseidon return Zeus's property?'

'If Poseidon doesn't have it, where is the thing?'

'I believe I know.' Chiron's expression was grim. 'Part of a prophecy I had years ago . . . well, some of the lines make sense to me, now. But before I can say more, you must officially take up the quest. You must seek the counsel of the Oracle.'

'Why can't you tell me where the bolt is beforehand?'

'Because if I did, you would be too afraid to accept the challenge.'

I swallowed. 'Good reason.'

'You agree then?'

I looked at Grover, who nodded encouragingly.

Easy for him. I was the one Zeus wanted to kill.

'All right,' I said. 'It's better than being turned into a dolphin.'

'Then it's time you consulted the Oracle,' Chiron said. 'Go upstairs, Percy Jackson, to the attic. When you come back down, assuming you're still sane, we will talk more.'

Four flights up, the stairs ended under a green trap-door.

I pulled the cord. The door swung down, and a wooden ladder clattered into place.

The warm air from above smelled like mildew and rotten wood and something else . . . a smell I remembered from biology class. Reptiles. The smell of snakes.

I held my breath and climbed.

The attic was filled with Greek hero junk: armour stands covered in cobwebs; once-bright shields pitted with rust; old leather steamer trunks plastered with stickers saying ITHAKA, CIRCE'S ISLE and LAND OF THE AMAZONS. One long table was stacked with glass jars filled with pickled *things* – severed hairy claws, huge yellow eyes, various other parts of monsters. A dusty mounted trophy on the wall looked like a giant snake's head, but with horns and a full set of shark's teeth. The plaque read: HYDRA HEAD NO. I, WOODSTOCK, NY, 1969.

By the window, sitting on a wooden tripod stool, was the most gruesome memento of all: a mummy. Not the wrapped-in-cloth kind, but a human female body shrivelled to a husk. She wore a tie-dyed sundress, lots of beaded necklaces, and a headband over long black hair. The skin of her face was thin and leathery over her skull, and her eyes were glassy white slits, as if the real eyes had been replaced by marbles; she'd been dead a long, long time.

Looking at her sent chills up my back. And that was before she sat up on her stool and opened her mouth. A green mist poured from the mummy's mouth, coiling over the floor in thick tendrils, hissing like twenty-thousand snakes. I stumbled over myself trying to get to the trap-door, but it slammed shut. Inside my head, I heard a voice, slithering into one ear and coiling around my brain: *I am the spirit of Delphi, speaker of the prophecies of Phoebus Apollo, slayer of the mighty Python. Approach, seeker, and ask.*

I wanted to say, *No thanks, wrong door, just looking for the bathroom.* But I forced myself to take a deep breath.

The mummy wasn't alive. She was some kind of grue-some receptacle for something else, the power that was now swirling around me in the green mist. But its presence didn't feel evil, like my demonic maths teacher Mrs Dodds or the Minotaur. It felt more like the Three Fates I'd seen knitting the yarn outside the highway fruit stand: ancient, powerful and definitely *not* human. But not particularly interested in killing me, either.

I got up the courage to ask, 'What is my destiny?'

The mist swirled more thickly, collecting right in front of me and around the table with the pickled monster-part jars. Suddenly there were four men sitting around the table, playing cards. Their faces became clearer. It was Smelly Gabe and his buddies.

My fists clenched, though I knew this poker party couldn't be real. It was an illusion, made out of mist.

Gabe turned towards me and spoke in the rasping voice of the Oracle: *You shall go west, and face the god who has turned.*

His buddy on the right looked up and said in the same voice: *You shall find what was stolen, and see it safely returned.*

The guy on the left threw in two poker chips, then said: *You shall be betrayed by one who calls you a friend.*

Finally, Eddie, our building super, delivered the worst line of all: *And you shall fail to save what matters most, in the end.*

The figures began to dissolve. At first I was too stunned to say anything, but as the mist retreated, coiling into a huge green serpent and slithering back into the mouth of the mummy, I cried, 'Wait! What do you mean? What friend? What will I fail to save?'

The tail of the mist snake disappeared into the

mummy's mouth. She reclined back against the wall. Her mouth closed tight, as if it hadn't been open in a hundred years. The attic was silent again, abandoned, nothing but a room full of mementos.

I got the feeling that I could stand here until I had cobwebs, too, and I wouldn't learn anything else.

My audience with the Oracle was over.

'Well?' Chiron asked me.

I slumped into a chair at the pinochle table. 'She said I would retrieve what was stolen.'

Grover sat forward, chewing excitedly on the remains of a Diet Coke can. 'That's great!'

'What did the Oracle say *exactly*?' Chiron pressed. 'This is important.'

My ears were still tingling from the reptilian voice. 'She . . . she said I would go west and face a god who had turned. I would retrieve what was stolen and see it safely returned.'

'I knew it,' Grover said.

Chiron didn't look satisfied. 'Anything else?'

I didn't want to tell him.

What friend would betray me? I didn't have that many.

And the last line — I would fail to save what mattered most. What kind of Oracle would send me on a quest and tell me, *Oh, by the way, you'll fail.*

How could I confess that?

'No,' I said. 'That's about it.'

He studied my face. 'Very well, Percy. But know this: the Oracle's words often have double meanings. Don't dwell on them too much. The truth is not always clear until events come to pass.'

I got the feeling he knew I was holding back something bad, and he was trying to make me feel better.

'Okay,' I said, anxious to change topics. 'So where do I go? Who's this god in the west?'

'Ah, think, Percy,' Chiron said. 'If Zeus and Poseidon weaken each other in a war, who stands to gain?'

'Somebody else who wants to take over?' I guessed.

'Yes, quite. Someone who harbours a grudge, who has been unhappy with his lot since the world was divided aeons ago, whose kingdom would grow powerful with the deaths of millions. Someone who hates his brothers for forcing him into an oath to have no more children, an oath that both of them have now broken.'

I thought about my dreams, the evil voice that had spoken from under the ground. 'Hades.'

Chiron nodded. 'The Lord of the Dead is the only possibility.'

A scrap of aluminium dribbled out of Grover's mouth. 'Whoa, wait. Wh-what?'

'A Fury came after Percy,' Chiron reminded him. 'She watched the young man until she was sure of his identity, then tried to kill him. Furies obey only one lord: Hades.'

'Yes, but – but Hades hates *all* heroes,' Grover protested. 'Especially if he has found out Percy is a son of Poseidon . . .'

'A hellhound got into the forest,' Chiron continued.

'Those can only be summoned from the Fields of Punishment, and it had to be summoned by someone within the camp. Hades must have a spy here. He must suspect Poseidon will try to use Percy to clear his name. Hades would very much like to kill this young half-blood before he can take on the quest.'

'Great,' I muttered. 'That's two major gods who want to kill me.'

'But a quest to . . .' Grover swallowed. 'I mean, couldn't the master bolt be in some place like Maine? Maine's very nice this time of year.'

'Hades sent a minion to steal the master bolt,' Chiron insisted. 'He hid it in the Underworld, knowing full well that Zeus would blame Poseidon. I don't pretend to understand the Lord of the Dead's motives perfectly, or why he chose this time to start a war, but one thing is certain. Percy must go to the Underworld, find the master bolt, and reveal the truth.'

A strange fire burned in my stomach. The weirdest thing was: it wasn't fear. It was anticipation. The desire for revenge. Hades had tried to kill me three times so far, with the Fury, the Minotaur and the hellhound. It was his fault my mother had disappeared in a flash of light. Now he was trying to frame me and my dad for a theft we hadn't committed.

I was ready to take him on.

Besides, if my mother was in the Underworld . . .

Whoa, boy, said the small part of my brain that was still sane. You're a kid. Hades is a god.

Grover was trembling. He'd started eating pinochle cards like potato crisps.

The poor guy needed to complete a quest with me so he could get his searcher's licence, whatever that was, but how could I ask him to do this quest, especially when the Oracle said I was destined to fail? This was suicide.

'Look, if we know it's Hades,' I told Chiron, 'why can't we just tell the other gods? Zeus or Poseidon could go down to the Underworld and bust some heads.'

'Suspecting and knowing are not the same,' Chiron said. 'Besides, even if the other gods suspect Hades – and I imagine Poseidon does – they couldn't retrieve the bolt themselves. Gods cannot cross each other's territories except by invitation. That is another ancient rule. Heroes, on the other hand, have certain privileges. They can go anywhere, challenge anyone, as long as they're bold enough and strong enough to do it. No god can be held responsible for a hero's actions. Why do you think the gods always operate through humans?'

'You're saying I'm being used.'

'I'm saying it's no accident Poseidon has claimed you now. It's a very risky gamble, but he's in a desperate situation. He needs you.'

My dad needs me.

Emotions rolled around inside me like bits of glass in a kaleidoscope. I didn't know whether to feel resentful or grateful or happy or angry. Poseidon had ignored me for twelve years. Now suddenly he needed me.

I looked at Chiron. 'You've known I was Poseidon's son all along, haven't you?'

'I had my suspicions. As I said ... I've spoken to the Oracle, too.'

I got the feeling there was a lot he wasn't telling me about his prophecy, but I decided I couldn't worry about that right now. After all, I was holding back information too.

'So let me get this straight,' I said. 'I'm supposed go to the Underworld and confront the Lord of the Dead.'

'Check,' Chiron said.

'Find the most powerful weapon in the universe.'

'Check.'

'And get it back to Olympus before the summer solstice, in ten days.'

'That's about right.'

I looked at Grover, who gulped down the ace of hearts.

'Did I mention that Maine is very nice this time of year?' he asked weakly.

'You don't have to go,' I told him. 'I can't ask that of you.'

'Oh ...' He shifted his hooves. 'No ... it's just that satyrs and underground places ... well ...'

He took a deep breath, then stood, brushing the shredded cards and aluminium bits off his T-shirt. 'You saved my life, Percy. If ... if you're serious about wanting me along, I won't let you down.'

I felt so relieved I wanted to cry, though I didn't think that would be very heroic. Grover was the only friend I'd ever had for longer than a few months. I wasn't sure what good a satyr could do against the forces of the dead, but I felt better knowing he'd be with me.

'All the way, G-man.' I turned to Chiron. 'So where do we go? The Oracle just said to go west.'

'The entrance to the Underworld is always in the west. It moves from age to age, just like Olympus. Right now, of course, it's in America.'

'Where?'

Chiron looked surprised. 'I thought that would be obvious enough. The entrance to the Underworld is in Los Angeles.'

'Oh,' I said. 'Naturally. So we just get on a plane –'

'No!' Grover shrieked. 'Percy, what are you thinking? Have you ever been on a plane in your life?'

I shook my head, feeling embarrassed. My mom had never taken me anywhere by plane. She'd always said we didn't have the money. Besides, her parents had died in a plane crash.

'Percy, think,' Chiron said. 'You are the son of the Sea God. Your father's bitterest rival is Zeus, Lord of the Sky. Your mother knew better than to trust you in an aeroplane. You would be in Zeus's domain. You would never come down again alive.'

Overhead, lightning crackled. Thunder boomed.

'Okay,' I said, determined not to look at the storm. 'So, I'll travel overland.'

'That's right,' Chiron said. 'Two companions may accompany you. Grover is one. The other has already volunteered, if you will accept her help.'

'Gee,' I said, feigning surprise. 'Who else would be stupid enough to volunteer for a quest like this?'

The air shimmered behind Chiron.

Annabeth became visible, stuffing her Yankees cap into her back pocket.

'I've been waiting a long time for a quest, Seaweed Brain,' she said. 'Athena is no fan of Poseidon, but if you're going to save the world, I'm the best person to keep you from messing up.'

'If you do say so yourself,' I said. 'I suppose you have a plan, Wise Girl?'

Her cheeks coloured. 'Do you want my help or not?'

The truth was, I did. I needed all the help I could get.

'A trio,' I said. 'That'll work.'

'Excellent,' Chiron said. 'This afternoon, we can take you as far as the bus terminal in Manhattan. After that, you are on your own.'

Lightning flashed. Rain poured down on the meadows that were never supposed to have violent weather.

'No time to waste,' Chiron said. 'I think you should all get packing.'

10 I RUIN A PERFECTLY GOOD BUS

It didn't take me long to pack. I decided to leave the Minotaur horn in my cabin, which left me only an extra change of clothes and a toothbrush to stuff in a backpack Grover had found for me.

The camp store loaned me one hundred dollars in mortal money and twenty golden drachmas. These coins were as big as Girl Scout cookies and had images of various Greek gods stamped on one side and the Empire State Building on the other. The ancient mortal drachmas had been silver, Chiron told us, but Olympians never used less than pure gold. Chiron said the coins might come in handy for nonmortal transactions — whatever that meant. He gave Annabeth and me each a flask of nectar and an airtight bag full of ambrosia squares, to be used only in emergencies, if we were seriously hurt. It was god food, Chiron reminded us. It would cure us of almost any injury, but it was lethal to mortals. Too much of it would make a half-blood very, very feverish. An overdose would burn us up, literally.

Annabeth was bringing her magic Yankees cap, which she told me had been a twelfth-birthday present from her mom. She carried a book on famous classical architecture, written in Ancient Greek, to read when she got bored, and

[149]

a long bronze knife, hidden in her shirt sleeve. I was sure the knife would get us busted the first time we went through a metal detector.

Grover wore his fake feet and his trousers to pass as human. He wore a green rasta-style cap, because when it rained his curly hair flattened and you could just see the tips of his horns. His bright orange backpack was full of scrap metal and apples to snack on. In his pocket was a set of reed pipes his daddy goat had carved for him, even though he only knew two songs: Mozart's Piano Concerto no. 12 and Hilary Duff's 'So Yesterday', both of which sounded pretty bad on reed pipes.

We waved goodbye to the other campers, took one last look at the strawberry fields, the ocean and the Big House, then hiked up Half-Blood Hill to the tall pine tree that used to be Thalia, daughter of Zeus.

Chiron was waiting for us in his wheelchair. Next to him stood the surfer dude I'd seen when I was recovering in the sick room. According to Grover, the guy was the camp's head of security. He supposedly had eyes all over his body so he could never be surprised. Today, though, he was wearing a chauffeur's uniform, so I could only see extra peepers on his hands, face and neck.

'This is Argus,' Chiron told me. 'He will drive you into the city, and, er, well, keep an eye on things.'

I heard footsteps behind us.

Luke came running up the hill, carrying a pair of basketball shoes.

'Hey!' he panted. 'Glad I caught you.'

Annabeth blushed, the way she always did when Luke was around.

'Just wanted to say good luck,' Luke told me. 'And I thought . . . um, maybe you could use these.'

He handed me the sneakers, which looked pretty normal. They even smelled kind of normal.

Luke said, *'Maia!'*

White bird's wings sprouted out of the heels, startling me so much, I dropped them. The shoes flapped around on the ground until the wings folded up and disappeared.

'Awesome!' Grover said.

Luke smiled. 'Those served me well when I was on my quest. Gift from Dad. Of course, I don't use them much these days . . .' His expression turned sad.

I didn't know what to say. It was cool enough that Luke had come to say goodbye. I'd been afraid he might resent me for getting so much attention the last few days. But here he was giving me a magic gift . . . It made me blush almost as much as Annabeth.

'Hey, man,' I said. 'Thanks.'

'Listen, Percy . . .' Luke looked uncomfortable. 'A lot of hopes are riding on you. So just . . . kill some monsters for me, okay?'

We shook hands. Luke patted Grover's head between his horns, then gave a goodbye hug to Annabeth, who looked like she might pass out.

After Luke was gone, I told her, 'You're hyper-ventilating.'

'Am not.'

'You let him capture the flag instead of you, didn't you?'

'Oh . . . why do I want to go anywhere with you, Percy?'

She stomped down the other side of the hill, where a white SUV waited on the shoulder of the road. Argus followed, jingling his car keys.

I picked up the flying shoes and had a sudden bad feeling. I looked at Chiron. 'I won't be able to use these, will I?'

He shook his head. 'Luke meant well, Percy. But taking to the air . . . that would not be wise for you.'

I nodded, disappointed, but then I got an idea. 'Hey, Grover. You want a magic item?'

His eyes lit up. 'Me?'

Pretty soon we'd laced the sneakers over his fake feet, and the world's first flying goat boy was ready for launch.

'*Maia!*' he shouted.

He got off the ground okay, but then fell over sideways so his backpack dragged through the grass. The winged shoes kept bucking up and down like tiny broncos.

'Practice,' Chiron called after him. 'You just need practice!'

'Aaaaa!' Grover went flying sideways down the hill like a possessed lawn mower, heading towards the van.

Before I could follow, Chiron caught my arm. 'I should have trained you better, Percy,' he said. 'If only I had more time. Hercules, Jason – they all got more training.'

'That's okay. I just wish –'

I stopped myself because I was about to sound like a

brat. I was wishing my dad had given me a cool magic item to help on the quest, something as good as Luke's flying shoes, or Annabeth's invisible cap.

'What am I thinking?' Chiron cried. 'I can't let you get away without this.'

He pulled a pen from his coat pocket and handed it to me. It was an ordinary disposable ballpoint, black ink, removable cap. Probably cost thirty cents.

'Gee,' I said. 'Thanks.'

'Percy, that's a gift from your father. I've kept it for years, not knowing you were who I was waiting for. But the prophecy is clear to me now. You are the one.'

I remembered the field trip to the Metropolitan Museum of Art, when I'd vaporized Mrs Dodds. Chiron had thrown me a pen that turned into a sword. Could this be . . . ?

I took off the cap, and the pen grew longer and heavier in my hand. In half a second, I held a shimmering bronze sword with a double-edged blade, a leather-wrapped grip and a flat hilt riveted with gold studs. It was the first weapon that actually felt balanced in my hand.

'The sword has a long and tragic history that we need not go into,' Chiron told me. 'Its name is Anaklusmos.'

'"Riptide",' I translated, surprised the Ancient Greek came so easily.

'Use it only for emergencies,' Chiron said, 'and only against monsters. No hero should harm mortals unless absolutely necessary, of course, but this sword wouldn't harm them in any case.'

I looked at the wickedly sharp blade. 'What do you mean it wouldn't harm mortals? How could it not?'

'The sword is celestial bronze. Forged by the Cyclopes, tempered in the heart of Mount Etna, cooled in the River Lethe. It's deadly to monsters, to any creature from the Underworld, provided they don't kill you first. But the blade will pass through mortals like an illusion. They simply are not important enough for the blade to kill. And I should warn you: as a demigod, you can be killed by either celestial or normal weapons. You are twice as vulnerable.'

'Good to know.'

'Now recap the pen.'

I touched the pen cap to the sword tip and instantly Riptide shrank to a ballpoint pen again. I tucked it in my pocket, a little nervous, because I was famous for losing pens at school.

'You can't,' Chiron said.

'Can't what?'

'Lose the pen,' he said. 'It is enchanted. It will always reappear in your pocket. Try it.'

I was wary, but I threw the pen as far as I could down the hill and watched it disappear in the grass.

'It may take a few moments,' Chiron told me. 'Now check your pocket.'

Sure enough, the pen was there.

'Okay, that's *extremely* cool,' I admitted. 'But what if a mortal sees me pulling out a sword?'

Chiron smiled. 'Mist is a powerful thing, Percy.'

'Mist?'

'Yes. Read *The Iliad*. It's full of references to the stuff. Whenever divine or monstrous elements mix with the mortal world, they generate Mist, which obscures the vision of humans. You will see things just as they are, being a half-blood, but humans will interpret things quite differently. Remarkable, really, the lengths to which humans will go to fit things into their version of reality.'

I put Riptide back in my pocket.

For the first time, the quest felt real. I was actually leaving Half-Blood Hill. I was heading west with no adult supervision, no backup plan, not even a cell phone. (Chiron said cell phones were traceable by monsters; if we used one, it would be worse than sending up a flare.) I had no weapon stronger than a sword to fight off monsters and reach the Land of the Dead.

'Chiron . . .' I said. 'When you say the gods are immortal . . . I mean, there was a time *before* them, right?'

'Four ages before them, actually. The Time of the Titans was the Fourth Age, sometimes called the Golden Age, which is definitely a misnomer. This, the time of Western civilization and the rule of Zeus, is the Fifth Age.'

'So what was it like . . . before the gods?'

Chiron pursed his lips. 'Even I am not old enough to remember that, child, but I know it was a time of darkness and savagery for mortals. Kronos, the lord of the Titans, called his reign the Golden Age because men lived innocent and free of all knowledge. But that was mere propaganda. The Titan king cared nothing for your kind except as appetizers or a source of cheap entertainment. It was only in the early reign of Lord Zeus, when Prometheus the good Titan brought fire to mankind, that your species began to progress, and even then Prometheus was branded a radical thinker. Zeus punished him severely, as you may recall. Of course, eventually the gods warmed to humans, and Western civilization was born.'

'But the gods can't die now, right? I mean, as long as Western civilization is alive, they're alive. So ... even if I failed, nothing could happen so bad it would mess up *everything*, right?'

Chiron gave me a melancholy smile. 'No one knows how long the Age of the West will last, Percy. The gods are immortal, yes. But then, so were the Titans. *They* still exist, locked away in their various prisons, forced to endure endless pain and punishment, reduced in power, but still very much alive. May the Fates forbid that the gods should ever suffer such a doom, or that we should ever return to the darkness and chaos of the past. All we can do, child, is follow our destiny.'

'Our destiny ... assuming we know what that is.'

'Relax,' Chiron told me. 'Keep a clear head. And remember, you may be about to prevent the biggest war in human history.'

'Relax,' I said. 'I'm very relaxed.'

When I got to the bottom of the hill, I looked back. Under the pine tree that used to be Thalia, daughter of Zeus, Chiron was now standing in full horse-man form, holding his bow high in salute. Just your typical summer-camp send-off by your typical centaur.

Argus drove us out of the countryside and into western Long Island. It felt weird to be on a highway again, Annabeth and Grover sitting next to me as if we were normal carpoolers. After two weeks at Half-Blood Hill, the real world seemed like a fantasy. I found myself staring at every McDonald's, every kid in the back of his parents' car, every billboard and shopping mall.

'So far so good,' I told Annabeth. 'Ten miles and not a single monster.'

She gave me an irritated look. 'It's bad luck to talk that way, seaweed brain.'

'Remind me again – why do you hate me so much?'

'I don't hate you.'

'Could've fooled me.'

She folded her cap of invisibility. 'Look . . . we're just not supposed to get along, okay? Our parents are rivals.'

'Why?'

She sighed. 'How many reasons do you want? One time my mom caught Poseidon with his girlfriend in Athena's temple, which is *hugely* disrespectful. Another time, Athena and Poseidon competed to be the patron god for the city of Athens. Your dad created some stupid saltwater spring for his gift. My mom created the olive tree. The people saw that her gift was better, so they named the city after her.'

'They must really like olives.'

'Oh, forget it.'

'Now, if she'd invented pizza – *that* I could understand.'

'I said, forget it!'

In the front seat, Argus smiled. He didn't say anything, but one blue eye on the back of his neck winked at me.

Traffic slowed us down in Queens. By the time we got into Manhattan it was sunset and starting to rain.

Argus dropped us at the Greyhound Station on the Upper East Side, not far from my mom and Gabe's apartment. Taped to a mailbox was a soggy flyer with my picture on it: HAVE YOU SEEN THIS BOY?

I ripped it down before Annabeth and Grover could notice.

Argus unloaded our bags, made sure we got our bus tickets, then drove away, the eye on the back of his hand opening to watch us as he pulled out of the parking lot.

I thought about how close I was to my old apartment. On a normal day, my mom would be home from the candy store by now. Smelly Gabe was probably up there right now, playing poker, not even missing her.

Grover shouldered his backpack. He gazed down the street in the direction I was looking. 'You want to know why she married him, Percy?'

I stared at him. 'Were you reading my mind or something?'

'Just your emotions.' He shrugged. 'Guess I forgot to tell you satyrs can do that. You were thinking about your mom and your stepdad, right?'

I nodded, wondering what else Grover might've forgotten to tell me.

'Your mom married Gabe for *you*,' Grover told me. 'You call him "Smelly", but you've got no idea. The guy has this aura . . . Yuck. I can smell him from here. I can smell traces of him on you, and you haven't been near him for a fortnight.'

'Thanks,' I said. 'Where's the nearest shower?'

'You should be grateful, Percy. Your stepfather smells so repulsively human he could mask the presence of any demigod. As soon as I took a whiff inside his Camaro, I knew: Gabe has been covering your scent for years. If you hadn't lived with him every summer, you probably would've been found by monsters a long time ago. Your mom stayed with him to protect you. She was a smart lady. She must've loved you a lot to put up with that guy – if that makes you feel any better.'

It didn't, but I forced myself not to show it. I'll see her again, I thought. She isn't gone.

I wondered if Grover could still read my emotions, mixed up as they were. I was glad he and Annabeth were with me, but I felt guilty that I hadn't been straight with them. I hadn't told them the real reason I'd said yes to this crazy quest.

The truth was, I didn't care about retrieving Zeus's lightning bolt, or saving the world, or even helping my father out of trouble. The more I thought about it, I resented Poseidon for never visiting me, never helping my mom, never even sending a lousy child-support cheque. He'd only claimed me because he needed a job done.

All I cared about was my mom. Hades had taken her unfairly, and Hades was going to give her back.

You will be betrayed by one who calls you a friend, the Oracle whispered in my mind. *You will fail to save what matters most in the end.*

Shut up, I told it.

The rain kept coming down.

We got restless waiting for the bus and decided to play some Hacky Sack with one of Grover's apples. Annabeth was unbelievable. She could bounce the apple off her knee, her elbow, her shoulder, whatever. I wasn't too bad myself.

The game ended when I tossed the apple towards Grover and it got too close to his mouth. In one mega goat bite, our Hacky Sack disappeared – core, stem and all.

Grover blushed. He tried to apologize, but Annabeth and I were too busy cracking up.

Finally the bus came. As we stood in line to board, Grover started looking around, sniffing the air like he smelled his favourite school cafeteria delicacy – enchiladas.

'What is it?' I asked.

'I don't know,' he said tensely. 'Maybe it's nothing.'

But I could tell it wasn't nothing. I started looking over my shoulder, too.

I was relieved when we finally got on board and found seats together in the back of the bus. We stowed our backpacks. Annabeth kept slapping her Yankees cap nervously against her thigh.

As the last passengers got on, Annabeth clamped her hand onto my knee. 'Percy.'

An old lady had just boarded the bus. She wore a crumpled velvet dress, lace gloves and a shapeless orange-knit hat that shadowed her face, and she carried a big paisley purse. When she tilted her head up, her black eyes glittered, and my heart skipped a beat.

It was Mrs Dodds. Older, more withered, but definitely the same evil face.

I scrunched down in my seat.

Behind her came two more old ladies: one in a green hat, one in a purple hat. Otherwise they looked exactly like Mrs Dodds — same gnarled hands, paisley handbags, wrinkled velvet dresses. Triplet demon grandmothers.

They sat in the front row, right behind the driver. The two on the aisle crossed their legs over the walkway, making an X. It was casual enough, but it sent a clear message: nobody leaves.

The bus pulled out of the station, and we headed through the slick streets of Manhattan. 'She didn't stay dead long,' I said, trying to keep my voice from quivering. 'I thought you said they could be dispelled for a lifetime.'

'I said if you're *lucky*,' Annabeth said. 'You're obviously not.'

'All three of them,' Grover whimpered. *'Di immortales!'*

'It's okay,' Annabeth said, obviously thinking hard. 'The Furies. The three worst monsters from the Underworld. No problem. No problem. We'll just slip out the windows.'

'They don't open,' Grover moaned.

'A back exit?' she suggested.

There wasn't one. Even if there had been, it wouldn't

have helped. By that time, we were on Ninth Avenue, heading for the Lincoln Tunnel.

'They won't attack us with witnesses around,' I said. 'Will they?'

'Mortals don't have good eyes,' Annabeth reminded me. 'Their brains can only process what they see through the Mist.'

'They'll see three old ladies killing us, won't they?'

She thought about it. 'Hard to say. But we can't count on mortals for help. Maybe an emergency exit in the roof . . . ?'

We hit the Lincoln Tunnel, and the bus went dark except for the running lights down the aisle. It was eerily quiet without the sound of the rain.

Mrs Dodds got up. In a flat voice, as if she'd rehearsed it, she announced to the whole bus: 'I need to use the restroom.'

'So do I,' said the second sister.

'So do I,' said the third sister.

They all started coming down the aisle.

'I've got it,' Annabeth said. 'Percy, take my hat.'

'What?'

'You're the one they want. Turn invisible and go up the aisle. Let them pass you. Maybe you can get to the front and get away.'

'But you guys –'

'There's an outside chance they might not notice us,' Annabeth said. 'You're a son of one of the Big Three. Your smell might be overpowering.'

'I can't just leave you.'

'Don't worry about us,' Grover said. 'Go!'

My hands trembled. I felt like a coward, but I took the Yankees cap and put it on.

When I looked down, my body wasn't there any more.

I started creeping up the aisle. I managed to get up ten rows, then duck into an empty seat just as the Furies walked past.

Mrs Dodds stopped, sniffing, and looked straight at me. My heart was pounding.

Apparently she didn't see anything. She and her sisters kept going.

I was free. I made it to the front of the bus. We were almost through the Lincoln Tunnel now. I was about to press the emergency stop button when I heard hideous wailing from the back row.

The old ladies were not old ladies any more. Their faces were still the same – I guess those couldn't get any uglier – but their bodies had shrivelled into leathery brown hag bodies with bat's wings and hands and feet like gargoyle claws. Their handbags had turned into fiery whips.

The Furies surrounded Grover and Annabeth, lashing their whips, hissing: 'Where is it? Where?'

The other people on the bus were screaming, cowering in their seats. They saw *something*, all right.

'He's not here!' Annabeth yelled. 'He's gone!'

The Furies raised their whips.

Annabeth drew her bronze knife. Grover grabbed a tin can from his snack bag and prepared to throw it.

What I did next was so impulsive and dangerous I should've been named ADHD poster child of the year.

The bus driver was distracted, trying to see what was going on in his rearview mirror.

Still invisible, I grabbed the wheel from him and jerked it to the left. Everybody howled as they were thrown to the right, and I heard what I hoped was the sound of three Furies smashing against the windows.

'Hey!' the driver yelled. 'Hey – whoa!'

We wrestled for the wheel. The bus slammed against the side of the tunnel, grinding metal, throwing sparks a mile behind us.

We careened out of the Lincoln Tunnel and back into the rainstorm, people and monsters tossed around the bus, cars ploughed aside like bowling pins.

Somehow the driver found an exit. We shot off the highway, through half a dozen traffic lights, and ended up barrelling down one of those New Jersey rural roads where you can't believe there's so much nothing right across the river from New York. There were woods to our left, the Hudson River to our right and the driver seemed to be veering towards the river.

Another great idea: I hit the emergency brake.

The bus wailed, spun a full circle on the wet tar and crashed into the trees. The emergency lights came on. The door flew open. The bus driver was the first out, the passengers yelling as they stampeded after him. I stepped into the driver's seat and let them pass.

The Furies regained their balance. They lashed their

whips at Annabeth while she waved her knife and yelled in Ancient Greek, telling them to back off. Grover threw tin cans.

I looked at the open doorway. I was free to go, but I couldn't leave my friends. I took off the invisible cap. 'Hey!'

The Furies turned, baring their yellow fangs at me, and the exit suddenly sounded like an excellent idea. Mrs Dodds stalked up the aisle, just as she used to do in class, about to deliver my F- maths test. Every time she flicked her whip, red flames danced along the barbed leather.

Her two ugly sisters hopped on top of the seats on either side of her and crawled towards me like huge nasty lizards.

'Perseus Jackson,' Mrs Dodds said, in an accent that was definitely from somewhere further south than Georgia. 'You have offended the gods. You shall die.'

'I liked you better as a maths teacher,' I told her.

She growled.

Annabeth and Grover moved up behind the Furies cautiously, looking for an opening.

I took the ballpoint pen out of my pocket and uncapped it. Riptide elongated into a shimmering double-edged sword.

The Furies hesitated.

Mrs Dodds had felt Riptide's blade before. She obviously didn't like seeing it again.

'Submit now,' she hissed. 'And you will not suffer eternal torment.'

'Nice try,' I told her.

'Percy, look out!' Annabeth cried.

Mrs Dodds lashed her whip around my sword hand while the Furies on the either side lunged at me.

My hand felt like it was wrapped in molten lead, but I managed not to drop Riptide. I struck the Fury on the left with its hilt, sending her toppling backwards into a seat. I turned and sliced the Fury on the right. As soon as the blade connected with her neck, she screamed and exploded into dust. Annabeth got Mrs Dodds in a wrestler's hold and yanked her backwards while Grover ripped the whip out of her hands.

'Ow!' he yelled. 'Ow! Hot! Hot!'

The Fury I'd hilt-slammed came at me again, talons ready, but I swung Riptide and she broke open like a piñata.

Mrs Dodds was trying to get Annabeth off her back. She kicked, clawed, hissed and bit, but Annabeth held on while Grover got Mrs Dodds's legs tied up in her own whip. Finally they both shoved her backwards into the aisle. Mrs Dodds tried to get up, but she didn't have room to flap her bat wings, so she kept falling down.

'Zeus will destroy you!' she promised. 'Hades will have your soul!'

'*Braccas meas vescimini!*' I yelled.

I wasn't sure where the Latin came from. I think it meant 'Eat my pants!'

Thunder shook the bus. The hair rose on the back of my neck.

'Get out!' Annabeth yelled at me. 'Now!' I didn't need any encouragement.

We rushed outside and found the other passengers wandering around in a daze, arguing with the driver, or running around in circles yelling, 'We're going to die!' A Hawaiian-shirted tourist with a camera snapped my photograph before I could recap my sword.

'Our bags!' Grover realized. 'We left our –'

BOOOOOM!

The windows of the bus exploded as the passengers ran for cover. Lightning shredded a huge crater in the roof, but an angry wail from inside told me Mrs Dodds was not yet dead.

'Run!' Annabeth said. 'She's calling for reinforcements! We have to get out of here!'

We plunged into the woods as the rain poured down, the bus in flames behind us and nothing but darkness ahead.

II ⚡ WE VISIT THE GARDEN GNOME EMPORIUM

In a way, it's nice to know there are Greek gods out there, because you have somebody to blame when things go wrong. For instance, when you're walking away from a bus that's just been attacked by monster hags and blown up by lightning, and it's raining on top of everything else, most people might think that's just really bad luck; when you're a half-blood, you understand that some divine force really is trying to mess up your day.

So there we were, Annabeth and Grover and I, walking through the woods on the New Jersey riverbank, the glow of New York City making the night sky yellow behind us and the smell of the Hudson reeking in our noses.

Grover was shivering and braying, his big goat eyes turned slit-pupilled and full of terror. 'Three Kindly Ones. All three at once.'

I was pretty much in shock myself. The explosion of bus windows still rang in my ears. But Annabeth kept pulling us along, saying: 'Come on! The further away we get, the better.'

'All our money was back there,' I reminded her. 'Our food and clothes. Everything.'

'Well, maybe if you hadn't decided to jump into the fight —'

'What did you want me to do? Let you get killed?'

'You didn't need to protect me, Percy. I would've been fine.'

'Sliced like sandwich bread,' Grover put in, 'but fine.'

'Shut up, goat boy,' said Annabeth.

Grover brayed mournfully. 'Tin cans . . . a perfectly good bag of tin cans.'

We sloshed across mushy ground, through nasty twisted trees that smelled like sour laundry.

After a few minutes, Annabeth fell into line next to me. 'Look, I . . .' Her voice faltered. 'I appreciate your coming back for us, okay? That was really brave.'

'We're a team, right?'

She was silent for a few more steps. 'It's just that if you died . . . aside from the fact that it would really suck for you, it would mean the quest was over. This may be my only chance to see the real world.'

The thunderstorm had finally let up. The city glow faded behind us, leaving us in almost total darkness. I couldn't see anything of Annabeth except a glint of her blonde hair.

'You haven't left Camp Half-Blood since you were seven?' I asked her.

'No . . . only short field trips. My dad —'

'The history professor.'

'Yeah. It didn't work out for me living at home. I mean, Camp Half-Blood *is* my home.' She was rushing her words out now, as if she were afraid somebody might try to stop her. 'At camp you train and train. And that's all cool and everything, but the real world is where the monsters are. That's where you learn whether you're any good or not.'

If I didn't know better, I could've sworn I heard doubt in her voice.

'You're pretty good with that knife,' I said.

'You think so?'

'Anybody who can piggyback-ride a Fury is okay by me.'

I couldn't really see, but I thought she might've smiled.

'You know,' she said, 'maybe I should tell you . . . Something funny back on the bus . . .'

Whatever she wanted to say was interrupted by a shrill *toot-toot-toot*, like the sound of an owl being tortured.

'Hey, my reed pipes still work!' Grover cried. 'If I could just remember a "find path" song, we could get out of these woods!'

He puffed out a few notes, but the tune still sounded suspiciously like Hilary Duff.

Instead of finding a path, I immediately slammed into a tree and got a nice-size knot on my head.

Add to the list of superpowers I did *not* have: infrared vision.

After tripping and cursing and generally feeling miserable for another mile or so, I started to see light up ahead: the colours of a neon sign. I could smell food. Fried, greasy, excellent food. I realized I hadn't eaten anything unhealthy since I'd arrived at Half-Blood Hill, where we lived on grapes, bread, cheese and extra-lean-cut nymph-prepared barbecue. This boy needed a double cheeseburger.

We kept walking until I saw a deserted two-lane road through the trees. On the other side was a closed-down gas station, a tattered billboard for a 1990s movie and one open business, which was the source of the neon light and the good smell.

It wasn't a fast-food restaurant like I'd hoped. It was one of those weird roadside curio shops that sell lawn flamingos and wooden Indians and cement grizzly bears and stuff like that. The main building was a long, low warehouse, surrounded by acres of statuary. The neon sign above the gate was impossible for me to read, because if there's anything worse for my dyslexia than regular English, it's red cursive neon English.

To me, it looked like: *ATNYU MES GDERAN GOMEN MEPROIUM.*

'What the heck does that say?' I asked.

'I don't know,' Annabeth said.

She loved reading so much, I'd forgotten she was dyslexic, too.

Grover translated: 'Aunty Em's Garden Gnome Emporium.'

Flanking the entrance, as advertised, were two cement garden gnomes, ugly bearded little runts, smiling and waving, as if they were about to get their picture taken.

I crossed the street, following the smell of the hamburgers.

'Hey ...' Grover warned.

'The lights are on inside,' Annabeth said. 'Maybe it's open.'

'Snack bar,' I said wistfully.

'Snack bar,' she agreed.

'Are you two crazy?' Grover said. 'This place is weird.'

We ignored him.

The front garden was a forest of statues: cement animals, cement children, even a cement satyr playing the pipes, which gave Grover the creeps.

'Bla-ha-ha!' he bleated. 'Looks like my Uncle Ferdinand!'

We stopped at the warehouse door.

'Don't knock,' Grover pleaded. 'I smell monsters.'

'Your nose is clogged up from the Furies,' Annabeth told him. 'All I smell is burgers. Aren't you hungry?'

'Meat!' he said scornfully. 'I'm a vegetarian.'

'You eat cheese enchiladas and aluminium cans,' I reminded him.

'Those are vegetables. Come on. Let's leave. These statues are . . . looking at me.'

Then the door creaked open, and standing in front of us was a tall Middle Eastern woman – at least, I assumed she was Middle Eastern, because she wore a long black gown that covered everything but her hands, and her head was completely veiled. Her eyes glinted behind a curtain of black gauze, but that was about all I could make out. Her coffee-coloured hands looked old, but well-manicured and elegant, so I imagined she was a grandmother who had once been a beautiful lady.

Her accent sounded vaguely Middle Eastern, too. She

said, 'Children, it is too late to be out all alone. Where are your parents?'

'They're . . . um . . .' Annabeth started to say.

'We're orphans,' I said.

'Orphans?' the woman said. The word sounded alien in her mouth. 'But, my dears! Surely not!'

'We got separated from our caravan,' I said. 'Our circus caravan. The ringmaster told us to meet him at the gas station if we got lost, but he may have forgotten, or maybe he meant a different gas station. Anyway, we're lost. Is that food I smell?'

'Oh, my dears,' the woman said. 'You must come in, poor children. I am Aunty Em. Go straight through to the back of the warehouse, please. There is a dining area.'

We thanked her and went inside.

Annabeth muttered to me, 'Circus caravan?'

'Always have a strategy, right?'

'Your head is full of kelp.'

The warehouse was filled with more statues – people in all different poses, wearing all different outfits and with different expressions on their faces. I was thinking you'd have to have a pretty huge garden to fit even one of these statues, because they were all life-size. But mostly I was thinking about food.

Go ahead, call me an idiot for walking into a strange lady's shop like that just because I was hungry, but I do impulsive stuff sometimes. Plus, you've never smelled Aunty Em's burgers. The aroma was like laughing gas in the dentist's chair – it made everything else go away. I barely noticed Grover's nervous whimpers, or the way the statues' eyes seemed to follow me, or the fact that Aunty Em had locked the door behind us.

All I cared about was finding the dining area. And, sure enough, there it was at the back of the warehouse, a fast-food counter with a grill, a soda fountain, a pretzel heater and a nacho cheese dispenser. Everything you could want, plus a few steel picnic tables out front.

'Please, sit down,' Aunty Em said.

'Awesome,' I said.

'Um,' Grover said reluctantly, 'we don't have any money, ma'am.'

Before I could jab him in the ribs, Aunty Em said, 'No, no, children. No money. This is a special case, yes? It is my treat, for such nice orphans.'

'Thank you, ma'am,' Annabeth said.

Aunty Em stiffened, as if Annabeth had done some-thing wrong, but then the old woman relaxed just as quickly, so I figured it must've been my imagination.

'Quite all right, Annabeth,' she said. 'You have such beautiful grey eyes, child.' Only later did I wonder how she knew Annabeth's name, even though we had never introduced ourselves.

Our hostess disappeared behind the snack counter and started cooking. Before we knew it, she'd brought us plastic trays heaped with double cheeseburgers, vanilla shakes and XXL servings of French fries.

I was halfway through my burger before I remembered to breathe.

Annabeth slurped her shake.

Grover picked at the fries, and eyed the tray's waxed paper liner as if he might go for that, but he still looked too nervous to eat.

'What's that hissing noise?' he asked.

I listened, but didn't hear anything. Annabeth shook her head.

'Hissing?' Aunty Em asked. 'Perhaps you hear the deep-fryer oil. You have keen ears, Grover.'

'I take vitamins. For my ears.'

'That's admirable,' she said. 'But please, relax.'

Aunty Em ate nothing. She hadn't taken off her head-dress, even to cook, and now she sat forward and interlaced her fingers and watched us eat. It was a little unsettling, having someone stare at me when I couldn't see her face, but I was feeling satisfied after the burger, and a little sleepy, and I figured the least I could do was try to make small talk with our hostess.

'So, you sell gnomes,' I said, trying to sound interested.

'Oh, yes,' Aunty Em said. 'And animals. And people. Anything for the garden. Custom orders. Statuary is very popular, you know.'

'A lot of business on this road?'

'Not so much, no. Since the highway was built . . . most cars, they do not go this way now. I must cherish every customer I get.'

My neck tingled, as if somebody else was looking at me. I turned, but it was just a statue of a young girl holding an Easter basket. The detail was incredible, much better than you see in most garden statues. But something was wrong with her face. It looked as if she were startled, or even terrified.

'Ah,' Aunty Em said sadly. 'You notice some of my creations do not turn out well. They are marred. They do not sell. The face is the hardest to get right. Always the face.'

'You make these statues yourself?' I asked.

'Oh, yes. Once upon a time, I had two sisters to help me in the business, but they have passed on, and Aunty Em is alone. I have only my statues. This is why I make them, you see. They are my company.' The sadness in her voice sounded so deep and so real that I couldn't help feeling sorry for her.

Annabeth had stopped eating. She sat forward and said, 'Two sisters?'

'It's a terrible story,' Aunty Em said. 'Not one for children, really. You see, Annabeth, a bad woman was jealous of me, long ago, when I was young. I had a . . . a boyfriend, you know, and this bad woman was determined to break us apart. She caused a terrible accident. My sisters stayed by me. They shared my bad fortune as long as they could, but eventually they passed on. They faded away. I alone have survived, but at a price. Such a price.'

I wasn't sure what she meant, but I felt bad for her. My eyelids kept getting heavier, my full stomach making me sleepy. Poor old lady. Who would want to hurt somebody so nice?

'Percy?' Annabeth was shaking me to get my attention.

'Maybe we should go. I mean, the ringmaster will be waiting.'

She sounded tense. I wasn't sure why. Grover was eating the waxed paper off the tray now, but if Aunty Em found that strange, she didn't say anything.

'Such beautiful grey eyes,' Aunty Em told Annabeth again. 'My, yes, it has been a long time since I've seen grey eyes like those.'

She reached out as if to stroke Annabeth's cheek, but Annabeth stood up abruptly.

'We really should go.'

'Yes!' Grover swallowed his waxed paper and stood up. 'The ringmaster is waiting! Right!'

I didn't want to leave. I felt full and content. Aunty Em was so nice. I wanted to stay with her a while.

'Please, dears,' Aunty Em pleaded. 'I so rarely get to be with children. Before you go, won't you at least sit for a pose?'

'A pose?' Annabeth asked warily.

'A photograph. I will use it to model a new statue set. Children are so popular, you see. Everyone loves children.'

Annabeth shifted her weight from foot to foot. 'I don't think we can, ma'am. Come on, Percy —'

'Sure we can,' I said. I was irritated with Annabeth for being so bossy, so rude to an old lady who'd just fed us for free. 'It's just a photo, Annabeth. What's the harm?'

'Yes, Annabeth,' the woman purred. 'No harm.'

I could tell Annabeth didn't like it, but she allowed

Aunty Em to lead us back out the front door, into the garden of statues.

Aunty Em directed us to a park bench next to the stone satyr. 'Now,' she said, 'I'll just position you correctly. The young girl in the middle, I think, and the two young gentlemen on either side.'

'Not much light for a photo,' I remarked.

'Oh, enough,' Aunty Em said. 'Enough for us to see each other, yes?'

'Where's your camera?' Grover asked.

Aunty Em stepped back, as if to admire the shot. 'Now, the face is the most difficult. Can you smile for me please, everyone? A large smile?'

Grover glanced at the cement satyr next to him, and mumbled, 'That sure does look like Uncle Ferdinand.'

'Grover,' Aunty Em chastised, 'look this way, dear.'

She still had no camera in her hands.

'Percy —' Annabeth said.

Some instinct warned me to listen to Annabeth, but I was fighting the sleepy feeling, the comfortable lull that came from the food and the old lady's voice.

'I will just be a moment,' Aunty Em said. 'You know, I can't see you very well in this cursed veil . . .'

'Percy, something's wrong,' Annabeth insisted.

'Wrong?' Aunty Em said, reaching up to undo the wrap around her head. 'Not at all, dear. I have such noble company tonight. What could be wrong?'

'That *is* Uncle Ferdinand!' Grover gasped.

'Look away from her!' Annabeth shouted. She whipped

her Yankees cap on to her head and vanished. Her invisible hands pushed Grover and me both off the bench.

I was on the ground, looking at Aunt Em's sandalled feet.

I could hear Grover scrambling off in one direction, Annabeth in another. But I was too dazed to move.

Then I heard a strange, rasping sound above me. My eyes rose to Aunty Em's hands, which had turned gnarled and warty, with sharp bronze talons for fingernails.

I almost looked higher, but somewhere off to my left Annabeth screamed, 'No! Don't!'

More rasping – the sound of tiny snakes, right above me, from . . . from about where Aunty Em's head would be.

'Run!' Grover bleated. I heard him racing across the gravel, yelling, *'Maia!'* to kick-start his flying sneakers.

I couldn't move. I stared at Aunty Em's gnarled claws, and tried to fight the groggy trance the old woman had put me in.

'Such a pity to destroy a handsome young face,' she told me soothingly. 'Stay with me, Percy. All you have to do is look up.'

I fought the urge to obey. Instead I looked to one side and saw one of those glass spheres people put in gardens – a gazing ball. I could see Aunty Em's dark reflection in the orange glass; her headdress was gone, revealing her face as a shimmering pale circle. Her hair was moving, writhing like serpents.

Aunty Em.

Aunty 'M'.

How could I have been so stupid?

Think, I told myself. How did Medusa die in the myth?

But I couldn't think. Something told me that in the myth Medusa had been asleep when she was attacked by my namesake, Perseus. She wasn't anywhere near asleep now. If she wanted, she could take those talons right now and rake open my face.

'The Grey-Eyed One did this to me, Percy,' Medusa said, and she didn't sound anything like a monster. Her voice invited me to look up, to sympathize with a poor old grandmother. 'Annabeth's mother, the cursed Athena, turned me from a beautiful woman into this.'

'Don't listen to her!' Annabeth's voice shouted, somewhere in the statuary. 'Run, Percy!'

'Silence!' Medusa snarled. Then her voice modulated back to a comforting purr. 'You see why I must destroy the girl, Percy. She is my enemy's daughter. I shall crush her statue to dust. But you, dear Percy, you need not suffer.'

'No,' I muttered. I tried to make my legs move.

'Do you really want to help the gods?' Medusa asked. 'Do you understand what awaits you on this foolish quest, Percy? What will happen if you reach the Underworld? Do not be a pawn of the Olympians, my dear. You would be better off as a statue. Less pain. Less pain.'

'Percy!' Behind me, I heard a buzzing sound, like a ninety-kilogram hummingbird in a nosedive. Grover yelled, 'Duck!'

I turned, and there he was in the night sky, flying in from twelve o'clock with his winged shoes fluttering –

Grover, holding a tree branch the size of a baseball bat. His eyes were shut tight, his head twitched from side to side. He was navigating by ears and nose alone.

'Duck!' he yelled again. 'I'll get her!'

That finally jolted me into action. Knowing Grover, I was sure he'd miss Medusa and nail me. I dove to one side.

Thwack!

At first I figured it was the sound of Grover hitting a tree. Then Medusa roared with rage.

'You miserable satyr,' she snarled. 'I'll add you to my collection!'

'That was for Uncle Ferdinand!' Grover yelled back.

I scrambled away and hid in the statuary while Grover swooped down for another pass.

Ker-whack!

'Arrgh!' Medusa yelled, her snake-hair hissing and spitting.

Right next to me, Annabeth's voice said, 'Percy!'

I jumped so high my feet nearly cleared a garden gnome. 'Jeez! Don't do that!'

Annabeth took off her Yankees cap and became visible. 'You have to cut her head off.'

'What? Are you crazy? Let's get out of here.'

'Medusa is a menace. She's evil. I'd kill her myself, but . . .' Annabeth swallowed, as if she were about to make a difficult admission. 'But you've got the better weapon. Besides, I'd never get close to her. She'd slice me to bits because of my mother. You — you've got a chance.'

'What? I can't —'

'Look, do you want her turning more innocent people into statues?'

She pointed to a pair of statue lovers, a man and a woman with their arms around each other, turned to stone by the monster.

Annabeth grabbed a green gazing ball from a nearby pedestal. 'A polished shield would be better.' She studied the sphere critically. 'The convexity will cause some distortion. The reflection's size should be off by a factor of –'

'Would you speak English?'

'I *am!*' She tossed me the glass ball. 'Just look at her in the glass. *Never* look at her directly.'

'Hey, guys!' Grover yelled somewhere above us. 'I think she's unconscious!'

'*Roooaaarrr!*'

'Maybe not,' Grover corrected. He went in for another pass with the tree branch.

'Hurry,' Annabeth told me. 'Grover's got a great nose, but he'll eventually crash.'

I took out my pen and uncapped it. The bronze blade of Riptide elongated in my hand.

I followed the hissing and spitting sounds of Medusa's hair.

I kept my eyes locked on the gazing ball so I would only glimpse Medusa's reflection, not the real thing. Then, in the green tinted glass, I saw her.

Grover was coming in for another turn at bat, but this time he flew a little too low. Medusa grabbed the stick and pulled him off course. He tumbled through the air and crashed into the arms of a stone grizzly bear with a painful 'Ummphh!'

Medusa was about to lunge at him when I yelled, 'Hey!'

I advanced on her, which wasn't easy, holding a sword and a glass ball. If she charged, I'd have a hard time defending myself.

But she let me approach – ten metres, five metres.

I could see the reflection of her face now. Surely it wasn't really *that* ugly. The green swirls of the gazing ball must be distorting it, making it look worse.

'You wouldn't harm an old woman, Percy,' she crooned. 'I know you wouldn't.'

I hesitated, fascinated by the face I saw reflected in the glass – the eyes that seemed to burn straight through the green tint, making my arms go weak.

From the cement grizzly, Grover moaned, 'Percy, don't listen to her!'

Medusa cackled. 'Too late.'

She lunged at me with her talons.

I slashed up with my sword, heard a sickening *shlock!*, then a hiss like wind rushing out of a cavern – the sound of a monster disintegrating.

Something fell to the ground next to my foot. It took all my willpower not to look. I could feel warm ooze soaking into my sock, little dying snake heads tugging at my shoelaces.

'Oh, yuck,' Grover said. His eyes were still tightly closed, but I guess he could hear the thing gurgling and steaming. 'Mega-yuck.'

Annabeth came up next to me, her eyes fixed on the sky. She was holding Medusa's black veil. She said, 'Don't move.'

Very, very carefully, without looking down, she knelt and draped the monster's head in black cloth, then picked it up. It was still dripping green juice.

'Are you okay?' she asked me, her voice trembling.

'Yeah,' I decided, though I felt like throwing up my double cheeseburger. 'Why didn't ... why didn't the head evaporate?'

'Once you sever it, it becomes a spoil of war,' she said. 'Same as your Minotaur horn. But don't unwrap the head. It can still petrify you.'

Grover moaned as he climbed down from the grizzly statue. He had a big welt on his forehead. His green rasta cap hung from one of his little goat horns, and his fake feet had been knocked off his hooves. The magic sneakers were flying aimlessly around his head.

'The Red Baron,' I said. 'Good job, man.'

He managed a bashful grin. 'That really was *not* fun, though. Well, the hitting-her-with-a-stick part, that was fun. But crashing into a concrete bear? *Not* fun.'

He snatched his shoes out of the air. I recapped my sword. Together, the three of us stumbled back to the warehouse.

We found some old plastic grocery bags behind the snack counter and double-wrapped Medusa's head. We plopped it on the table where we'd eaten dinner and sat around it, too exhausted to speak.

Finally I said, 'So we have Athena to thank for this monster?'

Annabeth flashed me an irritated look. 'Your dad, actually. Don't you remember? Medusa was Poseidon's girlfriend. They decided to meet in my mother's temple. That's why Athena turned her into a monster. Medusa and her two sisters who had helped her get into the temple, they became the three gorgons. That's why Medusa wanted to slice me up, but she wanted to preserve you as a nice statue. She's still sweet on your dad. You probably reminded her of him.'

My face was burning. 'Oh, so now it's *my* fault we met Medusa.'

Annabeth straightened. In a bad imitation of my voice, she said: '"It's just a photo, Annabeth. What's the harm?"'

'Forget it,' I said. 'You're impossible.'

'You're insufferable.'

'You're —'

'Hey!' Grover interrupted. 'You two are giving me a migraine, and satyrs don't even *get* migraines. What are we going to do with the head?'

I stared at the thing. One little snake was hanging out of a hole in the plastic. The words printed on the side of the bag said: WE APPRECIATE YOUR BUSINESS!

I was angry, not just with Annabeth or her mom, but with all the gods for this whole quest, for getting us blown off the road and in two major fights the very first day out from camp. At this rate, we'd never make it to L.A. alive, much less before the summer solstice.

What had Medusa said?

Do not be a pawn of the Olympians, my dear. You would be better off as a statue.

I got up. 'I'll be back.'

'Percy,' Annabeth called after me. 'What are you —'

I searched the back of the warehouse until I found Medusa's office. Her account book showed her six most recent sales, all shipments to the Underworld to decorate Hades and Persephone's garden. According to one freight bill, the Underworld's billing address was DOA Recording Studios, West Hollywood, California. I folded up the bill and stuffed it in my pocket.

In the cash register I found twenty dollars, a few golden drachmas and some packing slips for Hermes Overnight Express, each with a little leather bag attached for coins. I rummaged around the rest of the office until I found the right-size box.

I went back to the picnic table, packed up Medusa's head, and filled out a delivery slip:

The Gods
Mount Olympus
600th Floor,
Empire State Building
New York, NY

With best wishes,
PERCY JACKSON

'They're not going to like that,' Grover warned. 'They'll think you're impertinent.'

I poured some golden drachmas in the pouch. As soon as I closed it, there was a sound like a cash register. The package floated off the table and disappeared with a *pop!*

'I *am* impertinent,' I said.

I looked at Annabeth, daring her to criticize.

She didn't. She seemed resigned to the fact that I had a major talent for ticking off the gods. 'Come on,' she muttered. 'We need a new plan.'

12 ⚡ WE GET ADVICE
FROM A POODLE

We were pretty miserable that night.

We camped out in the woods, a hundred metres from the main road, in a marshy clearing that local kids had obviously been using for parties. The ground was littered with flattened soda cans and fast-food wrappers.

We'd taken some food and blankets from Aunty Em's, but we didn't dare light a fire to dry our damp clothes. The Furies and Medusa had provided enough excitement for one day. We didn't want to attract anything else.

We decided to sleep in shifts. I volunteered to take first watch.

Annabeth curled up on the blankets and was snoring as soon as her head hit the ground. Grover fluttered with his flying shoes to the lowest bough of a tree, put his back to the trunk, and stared at the night sky.

'Go ahead and sleep,' I told him. 'I'll wake you if there's trouble.'

He nodded, but still didn't close his eyes. 'It makes me sad, Percy.'

'What does? The fact that you signed up for this stupid quest?'

'No. *This* makes me sad.' He pointed at all the garbage on

the ground. 'And the sky. You can't even see the stars. They've polluted the sky. This is a terrible time to be a satyr.'

'Oh, yeah. I guess you'd be an environmentalist.'

He glared at me. 'Only a human wouldn't be. Your species is clogging up the world so fast . . . ah, never mind. It's useless to lecture a human. At the rate things are going, I'll never find Pan.'

'Pam? Like the cooking spray?'

'Pan!' he cried indignantly. 'P-A-N. The great god Pan! What do you think I want a searcher's licence for?'

A strange breeze rustled through the clearing, temporarily overpowering the stink of trash and muck. It brought the smell of berries and wildflowers and clean rainwater, things that might've once been in these woods. Suddenly I was nostalgic for something I'd never known.

'Tell me about the search,' I said.

Grover looked at me cautiously, as if he were afraid I was just making fun.

'The God of Wild Places disappeared two thousand years ago,' he told me. 'A sailor off the coast of Ephesos heard a mysterious voice crying out from the shore, "Tell them that the great god Pan has died!" When humans heard the news, they believed it. They've been pillaging Pan's kingdom ever since. But for the satyrs, Pan was our lord and master. He protected us and the wild places of the earth. We refuse to believe that he died. In every generation, the bravest satyrs pledge their lives to finding Pan. They search the earth, exploring all the wildest places, hoping to find where he is hidden and wake him from his sleep.'

'And you want to be a searcher.'

'It's my life's dream,' he said. 'My father was a searcher. And my Uncle Ferdinand ... the statue you saw back there –'

'Oh, right, sorry.'

Grover shook his head. 'Uncle Ferdinand knew the risks. So did my dad. But I'll succeed. I'll be the first searcher to return alive.'

'Hang on – *the first?*'

Grover took his reed pipes out of his pocket. 'No searcher has ever come back. Once they set out, they disappear. They're never seen alive again.'

'Not once in two thousand years?'

'No.'

'And your dad? You have no idea what happened to him?'

'None.'

'But you still want to go,' I said, amazed. 'I mean, you really think you'll be the one to find Pan?'

'I have to believe that, Percy. Every searcher does. It's the only thing that keeps us from despair when we look at what humans have done to the world. I have to believe Pan can still be awakened.'

I stared at the orange haze of the sky and tried to understand how Grover could pursue a dream that seemed so hopeless. Then again, was I any better?

'How are we going to get into the Underworld?' I asked him. 'I mean, what chance do we have against a god?'

'I don't know,' he admitted. 'But back at Medusa's,

when you were searching her office? Annabeth was telling me –'

'Oh, I forgot. Annabeth will have a plan all figured out.'

'Don't be so hard on her, Percy. She's had a tough life, but she's a good person. After all, she forgave me . . .' His voice faltered.

'What do you mean?' I asked. 'Forgave you for what?'

Suddenly, Grover seemed very interested in playing notes on his pipes.

'Wait a minute,' I said. 'Your first keeper job was five years ago. Annabeth has been at camp five years. She wasn't . . . I mean, your first assignment that went wrong –'

'I can't talk about it,' Grover said, and his quivering lower lip suggested he'd start crying if I pressed him. 'But as I was saying, back at Medusa's, Annabeth and I agreed there's something strange going on with this quest. Something isn't what it seems.'

'Well, duh. I'm getting blamed for stealing a thunderbolt that Hades took.'

'That's not what I mean,' Grover said. 'The Fu – The Kindly Ones were sort of holding back. Like Mrs Dodds at Yancy Academy . . . why did she wait so long to try to kill you? Then on the bus, they just weren't as aggressive as they could've been.'

'They seemed plenty aggressive to me.'

Grover shook his head. 'They were screeching at us: "Where is it? Where?"'

'Asking about me,' I said.

'Maybe ... but Annabeth and I, we both got the feeling they weren't asking about a person. They said "Where is *it*?" They seemed to be asking about an object.'

'That doesn't make sense.'

'I know. But if we've misunderstood something about this quest, and we only have nine days to find the master bolt . . .' He looked at me like he was hoping for answers, but I didn't have any.

I thought about what Medusa had said: I was being used by the gods. What lay ahead of me was worse than petrification. 'I haven't been straight with you,' I told Grover. 'I don't care about the master bolt. I agreed to go to the Underworld so I could bring back my mother.'

Grover blew a soft note on his pipes. 'I know that, Percy. But are you sure that's the only reason?'

'I'm not doing it to help my father. He doesn't care about me. I don't care about him.'

Grover gazed down from his tree branch. 'Look, Percy, I'm not as smart as Annabeth. I'm not as brave as you. But I'm pretty good at reading emotions. You're glad your dad is alive. You feel good that he's claimed you, and part of you wants to make him proud. That's why you mailed Medusa's head to Olympus. You wanted him to notice what you'd done.'

'Yeah? Well maybe satyr emotions work differently than human emotions. Because you're wrong. I don't care what he thinks.'

Grover pulled his feet up onto the branch. 'Okay, Percy. Whatever.'

'Besides, I haven't done anything worth bragging about. We barely got out of New York and we're stuck here with no money and no way west.'

Grover looked at the night sky, like he was thinking about that problem. 'How about *I* take first watch, huh? You get some sleep.'

I wanted to protest, but he started to play Mozart, soft and sweet, and I turned away, my eyes stinging. After a few bars of Piano Concerto no. 12, I was asleep.

In my dreams, I stood in a dark cavern before a gaping pit. Grey mist creatures churned all around me, whispering rags of smoke that I somehow knew were the spirits of the dead.

They tugged at my clothes, trying to pull me back, but I felt compelled to walk forward to the very edge of the chasm.

Looking down made me dizzy.

The pit yawned so wide and was so completely black, I knew it must be bottomless. Yet I had a feeling that something was trying to rise from the abyss, something huge and evil.

The little hero, an amused voice echoed far down in the darkness. *Too weak, too young, but perhaps you will do.*

The voice felt ancient – cold and heavy. It wrapped around me like sheets of lead.

They have misled you, boy, it said. *Barter with me. I will give you what you want.*

A shimmering image hovered over the void: my mother, frozen at the moment she'd dissolved in a shower of gold.

Her face was distorted with pain, as if the Minotaur were still squeezing her neck. Her eyes looked directly at me, pleading: *Go!*

I tried to cry out, but my voice wouldn't work.

Cold laughter echoed from the chasm.

An invisible force pulled me forward. It would drag me into the pit unless I stood firm.

Help me rise, boy. The voice became hungrier. *Bring me the bolt. Strike a blow against the treacherous gods!*

The spirits of the dead whispered around me, *No! Wake!*

The image of my mother began to fade. The thing in the pit tightened its unseen grip around me.

I realized it wasn't interested in pulling me in. It was using me to pull itself *out*.

Good, it murmured. *Good.*

Wake! the dead whispered. *Wake!*

Someone was shaking me.

My eyes opened, and it was daylight.

'Well,' Annabeth said, 'the zombie lives.'

I was trembling from the dream. I could still feel the grip of the chasm monster around my chest. 'How long was I asleep?'

'Long enough for me to cook breakfast.' Annabeth tossed me a bag of nacho-flavoured corn chips from Aunty Em's snack bar. 'And Grover went exploring. Look, he found a friend.'

My eyes had trouble focusing.

Grover was sitting cross-legged on a blanket with

something fuzzy in his lap, a dirty, unnaturally pink stuffed animal.

No. It wasn't a stuffed animal. It was a pink poodle.

The poodle yapped at me suspiciously. Grover said, 'No, he's not.'

I blinked. 'Are you . . . talking to that thing?'

The poodle growled.

'This *thing*,' Grover warned, 'is our ticket west. Be nice to him.'

'You can talk to animals?'

Grover ignored the question. 'Percy, meet Gladiola. Gladiola, Percy.'

I stared at Annabeth, figuring she'd crack up at this practical joke they were playing on me, but she looked deadly serious.

'I'm not saying hello to a pink poodle,' I said. 'Forget it.'

'Percy,' Annabeth said. 'I said hello to the poodle. You say hello to the poodle.'

The poodle growled.

I said hello to the poodle.

Grover explained that he'd come across Gladiola in the woods and they'd struck up a conversation. The poodle had run away from a rich local family, who'd posted a $200 reward for his return. Gladiola didn't really want to go back to his family, but he was willing to if it meant helping Grover.

'How does Gladiola know about the reward?' I asked.

'He read the signs,' Grover said. 'Duh.'

'Of course,' I said. 'Silly me.'

'So we turn in Gladiola,' Annabeth explained in her best strategy voice, 'we get money and we buy tickets to Los Angeles. Simple.'

I thought about my dream – the whispering voices of the dead, the thing in the chasm and my mother's face, shimmering as it dissolved into gold. All that might be waiting for me in the West.

'Not another bus,' I said warily.

'No,' Annabeth agreed.

She pointed downhill, towards train tracks I hadn't been able to see last night in the dark. 'There's an Amtrack station half a mile that way. According to Gladiola, the westbound train leaves at noon.'

13 ⚡ I PLUNGE TO MY DEATH

We spent two days on the Amtrak train, heading west through hills, over rivers, past amber waves of grain.

We weren't attacked once, but I didn't relax. I felt that we were travelling around in a display case, being watched from above and maybe from below, that something was waiting for the right opportunity.

I tried to keep a low profile because my name and picture were splattered over the front pages of several East Coast newspapers. The *Trenton Register-News* showed a photo taken by a tourist as I got off the Greyhound bus. I had a wild look in my eyes. My sword was a metallic blur in my hands. It might've been a baseball bat or a lacrosse stick.

The picture's caption read:

> *Twelve-year-old Percy Jackson, wanted for questioning in the Long Island disappearance of his mother two weeks ago, is shown here fleeing from the bus where he accosted several elderly female passengers. The bus exploded on an east New Jersey roadside shortly after Jackson fled the scene. Based on eyewitness accounts, police believe the boy may be travelling with two teenage accomplices. His stepfather, Gabe Ugliano, has offered a cash reward for information leading to his capture.*

'Don't worry,' Annabeth told me. 'Mortal police could never find us.' But she didn't sound so sure.

The rest of the day I spent alternately pacing the length of the train (because I had a really hard time sitting still), or looking out the windows.

Once, I spotted a family of centaurs galloping across a wheat field, bows at the ready, as they hunted lunch. The little boy centaur, who was the size of a second-grader on a pony, caught my eye and waved. I looked around the passenger car, but nobody else had noticed. The adult riders all had their faces buried in laptop computers or magazines.

Another time, towards evening, I saw something huge moving through the woods. I could've sworn it was a lion, except that lions don't live wild in America, and this thing was the size of a tank. Its fur glinted gold in the evening light. Then it leaped through the trees and was gone.

Our reward money for returning Gladiola the poodle had only been enough to purchase tickets as far as Denver. We couldn't get berths in the sleeper car, so we dozed in our seats. My neck got stiff. I tried not to drool in my sleep, since Annabeth was sitting right next to me.

Grover kept snoring and bleating and waking me up. Once, he shuffled around and his fake foot fell off. Annabeth and I had to stick it back on before any of the other passengers noticed.

'So,' Annabeth asked me, once we'd got Grover's trainer readjusted. 'Who wants your help?'

'What do you mean?'

'When you were asleep just now, you mumbled, "I won't help you." Who were you dreaming about?'

I was reluctant to say anything. It was the second time I'd dreamed about the evil voice from the pit. But it bothered me so much I finally told her.

Annabeth was quiet for a long time. 'That doesn't sound like Hades. He always appears on a black throne, and he never laughs.'

'He offered my mother in trade. Who else could do that?'

'I guess ... if he meant, "Help me rise from the Underworld." If he wants war with the Olympians. But why ask you to bring him the master bolt if he already has it?'

I shook my head, wishing I knew the answer. I thought about what Grover had told me, that the Furies on the bus seemed to have been looking for something.

Where is it? Where?

Maybe Grover sensed my emotions. He snorted in his sleep, muttered something about vegetables and turned his head.

Annabeth readjusted his cap so it covered his horns. 'Percy, you can't barter with Hades. You know that, right? He's deceitful, heartless and greedy. I don't care if his Kindly Ones weren't as aggressive this time –'

'This time?' I asked. 'You mean you've run into them before?'

Her hand crept up to her necklace. She fingered a glazed white bead painted with the image of a pine tree, one of her clay end-of-summer tokens. 'Let's just say I've got no love for the Lord of the Dead. You can't be tempted to make a deal for your mom.'

'What would you do if it was your dad?'

'That's easy,' she said. 'I'd leave him to rot.'

'You're not serious?'

Annabeth's grey eyes fixed on me. She wore the same expression she'd worn in the woods at camp, the moment she drew her sword against the hellhound. 'My dad's resented me since the day I was born, Percy,' she said. 'He never wanted a baby. When he got me, he asked Athena to take me back and raise me on Olympus because he was too busy with his work. She wasn't happy about that. She told him heroes had to be raised by their mortal parent.'

'But how ... I mean, I guess you weren't born in a hospital ...'

'I appeared on my father's doorstep, in a golden cradle, carried down from Olympus by Zephyr the West Wind. You'd think my dad would remember that as a miracle, right? Like, maybe he'd take some digital photos or something. But he always talked about my arrival as if it were the most inconvenient thing that had ever happened to him. When I was five he got married and totally forgot about Athena. He got a "regular" mortal wife, and had two "regular" mortal kids, and tried to pretend I didn't exist.'

I stared out the train window. The lights of a sleeping town were drifting by. I wanted to make Annabeth feel better, but I didn't know how.

'My mom married a really awful guy,' I told her. 'Grover said she did it to protect me, to hide me in the scent of a human family. Maybe that's what your dad was thinking.'

Annabeth kept worrying at her necklace. She was pinching the gold college ring that hung with the beads. It occurred to me that the ring must be her father's. I wondered why she wore it if she hated him so much.

'He doesn't care about me,' she said. 'His wife – my stepmom – treated me like a freak. She wouldn't let me play with her children. My dad went along with her. Whenever something dangerous happened – you know, something with monsters – they would both look at me resentfully, like, "How dare you put our family at risk!" Finally, I took the hint. I wasn't wanted. I ran away.'

'How old were you?'

'Same age as when I started camp. Seven.'

'But . . . you couldn't have got all the way to Half-Blood Hill by yourself.'

'Not alone, no. Athena watched over me, guided me towards help. I made a couple of unexpected friends who took care of me, for a short time, anyway.'

I wanted to ask what happened, but Annabeth seemed lost in sad memories. So I listened to the sound of Grover snoring and gazed out the train windows as the dark fields of Ohio raced by.

Towards the end of our second day on the train, June 13, eight days before the summer solstice, we passed through some golden hills and over the Mississippi River into St Louis.

Annabeth craned her neck to see the Gateway Arch, which looked to me like a huge shopping-bag handle stuck on the city.

'I want to do that,' she sighed.

'What?' I asked.

'Build something like that. You ever see the Parthenon, Percy?'

'Only in pictures.'

'Someday, I'm going to see it in person. I'm going to build the greatest monument to the gods ever. Something that'll last a thousand years.'

I laughed. 'You? An architect?'

I don't know why, but I found it funny. Just the idea of Annabeth trying to sit quietly and draw all day.

Her cheeks flushed. 'Yes, an architect. Athena expects her children to create things, not just tear them down, like a certain god of earthquakes I could mention.'

I watched the churning brown water of the Mississippi below.

'Sorry,' Annabeth said. 'That was mean.'

'Can't we work together a little?' I pleaded. 'I mean, didn't Athena and Poseidon ever cooperate?'

Annabeth had to think about it. 'I guess . . . the chariot,' she said tentatively. 'My mom invented it, but Poseidon created horses out of the crests of waves. So they had to work together to make it complete.'

'Then we can cooperate, too. Right?'

We rode into the city, Annabeth watching as the Arch disappeared behind a hotel.

'I suppose,' she said at last.

We pulled into the Amtrak station downtown. The intercom told us we'd have a three-hour stopover before departing for Denver.

Grover stretched. Before he was even fully awake, he said, 'Food.'

'Come on, goat boy,' Annabeth said. 'Sightseeing.'

'Sightseeing?'

'The Gateway Arch,' she said. 'This may be my only chance to ride to the top. Are you coming or not?'

Grover and I exchanged looks.

I wanted to say no, but I figured that if Annabeth was going, we couldn't very well let her go alone.

Grover shrugged. 'As long as there's a snack bar without monsters.'

The Arch was about a mile from the train station. Late in the day the lines to get in weren't that long. We threaded our way through the underground museum, looking at covered wagons and other junk from the 1800s. It wasn't all that thrilling, but Annabeth kept telling us interesting facts about how the Arch was built, and Grover kept passing me jelly beans, so I was okay.

I kept looking around, though, at the other people in line. 'You smell anything?' I murmured to Grover.

He took his nose out of the jelly-bean bag long enough to sniff. 'Underground,' he said distastefully. 'Underground air always smells like monsters. Probably doesn't mean anything.'

But something felt wrong to me. I had a feeling we shouldn't be here.

'Guys,' I said. 'You know the gods' symbols of power?'

Annabeth had been in the middle of reading about the construction equipment used to build the Arch, but she looked over. 'Yeah?'

'Well, Hade —'

Grover cleared his throat. 'We're in a public place . . . You mean, our friend downstairs?'

'Um, right,' I said. 'Our friend *way* downstairs. Doesn't he have a hat like Annabeth's?'

'You mean the Helm of Darkness,' Annabeth said. 'Yeah, that's his symbol of power. I saw it next to his seat during the winter solstice council meeting.'

'He was there?' I asked.

She nodded. 'It's the only time he's allowed to visit Olympus — the darkest day of the year. But his helmet is a lot more powerful than my invisibility hat, if what I've heard is true . . .'

'It allows him to become darkness,' Grover confirmed. 'He can melt into shadow or pass through walls. He can't be touched, or seen, or heard. And he can radiate fear so intense it can drive you insane or stop your heart. Why do you think all rational creatures fear the dark?'

'But then . . . how do we know he's not here right now, watching us?' I asked.

Annabeth and Grover exchanged looks.

'We don't,' Grover said.

'Thanks, that makes me feel a lot better,' I said. 'Got any blue jelly beans left?'

I'd almost mastered my jumpy nerves when I saw the tiny little elevator car we were going to ride to the top of the Arch, and I knew I was in trouble. I hate confined places. They make me nuts.

We got shoehorned into the car with this big fat lady and her dog, a Chihuahua with a rhinestone collar. I figured maybe the dog was a seeing-eye Chihuahua, because none of the guards said a word about it.

We started going up, inside the Arch. I'd never been in an elevator that went in a curve, and my stomach wasn't too happy about it.

'No parents?' the fat lady asked us.

She had beady eyes; pointy, coffee-stained teeth; a floppy denim hat, and a denim dress that bulged so much she looked like a blue-jean blimp.

'They're below,' Annabeth told her. 'Scared of heights.'

'Oh, the poor darlings.'

The Chihuahua growled. The woman said, 'Now, now, sonny. Behave.' The dog had beady eyes like its owner, intelligent and vicious.

I said, 'Sonny. Is that his name?'

'No,' the lady told me.

She smiled, as if that cleared everything up.

At the top of the Arch, the observation deck reminded me of a tin can with carpeting. Rows of tiny windows looked out over the city on one side and the river on the other. The view was okay, but if there's anything I like less than a confined space, it's a confined space two hundred metres in the air. I was ready to go pretty quick.

Annabeth kept talking about structural supports, and how she would've made the windows bigger, and designed a see-through floor. She probably could've stayed up there for hours, but luckily for me the park ranger announced that the observation deck would be closing in a few minutes.

I steered Grover and Annabeth towards the exit, loaded them into the elevator and I was about to get in myself when I realized there were already two other tourists inside. No room for me.

The park ranger said, 'Next car, sir.'

'We'll get out,' Annabeth said. 'We'll wait with you.'

But that was going to mess everybody up and take even more time, so I said, 'Naw, it's okay. I'll see you guys at the bottom.'

Grover and Annabeth both looked nervous, but they let the elevator door slide shut. Their car disappeared down the ramp.

Now the only people left on the observation deck were me, a little boy with his parents, the park ranger and the fat lady with her Chihuahua.

I smiled uneasily at the fat lady. She smiled back, her forked tongue flickering between her teeth.

Wait a minute.

Forked tongue?

Before I could decide if I'd really seen that, her Chihuahua jumped down and started yapping at me.

'Now, now, sonny,' the lady said. 'Does this look like a good time? We have all these nice people here.'

'Doggie!' said the little boy. 'Look, a doggie!'

His parents pulled him back.

The Chihuahua bared his teeth at me, foam dripping from his black lips.

'Well, son,' the fat lady sighed. 'If you insist.'

Ice started forming in my stomach. 'Um, did you just call that Chihuahua your son?'

'*Chimera*, dear,' the fat lady corrected. 'Not a Chihuahua. It's an easy mistake to make.'

She rolled up her denim sleeves, revealing that the skin of her arms was scaly and green. When she smiled, I saw that her teeth were fangs. The pupils of her eyes were sideways slits, like a reptile's.

The Chihuahua barked louder, and with each bark, it grew. First to the size of a Dobermann, then to a lion. The bark became a roar.

The little boy screamed. His parents pulled him back towards the exit, straight into the park ranger, who stood, paralysed, gaping at the monster.

The Chimera was now so tall its back rubbed against the roof. It had the head of a lion with a blood-caked mane, the body and hooves of a giant goat, and a serpent for a tail, a three-metre-long diamondback growing right out of its shaggy behind. The rhinestone dog collar still hung around its neck, and the plate-sized dog tag was now easy to read: CHIMERA – RABID, FIRE-BREATHING, POISONOUS – IF FOUND, PLEASE CALL TARTARUS – EXT. 954.

I realized I hadn't even uncapped my sword. My hands were numb. I was three metres away from the Chimera's bloody maw, and I knew that as soon as I moved, the creature would lunge.

The snake lady made a hissing noise that might've been laughter. 'Be honoured, Percy Jackson. Lord Zeus rarely allows me to test a hero with one of my brood. For I am the Mother of Monsters, the terrible Echidna!'

I stared at her. All I could think to say was: 'Isn't that a kind of anteater?'

She howled, her reptilian face turning brown and green with rage. 'I hate it when people say that! I hate Australia! Naming that ridiculous animal after me. For that, Percy Jackson, my son shall destroy you!'

The Chimera charged, its lion teeth gnashing. I managed to leap aside and dodge the bite.

I ended up next to the family and the park ranger, who were all screaming now, trying to pry open the emergency exit doors.

I couldn't let them get hurt. I uncapped my sword, ran to the other side of the deck, and yelled, 'Hey, Chihuahua!'

The Chimera turned faster than I would've thought possible.

Before I could swing my sword, it opened its mouth, emitting a stench like the world's largest barbecue pit, and shot a column of flame straight at me.

I dived through the explosion. The carpet burst into flames; the heat was so intense, it seared off my eyebrows.

Where I had been standing a moment before was a

ragged hole in the side of the Arch, with melted metal steaming around the edges.

Great, I thought. We just blowtorched a national monument.

Riptide was now a shining bronze blade in my hands, and as the Chimera turned, I slashed at its neck.

That was my fatal mistake. The blade sparked harmlessly off the dog collar. I tried to regain my balance, but I was so worried about defending myself against the fiery lion's mouth, I completely forgot about the serpent tail until it whipped around and sank its fangs into my calf.

My whole leg was on fire. I tried to jab Riptide into the Chimera's mouth, but the serpent tail wrapped around my ankles and pulled me off balance, and my blade flew out of my hand, spinning out of the hole in the Arch and down towards the Mississippi River.

I managed to get to my feet, but I knew I had lost. I was weaponless. I could feel deadly poison racing up to my chest. I remembered Chiron saying that Anaklusmos would always return to me, but there was no pen in my pocket. Maybe it had fallen too far away. Maybe it only returned when it was in pen form. I didn't know, and I wasn't going to live long enough to figure it out.

I backed into the hole in the wall. The Chimera advanced, growling, smoke curling from its lips. The snake lady, Echidna, cackled. 'They don't make heroes like they used to, eh, son?'

The monster growled. It seemed in no hurry to finish me off now that I was beaten.

I glanced at the park ranger and the family. The little boy was hiding behind his father's legs. I had to protect these people. I couldn't just ... die. I tried to think, but my whole body was on fire. My head felt dizzy. I had no sword. I was facing a massive, fire-breathing monster and its mother. And I was scared.

There was no place else to go, so I stepped to the edge of the hole. Far, far below, the river glittered.

If I died, would the monsters go away? Would they leave the humans alone?

'If you are the son of Poseidon,' Echidna hissed, 'you would not fear water. Jump, Percy Jackson. Show me that water will not harm you. Jump and retrieve your sword. Prove your bloodline.'

Yeah, right, I thought. I'd read somewhere that jumping into water from a couple of stories up was like jumping onto solid tar. From here, I'd splatter on impact.

The Chimera's mouth glowed red, heating up for another blast.

'You have no faith,' Echidna told me. 'You do not trust the gods. I cannot blame you, little coward. Better you die now. The gods are faithless. The poison is in your heart.'

She was right: I was dying. I could feel my breath slowing down. Nobody could save me, not even the gods.

I backed up and looked down at the water. I remembered the warm glow of my father's smile when I was a baby. He must have seen me. He must have visited me when I was in my cradle.

I remembered the swirling green trident that had

appeared above my head the night of capture the flag, when Poseidon had claimed me as his son.

But this wasn't the sea. This was the Mississippi, dead centre of the USA. There was no sea god here.

'Die, faithless one,' Echidna rasped, and the Chimera sent a column of flame towards my face.

'Father, help me,' I prayed.

I turned and jumped. My clothes on fire, poison coursing through my veins, I plummeted towards the river.

14 ⚡ I BECOME A KNOWN FUGITIVE

I'd love to tell you I had some deep revelation on my way down, that I came to terms with my own mortality, laughed in the face of death, et cetera.

The truth? My only thought was: Aaaaggghhhhh!

The river raced towards me at the speed of a truck. Wind ripped the breath from my lungs. Steeples and skyscrapers and bridges tumbled in and out of my vision.

And then: *Flaaa-boooom!*

A whiteout of bubbles. I sank through the murk, sure that I was about to end up embedded in fifty metres of mud and lost forever.

But my impact with the water hadn't hurt. I was falling slowly now, bubbles trickling up through my fingers. I settled on the river bottom soundlessly. A catfish the size of my stepfather lurched away into the gloom. Clouds of silt and disgusting garbage – beer bottles, old shoes, plastic bags – swirled up all around me.

At that point, I realized a few things: first, I had not been flattened into a pancake. I had not been barbecued. I couldn't even feel the Chimera poison boiling in my veins any more. I was alive, which was good.

Second realization: I wasn't wet. I mean, I could feel the

coolness of the water. I could see where the fire on my clothes had been quenched. But when I touched my own shirt, it felt perfectly dry.

I looked at the garbage floating by and snatched an old cigarette lighter.

No way, I thought.

I flicked the lighter. It sparked. A tiny flame appeared, right there at the bottom of the Mississippi.

I grabbed a soggy hamburger wrapper out of the current and immediately the paper turned dry. I lit it with no problem. As soon as I let it go, the flames sputtered out. The wrapper turned back into a slimy rag. Weird.

But the strangest thought occurred to me only last: I was breathing. I was underwater, and I was breathing normally.

I stood up, thigh-deep in mud. My legs felt shaky. My hands trembled. I should've been dead. The fact that I wasn't seemed like . . . well, a miracle. I imagined a woman's voice, a voice that sounded a bit like my mother: *Percy, what do you say?*

Um . . . thanks. Underwater, I sounded like I did on recordings, like a much older kid. *Thank you . . . Father.*

No response. Just the dark drift of garbage downriver, the enormous catfish gliding by, the flash of sunset on the water's surface far above, turning everything the colour of butterscotch.

Why had Poseidon saved me? The more I thought about it, the more ashamed I felt. So I'd got lucky a few times before. Against a thing like the Chimera, I had never stood a chance. Those poor people in the Arch were probably toast. I couldn't protect them. I was no hero. Maybe I should just stay down here with the catfish, join the bottom feeders.

Fump-fump-fump. A riverboat's paddlewheel churned above me, swirling the silt around.

There, not two metres in front of me, was my sword, its gleaming bronze hilt sticking up in the mud.

I heard that woman's voice again: *Percy, take the sword. Your father believes in you.* This time, I knew the voice wasn't in my head. I wasn't imagining it. Her words seemed to come from everywhere, rippling through the water like dolphin sonar.

'Where are you?' I called aloud.

Then, through the gloom, I saw her — a woman the colour of the water, a ghost in the current, floating just above the sword. She had long billowing hair, and her eyes, barely visible, were green like mine.

A lump formed in my throat. I said, 'Mom?'

No, child, only a messenger, though your mother's fate is not as hopeless as you believe. Go to the beach in Santa Monica.

'What?'

It is your father's will. Before you descend into the Underworld, you must go to Santa Monica. Please, Percy, I cannot stay long. The river here is too foul for my presence.

'But . . .' I was sure this woman was my mother, or a vision of her, anyway. 'Who — how did you —'

There was so much I wanted to ask, the words jammed up in my throat.

I cannot stay, brave one, the woman said. She reached out, and I felt the current brush my face like a caress. *You must go to Santa Monica! And, Percy, do not trust the gifts . . .*

Her voice faded.

'Gifts?' I asked. 'What gifts? Wait!'

She made one more attempt to speak, but the sound was gone. Her image melted away. If it was my mother, I had lost her again.

I felt like drowning myself. The only problem: I was immune to drowning.

Your father believes in you, she had said.

She'd also called me brave . . . unless she was talking to the catfish.

I waded towards Riptide and grabbed it by the hilt. The Chimera might still be up there with its snaky fat mother, waiting to finish me off. At the very least, the mortal police would be arriving, trying to figure out who had blown a hole in the Arch. If they found me, they'd have some questions.

I capped my sword, stuck the ballpoint pen in my pocket. 'Thank you, Father,' I said again to the dark water.

Then I kicked up through the muck and swam for the surface.

I came ashore next to a floating McDonald's.

A block away, every emergency vehicle in St Louis was surrounding the Arch. Police helicopters circled overhead. The crowd of onlookers reminded me of Times Square on New Year's Eve.

A little girl said, 'Mama! That boy walked out of the river.'

'That's nice, dear,' her mother said, craning her neck to watch the ambulances.

'But he's dry!'

'That's nice, dear.'

A news lady was talking for the camera: 'Probably not a terrorist attack, we're told, but it's still very early in the investigation. The damage, as you can see, is very serious. We're trying to get to some of the survivors, to question them about eyewitness reports of someone falling from the Arch.'

Survivors. I felt a surge of relief. Maybe the park ranger and that family made it out safely. I hoped Annabeth and Grover were okay.

I tried to push through the crowd to see what was going on inside the police line.

'. . . an adolescent boy,' another reporter was saying. 'Channel Five has learned that surveillance cameras show an adolescent boy going wild on the observation deck, somehow setting off this freak explosion. Hard to believe, John, but that's what we're hearing. Again, no confirmed fatalities . . .'

I backed away, trying to keep my head down. I had to go a long way around the police perimeter. Uniformed officers and news reporters were everywhere.

I'd almost lost hope of ever finding Annabeth and Grover when a familiar voice bleated, 'Perrr-cy!'

I turned and got tackled by Grover's bear hug — or goat hug. He said, 'We thought you'd gone to Hades the hard way!'

Annabeth stood behind him, trying to look angry, but even she seemed relieved to see me. 'We can't leave you alone for five minutes! What happened?'

'I sort of fell.'

'Percy! Two hundred metres?'

Behind us, a cop shouted, 'Gangway!' The crowd parted, and a couple of paramedics hustled out, rolling a woman on a stretcher. I recognized her immediately as the mother of the little boy who'd been on the observation deck. She was saying, 'And then this huge dog, this huge fire-breathing Chihuahua –'

'Okay, ma'am,' the paramedic said. 'Just calm down. Your family is fine. The medication is starting to kick in.'

'I'm not crazy! This boy jumped out of the hole and the monster disappeared.' Then she saw me. 'There he is! That's the boy!'

I turned quickly and pulled Annabeth and Grover after me. We disappeared into the crowd.

'What's going on?' Annabeth demanded. 'Was she talking about the Chihuahua on the elevator?'

I told them the whole story of the Chimera, Echidna, my high-dive act, the underwater lady's message.

'Whoa,' said Grover. 'We've got to get you to Santa Monica! You can't ignore a summons from your dad.'

Before Annabeth could respond, we passed another reporter doing a news break, and I almost froze in my tracks when he said, 'Percy Jackson. That's right, Dan. Channel Twelve has learned that the boy who may have caused this explosion fits the description of a young man wanted by the authorities for a serious New Jersey bus accident three days ago. *And* the boy is believed to be travelling west. For our viewers at home, here is a photo of Percy Jackson.'

We ducked around the news van and slipped into an alley.

'First things first,' I told Grover. 'We've got to get out of town!'

Somehow, we made it back to the Amtrak station without getting spotted. We got on board the train just before it pulled out for Denver. The train trundled west as darkness fell, police lights still pulsing against the St Louis skyline behind us.

15 ⚡ A GOD BUYS US CHEESEBURGERS

The next afternoon, June 14, seven days before the solstice, our train rolled into Denver. We hadn't eaten since the night before in the dining car, somewhere in Kansas. We hadn't taken a shower since Half-Blood Hill, and I was sure that was obvious.

'Let's try to contact Chiron,' Annabeth said. 'I want to tell him about your talk with the river spirit.'

'We can't use phones, right?'

'I'm not talking about phones.'

We wandered through downtown for about half an hour, though I wasn't sure what Annabeth was looking for. The air was dry and hot, which felt weird after the humidity of St Louis. Everywhere we turned, the Rocky Mountains seemed to be staring at me, like a tidal wave about to crash into the city.

Finally we found an empty do-it-yourself car wash. We veered towards the stall furthest from the street, keeping our eyes open for patrol cars. We were three adolescents hanging out at a car wash without a car; any cop worth his doughnuts would figure we were up to no good.

'What exactly are we doing?' I asked, as Grover took out the spray gun.

'It's seventy-five cents,' he grumbled. 'I've only got two quarters left. Annabeth?'

'Don't look at me,' she said. 'The dining car wiped me out.'

I fished out my last bit of change and passed Grover a quarter, which left me two nickels and one drachma from Medusa's place.

'Excellent,' Grover said. 'We could do it with a spray bottle, of course, but the connection isn't as good, and my arm gets tired of pumping.'

'What are you talking about?'

He fed in the quarters and set the knob to *fine mist*. 'I-M'ing.'

'Instant messaging?'

'*Iris*-messaging,' Annabeth corrected. 'The rainbow goddess Iris carries messages for the gods. If you know how to ask, and she's not too busy, she'll do the same for half-bloods.'

'You summon the goddess with a spray gun?'

Grover pointed the nozzle in the air and water hissed out in a thick white mist. 'Unless you know an easier way to make a rainbow.'

Sure enough, late afternoon light filtered through the vapour and broke into colours.

Annabeth held her palm out to me. 'Drachma, please.'

I handed it over.

She raised the coin over her head. 'O goddess, accept our offering.'

She threw the drachma into the rainbow. It disappeared in a golden shimmer.

'Half-Blood Hill,' Annabeth requested.

For a moment, nothing happened.

Then I was looking through the mist at strawberry fields, and the Long Island Sound in the distance. We seemed to be on the porch of the Big House. Standing with his back to us at the railing was a sandy-haired guy in shorts and an orange tank top. He was holding a bronze sword and seemed to be staring intently at something down in the meadow.

'Luke!' I called.

He turned, eyes wide. I could swear he was standing a metre in front of me through a screen of mist, except I could only see the part of him that appeared in the rainbow.

'Percy!' His scarred face broke into a grin. 'Is that Annabeth, too? Thank the gods! Are you guys okay?'

'We're ... uh ... fine,' Annabeth stammered. She was madly straightening her dirty T-shirt, trying to comb the loose hair out of her face. 'We thought – Chiron – I mean –'

'He's down at the cabins.' Luke's smile faded. 'We're having some issues with the campers. Listen, is everything cool with you? Is Grover all right?'

'I'm right here,' Grover called. He held the nozzle out to one side and stepped into Luke's line of vision. 'What kind of issues?'

Just then a big Lincoln Continental pulled into the car wash with its stereo turned to maximum hip-hop. As the car slid into the next stall, the bass from the subwoofers vibrated so much, it shook the pavement.

'Chiron had to – what's that noise?' Luke yelled.

'I'll take care of it!' Annabeth yelled back, looking very relieved to have an excuse to get out of sight. 'Grover, come on!'

'What?' Grover said. 'But –'

'Give Percy the nozzle and come on!' she ordered.

Grover muttered something about girls being harder to understand than the Oracle at Delphi, then he handed me the spray gun and followed Annabeth.

I readjusted the hose so I could keep the rainbow going and still see Luke.

'Chiron had to break up a fight,' Luke shouted to me over the music. 'Things are pretty tense here, Percy. Word leaked out about the Zeus–Poseidon stand-off. We're still not sure how – probably the same scumbag who summoned the hellhound. Now the campers are starting to take sides. It's shaping up like the Trojan War all over again. Aphrodite, Ares and Apollo are backing Poseidon, more or less. Athena is backing Zeus.'

I shuddered to think that Clarisse's cabin would ever be on my dad's side for anything. In the next stall, I heard Annabeth and some guy arguing with each other, then the music's volume decreased drastically.

'So what's your status?' Luke asked me. 'Chiron will be sorry he missed you.'

I told him pretty much everything, including my dreams. It felt so good to see him, to feel like I was back at camp even for a few minutes, that I didn't realize how long I had talked until the beeper went off on the spray machine,

[222]

and I realized I only had one more minute before the water shut off.

'I wish I could be there,' Luke told me. 'We can't help from here, I'm afraid, but listen . . . it had to be Hades who took the master bolt. He was there at Olympus at the winter solstice. I was chaperoning a field trip and we saw him.'

'But Chiron said the gods can't take each other's magic items directly.'

'That's true,' Luke said, looking troubled. 'Still . . . Hades has the helmet of darkness. How could anybody else sneak into the throne room and steal the master bolt? You'd have to be invisible.'

We were both silent, until Luke seemed to realize what he'd said.

'Oh, hey,' he protested. 'I didn't mean Annabeth. She and I have known each other forever. She would never . . . I mean, she's like a little sister to me.'

I wondered if Annabeth would like that description. In the stall next to us, the music stopped completely. A man screamed in terror, car doors slammed and the Lincoln peeled out of the car wash.

'You'd better go see what that was,' Luke said. 'Listen, are you wearing the flying shoes? I'll feel better if I know they've done you some good.'

'Oh . . . uh, yeah!' I tried not to sound like a guilty liar. 'Yeah, they've come in handy.'

'Really?' He grinned. 'They fit and everything?'

The water shut off. The mist started to evaporate.

'Well, take care of yourself out there in Denver,' Luke

called, his voice getting fainter. 'And tell Grover it'll be better this time! Nobody will get turned into a pine tree if he just –'

But the mist was gone, and Luke's image faded to nothing. I was alone in a wet, empty car-wash stall.

Annabeth and Grover came around the corner, laughing, but stopped when they saw my face. Annabeth's smile faded. 'What happened, Percy? What did Luke say?'

'Not much,' I lied, my stomach feeling as empty as a Big Three cabin. 'Come on, let's find some dinner.'

A few minutes later, we were sitting at a booth in a gleaming chrome diner. All around us, families were eating burgers and drinking milkshakes and sodas.

Finally the waitress came over. She raised her eyebrow sceptically. 'Well?'

I said, 'We, um, want to order dinner.'

'You kids have money to pay for it?'

Grover's lower lip quivered. I was afraid he would start bleating, or worse, start eating the linoleum. Annabeth looked ready to pass out from hunger.

I was trying to think up a sob story for the waitress when a rumble shook the whole building; a motorcycle the size of a baby elephant had pulled up to the kerb.

All conversation in the diner stopped. The motorcycle's headlight glared red. Its gas tank had flames painted on it, and a shotgun holster riveted to either side, complete with shotguns. The seat was leather – but leather that looked like . . . well, Caucasian human skin.

The guy on the bike would've made pro wrestlers run for Mama. He was dressed in a red muscle shirt and black jeans and a black leather duster, with a hunting knife strapped to his thigh. He wore red wraparound shades, and he had the cruellest, most brutal face I'd ever seen — handsome, I guess, but wicked – with an oily black crewcut and cheeks that were scarred from many, many fights. The weird thing was, I felt like I'd seen his face somewhere before.

As he walked into the diner, a hot, dry wind blew through the place. All the people rose, as if they were hypnotized, but the biker waved his hand dismissively and they all sat down again. Everybody went back to their conversations. The waitress blinked, as if somebody had just pressed the rewind button on her brain. She asked us again, 'You kids have money to pay for it?'

The biker said, 'It's on me.' He slid into our booth, which was way too small for him, and crowded Annabeth against the window.

He looked up at the waitress, who was gaping at him, and said, 'Are you still here?'

He pointed at her, and she stiffened. She turned as if she'd been spun around, then marched back towards the kitchen.

The biker looked at me. I couldn't see his eyes behind the red shades, but bad feelings started boiling in my stomach. Anger, resentment, bitterness. I wanted to hit a wall. I wanted to pick a fight with somebody. Who did this guy think he was?

He gave me a wicked grin. 'So you're old Seaweed's kid, huh?'

I should've been surprised, or scared, but instead I felt like I was looking at my stepdad, Gabe. I wanted to rip this guy's head off. 'What's it to you?'

Annabeth's eyes flashed me a warning. 'Percy, this is —'

The biker raised his hand.

'S'okay,' he said. 'I don't mind a little attitude. Long as you remember who's the boss. You know who I am, little cousin?'

Then it struck me why this guy looked familiar. He had the same vicious sneer as some of the kids at Camp Half-Blood, the ones from cabin five.

'You're Clarisse's dad,' I said. 'Ares, god of war.'

Ares grinned and took off his shades. Where his eyes should've been, there was only fire, empty sockets glowing with miniature nuclear explosions. 'That's right, punk. I heard you broke Clarisse's spear.'

'She was asking for it.'

'Probably. That's cool. I don't fight my kids' fights, you know? What I'm here for — I heard you were in town. I got a little proposition for you.'

The waitress came back with heaping trays of food — cheeseburgers, fries, onion rings and chocolate shakes.

Ares handed her a few gold drachmas.

She looked nervously at the coins. 'But, these aren't . . .'

Ares pulled out his huge knife and started cleaning his fingernails. 'Problem, sweetheart?'

The waitress swallowed, then left with the gold.

'You can't do that,' I told Ares. 'You can't just threaten people with a knife.'

Ares laughed. 'Are you kidding? I love this country. Best place since Sparta. Don't you carry a weapon, punk? You should. Dangerous world out there. Which brings me to my proposition. I need you to do me a favour.'

'What favour could I do for a god?'

'Something a god doesn't have time to do himself. It's nothing much. I left my shield at an abandoned water park here in town. I was going on a little . . . date with my girlfriend. We were interrupted. I left my shield behind. I want you to fetch it for me.'

'Why don't you go back and get it yourself?'

The fire in his eye sockets glowed a little hotter.

'Why don't I turn you into prairie dog and run you over with my Harley? Because I don't feel like it. A god is giving you an opportunity to prove yourself, Percy Jackson. Will you prove yourself a coward?' He leaned forward. 'Or maybe you only fight when there's a river to dive into, so your daddy can protect you.'

I wanted to punch this guy, but somehow, I knew he was waiting for that. Ares's power was causing my anger. He'd love it if I attacked. I didn't want to give him the satisfaction.

'We're not interested,' I said. 'We've already got a quest.'

Ares's fiery eyes made me see things I didn't want to see – blood and smoke and corpses on the battlefield. 'I know all about your quest, punk. When that *item* was first stolen, Zeus sent his best out looking for it: Apollo, Athena, Artemis and me, naturally. If I couldn't sniff out a weapon that powerful . . .' He licked his lips, as if the very thought of the master bolt made him hungry. 'Well . . . if I couldn't find it, you got no hope. Nevertheless, I'm trying to give you the benefit of a doubt. Your dad and I go way back. After all, I'm the one who told him my suspicions about old Corpse Breath.'

'You told him Hades stole the bolt?'

'Sure. Framing somebody to start a war. Oldest trick in the book. I recognized it immediately. In a way, you got me to thank for your little quest.'

'Thanks,' I grumbled.

'Hey, I'm a generous guy. Just do my little job, and I'll help you on your way. I'll arrange a ride west for you and your friends.'

'We're doing fine on our own.'

'Yeah, right. No money. No wheels. No clue what you're up against. Help me out, and maybe I'll tell you something you need to know. Something about your mom.'

'My mom?'

He grinned. 'That got your attention. The water park is a mile west on Delancy. You can't miss it. Look for the Tunnel of Love ride.'

'What interrupted your date?' I asked. 'Something scare you off?'

Ares bared his teeth, but I'd seen his threatening look before on Clarisse. There was something false about it, almost like he was nervous.

'You're lucky you met me, punk, and not one of the other Olympians. They're not as forgiving of rudeness as I am. I'll meet you back here when you're done. Don't disappoint me.'

After that I must have fainted, or fallen into a trance, because when I opened my eyes again Ares was gone. I might've thought the conversation had been a dream, but Annabeth and Grover's expressions told me otherwise.

'Not good,' Grover said. 'Ares sought you out, Percy. This is not good.'

I stared out the window. The motorcycle had disappeared.

Did Ares really know something about my mom, or was he just playing with me? Now that he was gone, all the anger had drained out of me. I realized Ares must love to mess with people's emotions. That was his power — cranking up the passions so badly, they clouded your ability to think.

'It's probably some kind of trick,' I said. 'Forget Ares. Let's just go.'

'We can't,' Annabeth said. 'Look, I hate Ares as much as anybody, but you don't ignore the gods unless you want serious bad fortune. He wasn't kidding about turning you into a rodent.'

I looked down at my cheeseburger, which suddenly didn't seem so appetizing. 'Why does he need us?'

'Maybe it's a problem that requires brains,' Annabeth said. 'Ares has strength. That's all he has. Even strength has to bow to wisdom sometimes.'

'But this water park . . . he acted almost scared. What would make a war god run away like that?'

Annabeth and Grover glanced nervously at each other.

Annabeth said, 'I'm afraid we'll have to find out.'

The sun was sinking behind the mountains by the time we found the water park. Judging from the sign, it once had been called WATERLAND, but now some of the letters were smashed out, so it read WAT R A D.

The main gate was padlocked and topped with barbed wire. Inside, huge dry waterslides and tubes and pipes curled everywhere, leading to empty pools. Old tickets and advertisements fluttered around the tarmac. With night coming on, the place looked sad and creepy.

'If Ares brings his girlfriend here for a date,' I said, staring up at the barbed wire, 'I'd hate to see what she looks like.'

'Percy,' Annabeth warned. 'Be more respectful.'

'Why? I thought you hated Ares.'

'He's still a god. And his girlfriend is very temperamental.'

'You don't want to insult her looks,' Grover added.

'Who is she? Echidna?'

'No, Aphrodite,' Grover said, a little dreamily. 'Goddess of love.'

'I thought she was married to somebody,' I said. 'Hephaestus.'

'What's your point?' he asked.

'Oh.' I suddenly felt the need to change the subject. 'So how do we get in?'

'*Maia!*' Grover's shoes sprouted wings.

He flew over the fence, did an unintended somersault in midair, then stumbled to a landing on the opposite side. He dusted off his jeans, as if he'd planned the whole thing. 'You guys coming?'

Annabeth and I had to climb the old-fashioned way, holding down the barbed wire for each other as we crawled over the top.

The shadows grew long as we walked through the park, checking out the attractions. There was Ankle Biter Island, Head Over Wedgie and Dude, Where's My Swimsuit?

No monsters came to get us. Nothing made the slightest noise.

We found a souvenir shop that had been left open. Merchandise still lined the shelves: snow globes, pencils, postcards and racks of –

'Clothes,' Annabeth said. 'Fresh clothes.'

'Yeah,' I said. 'But you can't just –'

'Watch me.'

She snatched an entire row of stuff off the racks and disappeared into the changing room. A few minutes later she came out in Waterland flower-print shorts, a big red Waterland T-shirt and commemorative Waterland surf shoes. A Waterland backpack was slung over her shoulder, obviously stuffed with more goodies.

'What the heck.' Grover shrugged. Soon, all three of us were decked out like walking advertisements for the defunct theme park.

We continued searching for the Tunnel of Love. I got

the feeling that the whole park was holding its breath. 'So Ares and Aphrodite,' I said, to keep my mind off the growing dark, 'they have a thing going?'

'That's old gossip, Percy,' Annabeth told me. 'Three-thousand-year-old gossip.'

'What about Aphrodite's husband?'

'Well, you know,' she said. 'Hephaestus. The blacksmith. He was crippled when he was a baby, thrown off Mount Olympus by Zeus. So he isn't exactly handsome. Clever with his hands and all, but Aphrodite isn't into brains and talent, you know?'

'She likes bikers.'

'Whatever.'

'Hephaestus knows?'

'Oh sure,' Annabeth said. 'He caught them together once. I mean, literally caught them, in a golden net, and invited all the gods to come and laugh at them. Hephaestus is always trying to embarrass them. That's why they meet in out-of-the-way places, like . . .'

She stopped, looking straight ahead. 'Like that.'

In front of us was an empty pool that would've been awesome for skateboarding. It was at least fifty metres across and shaped like a bowl.

Around the rim, a dozen bronze statues of Cupid stood guard with wings spread and bows ready to fire. On the opposite side from us, a tunnel opened up, probably where the water flowed into when the pool was full. The sign above it read: THRILL RIDE O' LOVE: THIS IS NOT YOUR PARENTS' TUNNEL OF LOVE!

Grover crept towards the edge. 'Guys, look.'

Marooned at the bottom of the pool was a pink-and-white two-seater boat with a canopy over the top and little hearts painted all over it. In the left seat, glinting in the fading light, was Ares's shield, a polished circle of bronze.

'This is too easy,' I said. 'So we just walk down there and get it?'

Annabeth ran her fingers along the base of the nearest Cupid statue.

'There's a Greek letter carved here,' she said. 'Eta. I wonder . . .'

'Grover,' I said, 'you smell any monsters?'

He sniffed the wind. 'Nothing.'

'Nothing — like, in-the-Arch-and-you-didn't-smell-Echidna nothing, or really nothing?'

Grover looked hurt. 'I told you, that was underground.'

'Okay, I'm sorry.' I took a deep breath. 'I'm going down there.'

'I'll go with you.' Grover didn't sound too enthusiastic, but I got the feeling he was trying to make up for what had happened in St Louis.

'No,' I told him. 'I want you to stay up top with the flying shoes. You're the Red Baron, remember? I'll be counting on you for backup, in case something goes wrong.'

Grover puffed up his chest a little. 'Sure. But what could go wrong?'

'I don't know. Just a feeling. Annabeth, come with me —'

'Are you kidding?' She looked at me as if I'd just dropped from the moon. Her cheeks were bright red.

'What's the problem now?' I demanded.

'Me, go with you to the . . . the "Thrill Ride of Love"? How embarrassing is that? What if somebody saw me?'

'Who's going to see you?' But my face was burning now, too. Leave it to a girl to make everything complicated. 'Fine,' I told her. 'I'll do it myself.' But when I started down the side of the pool, she followed me, muttering about how boys always messed things up.

We reached the boat. The shield was propped on one seat, and next to it was a lady's silk scarf. I tried to imagine Ares and Aphrodite here, a couple of gods meeting in a junked-out amusement-park ride. Why? Then I noticed something I hadn't seen from up top: mirrors all the way around the rim of the pool, facing this spot. We could see ourselves no matter which direction we looked. That must be it. While Ares and Aphrodite were smooching with each other they could look at their favourite people: themselves.

I picked up the scarf. It shimmered pink, and the perfume was indescribable – rose, or mountain laurel. Something good. I smiled, a little dreamy, and was about to rub the scarf against my cheek when Annabeth ripped it out of my hand and stuffed it in her pocket. 'Oh, no you don't. Stay away from that love magic.'

'What?'

'Just get the shield, Seaweed Brain, and let's get out of here.'

The moment I touched the shield, I knew we were in trouble. My hand broke through something that had been connecting it to the dashboard. A cobweb, I thought, but then I looked at a strand of it on my palm and saw it was some kind of metal filament, so fine it was almost invisible. A tripwire.

'Wait,' Annabeth said.

'Too late.'

'There's another Greek letter on the side of the boat, another Eta. This is a trap.'

Noise erupted all around us, of a million gears grinding, as if the whole pool were turning into one giant machine.

Grover yelled, 'Guys!'

Up on the rim, the Cupid statues were drawing their bows into firing position. Before I could suggest taking cover, they shot, but not at us. They fired at each other, across the rim of the pool. Silky cables trailed from the arrows, arcing over the pool and anchoring where they landed to form a huge golden asterisk. Then smaller metallic threads started weaving together magically between the main strands, making a net.

'We have to get out,' I said.

'Duh!' Annabeth said.

I grabbed the shield and we ran, but going up the slope of the pool was not as easy as going down.

'Come on!' Grover shouted.

He was trying to hold open a section of the net for us, but wherever he touched it, the golden threads started to wrap around his hands.

The Cupids' heads popped open. Out came video cameras. Spotlights rose up all around the pool, blinding us with illumination, and a loudspeaker voice boomed: 'Live to Olympus in one minute . . . Fifty-nine seconds, fifty-eight . . .'

'Hephaestus!' Annabeth screamed. 'I'm so stupid! Eta is "H". He made this trap to catch his wife with Ares. Now we're going to be broadcast live to Olympus and look like absolute fools!'

We'd almost made it to the rim when the row of mirrors opened like hatches and thousands of tiny metallic . . . things poured out.

Annabeth screamed.

It was an army of wind-up creepy-crawlies: bronze-gear bodies, spindly legs, little pincer mouths, all scuttling towards us in a wave of clacking, whirring metal.

'Spiders!' Annabeth said. 'Sp – sp – aaaah!'

I'd never seen her like this before. She fell backwards in terror and almost got overwhelmed by the spider robots before I pulled her up and dragged her back towards the boat.

The things were coming out from all around the rim now, millions of them, flooding towards the centre of the pool, completely surrounding us. I told myself they probably weren't programmed to kill, just corral us and bite us and make us look stupid. Then again, this was a trap meant for gods. And we weren't gods.

Annabeth and I climbed into the boat. I started kicking away the spiders as they swarmed aboard. I yelled at

Annabeth to help me, but she was too paralysed to do much more than scream.

'Thirty, twenty-nine,' called the loudspeaker.

The spiders started spitting out strands of metal thread, trying to tie us down. The strands were easy enough to break at first, but there were so many of them, and the spiders just kept coming. I kicked one away from Annabeth's leg and its pincers took a chunk out of my new surf shoe.

Grover hovered above the pool in his flying trainers, trying to pull the net loose, but it wouldn't budge.

Think, I told myself. Think.

The tunnel of love entrance was under the net. We could use it as an exit, except that it was blocked by a million robot spiders.

'Fifteen, fourteen,' the loudspeaker called.

Water, I thought. Where does the ride's water come from?

Then I saw them: huge water pipes behind the mirrors, where the spiders had come from. And up above the net, next to one of the Cupids, a glass-windowed booth that must be the controller's station.

'Grover!' I yelled. 'Get into that booth! Find the "on" switch!'

'But –'

'Do it!' It was a crazy hope, but it was our only chance. The spiders were all over the prow of the boat now. Annabeth was screaming her head off. I had to get us out of here.

Grover was in the controller's booth now, slamming away at the buttons.

'Five, four –'

Grover looked up at me hopelessly, raising his hands. He was letting me know that he'd pushed every button, but still nothing was happening.

I closed my eyes and thought about waves, rushing water, the Mississippi River. I felt a familiar tug in my gut. I tried to imagine that I was dragging the ocean all the way to Denver.

'Two, one, *zero!*'

Water exploded out of the pipes. It roared into the pool, sweeping away the spiders. I pulled Annabeth into the seat next to me and fastened her seatbelt just as the tidal wave slammed into our boat, over the top, whisking the spiders away and dousing us completely, but not capsizing us. The boat turned, lifted in the flood, and spun in circles around the whirlpool.

The water was full of short-circuiting spiders, some of them smashing against the pool's concrete wall with such force they burst.

Spotlights glared down at us. The Cupid-cams were rolling, live to Olympus.

But I could only concentrate on controlling the boat. I willed it to ride the current, to keep away from the wall. Maybe it was my imagination, but the boat seemed to respond. At least, it didn't break into a million pieces. We spun around one last time, the water level now almost high enough to shred us against the metal net. Then the boat's nose turned towards the tunnel and we rocketed through into the darkness.

Annabeth and I held tight, both of us screaming as the boat shot curls and hugged corners and took forty-five degree plunges past pictures of Romeo and Juliet and a bunch of other Valentine's Day stuff.

Then we were out of the tunnel, the night air whistling through our hair as the boat barrelled straight towards the exit.

If the ride had been in working order, we would've sailed off a ramp between the golden Gates of Love and splashed down safely in the exit pool. But there was a problem. The Gates of Love were chained. Two boats that had been washed out of the tunnel before us were now piled against the barricade – one submerged, the other cracked in half.

'Unfasten your seat belt,' I yelled to Annabeth.

'Are you crazy?'

'Unless you want to get smashed to death.' I strapped Ares's shield to my arm. 'We're going to have to jump for it.' My idea was simple and insane. As the boat struck, we would use its force like a springboard to jump the gate. I'd heard of people surviving car crashes that way, getting thrown ten or fifteen metres away from an accident. With luck, we would land in the pool.

Annabeth seemed to understand. She gripped my hand as the gates got closer.

'When I say go,' I said.

'No! When I say go!'

'What?'

'Simple physics!' she yelled. 'Force times the trajectory angle –'

'Fine!' I shouted. 'When *you* say go!'

She hesitated . . . hesitated . . . then yelled, 'Now!'

Crack!

Annabeth was right. If we'd jumped when I thought we should've, we would've crashed into the gates. She got us maximum lift.

Unfortunately, that was a little more than we needed. Our boat smashed into the pileup and we were thrown into the air, straight over the gates, over the pool, and down towards solid tarmac.

Something grabbed me from behind.

Annabeth yelled, 'Ouch!'

Grover!

In midair, he had grabbed me by the shirt, and Annabeth by the arm, and was trying to pull us out of a crash landing, but Annabeth and I had all the momentum.

'You're too heavy!' Grover said. 'We're going down!'

We spiralled towards the ground, Grover doing his best to slow the fall.

We smashed into a photo-board, Grover's head going straight into the hole where tourists would put their faces, pretending to be Noo-Noo the Friendly Whale. Annabeth and I tumbled to the ground, banged up but alive. Ares's shield was still on my arm.

Once we caught our breath, Annabeth and I got Grover out of the photo-board and thanked him for saving our lives. I looked back at the Thrill Ride of Love. The water was subsiding. Our boat had been smashed to pieces against the gates.

A hundred metres away, at the entrance pool, the Cupids were still filming. The statues had swivelled so that their cameras were trained straight on us, the spotlights in our faces.

'Show's over!' I yelled. 'Thank you! Goodnight!'

The Cupids turned back to their original positions. The lights shut off. The park went quiet and dark again, except for the gentle trickle of water into the Thrill Ride of Love's exit pool. I wondered if Olympus had gone to a commercial break, or if our ratings had been any good.

I hated being teased. I hated being tricked. And I had plenty of experience handling bullies who liked to do that stuff to me. I hefted the shield on my arm and turned to my friends. 'We need to have a little talk with Ares.'

The war god was waiting for us in the diner parking lot.

'Well, well,' he said. 'You didn't get yourself killed.'

'You knew it was a trap,' I said.

Ares gave me a wicked grin. 'Bet that crippled blacksmith was surprised when he netted a couple of stupid kids. You looked good on TV.'

I shoved his shield at him. 'You're a jerk.'

Annabeth and Grover caught their breath.

Ares grabbed the shield and spun it in the air like pizza dough. It changed form, melting into a bulletproof vest. He slung it across his back.

'See that truck over there?' He pointed to an eighteen-wheeler parked across the street from the diner. 'That's your ride. Take you straight to L.A., with one stop in Vegas.'

The eighteen-wheeler had a sign on the back, which I could read only because it was reverse-printed white on black, a good combination for dyslexia: KINDNESS INTER-NATIONAL: HUMANE ZOO TRANSPORT. WARNING: LIVE WILD ANIMALS.

I said, 'You're kidding.'

Ares snapped his fingers. The back door of the truck

unlatched. 'Free ride west, punk. Stop complaining. And here's a little something for doing the job.'

He slung a blue nylon backpack off his handlebars and tossed it to me.

Inside were fresh clothes for all of us, twenty bucks in cash, a pouch full of golden drachmas and a bag of Double Stuf Oreos.

I said, 'I don't want your lousy –'

'Thank you, Lord Ares,' Grover interrupted, giving me his best red-alert warning look. 'Thanks a lot.'

I gritted my teeth. It was probably a deadly insult to refuse something from a god, but I didn't want anything that Ares had touched. Reluctantly, I slung the backpack over my shoulder. I knew my anger was being caused by the war god's presence, but I was still itching to punch him in the nose. He reminded me of every bully I'd ever faced: Nancy Bobofit, Clarisse, Smelly Gabe, sarcastic teachers – every jerk who'd called me stupid in school or laughed at me when I'd got expelled.

I looked back at the diner, which had only a couple of customers now. The waitress who'd served us dinner was watching nervously out the window, like she was afraid Ares might hurt us. She dragged the cook out from the kitchen to see. She said something to him. He nodded, held up a little disposable camera and snapped a picture of us.

Great, I thought. We'll make the papers again tomorrow.

I imagined the headline: TWELVE-YEAR-OLD OUTLAW BEATS UP DEFENCELESS BIKER.

'You owe me one more thing,' I told Ares, trying to

keep my voice level. 'You promised me information about my mother.'

'You sure you can handle the news?' He kick-started his motorcycle. 'She's not dead.'

The ground seemed to spin beneath me. 'What do you mean?'

'I mean she was taken away from the Minotaur before she could die. She was turned into a shower of gold, right? That's metamorphosis. Not death. She's being kept.'

'Kept. Why?'

'You need to study war, punk. Hostages. You take somebody to control somebody else.'

'Nobody's controlling me.'

He laughed. 'Oh yeah? See you around, kid.'

I balled up my fists. 'You're pretty smug, Lord Ares, for a guy who runs from Cupid statues.'

Behind his sunglasses, fire glowed. I felt a hot wind in my hair. 'We'll meet again, Percy Jackson. Next time you're in a fight, watch your back.'

He revved his Harley, then roared off down Delancy Street.

Annabeth said, 'That was not smart, Percy.'

'I don't care.'

'You don't want a god as your enemy. Especially not that god.'

'Hey, guys,' Grover said. 'I hate to interrupt, but . . .'

He pointed towards the diner. At the cash register, the last two customers were paying their bill, two men in identical black coveralls, with a white logo on their backs that matched the one on the KINDNESS INTERNATIONAL truck.

'If we're taking the zoo express,' Grover said, 'we need to hurry.'

I didn't like it, but we had no better option. Besides, I'd seen enough of Denver.

We ran across the street and climbed in the back of the big lorry, closing the doors behind us.

The first thing that hit me was the smell. It was like the world's biggest pan of kitty litter.

The trailer was dark inside until I uncapped Anaklusmos. The blade cast a faint bronze light over a very sad scene. Sitting in a row of filthy metal cages were three of the most pathetic zoo animals I'd ever beheld: a zebra, a male albino lion and some weird antelope thing I didn't know the name for.

Someone had thrown the lion a sack of turnips, which he obviously didn't want to eat. The zebra and the antelope had each got a polystyrene tray of hamburger meat. The zebra's mane was matted with chewing gum, like somebody had been spitting on it in their spare time. The antelope had a stupid silver birthday balloon tied to one of his horns that read OVER THE HILL!

Apparently, nobody had wanted to get close enough to the lion to mess with him, but the poor thing was pacing around on soiled blankets, in a space way too small for him, panting from the stuffy heat of the trailer. He had flies buzzing around his pink eyes and his ribs showed through his white fur.

'This is kindness?' Grover yelled. 'Humane zoo transport?'

He probably would've gone right back outside to beat up the truckers with his reed pipes, and I would've helped him, but just then the truck's engine roared to life, the trailer started shaking, and we were forced to sit down or fall down.

We huddled in the corner on some mildewed feed sacks, trying to ignore the smell and the heat and the flies. Grover talked to the animals in a series of goat bleats, but they just stared at him sadly. Annabeth was in favour of breaking the cages and freeing them on the spot, but I pointed out it wouldn't do much good until the truck stopped moving. Besides, I had a feeling we might look a lot better to the lion than those turnips.

I found a water jug and refilled their bowls, then used Anaklusmos to drag the mismatched food out of their cages. I gave the meat to the lion and the turnips to the zebra and the antelope.

Grover calmed the antelope down, while Annabeth used her knife to cut the balloon off his horn. She wanted to cut the gum out of the zebra's mane, too, but we decided that would be too risky with the truck bumping around. We told Grover to promise the animals we'd help them more in the morning, then we settled in for the night.

Grover curled up on a turnip sack; Annabeth opened our bag of Double Stuf Oreos and nibbled on one half-heartedly; I tried to cheer myself up by concentrating on the fact that we were halfway to Los Angeles. Halfway to our destination. It was only June fourteenth. The solstice wasn't until the twenty-first. We could make it in plenty of time.

On the other hand, I had no idea what to expect next. The gods kept toying with me. At least Hephaestus had the decency to be honest about it – he'd put up cameras and advertised me as entertainment. But even when the cameras weren't rolling, I had a feeling my quest was being watched. I was a source of amusement for the gods.

'Hey,' Annabeth said, 'I'm sorry for freaking out back at the water park, Percy.'

'That's okay.'

'It's just . . .' She shuddered. 'Spiders.'

'Because of the Arachne story,' I guessed. 'She got turned into a spider for challenging your mom to a weaving contest, right?'

Annabeth nodded. 'Arachne's children have been taking revenge on the children of Athena ever since. If there's a spider within a mile of me, it'll find me. I hate the creepy little things. Anyway, I owe you.'

'We're a team, remember?' I said. 'Besides, Grover did the fancy flying.'

I thought he was asleep, but he mumbled from the corner, 'I was pretty amazing, wasn't I?'

Annabeth and I laughed.

She pulled apart an Oreo, handed me half. 'In the Iris message . . . did Luke really say nothing?'

I munched my cookie and thought about how to answer. The conversation via rainbow had bothered me all evening. 'Luke said you and he go way back. He also said Grover wouldn't fail this time. Nobody would turn into a pine tree.'

In the dim bronze light of the sword blade, it was hard to read their expressions.

Grover let out a mournful bray.

'I should've told you the truth from the beginning.' His voice trembled. 'I thought if you knew what a failure I was, you wouldn't want me along.'

'You were the satyr who tried to rescue Thalia, the daughter of Zeus.'

He nodded glumly.

'And the other two half-bloods Thalia befriended, the ones who got safely to camp . . .' I looked at Annabeth. 'That was you and Luke, wasn't it?'

She put down her Oreo, uneaten. 'Like you said, Percy, a seven-year-old half-blood wouldn't have made it very far alone. Athena guided me towards help. Thalia was twelve. Luke was fourteen. They'd both run away from home, like me. They were happy to take me with them. They were . . . amazing monster-fighters, even without training. We travelled north from Virginia without any real plans, fending off monsters for about two weeks before Grover found us.'

'I was supposed to escort Thalia to camp,' he said, sniffling. 'Only Thalia. I had strict orders from Chiron: don't do anything that would slow down the rescue. We knew Hades was after her, see, but I couldn't just leave Luke and Annabeth by themselves. I thought . . . I thought I could lead all three of them to safety. It was my fault the Kindly Ones caught up with us. I froze. I got scared on the way back to camp and took some wrong turns. If I'd just been a little quicker . . .'

'Stop it,' Annabeth said. 'No one blames you. Thalia didn't blame you either.'

'She sacrificed herself to save us,' he said miserably. 'Her death was my fault. The Council of Cloven Elders said so.'

'Because you wouldn't leave two other half-bloods behind?' I said. 'That's not fair.'

'Percy's right,' Annabeth said. 'I wouldn't be here today if it weren't for you, Grover. Neither would Luke. We don't care what the council says.'

Grover kept sniffling in the dark. 'It's just my luck. I'm the lamest satyr ever, and I find the two most powerful half-bloods of the century, Thalia and Percy.'

'You're not lame,' Annabeth insisted. 'You've got more courage than any satyr I've ever met. Name one other who would dare go to the Underworld. I bet Percy is really glad you're here right now.'

She kicked me in the shin.

'Yeah,' I said, which I would've done even without the kick. 'It's not luck that you found Thalia and me, Grover. You've got the biggest heart of any satyr ever. You're a natural searcher. That's why you'll be the one who finds Pan.'

I heard a deep, satisfied sigh. I waited for Grover to say something, but his breathing only got heavier. When the sound turned to snoring, I realized he'd fallen sleep.

'How does he do that?' I marvelled.

'I don't know,' Annabeth said. 'But that was really a nice thing you told him.'

'I meant it.'

We rode in silence for a few miles, bumping around on the feed sacks. The zebra munched a turnip. The lion licked the last of the hamburger meat off his lips and looked at me hopefully.

Annabeth rubbed her necklace like she was thinking deep, strategic thoughts.

'That pine-tree bead,' I said. 'Is that from your first year?'

She looked. She hadn't realized what she was doing.

'Yeah,' she said. 'Every August, the counsellors pick the most important event of the summer, and they paint it on that year's beads. I've got Thalia's pine tree, a Greek trireme on fire, a centaur in a prom dress – now *that* was a weird summer . . .'

'And the college ring is your father's?'

'That's none of your –' She stopped herself. 'Yeah. Yeah, it is.'

'You don't have to tell me.'

'No . . . it's okay.' She took a shaky breath. 'My dad sent it to me folded up in a letter, two summers ago. The ring was, like, his main keepsake from Athena. He wouldn't have got through his doctoral programme at Harvard without her . . . That's a long story. Anyway, he said he wanted me to have it. He apologized for being a jerk, said he loved me and missed me. He wanted me to come home and live with him.'

'That doesn't sound so bad.'

'Yeah, well . . . the problem was, I believed him. I tried

to go home for that school year, but my stepmom was the same as ever. She didn't want her kids put in danger by living with a freak. Monsters attacked. We argued. Monsters attacked. We argued. I didn't even make it through winter break. I called Chiron and came right back to Camp Half-Blood.'

'You think you'll ever try living with your dad again?'

She wouldn't meet my eyes. 'Please. I'm not into self-inflicted pain.'

'You shouldn't give up,' I told her. 'You should write him a letter or something.'

'Thanks for the advice,' she said coldly, 'but my father's made his choice about who he wants to live with.'

We passed another few miles of silence.

'So if the gods fight,' I said, 'will things line up the way they did with the Trojan War? Will it be Athena versus Poseidon?'

She put her head against the backpack Ares had given us, and closed her eyes. 'I don't know what my mom will do. I just know I'll fight next to you.'

'Why?'

'Because you're my friend, Seaweed Brain. Any more stupid questions?'

I couldn't think of an answer for that. Fortunately I didn't have to. Annabeth was asleep.

I had trouble following her example, with Grover snoring and an albino lion staring hungrily at me, but eventually I closed my eyes.

* * *

My nightmare started out as something I'd dreamed a million times before: I was being forced to take a standardized test while wearing a straitjacket. All the other kids were going out to recess, and the teacher kept saying, *Come on, Percy. You're not stupid are you? Pick up your pencil.*

Then the dream strayed from the usual.

I looked over at the next desk and saw a girl sitting there, also wearing a straitjacket. She was my age, with unruly black, punk-style hair, dark eyeliner around her stormy green eyes, and freckles across her nose. Somehow, I knew who she was. She was Thalia, daughter of Zeus.

She struggled against the straitjacket, glared at me in frustration and snapped, *Well, Seaweed Brain? One of us has to get out of here.*

She's right, my dream-self thought. I'm going back to that cavern. I'm going to give Hades a piece of my mind.

The straitjacket melted off me. I fell through the classroom floor. The teacher's voice changed until it was cold and evil, echoing from the depths of a great chasm.

Percy Jackson, it said. *Yes, the exchange went well, I see.*

I was back in the dark cavern, spirits of the dead drifting around me. Unseen in the pit, the monstrous thing was speaking, but this time it wasn't addressing me. The numbing power of its voice seemed directed somewhere else.

And he suspects nothing? it asked.

Another voice, one I almost recognized, answered at my shoulder. *Nothing, my lord. He is as ignorant as the rest.*

I looked over, but no one was there. The speaker was invisible.

Deception upon deception, the thing in the pit mused aloud. *Excellent.*

Truly, my lord, said the voice next to me, *you are well-named the Crooked One. But was it really necessary? I could have brought you what I stole directly —*

You? the monster said in scorn. *You have already shown your limits. You would have failed me completely had I not intervened.*

But, my lord —

Peace, little servant. Our six months have bought us much. Zeus's anger has grown. Poseidon has played his most desperate card. Now we shall use it against him. Shortly you shall have the reward you wish, and your revenge. As soon as both items are delivered into my hands . . . but wait. He is here.

What? The invisible servant suddenly sounded tense. *You summoned him, my lord?*

No. The full force of the monster's attention was now pouring over me, freezing me in place. *Blast his father's blood — he is too changeable, too unpredictable. The boy brought himself hither.*

Impossible! the servant cried.

For a weakling such as you, perhaps, the voice snarled. Then its cold power turned back on me. *So . . . you wish to dream of your quest, young half-blood? Then I will oblige.*

The scene changed.

I was standing in a vast throne room with black marble walls and bronze floors. The empty, horrid throne was made from human bones fused together. Standing at the foot of the dais was my mother, frozen in shimmering golden light, her arms outstretched.

I tried to step towards her, but my legs wouldn't move. I reached for her, only to realize that my hands were withering to bones. Grinning skeletons in Greek armour crowded around me, draping me with silk robes, wreathing my head with laurels that smoked with Chimera poison, burning into my scalp.

The evil voice began to laugh. *Hail, the conquering hero!*

I woke with a start.

Grover was shaking my shoulder. 'The truck's stopped,' he said. 'We think they're coming to check on the animals.'

'Hide!' Annabeth hissed.

She had it easy. She just put on her magic cap and disappeared. Grover and I had to dive behind feed sacks and hope we looked like turnips.

The trailer doors creaked open. Sunlight and heat poured in.

'Man!' one of the truckers said, waving his hand in front of his ugly nose. 'I wish I hauled appliances.' He climbed inside and poured some water from a jug into the animals' dishes.

'You hot, big boy?' he asked the lion, then splashed the rest of the bucket right in the lion's face.

The lion roared in indignation.

'Yeah, yeah, yeah,' the man said.

Next to me, under the turnip sacks, Grover tensed. For a peace-loving herbivore, he looked downright murderous.

The trucker threw the antelope a squashed-looking Happy Meal bag. He smirked at the zebra. 'How ya doin', Stripes? Least we'll be getting rid of *you* this stop. You like magic shows? You're gonna love this one. They're gonna saw you in half!'

The zebra, wild-eyed with fear, looked straight at me.

There was no sound, but as clear as day, I heard it say: *Free me, lord. Please.*

I was too stunned to react.

There was a loud *knock, knock, knock* on the side of the trailer.

The trucker inside with us yelled, 'What do you want, Eddie?'

A voice outside – it must've been Eddie's – shouted back, 'Maurice? What'd ya say?'

'What are you banging for?'

Knock, knock, knock.

Outside, Eddie yelled, 'What banging?'

Our guy Maurice rolled his eyes and went back outside, cursing at Eddie for being an idiot.

A second later, Annabeth appeared next to me. She must've done the banging to get Maurice out of the trailer. She said, 'This transport business can't be legal.'

'No kidding,' Grover said. He paused, as if listening. 'The lion says these guys are animal smugglers!'

That's right, the zebra's voice said in my mind.

'We've got to free them!' Grover said. He and Annabeth both looked at me, waiting for my lead.

I'd heard the zebra talk, but not the lion. Why? Maybe

it was another learning disability . . . I could only understand zebras? Then I thought: horses. What had Annabeth said about Poseidon creating horses? Was a zebra close enough to a horse? Was that why I could understand it?

The zebra said, *Open my cage, lord. Please. I'll be fine after that.*

Outside, Eddie and Maurice were still yelling at each other, but I knew they'd be coming inside to torment the animals again any minute. I grabbed Riptide and slashed the lock off the zebra's cage.

The zebra burst out. It turned to me and bowed. *Thank you, lord.*

Grover held up his hands and said something to the zebra in goat talk, like a blessing.

Just as Maurice was poking his head back inside to check out the noise, the zebra leaped over him and into the street. There was yelling and screaming and cars honking. We rushed to the doors of the trailer in time to see the zebra galloping down a wide boulevard lined with hotels and casinos and neon signs. We'd just released a zebra in Las Vegas.

Maurice and Eddie ran after it, with a few policemen running after them, shouting, 'Hey! You need a permit for that!'

'Now would be a good time to leave,' Annabeth said.

'The other animals first,' Grover said.

I cut the locks with my sword. Grover raised his hands and spoke the same goat-blessing he'd used for the zebra.

'Good luck,' I told the animals. The antelope and the lion burst out of their cages and went off together into the streets.

Some tourists screamed. Most just backed off and took pictures, probably thinking it was some kind of stunt by one of the casinos.

'Will the animals be okay?' I asked Grover. 'I mean, the desert and all –'

'Don't worry,' he said. 'I placed a satyr's sanctuary on them.'

'Meaning?'

'Meaning they'll reach the wild safely,' he said. 'They'll find water, food, shade, whatever they need until they find a safe place to live.'

'Why can't you place a blessing like that on us?' I asked.

'It only works on wild animals.'

'So it would only affect Percy,' Annabeth reasoned.

'Hey!' I protested.

'Kidding,' she said. 'Come on. Let's get out of this filthy truck.'

We stumbled out into the desert afternoon. It was forty degrees, easy, and we must've looked like deep-fried vagrants, but everybody was too interested in the wild animals to pay us much attention.

We passed the Monte Carlo and the MGM. We passed pyramids, a pirate ship and the Statue of Liberty, which was a pretty small replica, but still made me homesick.

I wasn't sure what we were looking for. Maybe just a place to get out of the heat for a few minutes, find a sandwich and a glass of lemonade, make a new plan for getting west.

We must have taken a wrong turn, because we found

ourselves at a deadend, standing in front of the Lotus Hotel and Casino. The entrance was a huge neon flower, the petals lighting up and blinking. No one was going in or out, but the glittering chrome doors were open, spilling out air conditioning that smelled like flowers – lotus blossom, maybe. I'd never smelled one, so I wasn't sure.

The doorman smiled at us. 'Hey, kids. You look tired. You want to come in and sit down?'

I'd learned to be suspicious, the last week or so. I figured anybody might be a monster or a god. You just couldn't tell. But this guy was normal. One look at him, and I could see. Besides, I was so relieved to hear somebody who sounded sympathetic that I nodded and said we'd love to come in. Inside, we took one look around, and Grover said, 'Whoa.'

The whole lobby was a giant game room. And I'm not talking about cheesy old Pac-Man games or slot machines. There was an indoor water slide snaking around the glass elevator, which went straight up at least forty floors. There was a climbing wall on the side of one building, and an indoor bungee-jumping bridge. There were virtual-reality suits with working laser guns. And hundreds of video games, each one the size of a widescreen TV. Basically, you name it, this place had it. There were a few other kids playing, but not that many. No waiting for any of the games. There were waitresses and snack bars all around, serving every kind of food you can imagine.

'Hey!' a bellhop said. At least I guessed he was a bellhop. He wore a white-and-yellow Hawaiian shirt with lotus designs, shorts and flip-flops. 'Welcome to the Lotus Casino. Here's your room key.'

I stammered, 'Um, but . . .'

'No, no,' he said, laughing. 'The bill's taken care of. No extra charges, no tips. Just go on up to the top floor, room 4001. If you need anything, like extra bubbles for the hot tub, or skeet targets for the shooting range, or whatever, just call the front desk. Here are your LotusCash cards. They work in the restaurants and on all the games and rides.'

He handed us each a green plastic credit card.

I knew there must be some mistake. Obviously he thought we were some millionaire's kids. But I took the card and said, 'How much is on here?'

His eyebrows knit together. 'What do you mean?'

'I mean, when does it run out of cash?'

He laughed. 'Oh, you're making a joke. Hey, that's cool. Enjoy your stay.'

We took the elevator upstairs and checked out our room. It was a suite with three separate bedrooms and a bar stocked with candy, sodas and crisps. A hotline to room service. Fluffy towels and waterbeds with feather pillows. A big-screen television with satellite and high-speed Internet. The balcony had its own hot tub and, sure enough, there was a skeet-shooting machine and a shotgun, so you could launch clay pigeons right out over the Las Vegas skyline and plug them with your gun. I didn't see how that could be legal, but I thought it was pretty cool. The view over the Strip and the desert was amazing, though I doubted we'd ever have time to look at the view with a room like this.

'Oh, goodness,' Annabeth said. 'This place is . . .'

'Sweet,' Grover said. 'Absolutely sweet.'

There were clothes in the closet, and they fitted me. I frowned, thinking that this was a little strange.

I threw Ares's backpack in the trash can. Wouldn't need that any more. When we left, I could just charge a new one at the hotel store.

I took a shower, which felt awesome after a week of grimy travel. I changed clothes, ate a bag of crisps, drank three Cokes and came out feeling better than I had in a long time. In the back of my mind, some small problem kept nagging me. I'd had a dream or something . . . I needed to talk to my friends. But I was sure it could wait.

I came out of the bedroom and found that Annabeth and Grover had also showered and changed clothes. Grover was eating crisps to his heart's content, while Annabeth cranked up the National Geographic Channel.

'All those stations,' I told her, 'and you turn on National Geographic. Are you insane?'

'It's interesting.'

'I feel good,' Grover said. 'I love this place.'

Without his even realizing it, the wings sprouted out of his shoes and lifted him a foot off the ground, then back down again.

'So what now?' Annabeth asked. 'Sleep?'

Grover and I looked at each other and grinned. We both held up our green plastic LotusCash cards.

'Play time,' I said.

I couldn't remember the last time I had so much fun. I came from a relatively poor family. Our idea of a splurge was eating out at Burger King and renting a video. A five-star Vegas hotel? Forget it.

I bungee-jumped the lobby five or six times, did the waterslide, snowboarded the artificial ski slope and played virtual-reality laser tag and FBI sharpshooter. I saw Grover a few times, going from game to game. He really liked the reverse hunter thing – where the deer go out and shoot the rednecks. I saw Annabeth playing trivia games and other brainiac stuff. They had this huge 3-D sim game where you build your own city, and you could actually see the holographic buildings rise on the display board. I didn't think much of it, but Annabeth loved it.

I'm not sure when I first realized something was wrong.

Probably, it was when I noticed the guy standing next to me at VR sharpshooters. He was about thirteen, I guess, but his clothes were weird. I thought he was some Elvis impersonator's son. He wore bell-bottoms and a red T-shirt with black piping, and his hair was permed and gelled like a New Jersey girl's on homecoming night.

We played a game of sharpshooters together and he said, 'Groovy, man. Been here two weeks, and the games keep getting better and better.'

Groovy?

Later, while we were talking, I said something "rocked", and he looked at me kind of puzzled, as if he'd never heard the word used that way before.

He said his name was Darrin, but as soon as I started asking him questions he got bored with me and started to go back to the computer screen.

I said, 'Hey, Darrin?'

'What?'

'What year is it?'

He frowned at me. 'In the game?'

'No. In real life.'

He had to think about it. '1977.'

'No,' I said, getting a little scared. 'Really.'

'Hey, man. Bad vibes. I got a game happening.'

After that he totally ignored me.

I started talking to people, and I found it wasn't easy. They were glued to the TV screen, or the video game, or their food, or whatever. I found a guy who told me it was 1985. Another guy told me it was 1993. They all claimed they hadn't been in here very long, a few days, a few weeks at most. They didn't really know and they didn't care.

Then it occurred to me: how long had I been here? It seemed like only a couple of hours, but was it?

I tried to remember why we were here. We were going to Los Angeles. We were supposed to find the entrance to the Underworld. My mother ... for a scary second, I had trouble remembering her name. Sally. Sally Jackson. I had to find her. I had to stop Hades from causing World War III.

I found Annabeth still building her city.

'Come on,' I told her. 'We've got to get out of here.'

No response.

I shook her. 'Annabeth?'

She looked up, annoyed. 'What?'

'We need to leave.'

'Leave? What are you talking about? I've just got the towers —'

'This place is a trap.'

She didn't respond until I shook her again. 'What?'

'Listen. The Underworld. Our quest!'

'Oh, come on, Percy. Just a few more minutes.'

'Annabeth, there are people here from 1977. Kids who have never aged. You check in, and you stay forever.'

'So?' she asked. 'Can you imagine a better place?'

I grabbed her wrist and yanked her away from the game.

'Hey!' She screamed and hit me, but nobody else even bothered looking at us. They were too busy.

I made her look directly in my eyes. I said, 'Spiders. Large, hairy spiders.'

That jarred her. Her vision cleared. 'Oh my gods,' she said. 'How long have we —'

'I don't know, but we've got to find Grover.'

We went searching, and found him still playing Virtual Deer Hunter.

'Grover!' we both shouted.

He said, 'Die, human! Die, silly polluting nasty person!'

'Grover!'

He turned the plastic gun on me and started clicking, as if I were just another image from the screen.

I looked at Annabeth, and together we took Grover by the arms and dragged him away. His flying shoes sprang to life and started tugging his legs in the other direction as he shouted, 'No! I just got to a new level! No!'

The Lotus bellhop hurried up to us. 'Well, now, are you ready for your platinum cards?'

'We're leaving,' I told him.

'Such a shame,' he said, and I got the feeling that he really meant it, that we'd be breaking his heart if we went. 'We just added an entire new floor full of games for platinum-card members.'

He held out the cards, and I wanted one. I knew that if I took one, I'd never leave. I'd stay here, happy forever, playing games forever, and soon I'd forget my mom, and my quest, and maybe even my own name. I'd be playing virtual rifleman with groovy Disco Darrin forever.

Grover reached for the card, but Annabeth yanked back his arm and said, 'No, thanks.'

We walked towards the door, and as we did, the smell of the food and the sounds of the games seemed to get more and more inviting. I thought about our room upstairs. We could just stay the night, sleep in a real bed for once . . .

Then we burst through the doors of the Lotus Casino and ran down the sidewalk. It felt like afternoon, about the same time of day we'd gone into the casino, but something was wrong. The weather had completely changed. It was stormy, with heat lightning flashing out in the desert.

Ares's backpack was slung over my shoulder, which was odd, because I was sure I had thrown it in the trash can in room 4001, but at the moment I had other problems to worry about.

I ran to the nearest newspaper stand and read the year first. Thank the gods, it was the same year it had been when we went in. Then I noticed the date: June twentieth.

We had been in the Lotus Casino for five days.

We had only one day left until the summer solstice. One day to complete our quest.

It was Annabeth's idea.

She loaded us into the back of a Vegas taxi as if we actually had money, and told the driver, 'Los Angeles, please.'

The cabbie chewed his cigar and sized us up. 'That's three hundred miles. For that, you gotta pay up front.'

'You accept casino debit cards?' Annabeth asked.

He shrugged. 'Some of 'em. Same as credit cards. I gotta swipe 'em through, first.'

Annabeth handed him her green LotusCash card.

He looked at it sceptically.

'Swipe it,' Annabeth invited.

He did.

His meter machine started rattling. The lights flashed. Finally an infinity symbol came up next to the dollar sign.

The cigar fell out of the driver's mouth. He looked back at us, his eyes wide. 'Where to in Los Angeles . . . uh, Your Highness?'

'The Santa Monica pier.' Annabeth sat up a little straighter. I could tell she liked the 'Your Highness' thing. 'Get us there fast, and you can keep the change.'

Maybe she shouldn't have told him that.

The cab's speedometer never dipped below ninety-five the whole way through the Mojave Desert.

On the road, we had plenty of time to talk. I told Annabeth and Grover about my latest dream, but the details got sketchier the more I tried to remember them. The Lotus Casino seemed to have short-circuited my memory. I couldn't recall what the invisible servant's voice had sounded like, though I was sure it was somebody I knew. The servant had called the monster in the pit something other than 'my lord' . . . some special name or title . . .

'The Silent One?' Annabeth suggested. 'The Rich One? Both of those are nicknames for Hades.'

'Maybe . . .' I said, though neither sounded quite right.

'That throne room sounds like Hades's,' Grover said. 'That's the way it's usually described.'

I shook my head. 'Something's wrong. The throne room wasn't the main part of the dream. And that voice from the pit . . . I don't know. It just didn't feel like a god's voice.'

Annabeth's eyes widened.

'What?' I asked.

'Oh . . . nothing. I was just — No, it *has* to be Hades. Maybe he sent this thief, this invisible person, to get the master bolt, and something went wrong —'

'Like what?'

'I — I don't know,' she said. 'But if he stole Zeus's symbol of power from Olympus, and the gods were hunting

[267]

him, I mean, a lot of things could go wrong. So this thief had to hide the bolt, or he lost it somehow. Anyway, he failed to bring it to Hades. That's what the voice said in your dream, right? The guy failed. That would explain what the Furies were searching for when they came after us on the bus. Maybe they thought we had retrieved the bolt.'

I wasn't sure what was wrong with her. She looked pale.

'But if I'd already retrieved the bolt,' I said, 'why would I be travelling to the Underworld?'

'To threaten Hades,' Grover suggested. 'To bribe or blackmail him into getting your mom back.'

I whistled. 'You have evil thoughts for a goat.'

'Why, thank you.'

'But the thing in the pit said it was waiting for *two* items,' I said. 'If the master bolt is one, what's the other?'

Grover shook his head, clearly mystified.

Annabeth was looking at me as if she knew my next question, and was silently willing me not to ask it.

'You have an idea what might be in that pit, don't you?' I asked her. 'I mean, if it isn't Hades?'

'Percy . . . let's not talk about it. Because if it isn't Hades . . . No. It has to be Hades.'

Wasteland rolled by. We passed a sign that said: CALIFORNIA STATE LINE, 12 MILES.

I got the feeling I was missing one simple, critical piece of information. It was like when I stared at a common word I should know, but I couldn't make sense of it because one or two letters were floating around. The more I thought about my quest, the more I was sure that confronting Hades wasn't the real answer. There was something else going on, something even more dangerous.

The problem was: we were hurtling towards the Underworld at ninety-five miles an hour, betting that Hades had the master bolt. If we got there and found out we were wrong, we wouldn't have time to correct ourselves. The solstice deadline would pass and war would begin.

'The answer is in the Underworld,' Annabeth assured me. 'You saw spirits of the dead, Percy. There's only one place that could be. We're doing the right thing.'

She tried to boost our morale by suggesting clever strategies for getting into the Land of the Dead, but my heart wasn't in it. There were just too many unknown factors. It was like cramming for a test without knowing the subject. And believe me, I'd done *that* enough times.

The cab sped west. Every gust of wind through Death Valley sounded like a spirit of the dead. Every time the brakes hissed on an eighteen-wheeler, it reminded me of Echidna's reptilian voice.

At sunset, the taxi dropped us at the beach in Santa Monica. It looked exactly the way L.A. beaches do in the movies, only it smelled worse. There were carnival rides lining the pier, palm trees lining the sidewalks, homeless guys sleeping in the sand dunes and surfer dudes waiting for the perfect wave.

Grover, Annabeth and I walked down to the edge of the surf.

'What now?' Annabeth asked.

The Pacific was turning gold in the setting sun. I thought about how long it had been since I'd stood on the beach at Montauk, on the opposite side of the country, looking out at a different sea.

How could there be a god who could control all that? What did my science teacher used to say — two-thirds of the earth's surface was covered in water? How could I be the son of someone that powerful?

I stepped into the surf.

'Percy?' Annabeth said. 'What are you doing?'

I kept walking, up to my waist, then my chest.

She called after me, 'You know how polluted that water is? There're all kinds of toxic —'

That's when my head went under.

I held my breath at first. It's difficult to intentionally inhale water. Finally I couldn't stand it any more. I gasped. Sure enough, I could breathe normally.

I walked down into the shoals. I shouldn't have been able to see through the murk, but somehow I could tell where everything was. I could sense the rolling texture of the bottom. I could make out sand-dollar colonies dotting the sandbars. I could even see the currents, warm and cold streams swirling together.

I felt something rub against my leg. I looked down and almost shot out of the water like a ballistic missile. Sliding along beside me was a two-metre-long mako shark.

But the thing wasn't attacking. It was nuzzling me. Heeling like a dog. Tentatively, I touched its dorsal fin. It bucked a little, as if inviting me to hold tighter. I grabbed the fin with both hands. It took off, pulling me along. The shark carried me down into the darkness. It deposited me at the edge of the ocean proper, where the sand bank dropped off into a huge chasm. It was like standing on the rim of the Grand Canyon at midnight, not being able to see much, but knowing the void was right there.

The surface shimmered maybe fifty metres above. I knew I should've been crushed by the pressure. Then again, I shouldn't have been able to breathe. I wondered if there was a limit to how deep I could go, if I could sink straight to the bottom of the Pacific.

Then I saw something glimmering in the darkness below, growing bigger and brighter as it rose towards me. A woman's voice, like my mother's, called: 'Percy Jackson.'

As she got closer, her shape became clearer. She had flowing black hair, a dress made of green silk. Light flickered around her, and her eyes were so distractingly beautiful I hardly noticed the stallion-sized sea horse she was riding.

She dismounted. The sea horse and the mako shark whisked off and started playing something that looked like tag. The underwater lady smiled at me. 'You've come far, Percy Jackson. Well done.'

I wasn't quite sure what to do, so I bowed. 'You're the woman who spoke to me in the Mississippi River.'

'Yes, child. I am a Nereid, a spirit of the sea. It was not easy to appear so far upriver, but the naiads, my freshwater cousins, helped sustain my life force. They honour Lord Poseidon, though they do not serve in his court.'

'And . . . you serve in Poseidon's court?'

She nodded. 'It has been many years since a child of the Sea God has been born. We have watched you with great interest.'

Suddenly I remembered faces in the waves off Montauk Beach when I was a little boy, reflections of smiling women. Like so many of the weird things in my life, I'd never given it much thought before.

'If my father is so interested in me,' I said, 'why isn't he here? Why doesn't he speak to me?'

A cold current rose out of the depths.

'Do not judge the Lord of the Sea too harshly,' the Nereid told me. 'He stands at the brink of an unwanted war. He has much to occupy his time. Besides, he is forbidden to help you directly. The gods may not show such favouritism.'

'Even to their own children?'

'Especially to them. The gods can work by indirect influence only. That is why I give you a warning, and a gift.'

She held out her hand. Three white pearls flashed in her palm.

'I know you journey to Hades's realm,' she said. 'Few mortals have ever done this and survived: Orpheus, who had great musical skill; Hercules, who had great strength; Houdini, who could escape even the depths of Tartarus. Do you have these talents?'

'Um . . . no, ma'am.'

'Ah, but you have something else, Percy. You have gifts you have only begun to know. The oracles have foretold a great and terrible future for you, should you survive to manhood. Poseidon would not have you die before your time. Therefore take these, and when you are in need, smash a pearl at your feet.'

'What will happen?'

'That,' she said, 'depends on the need. But remember: what belongs to the sea will always return to the sea.'

'What about the warning?'

Her eyes flickered with green light. 'Go with what your heart tells you, or you will lose all. Hades feeds on doubt and hopelessness. He will trick you if he can, make you mistrust your own judgement. Once you are in his realm, he will never willingly let you leave. Keep faith. Good luck, Percy Jackson.'

She summoned her sea horse and rode towards the void.

'Wait!' I called. 'At the river, you said not to trust the gifts. What gifts?'

'Goodbye, young hero,' she called back, her voice fading into the depths. 'You must listen to your heart.' She became a speck of glowing green, and then she was gone.

I wanted to follow her down into the darkness. I wanted to see the court of Poseidon. But I looked up at the sunset darkening on the surface. My friends were waiting. We had so little time . . .

I kicked upwards towards the shore.

When I reached the beach, I told Grover and Annabeth what had happened, and showed them the pearls.

Annabeth grimaced. 'No gift comes without a price.'

'They were free.'

'No.' She shook her head. '"There is no such thing as a free lunch." That's an ancient Greek saying that translated pretty well into American. There will be a price. You wait.'

On that happy thought, we turned our backs on the sea.

With some spare change from Ares's backpack, we took the bus into West Hollywood. I showed the driver the Underworld address slip I'd taken from Aunty Em's Garden Gnome Emporium, but he'd never heard of DOA Recording Studios.

'You remind me of somebody I saw on TV,' he told me. 'You a child actor or something?'

'Uh . . . I'm a stunt double . . . for a lot of child actors.'

'Oh! That explains it.'

We thanked him and got off quickly at the next stop.

We wandered for miles on foot, looking for DOA. Nobody seemed to know where it was. It didn't appear in the phone book.

Twice, we ducked into alleys to avoid cop cars.

I froze in front of an appliance store window because a television was playing an interview with somebody who looked very familiar – my stepdad, Smelly Gabe. He was talking to Barbara Walters – I mean, as if he were some kind of huge celebrity. She was interviewing him in our apartment, in the middle of a poker game, and there was a young blonde lady sitting next to him, patting his hand.

A fake tear glistened on his cheek. He was saying, 'Honest, Ms Walters, if it wasn't for Sugar here, my grief counsellor, I'd be a wreck. My stepson took everything I cared about. My wife ... my Camaro ... I – I'm sorry. I have trouble talking about it.'

'There you have it, America.' Barbara Walters turned to the camera. 'A man torn apart. An adolescent boy with serious issues. Let me show you, again, the last known photo of this troubled young fugitive, taken a week ago in Denver.'

The screen cut to a grainy shot of me, Annabeth and Grover standing outside the Colorado diner, talking to Ares.

'Who are the other children in this photo?' Barbara Walters asked dramatically. 'Who is the man with them? Is Percy Jackson a delinquent, a terrorist, or perhaps the brainwashed victim of a frightening new cult? When we come back, we chat with a leading child psychologist. Stay tuned, America.'

'C'mon,' Grover told me. He hauled me away before I could punch a hole in the appliance-store window.

It got dark, and hungry-looking characters started coming out on the streets to play. Now, don't get me wrong. I'm a New Yorker. I don't scare easy. But L.A. had a totally different feel from New York. Back home, everything seemed close. It didn't matter how big the city was, you could get anywhere without getting lost. The street pattern and the subway made sense. There was a system to how things worked. A kid could be safe as long as he wasn't stupid.

L.A. wasn't like that. It was spread out, chaotic, hard to move around. It reminded me of Ares. It wasn't enough for

L.A. to be big; it had to prove it was big by being loud and strange and difficult to navigate, too. I didn't know how we were ever going to find the entrance to the Underworld by tomorrow, the summer solstice.

We walked past gangbangers, bums and street hawkers, who looked at us like they were trying to figure if we were worth the trouble of mugging.

As we hurried passed the entrance of an alley, a voice from the darkness said, 'Hey, you.'

Like an idiot, I stopped.

Before I knew it, we were surrounded. A gang of kids had circled us. Six of them in all – white kids with expensive clothes and mean faces. Like the kids at Yancy Academy: rich brats playing at being bad boys.

Instinctively, I uncapped Riptide.

When the sword appeared out of nowhere, the kids backed off, but their leader was either really stupid or really brave, because he kept coming at me with a switchblade.

I made the mistake of swinging.

The kid yelped. But he must've been one hundred percent mortal, because the blade passed harmlessly right through his chest. He looked down. 'What the . . .'

I figured I had about three seconds before his shock turned to anger. 'Run!' I screamed at Annabeth and Grover.

We pushed two kids out of the way and raced down the street, not knowing where we were going. We turned a sharp corner.

'There!' Annabeth shouted.

Only one store on the block looked open, its windows glaring with neon. The sign above the door said something like: CRSTUY'S WATREBDE ALPACE.

'Crusty's Waterbed Palace?' Grover translated.

It didn't sound like a place I'd ever go except in an emergency, but this definitely qualified.

We burst through the doors, ran behind a waterbed, and ducked. A split second later, the gang kids ran past outside.

'I think we lost them,' Grover panted.

A voice behind us boomed, 'Lost who?'

We all jumped.

Standing behind us was a guy who looked like a raptor in a leisure suit. He was at least two metres tall, with absolutely no hair. He had grey leathery skin, thick-lidded eyes, and a cold reptilian smile. He moved towards us slowly, but I got the feeling he could move fast if he needed to.

His suit might've come from the Lotus Casino. It belonged back in the seventies, big time. The shirt was silk paisley, unbuttoned halfway down his hairless chest. The lapels on his velvet jacket were as wide as landing strips. The silver chains around his neck – I couldn't even count them.

'I'm Crusty,' he said, with a tartar-yellow smile.

I resisted the urge to say, *Yes, you are.*

'Sorry to barge in,' I told him. 'We were just, um, browsing.'

'You mean hiding from those no-good kids,' he grumbled. 'They hang around every night. I get a lot of people in here, thanks to them. Say, you want to look at a waterbed?'

I was about to say *No, thanks*, when he put a huge paw on my shoulder and steered me deeper into the showroom.

There was every kind of waterbed you could imagine: different kinds of wood, different patterns of sheets; queen-size, king-size, emperor-of-the-universe-size.

'This is my most popular model.' Crusty spread his hands proudly over a bed covered with black satin sheets, with built-in Lava Lamps on the headboard. The mattress vibrated, so it looked like oil-flavoured jelly.

'Million-hand massage,' Crusty told us. 'Go on, try it out. Shoot, take a nap. I don't care. No business today, anyway.'

'Um,' I said, 'I don't think . . .'

'Million-hand massage!' Grover cried, and dived in. 'Oh, you guys! This is cool.'

'Hmm,' Crusty said, stroking his leathery chin. 'Almost, almost.'

'Almost what?' I asked.

He looked at Annabeth. 'Do me a favour and try this one over here, honey. Might fit.'

Annabeth said, 'But what —'

He patted her reassuringly on the shoulder and led her over to the Safari Deluxe model with teakwood lions carved into the frame and a leopard-patterned bedspread. When Annabeth didn't want to lie down, Crusty pushed her.

'Hey!' she protested.

Crusty snapped his fingers. *'Ergo!'*

Ropes sprang from the sides of the bed, lashing around Annabeth, holding her to the mattress.

Grover tried to get up, but ropes sprang from his black-satin bed, too, and lashed him down.

'Not cool!' he yelled, his voice vibrating from the million-hand massage. 'Not cool at all!'

The giant looked at Annabeth, then turned towards me and grinned. 'Almost, darn it.'

I tried to step away, but his hand shot out and clamped around the back of my neck. 'Whoa, kid. Don't worry. We'll find you one in a sec.'

'Let my friends go.'

'Oh, sure I will. But I got to make them fit, first.'

'What do you mean?'

'All the beds are exactly six feet, see? Your friends are too short. Got to make them fit.'

Annabeth and Grover kept struggling.

'Can't stand imperfect measurements,' Crusty muttered. '*Ergo!*'

A new set of ropes leaped out from the top and bottom of the beds, wrapping around Grover and Annabeth's ankles, then around their armpits. The ropes started tightening, pulling my friends from both ends.

'Don't worry,' Crusty told me. 'These are stretching jobs. Maybe eight extra centimetres on their spines. They might even live. Now why don't we find a bed you like, huh?'

'Percy!' Grover yelled.

My mind was racing. I knew I couldn't take on this giant waterbed salesman alone. He would snap my neck before I ever got my sword out.

'Your real name's not Crusty, is it?' I asked.

'Legally, it's Procrustes,' he admitted.

'The Stretcher,' I said. I remembered the story: the giant who'd tried to kill Theseus with over-hospitality on his way to Athens.

'Yeah,' the salesman said. 'But who can pronounce "Procrustes"? Bad for business. Now "Crusty", anybody can say that.'

'You're right. It's got a good ring to it.'

His eyes lit up. 'You think so?'

'Oh, absolutely,' I said. 'And the workmanship on these beds? Fabulous!'

He grinned hugely, but his fingers didn't loosen on my neck. 'I tell my customers that. Every time. Nobody bothers to look at the workmanship. How many built-in Lava Lamp headboards have you seen?'

'Not too many.'

'That's right!'

'Percy!' Annabeth yelled. 'What are you doing?'

'Don't mind her,' I told Procrustes. 'She's impossible.'

The giant laughed. 'All my customers are. Never six feet exactly. So inconsiderate. And then they complain about the fitting.'

'What do you do if they're longer than six feet?'

'Oh, that happens all the time. It's a simple fix.'

He let go of my neck, but before I could react, he reached behind a nearby sales desk and brought out a huge double-bladed brass axe. He said, 'I just centre the subject as best I can and lop off whatever hangs over on either end.'

'Ah,' I said, swallowing hard. 'Sensible.'

'I'm so glad to come across an intelligent customer!'

The ropes were really stretching my friends now. Annabeth was turning pale. Grover made gurgling sounds like a strangled goose.

'So, Crusty . . .' I said, trying to keep my voice light. I glanced at the sales tag on the valentine-shaped Honeymoon Special. 'Does this one really have dynamic stabilizers to stop wave motion?'

'Absolutely. Try it out.'

'Yeah, maybe I will. But would it work even for a big guy like you? No waves at all?'

'Guaranteed.'

'No way.'

'Way.'

'Show me.'

He sat down eagerly on the bed, patted the mattress. 'No waves. See?'

I snapped my fingers. *Ergo.*

Ropes lashed around Crusty and flattened him against the mattress.

'Hey!' he yelled.

'Centre him just right,' I said.

The ropes readjusted themselves at my command. Crusty's whole head stuck out the top. His feet stuck out the bottom.

'No!' he said. 'Wait! This is just a demo.'

I uncapped Riptide. 'A few simple adjustments . . .'

I had no qualms about what I was about to do. If

Crusty were human, I couldn't hurt him anyway. If he was a monster, he deserved to turn into dust for a while.

'You drive a hard bargain,' he told me. 'I'll give you thirty percent off on selected floor models!'

'I think I'll start with the top.' I raised my sword.

'No money down! No interest for six months!'

I swung the sword. Crusty stopped making offers.

I cut the ropes on the other beds. Annabeth and Grover got to their feet, groaning and wincing and cursing me a lot.

'You look taller,' I said.

'Very funny,' Annabeth said. 'Be faster next time.'

I looked at the bulletin board behind Crusty's sales desk. There was an advertisement for Hermes Delivery Service, and another for the All-New Compendium of L.A. Area Monsters –'The only Monstrous Yellow Pages you'll ever need!' Under that, a bright orange flier for DOA Recording Studios, offering commissions for heroes' souls. 'We are always looking for new talent!' DOA's address was right underneath with a map.

'Come on,' I told my friends.

'Give us a minute,' Grover complained. 'We were almost stretched to death!'

'Then you're ready for the Underworld,' I said. 'It's only a block from here.'

18 ⚡ ANNABETH DOES OBEDIENCE SCHOOL

We stood in the shadows of Valencia Boulevard, looking up at gold letters etched in black marble: DOA RECORDING STUDIOS.

Underneath, stencilled on the glass doors: NO SOLICITORS. NO LOITERING. NO LIVING.

It was almost midnight, but the lobby was brightly lit and full of people. Behind the security desk sat a tough-looking guard with sunglasses and an earpiece.

I turned to my friends. 'Okay. You remember the plan.'

'The plan,' Grover gulped. 'Yeah. I love the plan.'

Annabeth said, 'What happens if the plan doesn't work?'

'Don't think negative.'

'Right,' she said. 'We're entering the Land of the Dead, and I shouldn't think negative.'

I took the pearls out of my pocket, the three milky spheres the Nereid had given me in Santa Monica. They didn't seem like much of a backup in case something went wrong.

Annabeth put her hand on my shoulder. 'I'm sorry, Percy. You're right, we'll make it. It'll be fine.'

She gave Grover a nudge.

'Oh, right!' he chimed in. 'We got this far. We'll find the master bolt and save your mom. No problem.'

I looked at them both, and felt really grateful. Only a few minutes before, I'd almost got them stretched to death on deluxe waterbeds, and now they were trying to be brave for my sake, trying to make me feel better.

I slipped the pearls back in my pocket. 'Let's whup some Underworld butt.'

We walked inside the DOA lobby.

Muzak played softly on hidden speakers. The carpet and walls were steel grey. Pencil cactuses grew in the corners like skeleton hands. The furniture was black leather, and every seat was taken. There were people sitting on couches, people standing up, people staring out the windows or waiting for the elevator. Nobody moved, or talked, or did much of anything. Out of the corner of my eye, I could see them all just fine, but if I focused on any one of them in particular, they started looking . . . transparent. I could see right through their bodies.

The security guard's desk was a raised podium, so we had to look up at him.

He was tall and elegant, with chocolate-coloured skin and bleached-blond hair shaved military style. He wore tortoiseshell shades and a silk Italian suit that matched his hair. A black rose was pinned to his lapel under a silver name tag.

I read the name tag, then looked at him in bewilderment. 'Your name is Chiron?'

He leaned across the desk. I couldn't see anything in his

glasses except my own reflection, but his smile was sweet and cold, like a python's, right before it eats you.

'What a precious young lad.' He had a strange accent – British, maybe, but also as if he had learned English as a second language. 'Tell me, mate, do I look like a centaur?'

'N-no.'

'Sir,' he added smoothly.

'Sir,' I said.

He pinched the name tag and ran his finger under the letters. 'Can you read this, mate? It says C-H-*A*-R-O-N. Say it with me: CARE-ON.'

'Charon.'

'Amazing! Now: *Mr* Charon.'

'Mr Charon,' I said.

'Well done.' He sat back. 'I *hate* being confused with that old horse-man. And now, how may I help you little dead ones?'

His question caught in my stomach like a fastball. I looked at Annabeth for support.

'We want to go the Underworld,' she said.

Charon's mouth twitched. 'Well, that's refreshing.'

'It is?' she asked.

'Straightforward and honest. No screaming. No "There must be a mistake, Mr Charon".' He looked us over. 'How did you die, then?'

I nudged Grover.

'Oh,' he said. 'Um . . . drowned . . . in the bathtub.'

'All three of you?' Charon asked.

We nodded.

'Big bathtub.' Charon looked mildly impressed. 'I don't suppose you have coins for passage. Normally, with adults, you see, I could charge your American Express, or add the ferry price to your last cable bill. But with children . . . alas, you never die prepared. Suppose you'll have to take a seat for a few centuries.'

'Oh, but we have coins.' I set three golden drachmas on the counter, part of the stash I'd found in Crusty's office desk.

'Well, now . . .' Charon moistened his lips. 'Real drachmas. Real golden drachmas. I haven't seen these in . . .'

His fingers hovered greedily over the coins.

We were so close.

Then Charon looked at me. That cold stare behind his glasses seemed to bore a hole through my chest. 'Here now,' he said. 'You couldn't read my name correctly. Are you dyslexic, lad?'

'No,' I said. 'I'm dead.'

Charon leaned forward and took a sniff. 'You're not dead. I should've known. You're a godling.'

'We have to get to the Underworld,' I insisted.

Charon made a growling sound deep in his throat.

Immediately, all the people in the waiting room got up and started pacing, agitated, lighting cigarettes, running hands through their hair, or checking their wristwatches.

'Leave while you can,' Charon told us. 'I'll just take these and forget I saw you.'

He started to go for the coins, but I snatched them back.

'No service, no tip.' I tried to sound braver than I felt.

Charon growled again – a deep, blood-chilling sound. The spirits of the dead started pounding on the elevator doors.

'It's a shame, too,' I sighed. 'We had more to offer.'

I held up the entire bag from Crusty's stash. I took out a fistful of drachmas and let the coins spill through my fingers.

Charon's growl changed into something more like a lion's purr. 'Do you think I can be bought, godling? Eh ... just out of curiosity, how much have you got there?'

'A lot,' I said. 'I bet Hades doesn't pay you well enough for such hard work.'

'Oh, you don't know the half of it. How would you like to babysit these spirits all day? Always "Please don't let me be dead" or "Please let me across for free". I haven't had a pay raise in three thousand years. Do you imagine suits like this come cheap?'

'You deserve better,' I agreed. 'A little appreciation. Respect. Good pay.'

With each word, I stacked another gold coin on the counter.

Charon glanced down at his silk Italian jacket, as if imagining himself in something even better. 'I must say, lad, you're making some sense now. Just a little.'

I stacked another few coins. 'I could mention a pay raise while I'm talking to Hades.'

He sighed. 'The boat's almost full, anyway. I might as well add you three and be off.'

He stood, scooped up our money, and said, 'Come along.'

We pushed through the crowd of waiting spirits, who started grabbing at our clothes like the wind, their voices whispering things I couldn't make out. Charon shoved them out of the way, grumbling, 'Freeloaders.'

He escorted us into the elevator, which was already crowded with souls of the dead, each one holding a green boarding pass. Charon grabbed two spirits who were trying to get on with us and pushed them back into the lobby.

'Right. Now, no one get any ideas while I'm gone,' he announced to the waiting room. 'And if anyone moves the dial off my easy-listening station again, I'll make sure you're here for another thousand years. Understand?'

He shut the doors. He put a key card into a slot in the elevator panel and we started to descend.

'What happens to the spirits waiting in the lobby?' Annabeth asked.

'Nothing,' Charon said.

'For how long?'

'Forever, or until I'm feeling generous.'

'Oh,' she said. 'That's . . . fair.'

Charon raised an eyebrow. 'Whoever said death was fair, young miss? Wait until it's your turn. You'll die soon enough, where you're going.'

'We'll get out alive,' I said.

'Ha.'

I got a sudden dizzy feeling. We weren't going down

any more, but forward. The air turned misty. Spirits around me started changing shape. Their modern clothes flickered, turning into grey hooded robes. The floor of the elevator began swaying.

I blinked hard. When I opened my eyes, Charon's creamy Italian suit had been replaced by a long black robe. His tortoiseshell glasses were gone. Where his eyes should've been were empty sockets – like Ares's eyes, except Charon's were totally dark, full of night and death and despair.

He saw me looking, and said, 'Well?'

'Nothing,' I managed.

I thought he was grinning, but that wasn't it. The flesh of his face was becoming transparent, letting me see straight through to his skull.

The floor kept swaying.

Grover said, 'I think I'm getting seasick.'

When I blinked again, the elevator wasn't an elevator any more. We were standing in a wooden barge. Charon was poling us across a dark, oily river, swirling with bones, dead fish and other, stranger things – plastic dolls, crushed carnations, soggy diplomas with gilt edges.

'The River Styx,' Annabeth murmured. 'It's so . . .'

'Polluted,' Charon said. 'For thousands of years, you humans have been throwing in everything as you come across – hopes, dreams, wishes that never came true. Irresponsible waste management, if you ask me.'

Mist curled off the filthy water. Above us, almost lost in the gloom, was a ceiling of stalactites. Ahead, the far shore glimmered with greenish light, the colour of poison.

Panic closed up my throat. What was I doing here? These people around me . . . they were dead.

Annabeth grabbed hold of my hand. Under normal circumstances, this would've embarrassed me, but I understood how she felt. She wanted reassurance that somebody else was alive on this boat.

I found myself muttering a prayer, though I wasn't quite sure who I was praying to. Down here, only one god mattered, and he was the one I had come to confront.

The shoreline of the Underworld came into view. Craggy rocks and black volcanic sand stretched inland about fifty metres to the base of a high stone wall, which marched off in either direction as far as we could see. A sound came from somewhere nearby in the green gloom, echoing off the stones – the howl of a large animal.

'Old Three-Face is hungry,' Charon said. His smile turned skeletal in the greenish light. 'Bad luck for you, godlings.'

The bottom of our boat slid onto the black sand. The dead began to disembark. A woman holding a little girl's hand. An old man and an old woman hobbling along arm in arm. A boy no older than I was, shuffling silently along in his grey robe.

Charon said, 'I'd wish you luck, mate, but there isn't any down here. Mind you, don't forget to mention my pay raise.'

He counted our golden coins into his pouch, then took

up his pole. He warbled something that sounded like a Barry Manilow song as he ferried the empty barge back across the river.

We followed the spirits up a well-worn path.

I'm not sure what I was expecting – Pearly Gates, or a big black portcullis, or something. But the entrance to the Underworld looked like a cross between airport security and the Jersey Turnpike.

There were three separate entrances under one huge black archway that said: YOU ARE NOW ENTERING EREBUS. Each entrance had a pass-through metal detector mounted with security cameras. Beyond this were tollbooths manned by black-robed ghouls like Charon.

The howling of the hungry animal was really loud now, but I couldn't see where it was coming from. The three-headed dog, Cerberus, who was supposed to guard Hades's door, was nowhere to be seen.

The dead queued up in the three lines, two marked: ATTENDANT ON DUTY, and one marked: EZ DEATH. The EZ DEATH line was moving right along. The other two were crawling.

'What do you figure?' I asked Annabeth.

'The fast line must go straight to Asphodel,' she said. 'No contest. They don't want to risk judgment from the court, because it might go against them.'

'There's a court for dead people?'

'Yeah. Three judges. They switch around who sits on the bench. King Minos, Thomas Jefferson, Shakespeare –

people like that. Sometimes they look at a life and decide that person needs a special reward – the Fields of Elysium. Sometimes they decide on punishment. But most people, well, they just lived. Nothing special, good or bad. So they go to the Fields of Asphodel.'

'And do what?'

Grover said, 'Imagine standing in a wheat field in Kansas. Forever.'

'Harsh,' I said.

'Not as harsh as that,' Grover muttered. 'Look.'

A couple of black-robed ghouls had pulled aside one spirit and were frisking him at the security desk. The face of the dead man looked vaguely familiar.

'He's that preacher who made the news, remember?' Grover asked.

'Oh, yeah.' I did remember now. We'd seen him on TV a couple of times at the Yancy Academy dorm. He was this annoying televangelist from upstate New York who'd raised millions of dollars for orphanages and then got caught spending the money on stuff for his mansion, like gold-plated toilet seats, and an indoor putt-putt golf course. He'd died in a police chase when his "Lamborghini for the Lord" went off a cliff.

I said, 'What're they doing to him?'

'Special punishment from Hades,' Grover guessed. 'The really bad people get his personal attention as soon as they arrive. The Fu – the Kindly Ones will set up an eternal torture for him.'

The thought of the Furies made me shudder. I realized

I was in their home territory now. Old Mrs Dodds would be licking her lips with anticipation.

'But if he's a preacher,' I said, 'and he believes in a different hell . . .'

Grover shrugged. 'Who says he's seeing this place the way we're seeing it? Humans see what they want to see. They're very stubborn – er, persistent, that way.'

We got closer to the gates. The howling was so loud now it shook the ground at my feet, but I still couldn't figure out where it was coming from.

Then, about fifteen metres in front of us, the green mist shimmered. Standing just where the path split into three lanes was an enormous shadowy monster.

I hadn't seen it before because it was half transparent, like the dead. Until it moved, it blended with whatever was behind it. Only its eyes and teeth looked solid. And it was staring straight at me.

My jaw hung open. All I could think to say was, 'He's a Rottweiler.'

I'd always imagined Cerberus as a big black mastiff. But he was obviously a purebred Rottweiler, except of course that he was twice the size of a woolly mammoth, mostly invisible, and had three heads.

The dead walked right up to him – no fear at all. The ATTENDANT ON DUTY lines parted on either side of him. The EZ DEATH spirits walked right between his front paws and under his belly, which they could do without even crouching.

'I'm starting to see him better,' I muttered. 'Why is that?'

'I think . . .' Annabeth moistened her lips. 'I'm afraid it's because we're getting closer to being dead.'

The dog's middle head craned towards us. It sniffed the air and growled.

'It can smell the living,' I said.

'But that's okay,' Grover said, trembling next to me. 'Because we have a plan.'

'Right,' Annabeth said. I'd never heard her voice sound quite so small. 'A plan.'

We moved towards the monster.

The middle head snarled at us, then barked so loud my eyeballs rattled.

'Can you understand it?' I asked Grover.

'Oh yeah,' he said. 'I can understand it.'

'What's it saying?'

'I don't think humans have a four-letter word that translates, exactly.'

I took the big stick out of my backpack – a bed post I'd broken off Crusty's Safari Deluxe floor model. I held it up, and tried to channel happy dog thoughts towards Cerberus – Alpo commercials, cute little puppies, fire hydrants. I tried to smile like I wasn't about to die.

'Hey, Big Fella,' I called up. 'I bet they don't play with you much.'

'GROWWWLLLL!'

'Good boy,' I said weakly.

I waved the stick. The dog's middle head followed the movement. The other two heads trained their eyes on me, completely ignoring the spirits. I had Cerberus's undivided attention. I wasn't sure that was a good thing.

'Fetch!' I threw the stick into the gloom, a good solid throw. I heard it go *ker-sploosh* in the River Styx.

Cerberus glared at me, unimpressed. His eyes were baleful and cold.

So much for the plan.

Cerberus was now making a new kind of growl, deeper down in his three throats.

'Um,' Grover said. 'Percy?'

'Yeah?'

'I just thought you'd want to know.'

'Yeah?'

'Cerberus? He's saying we've got ten seconds to pray to the god of our choice. After that . . . well . . . he's hungry.'

'Wait!' Annabeth said. She started rifling through her pack.

Uh-oh, I thought.

'Five seconds,' Grover said. 'Do we run now?'

Annabeth produced a red rubber ball the size of a grapefruit. It was labelled: WATERLAND, DENVER, CO. Before I could stop her, she raised the ball and marched straight up to Cerberus.

She shouted, 'See the ball? You want the ball, Cerberus? Sit!'

Cerberus looked as stunned as we were.

All three of his heads cocked sideways. Six nostrils dilated.

'Sit!' Annabeth called again.

I was sure that any moment she would become the world's largest Milkbone dog biscuit.

But instead, Cerberus licked his three sets of lips, shifted on his haunches, and sat, immediately crushing a dozen spirits who'd been passing underneath him in the EZ DEATH line. The spirits made muffled hisses as they dissipated, like the air let out of tyres.

Annabeth said, 'Good boy!'

She threw Cerberus the ball.

He caught it in his middle mouth. It was barely big enough for him to chew, and the other heads started snapping at the middle, trying to get the new toy.

'Drop it!' Annabeth ordered.

Cerberus's heads stopped fighting and looked at her. The ball was wedged between two of his teeth like a tiny piece of gum. He made a loud, scary whimper, then dropped the ball, now slimy and bitten nearly in half, at Annabeth's feet.

'Good boy.' She picked up the ball, ignoring the monster spit all over it.

She turned towards us. 'Go now. EZ DEATH line — it's faster.'

I said, 'But —'

'Now!' She ordered, in the same tone she was using on the dog.

Grover and I inched forward warily.

Cerberus started to growl.

'Stay!' Annabeth ordered the monster. 'If you want the ball, stay!'

Cerberus whimpered, but he stayed where he was.

'What about you?' I asked Annabeth as we passed her.

'I know what I'm doing, Percy,' she muttered. 'At least, I'm pretty sure . . .'

Grover and I walked between the monster's legs.

Please, Annabeth, I prayed. Don't tell him to sit again.

We made it through. Cerberus wasn't any less scary-looking from the back.

Annabeth said, 'Good dog!'

She held up the tattered red ball, and probably came to the same conclusion I did — if she rewarded Cerberus, there'd be nothing left for another trick.

She threw the ball anyway. The monster's left mouth immediately snatched it up, only to be attacked by the middle head while the right head moaned in protest.

While the monster was distracted, Annabeth walked briskly under its belly and joined us at the metal detector.

'How did you do that?' I asked her, amazed.

'Obedience school,' she said breathlessly, and I was surprised to see there were tears in her eyes. 'When I was little, at my dad's house, we had a Dobermann . . .'

'Never mind that,' Grover said, tugging at my shirt. 'Come on!'

We were about to bolt through the EZ DEATH line when Cerberus moaned pitifully from all three mouths. Annabeth stopped.

She turned to face the dog, which had done a one-eighty to look at us.

Cerberus panted expectantly, the tiny red ball in pieces in a puddle of drool at its feet.

'Good boy,' Annabeth said, but her voice sounded melancholy and uncertain.

The monster's heads turned sideways, as if worried about her.

'I'll bring you another ball soon,' Annabeth promised faintly. 'Would you like that?'

The monster whimpered. I didn't need to speak dog to know Cerberus was still waiting for the ball.

'Good dog. I'll come visit you soon. I – I promise.' Annabeth turned to us. 'Let's go.'

Grover and I pushed through the metal detector, which immediately screamed and set off flashing red lights. 'Unauthorized possessions! Magic detected!'

Cerberus started to bark.

We burst through the EZ DEATH gate, which started even more alarms blaring, and raced into the Underworld.

A few minutes later, we were hiding, out of breath, in the rotten trunk of an immense black tree as security ghouls scuttled past, yelling for backup from the Furies.

Grover murmured, 'Well, Percy, what have we learned today?'

'That three-headed dogs prefer red rubber balls over sticks?'

'No,' Grover told me. 'We've learned that your plans really, really bite!'

I wasn't sure about that. I thought maybe Annabeth and I had both had the right idea. Even here in the Underworld, everybody – even monsters – needed a little attention once in a while.

I thought about that as we waited for the ghouls to pass. I pretended not to see Annabeth wipe a tear from her cheek as she listened to the mournful keening of Cerberus in the distance, longing for his new friend.

19 ⚡ WE FIND OUT THE TRUTH, SORT OF

Imagine the largest concert crowd you've ever seen, a football field packed with a million fans.

Now imagine a field a million times that big, packed with people, and imagine the electricity has gone out, and there is no noise, no light, no beach ball bouncing around over the crowd. Something tragic has happened backstage. Whispering masses of people are just milling around in the shadows, waiting for a concert that will never start.

If you can picture that, you have a pretty good idea what the Fields of Asphodel looked like. The black grass had been trampled by aeons of dead feet. A warm, moist wind blew like the breath of a swamp. Black trees – Grover told me they were poplars – grew in clumps here and there.

The cavern ceiling was so high above us it might've been a bank of storm clouds, except for the stalactites, which glowed faint grey and looked wickedly pointed. I tried not to imagine they'd fall on us at any moment, but dotted around the fields were several that had fallen and impaled themselves in the black grass. I guess the dead didn't have to worry about little hazards like being speared by stalactites the size of booster rockets.

Annabeth, Grover and I tried to blend into the crowd,

keeping an eye out for security ghouls. I couldn't help looking for familiar faces among the spirits of Asphodel, but the dead are hard to look at. Their faces shimmer. They all look slightly angry or confused. They will come up to you and speak, but their voices sound like chatter, like bats twittering. Once they realize you can't understand them, they frown and move away.

The dead aren't scary. They're just sad.

We crept along, following the line of new arrivals that snaked from the main gates towards a black-tented pavilion with a banner that read:

JUDGMENTS FOR ELYSIUM AND ETERNAL DAMNATION
Welcome, Newly Deceased!

Out the back of the tent came two much smaller lines.

To the left, spirits flanked by security ghouls were marched down a rocky path towards the Fields of Punishment, which glowed and smoked in the distance, a vast, cracked wasteland with rivers of lava and minefields and miles of barbed wire separating the different torture areas. Even from far away, I could see people being chased by hellhounds, burned at the stake, forced to run naked through cactus patches or listen to opera music. I could just make out a tiny hill, with the ant-size figure of Sisyphus struggling to move his boulder to the top. And I saw worse tortures, too – things I don't want to describe.

The line coming from the right side of the judgment pavilion was much better. This one led down towards a small valley surrounded by walls – a gated community, which seemed to be the only happy part of the Underworld. Beyond the security gate were neighbourhoods of beautiful houses from every time period in history, Roman villas and mediaeval castles and Victorian mansions. Silver and gold flowers bloomed on the lawns. The grass rippled in rainbow colours. I could hear laughter and smell barbecue cooking.

Elysium.

In the middle of that valley was a glittering blue lake, with three small islands like a vacation resort in the Bahamas. The Isles of the Blest, for people who had chosen to be reborn three times, and three times achieved Elysium. Immediately I knew that's where I wanted to go when I died.

'That's what it's all about,' Annabeth said, like she was reading my thoughts. 'That's the place for heroes.'

But I thought of how few people there were in Elysium, how tiny it was compared to Asphodel or even Punishment. So few people did good in their lives. It was depressing.

We left the judgment pavilion and moved deeper into Asphodel. It got darker. The colours faded from our clothes. The crowds of chattering spirits began to thin.

After a few miles of walking, we began to hear a familiar screech in the distance. Looming on the horizon was a palace of glittering black obsidian. Above the parapets swirled three dark batlike creatures: the Furies. I got the feeling they were waiting for us.

'I suppose it's too late to turn back,' Grover said wistfully.

'We'll be okay.' I tried to sound confident.

'Maybe we should search some of the other places first,'

Grover suggested. 'Like, Elysium, for instance . . .'

'Come on, goat boy.' Annabeth grabbed his arm.

Grover yelped. His trainers sprouted wings and his legs shot forward, pulling him away from Annabeth. He landed flat on his back in the grass.

'Grover,' Annabeth chided. 'Stop messing around.'

'But I didn't –'

He yelped again. His shoes were flapping like crazy now. They levitated off the ground and started dragging him away from us.

'Maia!' he yelled, but the magic word seemed to have no effect. 'Maia, already! 911! Help!'

I got over being stunned and made a grab for Grover's hand, but too late. He was picking up speed, skidding downhill like a bobsled.

We ran after him.

Annabeth shouted, 'Untie the shoes!'

It was a smart idea, but I guess it's not so easy when your shoes are pulling you along feet-first at full speed. Grover tried to sit up, but he couldn't get close to the laces.

We kept after him, trying to keep him in sight as he zipped between the legs of spirits who chattered at him in annoyance.

I was sure Grover was going to barrel straight through the gates of Hades's palace, but his shoes veered sharply to the right and dragged him in the opposite direction.

The slope got steeper. Grover picked up speed. Annabeth and I had to sprint to keep up. The cavern walls narrowed on either side, and I realized we'd entered some kind of side tunnel. No black grass or trees now, just rock underfoot, and the dim light of the stalactites above.

'Grover!' I yelled, my voice echoing. 'Hold on to something!'

'What?' he yelled back.

He was grabbing at gravel, but there was nothing big enough to slow him down.

The tunnel got darker and colder. The hairs on my arms bristled. It smelled evil down here. It made me think of things I shouldn't even know about – blood spilled on an ancient stone altar, the foul breath of a murderer.

Then I saw what was ahead of us, and I stopped dead in my tracks.

The tunnel widened into a huge dark cavern, and in the middle was a chasm the size of a city block.

Grover was sliding straight towards the edge.

'Come on, Percy!' Annabeth yelled, tugging at my wrist.

'But that's –'

'I know!' she shouted. 'The place you described in your dream! But Grover's going to fall if we don't catch him.' She was right, of course. Grover's predicament got me moving again.

He was yelling, clawing at the ground, but the winged shoes kept dragging him towards the pit, and it didn't look like we could possibly get to him in time.

What saved him were his hooves.

The flying sneakers had always been a loose fit on him, and finally Grover hit a big rock and the left shoe came flying off. It sped into the darkness, down into the chasm.

The right shoe kept tugging him along, but not as fast. Grover was able to slow himself down by grabbing on to the big rock and using it like an anchor.

He was three metres from the edge of the pit when we caught him and hauled him back up the slope. The other winged shoe tugged itself off, circled around us angrily and kicked our heads in protest before flying off into the chasm to join its twin.

We all collapsed, exhausted, on the obsidian gravel. My limbs felt like lead. Even my backpack seemed heavier, as if somebody had filled it with rocks.

Grover was scratched up pretty bad. His hands were bleeding. His eyes had gone slit-pupilled, goat style, the way they did whenever he was terrified.

'I don't know how . . .' he panted. 'I didn't . . .'

'Wait,' I said. 'Listen.'

I heard something – a deep whisper in the darkness.

Another few seconds, and Annabeth said, 'Percy, this place –'

'Shh.' I stood.

The sound was getting louder, a muttering, evil voice from far, far below us. Coming from the pit.

Grover sat up. 'Wh – what's that noise?'

Annabeth heard it too, now. I could see it in her eyes. 'Tartarus. The entrance to Tartarus.'

I uncapped Anaklusmos.

The bronze sword expanded, gleaming in the darkness, and the evil voice seemed to falter, just for a moment, before resuming its chant.

I could almost make out words now, ancient, ancient words, older even than Greek. As if . . .

'Magic,' I said.

'We have to get out of here,' Annabeth said.

Together, we dragged Grover to his hooves and started back up the tunnel. My legs wouldn't move fast enough. My backpack weighed me down. The voice got louder and angrier behind us, and we broke into a run.

Not a moment too soon.

A cold blast of wind pulled at our backs, as if the entire pit were inhaling. For a terrifying moment, I lost ground, my feet slipping in the gravel. If we'd been any closer to the edge, we would've been sucked in.

We kept struggling forward, and finally reached the top of the tunnel, where the cavern widened out into the Fields of Asphodel. The wind died. A wail of outrage echoed from deep in the tunnel. Something was not happy we'd got away.

'What *was* that?' Grover panted, when we'd collapsed in the relative safety of a black poplar grove. 'One of Hades's pets?'

Annabeth and I looked at each other. I could tell she was nursing an idea, probably the same one she'd got during the taxi ride to L.A., but she was too scared to share it. That was enough to terrify me.

I capped my sword, put the pen back in my pocket. 'Let's keep going.' I looked at Grover. 'Can you walk?'

He swallowed. 'Yeah, sure. I never liked those shoes, anyway.'

He tried to sound brave about it, but he was trembling as badly as Annabeth and I were. Whatever was in that pit was nobody's pet. It was unspeakably old and powerful. Even Echidna hadn't given me that feeling. I was almost relieved to turn my back on that tunnel and head towards the palace of Hades.

Almost.

The Furies circled the parapets, high in the gloom. The outer walls of the fortress glittered black, and the two-storey-tall bronze gates stood wide open.

Up close, I saw that the engravings on the gates were scenes of death. Some were from modern times – an atomic bomb exploding over a city, a trench filled with gas mask-wearing soldiers, a line of African famine victims waiting with empty bowls – but all of them looked as if they'd been etched into the bronze thousands of years ago. I wondered if I was looking at prophecies that had come true.

Inside the courtyard was the strangest garden I'd ever seen. Multicoloured mushrooms, poisonous shrubs and weird luminous plants grew without sunlight. Precious jewels made up for the lack of flowers, piles of rubies as big as my fist, clumps of raw diamonds. Standing here and there like frozen party guests were Medusa's garden statues, petrified children, satyrs and centaurs, all smiling grotesquely.

In the centre of the garden was an orchard of pome-granate trees, their orange blooms neon bright in the dark. 'The garden of Persephone,' Annabeth said. 'Keep walking.'

I understood why she wanted to move on. The tart smell of those pomegranates was almost overwhelming. I had a sudden desire to eat them, but then I remembered the story of Persephone. One bite of Underworld food, and we would never be able to leave. I pulled Grover away to keep him from picking a big juicy one.

We walked up the steps of the palace, between black columns, through a black marble portico and into the house of Hades. The entry hall had a polished bronze floor, which seemed to boil in the reflected torchlight. There was no ceiling, just the cavern roof, far above. I guess they never had to worry about rain down here.

Every side doorway was guarded by a skeleton in military gear. Some wore Greek armour, some British redcoat uniforms, some camouflage with tattered American flags on the shoulders. They carried spears or muskets or M-16s. None of them bothered us, but their hollow eye sockets followed us as we walked down the hall, towards the big set of doors at the opposite end.

Two U.S. Marine skeletons guarded the doors. They grinned down at us, rocket-propelled grenade launchers held across their chests.

'You know,' Grover mumbled, 'I bet Hades doesn't have trouble with door-to-door salesmen.'

My backpack weighed a ton now. I couldn't figure out why. I wanted to open it, check to see if I had somehow picked up a stray bowling ball, but this wasn't the time.

'Well, guys,' I said. 'I suppose we should . . . knock?'

A hot wind blew down the corridor, and the doors swung open. The guards stepped aside.

'I guess that means *"entrez,"*,' Annabeth said.

The room inside looked just like in my dream, except this time the throne of Hades was occupied.

He was the third god I'd met, but the first who really struck me as godlike.

He was at least three metres tall, for one thing, and dressed in black silk robes and a crown of braided gold. His skin was albino white, his hair shoulder-length and jet black. He wasn't bulked up like Ares, but he radiated power. He lounged on his throne of fused human bones, looking lithe, graceful and dangerous as a panther.

I immediately felt like he should be giving the orders. He knew more than I did. He should be my master. Then I told myself to snap out of it.

Hades's aura was affecting me, just as Ares's had. The Lord of the Dead resembled pictures I'd seen of Adolph Hitler, or Napoleon, or the terrorist leaders who direct suicide bombers. Hades had the same intense eyes, the same kind of mesmerizing, evil charisma.

'You are brave to come here, Son of Poseidon,' he said in an oily voice. 'After what you have done to me, very brave indeed. Or perhaps you are simply very foolish.'

Numbness crept into my joints, tempting me to lie down and just take a little nap at Hades's feet. Curl up here and sleep forever.

I fought the feeling and stepped forward. I knew what I had to say. 'Lord and Uncle, I come with two requests.'

Hades raised an eyebrow. When he sat forward in his throne, shadowy faces appeared in the folds of his black robes, faces of torment, as if the garment were stitched of trapped souls from the Fields of Punishment, trying to get out. The ADHD part of me wondered, off-task, whether the rest of his clothes were made the same way. What horrible things would you have to do in your life to get woven into Hades's underwear?

'Only two requests?' Hades said. 'Arrogant child. As if you have not already taken enough. Speak, then. It amuses me not to strike you dead yet.'

I swallowed. This was going about as well as I'd feared.

I glanced at the empty, smaller throne next to Hades's. It was shaped like a black flower, gilded with gold. I wished Queen Persephone were here. I recalled something in the myths about how she could calm her husband's moods. But it was summer. Of course, Persephone would be above in the world of light with her mother, the goddess of agriculture Demeter. Her visits, not the tilt of the earth, created the seasons.

Annabeth cleared her throat. Her finger prodded me in the back.

'Lord Hades,' I said. 'Look, sir, there can't be a war among the gods. It would be . . . bad.'

'Really bad,' Grover added helpfully.

'Return Zeus's master bolt to me,' I said. 'Please, sir. Let me carry it to Olympus.'

Hades's eyes grew dangerously bright. 'You dare keep up this pretence, after what you have done?'

I glanced back at my friends. They looked as confused as I was.

'Um . . . Uncle,' I said. 'You keep saying "after what I've done". What exactly have I done?'

The throne room shook with a tremor so strong they probably felt it upstairs in Los Angeles. Debris fell from the cavern ceiling. Doors burst open all along the walls, and skeletal warriors marched in, hundreds of them, from every time period and nation in Western civilization. They lined the perimeter of the room, blocking the exits.

Hades bellowed, 'Do you think I *want* war, godling?'

I wanted to say, *Well, these guys don't look like peace activists.* But I thought that might be a dangerous answer.

'You are the Lord of the Dead,' I said carefully. 'A war would expand your kingdom, right?'

'A typical thing for my brothers to say! Do you think I need more subjects? Did you not see the sprawl of Asphodel?'

'Well . . .'

'Have you any idea how much my kingdom has swollen in this past century alone, how many subdivisions I've had to open?'

I opened my mouth to respond, but Hades was on a roll now.

'More security ghouls,' he moaned. 'Traffic problems at the judgment pavilion. Double overtime for the staff. I used to be a rich god, Percy Jackson. I control all the precious metals under the earth. But my expenses!'

'Charon wants a pay raise,' I blurted, just remembering

the fact. As soon as I said it, I wished I could sew up my mouth.

'Don't get me started on Charon!' Hades yelled. 'He's been impossible ever since he discovered Italian suits! Problems everywhere, and I've got to handle all of them personally. The commute time alone from the palace to the gates is enough to drive me insane! And the dead just keep arriving. *No*, godling. I need no help getting subjects! *I* did not ask for this war.'

'But you took Zeus's master bolt.'

'Lies!' More rumbling. Hades rose from his throne, towering to the height of a football goalpost. 'Your father may fool Zeus, boy, but I am not so stupid. I see his plan.'

'His plan?'

'*You* were the thief on the winter solstice,' he said. 'Your father thought to keep you his little secret. He directed you into the throne room on Olympus. You took the master bolt *and* my helmet. Had I not sent my Fury to discover you at Yancy Academy, Poseidon might have succeeded in hiding his scheme to start a war. But now you have been forced into the open. You will be exposed as Poseidon's thief, and I will have my helmet back!'

'But . . .' Annabeth spoke. I could tell her mind was going a million miles an hour. 'Lord Hades, your helmet of darkness is missing, too?'

'Do not play innocent with me, girl. You and the satyr have been helping this hero – coming here to threaten me in Poseidon's name, no doubt – to bring me an ultimatum. Does Poseidon think I can be blackmailed into supporting him?'

'No!' I said. 'Poseidon didn't – I didn't –'

'I have said nothing of the helmet's disappearance,' Hades snarled, 'because I had no illusions that anyone on Olympus would offer me the slightest justice, the slightest help. I can ill afford for word to get out that my most powerful weapon of fear is missing. So I searched for you myself, and when it was clear you were coming to me to deliver your threat, I did not try to stop you.'

'You didn't try to stop us? But –'

'Return my helmet now, or I will stop death,' Hades threatened. 'That is my counter-proposal. I will open the earth and have the dead pour back into the world. I will make your lands a nightmare. And you, Percy Jackson – *your* skeleton will lead my army out of Hades.'

The skeletal soldiers all took one step forward, making their weapons ready.

At that point, I probably should have been terrified. The strange thing was, I felt offended. Nothing gets me angrier than being accused of something I didn't do. I've had a lot of experience with that.

'You're as bad as Zeus,' I said. 'You think I stole from you? That's why you sent the Furies after me?'

'Of course,' Hades said.

'And the other monsters?'

Hades curled his lip. 'I had nothing to do with them. I wanted no quick death for you – I wanted you brought before me alive so you might face every torture in the Fields of Punishment. Why do you think I let you enter my kingdom so easily?'

'Easily?'

'Return my property!'

'But I don't have your helmet. I came for the master bolt.'

'Which you already possess!' Hades shouted. 'You came here with it, little fool, thinking you could you threaten me!'

'But I didn't!'

'Open your pack, then.'

A horrible feeling struck me. The weight in my backpack, like a bowling ball. It couldn't be . . .

I slung it off my shoulder and unzipped it. Inside was a sixty-centimetre-long metal cylinder, spiked on both ends, humming with energy.

'Percy,' Annabeth said. 'How —'

'I — I don't know. I don't understand.'

'You heroes are always the same,' Hades said. 'Your pride makes you foolish, thinking you could bring such a weapon before me. I did not ask for Zeus's master bolt, but since it is here, you will yield it to me. I am sure it will make an excellent bargaining tool. And now . . . my helmet. Where is it?'

I was speechless. I had no helmet. I had no idea how the master bolt had got into my backpack. I wanted to think Hades was pulling some kind of trick. Hades was the bad guy. But suddenly the world turned sideways. I realized I'd been played with. Zeus, Poseidon and Hades had been set at each other's throats by someone else. The master bolt had been in the backpack, and I'd got the backpack from . . .

'Lord Hades, wait,' I said. 'This is all a mistake.'

'A mistake?' Hades roared.

The skeletons aimed their weapons. From high above, there was a fluttering of leathery wings, and the three Furies swooped down to perch on the back of their master's throne. The one with Mrs Dodds's face grinned at me eagerly and flicked her whip.

'There is no mistake,' Hades said. 'I know why you have come – I know the *real* reason you brought the bolt. You came to bargain for *her*.'

Hades loosed a ball of gold fire from his palm. It exploded on the steps in front of me, and there was my mother, frozen in a shower of gold, just as she was at the moment when the Minotaur began to squeeze her to death.

I couldn't speak. I reached out to touch her, but the light was as hot as a bonfire.

'Yes,' Hades said with satisfaction. 'I took her. I knew, Percy Jackson, that you would come to bargain with me eventually. Return my helmet, and perhaps I will let her go. She is not dead, you know. Not yet. But if you displease me, that will change.'

I thought about the pearls in my pocket. Maybe they could get me out of this. If I could just get my mom free . . .

'Ah, the pearls,' Hades said, and my blood froze. 'Yes, my brother and his little tricks. Bring them forth, Percy Jackson.'

My hand moved against my will and brought out the pearls.

'Only three,' Hades said. 'What a shame. You do realize each only protects a single person. Try to take your mother, then, little godling. And which of your friends will you leave behind to spend eternity with me? Go on. Choose. Or give me the backpack and accept my terms.'

I looked at Annabeth and Grover. Their faces were grim.

'We were tricked,' I told them. 'Set up.'

'Yes, but why?' Annabeth asked. 'And the voice in the pit –'

'I don't know yet,' I said. 'But I intend to ask.'

'Decide, boy!' Hades yelled.

'Percy.' Grover put his hand on my shoulder. 'You can't give him the bolt.'

'I know that.'

'Leave me here,' he said. 'Use the third pearl on your mom.'

'No!'

'I'm a satyr,' Grover said. 'We don't have souls like humans do. He can torture me until I die, but he won't get me forever. I'll just be reincarnated as a flower or something. It's the best way.'

'No.' Annabeth drew her bronze knife. 'You two go on. Grover, you have to protect Percy. You have to get your searcher's licence and start your quest for Pan. Get his mom out of here. I'll cover you. I plan to go down fighting.'

'No way,' Grover said. 'I'm staying behind.'

'Think again, goat boy,' Annabeth said.

'Stop it, both of you!' I felt like my heart was being ripped in two. They had both been with me through so much. I remembered Grover dive-bombing Medusa in the statue garden, and Annabeth saving us from Cerberus; we'd survived Hephaestus's Waterland ride, the St Louis Arch, the Lotus Casino. I had spent thousands of miles worried that I'd be betrayed by a friend, but these friends would never do that. They had done nothing but save me, over and over, and now they wanted to sacrifice their lives for my mom.

'I know what to do,' I said. 'Take these.'

I handed them each a pearl.

Annabeth said, 'But, Percy . . .'

I turned and faced my mother. I desperately wanted to sacrifice myself and use the last pearl on her, but I knew what she would say. She would never allow it. I had to get the bolt back to Olympus and tell Zeus the truth. I had to stop the war. She would never forgive me if I saved her instead. I thought about the prophecy made at Half-Blood Hill what seemed like a million years ago. *You will fail to save what matters most in the end.*

'I'm sorry,' I told her. 'I'll be back. I'll find a way.'

The smug look on Hades's face faded. He said, 'Godling . . . ?'

'I'll find your helmet, Uncle,' I told him. 'I'll return it. Remember about Charon's pay raise.'

'Do not defy me –'

'And it wouldn't hurt to play with Cerberus once in a while. He likes red rubber balls.'

'Percy Jackson, you will not –'

I shouted, 'Now, guys!'

We smashed the pearls at our feet. For a scary moment, nothing happened.

Hades yelled, 'Destroy them!'

The army of skeletons rushed forward, swords out, guns clicking to full automatic. The Furies lunged, their whips bursting into flame.

Just as the skeletons opened fire, the pearl exploded at my feet with a burst of green light and a gust of fresh sea wind. I was encased in a milky white sphere, which was starting to float off the ground.

Annabeth and Grover were right behind me. Spears and bullets sparked harmlessly off the pearl bubbles as we floated up. Hades yelled with such rage, the entire fortress shook and I knew it was not going to be a peaceful night in L.A.

'Look up!' Grover yelled. 'We're going to crash!'

Sure enough, we were racing right towards the stalactites, which I figured would pop our bubbles and skewer us.

'How do you control these things?' Annabeth shouted.

'I don't think you do!' I shouted back.

We screamed as the bubbles slammed into the ceiling and . . . Darkness.

Were we dead?

No, I could still feel the racing sensation. We were going up, right through solid rock as easily as an air bubble in water. That was the power of the pearls, I realized – *What belongs to the sea will always return to the sea.*

For a few moments, I couldn't see anything outside the smooth walls of my sphere, then my pearl broke through on the ocean floor. The two other milky spheres, Annabeth and Grover, kept pace with me as we soared upward through the water. And *ker-blam!*

We exploded on the surface, in the middle of Los Angeles Bay, knocking a surfer off his board with an indignant, 'Dude!'

I grabbed Grover and hauled him over to a lifebuoy. I caught Annabeth and dragged her over too. A curious shark was circling us, a great white about three metres long.

I said, 'Beat it.'

The shark turned and raced away.

The surfer screamed something about bad mushrooms and paddled away from us as fast as he could.

Somehow, I knew what time it was: early morning, June 21, the day of the summer solstice.

In the distance, Los Angeles was on fire, plumes of smoke rising from neighbourhoods all over the city. There had been an earthquake, all right, and it was Hades's fault. He was probably sending an army of the dead after me right now.

But at the moment, the Underworld wasn't my biggest problem.

I had to get to shore. I had to get Zeus's thunderbolt back to Olympus. Most of all, I had to have a serious conversation with the god who'd tricked me.

20 ⚡ I BATTLE MY JERK RELATIVE

A Coast Guard boat picked us up, but they were too busy to keep us for long, or to wonder how three kids in street clothes had got out into the middle of the bay. There was a disaster to mop up. Their radios were jammed with distress calls.

They dropped us off at the Santa Monica pier with towels around our shoulders and water bottles that said I'M A JUNIOR COAST GUARD! and sped off to save more people.

Our clothes were sopping wet, even mine. When the Coast Guard boat had appeared, I'd silently prayed they wouldn't pick me out of the water and find me perfectly dry, which might've raised some eyebrows. So I'd willed myself to get soaked. Sure enough, my usual waterproof magic had abandoned me. I was also barefoot, because I'd given my shoes to Grover. Better the Coast Guard wonder why one of us was barefoot than wonder why one of us had hooves.

After reaching dry land, we stumbled down the beach, watching the city burn against a beautiful sunrise. I felt as if I'd just come back from the dead – which I had. My backpack was heavy with Zeus's master bolt. My heart was even heavier from seeing my mother.

'I don't believe it,' Annabeth said. 'We went all that way –'

'It was a trick,' I said. 'A strategy worthy of Athena.'

'Hey,' she warned.

'You get it, don't you?'

She dropped her eyes, her anger fading. 'Yeah. I get it.'

'Well, I don't!' Grover complained. 'Would somebody –'

'Percy . . .' Annabeth said. 'I'm sorry about your mother. I'm so sorry. . . .'

I pretended not to hear her. If I talked about my mother, I was going to start crying like a little kid.

'The prophecy was right,' I said. '"You shall go west and face the god who has turned." But it wasn't Hades. Hades didn't want war between the Big Three. Someone else pulled off the theft. Someone stole Zeus's master bolt, and Hades's helmet, and framed me because I'm Poseidon's kid. Poseidon will get blamed by both sides. By sundown today, there will be a three-way war. And I'll have caused it.'

Grover shook his head, mystified. 'But who would be that sneaky? Who would want war that bad?'

I stopped in my tracks, looking down the beach. 'Gee, let me think.'

There he was, waiting for us, in his black leather duster and his sunglasses, an aluminum baseball bat propped on his shoulder. His motorcycle rumbled beside him, its headlight turning the sand red.

'Hey, kid,' Ares said, seeming genuinely pleased to see me. 'You were supposed to die.'

'You tricked me,' I said. '*You* stole the helmet and the master bolt.'

Ares grinned. 'Well, now, I didn't steal them personally. Gods taking each other's symbols of power – that's a big no-no. But you're not the only hero in the world who can run errands.'

'Who did you use? Clarisse? She was there at the winter solstice.'

The idea seemed to amuse him. 'Doesn't matter. The point is, kid, you're impeding the war effort. See, you've got to die in the Underworld. Then Old Seaweed will be mad at Hades for killing you. Corpse Breath will have Zeus's master bolt, so Zeus'll be mad at *him*. And Hades is still looking for this . . .'

From his pocket he took out a ski cap – the kind bank robbers wear – and placed it between the handlebars of his bike. Immediately, the cap transformed into an elaborate bronze war helmet.

'The helmet of darkness,' Grover gasped.

'Exactly,' Ares said. 'Now where was I? Oh yeah, Hades will be mad at both Zeus and Poseidon, because he doesn't know who took this. Pretty soon, we got a nice little three-way slugfest going.'

'But they're your family!' Annabeth protested.

Ares shrugged. 'Best kind of war. Always the bloodiest. Nothing like watching your relatives fight, I always say.'

'You gave me the backpack in Denver,' I said. 'The master bolt was in there the whole time.'

'Yes and no,' Ares said. 'It's probably too complicated for your little mortal brain to follow, but the backpack is the master bolt's sheath, just morphed a bit. The bolt is connected to it, sort of like that sword you got, kid. It always returns to your pocket, right?'

I wasn't sure how Ares knew about that, but I guess a god of war had to make it his business to know about weapons.

'Anyway,' Ares continued, 'I tinkered with the magic a bit, so the bolt would only return to the sheath once you reached the Underworld. You get close to Hades . . . Bingo, you got mail. If you died along the way – no loss. I still had the weapon.'

'But why not just keep the master bolt for yourself?' I said. 'Why send it to Hades?'

Ares got a twitch in his jaw. For a moment, it was almost as if he were listening to another voice, deep inside his head. 'Why didn't I . . . yeah . . . with that kind of fire-power . . .'

He held the trance for one second . . . two seconds . . .

I exchanged nervous looks with Annabeth.

Ares's face cleared. 'I didn't want the trouble. Better to have you caught redhanded, holding the thing.'

'You're lying,' I said. 'Sending the bolt to the Underworld wasn't your idea, was it?'

'Of course it was!' Smoke drifted up from his sunglasses, as if they were about to catch fire.

'You didn't order the theft,' I guessed. 'Someone else sent a hero to steal the two items. Then, when Zeus sent you to hunt him down, you caught the thief. But you didn't turn him over to Zeus. Something convinced you to let him go.

You kept the items until another hero could come along and complete the delivery. That thing in the pit is ordering you around.'

'I am the god of war! I take orders from no one! I don't have dreams!'

I hesitated. 'Who said anything about dreams?'

Ares looked agitated, but he tried to cover it with a smirk.

'Let's get back to the problem at hand, kid. You're alive. I can't have you taking that bolt to Olympus. You just might get those hardheaded idiots to listen to you. So I've got to kill you. Nothing personal.'

He snapped his fingers. The sand exploded at his feet and out charged a wild boar, even larger and uglier than the one whose head hung above the door of cabin seven at Camp Half-Blood. The beast pawed the sand, glaring at me with beady eyes as it lowered its razor-sharp tusks and waited for the command to kill.

I stepped into the surf. 'Fight me yourself, Ares.'

He laughed, but I heard a little edge to his laughter . . . an uneasiness. 'You've only got one talent, kid, running away. You ran from the Chimera. You ran from the Underworld. You don't have what it takes.'

'Scared?'

'In your adolescent dreams.' But his sunglasses were starting to melt from the heat of his eyes. 'No direct involvement. Sorry, kid. You're not at my level.'

Annabeth said, 'Percy, run!'

The giant boar charged.

But I was done running from monsters. Or Hades, or Ares, or anybody.

As the boar rushed me, I uncapped my pen and sidestepped. Riptide appeared in my hands. I slashed upward. The boar's severed right tusk fell at my feet, while the disoriented animal charged into the sea.

I shouted, 'Wave!'

Immediately, a wave surged up from nowhere and engulfed the boar, wrapping around it like a blanket. The beast squealed once in terror. Then it was gone, swallowed by the sea.

I turned back to Ares. 'Are you going to fight me now?' I asked. 'Or are you going to hide behind another pet pig?'

Ares's face was purple with rage. 'Watch it, kid. I could turn you into –'

'A cockroach,' I said. 'Or a tapeworm. Yeah, I'm sure. That'd save you from getting your godly hide whipped, wouldn't it?'

Flames danced along the top of his glasses. 'Oh, man, you are really asking to be smashed into a grease spot.'

'If I lose, turn me into anything you want. Take the bolt. If I win, the helmet and the bolt are mine and *you* have to go away.'

Ares sneered.

He swung the baseball bat off his shoulder. 'How would you like to get smashed: classic or modern?'

I showed him my sword.

'That's cool, dead boy,' he said. 'Classic it is.' The

baseball bat changed into a huge, two-handed sword. The hilt was a large silver skull with a ruby in its mouth.

'Percy,' Annabeth said. 'Don't do this. He's a god.'

'He's a coward,' I told her.

She swallowed. 'Wear this, at least. For luck.'

She took off her necklace, with her five years' worth of camp beads and the ring from her father, and tied it around my neck.

'Reconciliation,' she said. 'Athena and Poseidon together.'

My face felt a little warm, but I managed a smile. 'Thanks.'

'And take this,' Grover said. He handed me a flattened tin can that he'd probably been saving in his pocket for a thousand miles. 'The satyrs stand behind you.'

'Grover . . . I don't know what to say.'

He patted me on the shoulder. I stuffed the tin can in my back pocket.

'You all done saying goodbye?' Ares came towards me, his black leather duster trailing behind him, his sword glinting like fire in the sunrise. 'I've been fighting for eternity, kid. My strength is unlimited and I cannot die. What have you got?'

A smaller ego, I thought, but I said nothing. I kept my feet in the surf, backing into the water up to my ankles. I thought back to what Annabeth had said at the Denver diner, so long ago: *Ares has strength. That's all he has. Even strength has to bow to wisdom sometimes.*

He cleaved downward at my head, but I wasn't there.

My body thought for me. The water seemed to push me into the air and I catapulted over him, slashing as I came down. But Ares was just as quick. He twisted, and the strike that should've caught him directly in the spine was deflected off the end of his sword hilt.

He grinned. 'Not bad, not bad.'

He slashed again and I was forced to jump onto dry land. I tried to sidestep, to get back to the water, but Ares seemed to know what I wanted. He outmanoeuvred me, pressing so hard I had to put all my concentration on not getting sliced into pieces. I kept backing away from the surf. I couldn't find any openings to attack. His sword had a reach a metre longer than Anaklusmos.

Get in close, Luke had told me once, back in our sword class. *When you've got the shorter blade, get in close.*

I stepped inside with a thrust, but Ares was waiting for that. He knocked my blade out of my hands and kicked me in the chest. I went airborne – fifteen, maybe twenty metres. I would've broken my back if I hadn't crashed into the soft sand of a dune.

'Percy!' Annabeth yelled. 'Cops!'

I was seeing double. My chest felt like it had just been hit with a battering ram, but I managed to get to my feet.

I couldn't look away from Ares for fear he'd slice me in half, but out of the corner of my eye I saw red lights flashing on the shoreline boulevard. Car doors were slamming.

'There, officer!' somebody yelled. 'See?'

A gruff cop voice: 'Looks like that kid on TV . . . what the heck . . .'

'That guy's armed,' another cop said. 'Call for backup.'

I rolled to one side as Ares's blade slashed the sand.

I ran for my sword, scooped it up, and launched a swipe at Ares's face, only to find my blade deflected again.

Ares seemed to know exactly what I was going to do the moment before I did it.

I stepped back towards the surf, forcing him to follow.

'Admit it, kid,' Ares said. 'You got no hope. I'm just toying with you.'

My senses were working overtime. I now understood what Annabeth had said about ADHD keeping you alive in battle. I was wide awake, noticing every little detail.

I could see where Ares was tensing. I could tell which way he would strike. At the same time, I was aware of Annabeth and Grover, ten metres to my left. I saw a second cop car pulling up, siren wailing. Spectators, people who had been wandering the streets because of the earthquake, were starting to gather. Among the crowd, I thought I saw a few who were walking with the strange, trotting gait of disguised satyrs. There were shimmering forms of spirits, too, as if the dead had risen from Hades to watch the battle. I heard the flap of leathery wings circling somewhere above.

More sirens.

I stepped further into the water, but Ares was fast. The tip of his blade ripped my sleeve and grazed my forearm.

A police voice on a megaphone said, 'Drop the guns! Set them on the ground. Now!'

Guns?

I looked at Ares's weapon, and it seemed to be flickering; sometimes it looked like a shotgun, sometimes a two-handed sword. I didn't know what the humans were seeing in my hands, but I was pretty sure it wouldn't make them like me.

Ares turned to glare at our spectators, which gave me a moment to breathe. There were five police cars now, and a line of officers crouching behind them, pistols trained on us.

'This is a private matter!' Ares bellowed. 'Be gone!'

He swept his hand, and a wall of red flame rolled across the patrol cars. The police barely had time to dive for cover before their vehicles exploded. The crowd behind them scattered, screaming.

Ares roared with laughter. 'Now, little hero. Let's add you to the barbecue.'

He slashed. I deflected his blade. I got close enough to strike, tried to fake him out with a feint, but my blow was knocked aside. The waves were hitting me in the back now. Ares was up to his thighs, wading in after me.

I felt the rhythm of the sea, the waves growing larger as the tide rolled in, and suddenly I had an idea. *Little waves*, I thought. And the water behind me seemed to recede. I was holding back the tide by force of will, but tension was building, like carbonation behind a cork.

Ares came towards me, grinning confidently. I lowered my blade, as if I were too exhausted to go on. *Wait for it*, I told the sea. The pressure now was almost lifting me off my feet. Ares raised his sword. I released the tide and jumped, rocketing straight over Ares on a wave.

A two-metre wall of water smashed him full in the face, leaving him cursing and sputtering with a mouth full of seaweed. I landed behind him with a splash and feinted towards his head, as I'd done before. He turned in time to raise his sword, but this time he was disoriented, he didn't anticipate the trick. I changed direction, lunged to the side and stabbed Riptide straight down into the water, sending the point through the god's heel.

The roar that followed made Hades's earthquake look like a minor event. The very sea was blasted back from Ares, leaving a wet circle of sand fifteen metres wide.

Ichor, the golden blood of the gods, flowed from a gash in the war god's boot. The expression on his face was beyond hatred. It was pain, shock, complete disbelief that he'd been wounded.

He limped towards me, muttering ancient Greek curses. Something stopped him.

It was as if a cloud covered the sun, but worse. Light faded. Sound and colour drained away. A cold, heavy presence passed over the beach, slowing time, dropping the temperature to freezing and making me feel like life was hopeless, fighting was useless.

The darkness lifted.

Ares looked stunned.

Police cars were burning behind us. The crowd of spectators had fled. Annabeth and Grover stood on the beach, in shock, watching the water flood back around Ares's feet, his glowing golden ichor dissipating in the tide.

Ares lowered his sword.

'You have made an enemy, godling,' he told me. 'You have sealed your fate. Every time you raise your blade in battle, every time you hope for success, you will feel my curse. Beware, Perseus Jackson. Beware.'

His body began to glow.

'Percy!' Annabeth shouted. 'Don't watch!'

I turned away as the god Ares revealed his true immortal form. I somehow knew that if I looked, I would disintegrate into ashes.

The light died.

I looked back. Ares was gone. The tide rolled out to reveal Hades's bronze helmet of darkness. I picked it up and walked towards my friends.

But before I got there, I heard the flapping of leathery wings. Three evil-looking grandmothers with lace hats and fiery whips drifted down from the sky and landed in front of me.

The middle Fury, the one who had been Mrs Dodds, stepped forward. Her fangs were bared, but for once she didn't look threatening. She looked more disappointed, as if she'd been planning to have me for supper, but had decided I might give her indigestion.

'We saw the whole thing,' she hissed. 'So . . . it truly was not you?'

I tossed her the helmet, which she caught in surprise.

'Return that to Lord Hades,' I said. 'Tell him the truth. Tell him to call off the war.'

She hesitated, then ran a forked tongue over her green, leathery lips. 'Live well, Percy Jackson. Become a true hero.

Because if you do not, if you ever come into my clutches again . . .'

She cackled, savouring the idea. Then she and her sisters rose on their bat's wings, fluttered into the smoke-filled sky and disappeared.

I joined Grover and Annabeth, who were staring at me in amazement.

'Percy . . .' Grover said. 'That was so incredibly . . .'

'Terrifying,' said Annabeth.

'Cool!' Grover corrected.

I didn't feel terrified. I certainly didn't feel cool. I was tired and sore and completely drained of energy.

'Did you guys feel that . . . whatever it was?' I asked.

They both nodded uneasily.

'Must've been the Furies overhead,' Grover said.

But I wasn't so sure. Something had stopped Ares from killing me, and whatever could do that was a lot stronger than the Furies.

I looked at Annabeth, and an understanding passed between us. I knew now what was in that pit, what had spoken from the entrance of Tartarus.

I reclaimed my backpack from Grover and looked inside. The master bolt was still there. Such a small thing to almost cause World War III.

'We have to get back to New York,' I said. 'By tonight.'

'That's impossible,' Annabeth said, 'unless we —'

'Fly,' I agreed.

She stared at me. 'Fly, like, in an aeroplane, which you

were warned never to do lest Zeus strike you out of the sky, *and* carrying a weapon that has more destructive power than a nuclear bomb?'

'Yeah,' I said. 'Pretty much exactly like that. Come on.'

⚡ I SETTLE
MY TAB

It's funny how humans can wrap their mind around things and fit them into their version of reality. Chiron had told me that long ago. As usual, I didn't appreciate his wisdom until much later.

According to the L.A. news, the explosion at the Santa Monica beach had been caused when a crazy kidnapper fired a shotgun at a police car. He accidentally hit a gas main that had ruptured during the earthquake.

This crazy kidnapper (a.k.a. Ares) was the same man who had abducted me and two other adolescents in New York and brought us across country on a ten-day odyssey of terror.

Poor little Percy Jackson wasn't an international criminal, after all. He'd caused a commotion on that Greyhound bus in New Jersey trying to get away from his captor (and afterwards, witnesses would even swear they had seen the leather-clad man on the bus – 'Why didn't I remember him before?') The crazy man had caused the explosion in the St Louis Arch. After all, no kid could've done that. A concerned waitress in Denver had seen the man threatening his abductees outside her diner, gotten a friend to take a photo and notified the police. Finally, brave Percy Jackson

(I was beginning to like this kid) had stolen a gun from his captor in Los Angeles and battled him shotgun-to-rifle on the beach. Police had arrived just in time. But in the spectacular explosion, five police cars had been destroyed and the captor had fled. No fatalities had occurred. Percy Jackson and his two friends were safely in police custody.

The reporters fed us this whole story. We just nodded and acted tearful and exhausted (which wasn't hard), and played victimized kids for the cameras.

'All I want,' I said, choking back my tears, 'is to see my loving stepfather again. Every time I saw him on TV, calling me a delinquent punk, I knew ... somehow ... we would be okay. And I know he'll want to reward each and every person in this beautiful city of Los Angeles with a free major appliance from his store. Here's the phone number.' The police and reporters were so moved that they passed around the hat and raised money for three tickets on the next plane to New York.

I knew there was no choice but to fly. I hoped Zeus would cut me some slack, considering the circumstances. But it was still hard to force myself on board the flight.

Takeoff was a nightmare. Every spot of turbulence was scarier than a Greek monster. I didn't unclench my hands from the armrests until we touched down safely at La Guardia. The local press was waiting for us outside security, but we managed to evade them thanks to Annabeth, who lured them away in her invisible Yankees cap, shouting, 'They're over by the frozen yogurt! Come on!', then rejoined us at baggage claim.

We split up at the taxi stand. I told Annabeth and Grover to get back to Half-Blood Hill and let Chiron know what had happened. They protested, and it was hard to let them go after all we'd been through, but I knew I had to do this last part of the quest by myself. If things went wrong, if the gods didn't believe me . . . I wanted Annabeth and Grover to survive to tell Chiron the truth.

I hopped in a taxi and headed into Manhattan.

Thirty minutes later, I walked into the lobby of the Empire State Building.

I must have looked like a homeless kid, with my tattered clothes and my scraped-up face. I hadn't slept in at least twenty-four hours.

I went up to the guard at the front desk and said, 'Six hundredth floor.'

He was reading a huge book with a picture of a wizard on the front. I wasn't much into fantasy, but the book must've been good, because the guard took a while to look up. 'No such floor, kiddo.'

'I need an audience with Zeus.'

He gave me a vacant smile. 'Sorry?'

'You heard me.'

I was about to decide this guy was just a regular mortal, and I'd better run for it before he called the straitjacket patrol, when he said, 'No appointment, no audience, kiddo. Lord Zeus doesn't see anyone unannounced.'

'Oh, I think he'll make an exception.' I slipped off my backpack and unzipped the top.

The guard looked inside at the metal cylinder, not getting what it was for a few seconds. Then his face went pale. 'That isn't . . .'

'Yes, it is,' I promised. 'You want me take it out and —'

'No! No!' He scrambled out of his seat, fumbled around his desk for a key card, then handed it to me. 'Insert this in the security slot. Make sure nobody else is in the elevator with you.'

I did as he told me. As soon as the elevator doors closed, I slipped the key into the slot. The card disappeared and a new button appeared on the console, a red one that said 600.

I pressed it and waited, and waited.

Muzak played. 'Raindrops keep falling on my head . . .'

Finally, *ding*. The doors slid open. I stepped out and almost had a heart attack.

I was standing on a narrow stone walkway in the middle of the air. Below me was Manhattan, from the height of an aeroplane. In front of me, white marble steps wound up the spine of a cloud, into the sky. My eyes followed the stairway to its end, where my brain just could not accept what I saw.

Look again, my brain said.

We're looking, my eyes insisted. It's really there.

From the top of the clouds rose the decapitated peak of a mountain, its summit covered with snow. Clinging to the mountainside were dozens of multilevelled palaces – a city of mansions – all with white-columned porticos, gilded terraces and bronze braziers glowing with a thousand fires.

Roads wound crazily up to the peak, where the largest palace gleamed against the snow. Precariously perched gardens bloomed with olive trees and rosebushes. I could make out an open-air market filled with colourful tents, a stone amphitheatre built on one side of the mountain, a hippodrome and a coliseum on the other. It was an Ancient Greek city, except it wasn't in ruins. It was new, and clean, and colourful, the way Athens must've looked twenty-five hundred years ago.

This place can't be here, I told myself. The tip of a mountain hanging over New York City like a billion-ton asteroid? How could something like that be anchored above the Empire State Building, in plain sight of millions of people, and not get noticed?

But here it was. And here I was.

My trip through Olympus was a daze. I passed some giggling wood nymphs who threw olives at me from their garden. Hawkers in the market offered to sell me ambrosia-on-a-stick, and a new shield, and a genuine glitter-weave replica of the Golden Fleece, as seen on Hephaestus-TV. The nine muses were tuning their instruments for a concert in the park while a small crowd gathered – satyrs and naiads and a bunch of good-looking teenagers who might've been minor gods and goddesses. Nobody seemed worried about an impending civil war. In fact, everybody seemed in a festive mood. Several of them turned to watch me pass, and whispered to themselves.

I climbed the main road, towards the big palace at the peak. It was a reverse copy of the palace in the Underworld.

There, everything had been black and bronze. Here, everything glittered white and silver.

I realized Hades must've built his palace to resemble this one. He wasn't welcomed in Olympus except on winter solstice, so he'd built his own Olympus underground. Despite my bad experience with him, I felt a little sorry for the guy. To be banished from this place seemed really unfair. It would make anybody bitter.

Steps led up to a central courtyard. Past that, the throne room.

Room really isn't the right word. The place made Grand Central Station look like a broom closet. Massive columns rose to a domed ceiling, which was gilded with moving constellations.

Twelve thrones, built for beings the size of Hades, were arranged in an inverted U, just like the cabins at Camp Half-Blood. An enormous fire crackled in the central hearth pit. The thrones were empty except for two at the end: the head throne on the right, and the one to its immediate left. I didn't have to be told who the two gods were that were sitting there, waiting for me to approach. I came towards them, my legs trembling.

The gods were in giant human form, as Hades had been, but I could barely look at them without feeling a tingle, as if my body were starting to burn. Zeus, the Lord of the Gods, wore a dark blue, pinstriped suit. He sat on a simple throne of solid platinum. He had a well-trimmed beard, marbled grey and black like a storm cloud. His face was proud and handsome and grim, his eyes rainy grey.

As I got nearer to him, the air crackled and smelled of ozone.

The god sitting next to him was his brother, without a doubt, but he was dressed very differently. He reminded me of a beachcomber from Key West. He wore leather sandals, khaki Bermuda shorts, and a Tommy Bahama shirt with coconuts and parrots all over it. His skin was deeply tanned, his hands scarred like an old-time fisherman's. His hair was black, like mine. His face had that same brooding look that had always got me branded a rebel. But his eyes, sea-green like mine, were surrounded by sun-crinkles that told me he smiled a lot, too.

His throne was a deep-sea fisherman's chair. It was the simple swivelling kind, with a black leather seat and a built-in holster for a fishing pole. Instead of a pole, the holster held a bronze trident, flickering with green light around the tips.

The gods weren't moving or speaking, but there was tension in the air, as if they'd just finished an argument.

I approached the fisherman's throne and knelt at his feet. 'Father.' I dared not look up. My heart was racing. I could feel the energy emanating from the two gods. If I said the wrong thing, I had no doubt they could blast me into dust.

To my left, Zeus spoke. 'Should you not address the master of this house first, boy?'

I kept my head down, and waited.

'Peace, brother,' Poseidon finally said. His voice stirred my oldest memories: that warm glow I remembered as a baby, the sensation of this god's hand on my forehead. 'The boy defers to his father. This is only right.'

'You still claim him then?' Zeus asked menacingly. 'You claim this child whom you sired against our sacred oath?'

'I have admitted my wrongdoing,' Poseidon said. 'Now I would hear him speak.'

Wrongdoing.

A lump welled up in my throat. Was that all I was? A wrongdoing? The result of a god's mistake?

'I have spared him once already,' Zeus grumbled. 'Daring to fly through my domain . . . pah! I should have blasted him out of the sky for his impudence.'

'And risk destroying your own master bolt?' Poseidon asked calmly. 'Let us hear him out, brother.'

Zeus grumbled some more. 'I shall listen,' he decided. 'Then I shall make up my mind whether or not to cast this boy down from Olympus.'

'Perseus,' Poseidon said. 'Look at me.'

I did, and I wasn't sure what I saw in his face. There was no clear sign of love or approval. Nothing to encourage me. It was like looking at the ocean: some days, you could tell what mood it was in. Most days, though, it was unreadable, mysterious.

I got the feeling Poseidon really didn't know what to think of me. He didn't know whether he was happy to have me as a son or not. In a strange way, I was glad that Poseidon was so distant. If he'd tried to apologize, or told me he loved me, or even smiled, it would've felt fake. Like a human dad, making some lame excuse for not being around. I could live with that. After all, I wasn't sure about him yet, either.

'Address Lord Zeus, boy,' Poseidon told me. 'Tell him your story.'

So I told Zeus everything, just as it had happened. I took out the metal cylinder, which began sparking in the Sky God's presence, and laid it at his feet.

There was a long silence, broken only by the crackle of the hearth fire.

Zeus opened his palm. The lightning bolt flew into it. As he closed his fist, the metallic points flared with electricity, until he was holding what looked more like the classic thunderbolt, a five-metre javelin of arcing, hissing energy that made the hairs on my scalp rise.

'I sense the boy tells the truth,' Zeus muttered. 'But that Ares would do such a thing . . . it is most unlike him.'

'He is proud and impulsive,' Poseidon said. 'It runs in the family.'

'Lord?' I asked.

They both said, 'Yes?'

'Ares didn't act alone. Someone else – something else – came up with the idea.'

I described my dreams, and the feeling I'd had on the beach, that momentary breath of evil that had seemed to stop the world and made Ares back off from killing me.

'In the dreams,' I said, 'the voice told me to bring the bolt to the Underworld. Ares hinted that he'd been having dreams, too. I think he was being used, just as I was, to start a war.'

'You are accusing Hades, after all?' Zeus asked.

'No,' I said. 'I mean, Lord Zeus, I've been in the presence of Hades. This feeling on the beach was different. It was the same thing I felt when I got close to that pit. That was the entrance to Tartarus, wasn't it? Something powerful and evil is stirring down there ... something even older than the gods.'

Poseidon and Zeus looked at each other. They had a quick, intense discussion in Ancient Greek. I only caught one word. *Father.*

Poseidon made some kind of suggestion, but Zeus cut him off. Poseidon tried to argue. Zeus held up his hand angrily. 'We will speak of this no more,' Zeus said. 'I must go personally to purify this thunderbolt in the waters of Lemnos, to remove the human taint from its metal.'

He rose and looked at me. His expression softened just a fraction of a degree. 'You have done me a service, boy. Few heroes could have accomplished as much.'

'I had help, sir,' I said. 'Grover Underwood and Annabeth Chase —'

'To show you my thanks, I shall spare your life. I do not trust you, Perseus Jackson. I do not like what your arrival means for the future of Olympus. But for the sake of peace in the family, I shall let you live.'

'Um ... thank you, sir.'

'Do not presume to fly again. Do not let me find you

here when I return. Otherwise you shall taste this bolt. And it shall be your last sensation.'

Thunder shook the palace. With a blinding flash of lightning, Zeus was gone.

I was alone in the throne room with my father.

'Your uncle,' Poseidon sighed, 'has always had a flair for dramatic exits. I think he would've done well as the god of theatre.'

An uncomfortable silence.

'Sir,' I said, 'what was in that pit?'

Poseidon regarded me. 'Have you not guessed?'

'Kronos,' I said. 'The king of the Titans.'

Even in the throne room of Olympus, far away from Tartarus, the name *Kronos* darkened the room, made the hearth fire seem not quite so warm on my back.

Poseidon gripped his trident. 'In the First War, Percy, Zeus cut our father, Kronos, into a thousand pieces, just as Kronos had done to his own father, Ouranos. Zeus cast Kronos's remains into the darkest pit of Tartarus. The Titan army was scattered, their mountain fortress on Etna destroyed, their monstrous allies driven to the furthest corners of the earth. And yet Titans cannot die, any more than we gods can. Whatever is left of Kronos is still alive in some hideous way, still conscious in his eternal pain, still hungering for power.'

'He's healing,' I said. 'He's coming back.'

Poseidon shook his head. 'From time to time, over the aeons, Kronos has stirred. He enters men's nightmares and breathes evil thoughts. He wakens restless monsters from the depths. But to suggest he could rise from the pit is another thing.'

'That's what he intends, Father. That's what he said.'

Poseidon was silent for a long time.

'Lord Zeus has closed discussion on this matter. He will not allow talk of Kronos. You have completed your quest, child. That is all you need to do.'

'But –' I stopped myself. Arguing would do no good. It would very possibly anger the only god who I had on my side. 'As . . . as you wish, Father.'

A faint smile played on his lips. 'Obedience does not come naturally to you, does it?'

'No . . . sir.'

'I must take some blame for that, I suppose. The sea does not like to be restrained.' He rose to his full height and took up his trident. Then he shimmered and became the size of a regular man, standing directly in front of me. 'You must go, child. But first, know that your mother has returned.'

I stared at him, completely stunned. 'My mother?'

'You will find her at home. Hades sent her when you recovered his helmet. Even the Lord of Death pays his debts.'

My heart was pounding. I couldn't believe it. 'Do you . . . would you . . .'

I wanted to ask if Poseidon would come with me to see her, but then I realized that was ridiculous. I imagined loading the God of the Sea into a taxi and taking him to the Upper East Side. If he'd wanted to see my mom all these years, he would have. And there was Smelly Gabe to think about.

Poseidon's eyes took on a little sadness. 'When you return home, Percy, you must make an important choice. You will find a package waiting in your room.'

'A package?'

'You will understand when you see it. No one can choose your path, Percy. You must decide.'

I nodded, though I didn't know what he meant.

'Your mother is a queen among women,' Poseidon said wistfully. 'I had not met such a mortal woman in a thousand years. Still ... I am sorry you were born, child. I have brought you a hero's fate, and a hero's fate is never happy. It is never anything but tragic.'

I tried not to feel hurt. Here was my own dad, telling me he was sorry I'd been born. 'I don't mind, Father.'

'Not yet, perhaps,' he said. 'Not yet. But it was an unforgivable mistake on my part.'

'I'll leave you then.' I bowed awkwardly. 'I – I won't bother you again.'

I was five steps away when he called, 'Perseus.'

I turned.

There was a different light in his eyes, a fiery kind of pride. 'You did well, Perseus. Do not misunderstand me. Whatever else you do, know that you are mine. You are a true son of the Sea God.'

As I walked back through the city of the gods, conversations stopped. The muses paused their concert. People and satyrs and naiads all turned towards me, their faces filled with respect and gratitude and, as I passed, they knelt, as if I were some kind of hero.

* * *

Fifteen minutes later, still in a trance, I was back on the streets of Manhattan.

I caught a taxi to my mom's apartment, rang the doorbell, and there she was – my beautiful mother, smelling of peppermint and licorice, the weariness and worry evaporating from her face as soon as she saw me.

'Percy! Oh, thank goodness. Oh, my baby.'

She crushed the air right out of me. We stood in the hallway as she cried and ran her hands through my hair.

I'll admit it – my eyes were a little misty, too. I was shaking, I was so relieved to see her.

She told me she'd just appeared at the apartment that morning, scaring Gabe half out of his wits. She didn't remember anything since the Minotaur, and couldn't believe it when Gabe told her I was a wanted criminal, travelling across the country, blowing up national monuments. She'd been going out of her mind with worry all day because she hadn't heard the news. Gabe had forced her to go into work, saying she had a month's salary to make up and she'd better get started.

I swallowed back my anger and told her my own story. I tried to make it sound less scary than it had been, but that wasn't easy. I was just getting to the fight with Ares when Gabe's voice interrupted from the living room. 'Hey, Sally! That meat loaf done yet or what?'

She closed her eyes. 'He isn't going to be happy to see you, Percy. The store got half a million phone calls today from Los Angeles . . . something about free appliances.'

'Oh, yeah. About that . . .'

She managed a weak smile. 'Just don't make him angrier, all right? Come on.'

In the month I'd been gone, the apartment had turned into Gabeland. Garbage was ankle-deep on the carpet. The sofa had been reupholstered in beer cans. Dirty socks and underwear hung off the lampshades.

Gabe and three of his big goony friends were playing poker at the table.

When Gabe saw me, his cigar dropped out of his mouth. His face got redder than lava. 'You got nerve coming here, you little punk. I thought the police –'

'He's not a fugitive after all,' my mom interjected. 'Isn't that wonderful, Gabe?'

Gabe looked back and forth between us. He didn't seem to think my homecoming was so wonderful.

'Bad enough I had to give back your life insurance money, Sally,' he growled. 'Get me the phone. I'll call the cops.'

'Gabe, no!'

He raised his eyebrows. 'Did you just say *"no"*? You think I'm gonna put up with this punk again? I can still press charges against him for ruining my Camaro.'

'But –'

He raised his hand, and my mother flinched.

For the first time, I realized something. Gabe had hit my mother. I didn't know when, or how much. But I was sure he'd done it. Maybe it had been going on for years, when I wasn't around.

A balloon of anger started expanding in my chest. I came towards Gabe, instinctively taking my pen out of my pocket.

He just laughed. 'What, punk? You gonna write on me? You touch me, and you are going to jail forever, you understand?'

'Hey, Gabe,' his friend Eddie interrupted. 'He's just a kid.'

Gabe looked at him resentfully and mimicked in a falsetto voice: *Just a kid.*'

His other friends laughed like idiots.

'I'll be nice to you, punk.' Gabe showed me his tobacco-stained teeth. 'I'll give you five minutes to get your stuff and clear out. After that, I call the police.'

'Gabe!' my mother pleaded.

'He ran away,' Gabe told her. 'Let him stay gone.'

I was itching to uncap Riptide but, even if I did, the blade wouldn't hurt humans. And Gabe, by the loosest definition, was human.

My mother took my arm. 'Please, Percy. Come on. We'll go to your room.'

I let her pull me away, my hands still trembling with rage.

My room had been completely filled with Gabe's junk. There were stacks of used car batteries, a rotting bouquet of sympathy flowers with a card from somebody who'd seen his Barbara Walters interview.

'Gabe is just upset, honey,' my mother told me. 'I'll talk to him later. I'm sure it will work out.'

'Mom, it'll never work out. Not as long as Gabe's here.'

She wrung her hands nervously. 'I can . . . I'll take you to work with me for the rest of the summer. In the autumn, maybe there's another boarding school —'

'Mom.'

She lowered her eyes. 'I'm trying, Percy. I just . . . I need some time.'

A package appeared on my bed. At least, I could've sworn it hadn't been there a moment before.

It was a battered cardboard box about the right size to fit a basketball. The address on the mailing slip was in my own handwriting:

> The Gods
> Mount Olympus
> 600th Floor,
> Empire State Building
> New York, NY
>
> With best wishes,
> PERCY JACKSON

Over the top in black marker, in a man's clear bold print, was the address of our apartment, and the words: RETURN TO SENDER.

Suddenly I understood what Poseidon had told me on Olympus.

A package. A decision.

Whatever else you do, know that you are mine. You are a true son of the Sea God.

I looked at my mother. 'Mom, do you want Gabe gone?'

'Percy, it isn't that simple. I –'

'Mom, just tell me. That jerk has been hitting you. Do you want him gone or not?'

She hesitated, then nodded almost imperceptibly. 'Yes, Percy. I do. And I'm trying to get up my courage to tell him. But you can't do this for me. You can't solve my problems.'

I looked at the box.

I *could* solve her problem. I wanted to slice that package open, plop it on the poker table, and take out what was inside. I could start my very own statue garden, right there in the living room.

That's what a Greek hero would do in the stories, I thought. That's what Gabe deserves.

But a hero's story always ended in tragedy. Poseidon had told me that.

I remembered the Underworld. I thought about Gabe's spirit drifting forever in the Fields of Asphodel, or condemned to some hideous torture behind the barbed wire of the Fields of Punishment – an eternal poker game, sitting up to his waist in boiling oil listening to opera music. Did I have the right to send someone there? Even Gabe?

A month ago, I wouldn't have hesitated. Now . . .

'I can do it,' I told my mom. 'One look inside this box, and he'll never bother you again.'

She glanced at the package, and seemed to understand immediately. 'No, Percy,' she said, stepping away. 'You can't.'

'Poseidon called you a queen,' I told her. 'He said he hadn't met a woman like you in a thousand years.'

Her cheeks flushed. 'Percy –'

'You deserve better than this, Mom. You should go to college, get your degree. You can write your novel, meet a nice guy maybe, live in a nice house. You don't need to protect me any more by staying with Gabe. Let me get rid of him.'

She wiped a tear off her cheek. 'You sound so much like your father,' she said. 'He offered to stop the tide for me once. He offered to build me a palace at the bottom of the sea. He thought he could solve all my problems with a wave of his hand.'

'What's wrong with that?'

Her multicoloured eyes seemed to search inside me. 'I think you know, Percy. I think you're enough like me to understand. If my life is going to mean anything, I have to live it myself. I can't let a god take care of me . . . or my son. I have to . . . find the courage on my own. Your quest has reminded me of that.'

We listened to the sound of poker chips, swearing and ESPN from the living-room television.

'I'll leave the box,' I said. 'If he threatens you . . .'

She looked pale, but she nodded. 'Where will you go, Percy?'

'Half-Blood Hill.'

'For the summer . . . or forever?'

'I guess that depends.'

We locked eyes, and I sensed that we had an agreement.

We would see how things stood at the end of the summer.

She kissed my forehead. 'You'll be a hero, Percy. You'll be the greatest of all.'

I took one last look around my bedroom. I had a feeling I'd never see it again. Then I walked with my mother to the front door.

'Leaving so soon, punk?' Gabe called after me. 'Good riddance.'

I had one last twinge of doubt. How could I turn down the perfect chance to take revenge on him? I was leaving here without saving my mother.

'Hey, Sally,' he yelled. 'What about that meat loaf, huh?'

A steely look of anger flared in my mother's eyes, and I thought, just maybe, I was leaving her in good hands after all. Her own.

'The meat loaf is coming right up, dear,' she told Gabe. 'Meat loaf surprise.'

She looked at me, and winked.

The last thing I saw as the door swung closed was my mother staring at Gabe, as if she were contemplating how he would look as a garden statue.

22 ⚡ THE PROPHECY COMES TRUE

We were the first heroes to return alive to Half-Blood Hill since Luke, so of course everybody treated us as if we'd won some reality TV contest. According to camp tradition, we wore laurel wreaths to a big feast prepared in our honour, then led a procession down to the bonfire, where we got to burn the burial shrouds our cabins had made for us in our absence.

Annabeth's shroud was so beautiful – grey silk with embroidered owls – I told her it seemed a shame not to bury her in it. She punched me and told me to shut up.

Being the son of Poseidon, I didn't have any cabin mates, so the Ares cabin had volunteered to make my shroud. They'd taken an old bedsheet and painted smiley faces with X'ed-out eyes around the border, and the word LOSER painted really big in the middle.

It was fun to burn.

As Apollo's cabin led the sing-along and passed out toasted marshmallows, I was surrounded by my old Hermes cabinmates, Annabeth's friends from Athena and Grover's satyr buddies, who were admiring the brand new searcher's licence he'd received from the Council of Cloven Elders. The council had called Grover's performance on the quest

'Brave to the point of indigestion. Horns-and-whiskers above anything we have seen in the past.'

The only ones not in a party mood were Clarisse and her cabinmates, whose poisonous looks told me they'd never forgive me for disgracing their dad.

That was okay with me.

Even Dionysus's welcome-home speech wasn't enough to dampen my spirits. 'Yes, yes, so the little brat didn't get himself killed and now he'll have an even bigger head. Well, huzzah for that. In other announcements, there will be *no* canoe races this Saturday . . .'

I moved back into cabin three, but it didn't feel so lonely any more. I had my friends to train with during the day. At night, I lay awake and listened to the sea, knowing my father was out there. Maybe he wasn't quite sure about me yet, maybe he hadn't even wanted me born, but he was watching. And so far, he was proud of what I'd done.

As for my mother, she had a chance at a new life. Her letter arrived a week after I got back to camp. She told me Gabe had left mysteriously – disappeared off the face of the planet, in fact. She'd reported him missing to the police, but she had a funny feeling they would never find him.

On a completely unrelated subject, she'd sold her first life-size concrete sculpture, entitled *The Poker Player*, to a collector, through an art gallery in Soho. She'd got so much money for it, she'd put a deposit down on a new apartment and made a payment on her first term's tuition at NYU. The Soho gallery was clamouring for more of her work, which they called 'a huge step forward in super-ugly neorealism'.

But don't worry, my mom wrote. *I'm done with sculpture. I've disposed of that box of tools you left me. It's time for me to turn to writing.*

At the bottom, she wrote a P.S.: *Percy, I've found a good private school here in the city. I've put a deposit down to hold you a spot, in case you want to enrol for seventh grade. You could live at home. But if you want to go year-round at Half-Blood Hill, I'll understand.*

I folded the note carefully and set it on my bedside table. Every night before I went to sleep, I read it again, and I tried to decide how to answer her.

On the Fourth of July, the whole camp gathered at the beach for a fireworks display by cabin nine. Being Hephaestus's kids, they weren't going to settle for a few lame red-white-and-blue explosions. They'd anchored a barge offshore and loaded it with rockets the size of Patriot missiles. According to Annabeth, who'd seen the show before, the blasts would be sequenced so tightly they'd look like frames of animation across the sky. The finale was supposed to be a couple of thirty-metre-tall Spartan warriors who would crackle to life above the ocean, fight a battle, then explode into a million colours.

As Annabeth and I were spreading a picnic blanket, Grover showed up to tell us goodbye. He was dressed in his usual jeans and T-shirt and trainers, but in the last few weeks he'd started to look older, almost high-school age. His goatee had got thicker. He'd put on weight. His horns had grown a few centimetres at least, so he now had to wear his rasta cap all the time to pass as human.

'I'm off,' he said. 'I just came to say . . . well, you know.'

I tried to feel happy for him. After all, it wasn't every day a satyr got permission to go look for the great god Pan. But it was hard saying goodbye. I'd only known Grover a year, yet he was my oldest friend.

Annabeth gave him a hug. She told him to keep his fake feet on.

I asked him where he was going to search first.

'Kind of a secret,' he said, looking embarrassed. 'I wish you could come with me, guys, but humans and Pan . . .'

'We understand,' Annabeth said. 'You got enough tin cans for the trip?'

'Yeah.'

'And you remembered your reed pipes?'

'Jeez, Annabeth,' he grumbled. 'You're like an old mama goat.'

But he didn't really sound annoyed.

He gripped his walking stick and slung a backpack over his shoulder. He looked like any hitchhiker you might see on an American highway – nothing like the little runty boy I used to defend from bullies at Yancy Academy.

'Well,' he said, 'wish me luck.'

He gave Annabeth another hug. He clapped me on the shoulder, then headed back through the dunes.

Fireworks exploded to life overhead: Hercules killing

the Nemean lion, Artemis chasing the boar, George Washington (who, by the way, was a son of Athena) crossing the Delaware.

'Hey, Grover,' I called.

He turned at the edge of the woods.

'Wherever you're going – I hope they make good enchiladas.'

Grover grinned, and then he was gone, the trees closing around him.

'We'll see him again,' Annabeth said.

I tried to believe it. The fact that no searcher had ever come back in two thousand years . . . well, I decided not to think about that. Grover would be the first. He had to be.

July passed.

I spent my days devising new strategies for capture-the-flag and making alliances with the other cabins to keep the banner out of Ares's hands. I got to the top of the climbing wall for the first time without getting scorched by lava.

From time to time, I'd walk past the Big House, glance up at the attic windows and think about the Oracle. I tried to convince myself that its prophecy had come to completion.

You shall go west, and face the god who has turned.

Been there, done that – even though the traitor god had turned out to be Ares rather than Hades.

You shall find what was stolen, and see it safely returned.

Check. One master bolt delivered. One helmet of darkness back on Hades's oily head.

You shall be betrayed by one who calls you a friend.

This line still bothered me. Ares had pretended to be my friend, then betrayed me. That must be what the Oracle meant. . . .

And you shall fail to save what matters most, in the end.

I *had* failed to save my mom, but only because I'd let her save herself, and I knew that was the right thing.

So why was I still uneasy?

The last night of the summer session came all too quickly.

The campers had one last meal together. We burned part of our dinner for the gods. At the bonfire, the senior counsellors awarded the end-of-summer beads.

I got my own leather necklace, and when I saw the bead for my first summer, I was glad the firelight covered my blushing. The design was pitch black, with a sea-green trident shimmering in the centre.

'The choice was unanimous,' Luke announced. 'This bead commemorates the first son of the Sea God at this camp, and the quest he undertook into the darkest part of the Underworld to stop a war!'

The entire camp got to their feet and cheered. Even Ares's cabin felt obliged to stand. Athena's cabin steered Annabeth to the front so she could share in the applause.

I'm not sure I'd ever felt as happy or sad as I did at that moment. I'd finally found a family, people who cared about me and thought I'd done something right. And in the morning, most of them would be leaving for the year.

* * *

The next morning, I found a form letter on my bedside table.

I knew Dionysus must've filled it out, because he stubbornly insisted on getting my name wrong:

> Dear _____ Peter Johnson _____ ,
> If you intend to stay at Camp Half-Blood year-
> round, you must inform the Big House by noon
> today. If you do not announce your intentions,
> we will assume you have vacated your cabin or
> died a horrible death. Cleaning harpies will begin
> work at sundown. They will be authorized to eat
> any unregistered campers. All personal articles
> left behind will be incinerated in the lava pit.
>
> Have a nice day!
> Mr D (Dionysus)
> Camp Director, Olympian Council no.12

That's another thing about ADHD. Deadlines just aren't real to me until I'm staring one in the face. Summer was over, and I still hadn't answered my mother, or the camp, about whether I'd be staying. Now I had only a few hours to decide.

The decision should have been easy. I mean, nine months of hero training or nine months of sitting in a classroom – duh.

But there was my mom to consider. For the first time, I had the chance to live with her for a whole year, without Gabe. I had a chance be at home and knock around the city in my free time. I remembered what Annabeth had said so long ago on our quest: *The real world is where the monsters are. That's where you learn whether you're any good or not.*

I thought about the fate of Thalia, daughter of Zeus. I wondered how many monsters would attack me if I left Half-Blood Hill. If I stayed in one place for a whole school year, without Chiron or my friends around to help me, would my mother and I even survive until the next summer? That was assuming the spelling tests and five-paragraph essays didn't kill me. I decided I'd go down to the arena and do some sword practice. Maybe that would clear my head.

The campgrounds were mostly deserted, shimmering in the August heat. All the campers were in their cabins packing up, or running around with brooms and mops, getting ready for final inspection. Argus was helping some of the Aphrodite kids haul their Gucci suitcases and makeup kits over the hill where the camp's shuttle bus would be waiting to take them to the airport.

Don't think about leaving yet, I told myself. Just train.

I got to the sword-fighters' arena and found that Luke had had the same idea. His gym bag was plopped at the edge of the stage. He was working solo, whacking away at battle dummies with a sword I'd never seen before. It must've been a regular steel blade, because he was slashing the dummies' heads right off, stabbing through their straw-stuffed guts. His orange counsellor's shirt was dripping with sweat. His expression was so intense, his life might've really been in danger. I watched, fascinated, as he disembowelled the whole row of dummies, hacking off limbs and basically reducing them to a pile of straw and armour.

They were only dummies, but I still couldn't help being awed by Luke's skill. The guy was an incredible fighter. It made me wonder, again, how he possibly could've failed at his quest.

Finally, he saw me, and stopped mid-swing. 'Percy.'

'Um, sorry,' I said, embarrassed. 'I just –'

'It's okay,' he said, lowering his sword. 'Just doing some last-minute practice.'

'Those dummies won't be bothering anybody any more.'

Luke shrugged. 'We build new ones every summer.'

Now that his sword wasn't swirling around, I could see something odd about it. The blade was two different types of metal – one edge bronze, the other steel.

Luke noticed me looking at it. 'Oh, this? New toy. This is Backbiter.'

'Backbiter?'

Luke turned the blade in the light so it glinted wickedly. 'One side is celestial bronze. The other is tempered steel. Works on mortals and immortals both.'

I thought about what Chiron had told me when I started my quest – that a hero should never harm mortals unless absolutely necessary.

'I didn't know they could make weapons like that.'

'*They* probably can't,' Luke agreed. 'It's one of a kind.'

He gave me a tiny smile, then slid the sword into its scabbard. 'Listen, I was going to come looking for you.

What do you say we go down to the woods one last time, look for something to fight?'

I don't know why I hesitated. I should've felt relieved that Luke was being so friendly. Ever since I'd got back from the quest, he'd been acting a little distant. I was afraid he might resent me for all the attention I'd had.

'You think it's a good idea?' I asked. 'I mean –'

'Aw, come on.' He rummaged in his gym bag and pulled out a six-pack of Cokes. 'Drinks are on me.'

I stared at the Cokes, wondering where the heck he'd got them. There were no regular mortal sodas at the camp store. No way to smuggle them in, unless you talked to a satyr maybe.

Of course, the magic dinner goblets would fill with anything you want, but it just didn't taste the same as a real Coke, straight out of the can.

Sugar and caffeine. My willpower crumbled.

'Sure,' I decided. 'Why not?'

We walked down to the woods and kicked around for some kind of monster to fight, but it was too hot. All the monsters with any sense must've been taking siestas in their nice cool caves.

We found a shady spot by the creek where I'd broken Clarisse's spear during my first capture the flag game. We sat on a big rock, drank our Cokes and watched the sunlight in the woods.

After a while Luke said, 'You miss being on a quest?'

'With monsters attacking me every metre? Are you kidding?'

Luke raised an eyebrow.

'Yeah, I miss it,' I admitted. 'You?'

A shadow passed over his face.

I was used to hearing from the girls how good-looking Luke was, but at the moment, he looked weary, and angry, and not at all handsome. His blond hair was grey in the sunlight. The scar on his face looked deeper than usual. I could imagine him as an old man.

'I've lived at Half-Blood Hill year-round since I was fourteen,' he told me. 'Ever since Thalia . . . well, you know. I trained, and trained, and trained. I never got to be a normal teenager, out there in the real world. Then they threw me one quest, and when I came back, it was like, 'Okay, ride's over. Have a nice life.''

He crumpled his Coke can and threw it into the creek, which really shocked me. One of the first things you learn at Camp Half-Blood is: don't litter. You'll hear from the nymphs and the naiads. They'll get even. You'll crawl into bed one night and find your sheets filled with centipedes and mud.

'The heck with laurel wreaths,' Luke said. 'I'm not going to end up like those dusty trophies in the Big House attic.'

'You make it sound like you're leaving.'

Luke gave me a twisted smile. 'Oh, I'm leaving, all right, Percy. I brought you down here to say goodbye.'

He snapped his fingers. A small fire burned a hole in the ground at my feet. Out crawled something glistening black, about the size of my hand. A scorpion.

I started to go for my pen.

'I wouldn't,' Luke cautioned. 'Pit scorpions can jump up to five metres. Its stinger can pierce right through your clothes. You'll be dead in sixty seconds.'

'Luke, what —'

Then it hit me.

You will be betrayed by one who calls you a friend.

'You,' I said.

He stood calmly and brushed off his jeans.

The scorpion paid him no attention. It kept its beady black eyes on me, clamping its pincers as it crawled onto my shoe.

'I saw a lot out there in the world, Percy,' Luke said. 'Didn't you feel it — the darkness gathering, the monsters growing stronger? Didn't you realize how useless it all is? All the heroics — being pawns of the gods. They should've been overthrown thousands of years ago, but they've hung on, thanks to us half-bloods.'

I couldn't believe this was happening.

'Luke . . . you're talking about our parents,' I said.

He laughed. 'That's supposed to make me love them? Their precious "Western civilization" is a disease, Percy. It's killing the world. The only way to stop it is to burn it to the ground, start over with something more honest.'

'You're as crazy as Ares.'

His eyes flared. 'Ares is a fool. He never realized the true master he was serving. If I had time, Percy, I could explain. But I'm afraid you won't live that long.'

The scorpion crawled onto my trouser leg.

There had to be a way out of this. I needed time to think.

'Kronos,' I said. 'That's who you serve.'

The air got colder.

'You should be careful with names,' Luke warned.

'Kronos got you to steal the master bolt and the helmet. He spoke to you in your dreams.'

Luke's eye twitched. 'He spoke to you, too, Percy. You should've listened.'

'He's brainwashing you, Luke.'

'You're wrong. He showed me that my talents are being wasted. You know what my quest was two years ago, Percy? My father, Hermes, wanted me to steal a golden apple from the Garden of the Hesperides and return it to Olympus. After all the training I'd done, *that* was the best he could think up.'

'That's not an easy quest,' I said. 'Hercules did it.'

'Exactly,' Luke said. 'Where's the glory in repeating what others have done? All the gods know how to do is replay their past. My heart wasn't in it. The dragon in the garden gave me this –' he pointed angrily at his scar – 'and when I came back, all I got was pity. I wanted to pull Olympus down stone by stone right then, but I bided my time. I began to dream of Kronos. He convinced me to steal something worthwhile, something no hero had ever had the courage to take. When we went on that winter-solstice field trip, while the other campers were asleep, I sneaked into the throne room and took Zeus's master bolt right from his chair. Hades's helmet of darkness, too. You wouldn't believe how easy it was. The Olympians are so arrogant; they never dreamed someone would dare steal from them. Their security is horrible. I was halfway across New Jersey before I heard the storms rumbling, and I knew they'd discovered my theft.'

The scorpion was sitting on my knee now, staring at me with its glittering eyes. I tried to keep my voice level. 'So why didn't you bring the items to Kronos?'

Luke's smile wavered. 'I ... I got overconfident. Zeus sent out his sons and daughters to find the stolen bolt – Artemis, Apollo, my father, Hermes. But it was Ares who caught me. I could have beaten him, but I wasn't careful enough. He disarmed me took the items of power, threatened to return them to Olympus and burn me alive. Then Kronos's voice came to me, and told me what to say. I put the idea in Ares's head about a great war between the gods. I said all he had to do was hide the items away for a while and watch the others fight. Ares got a wicked gleam in his eyes. I knew he was hooked. He let me go, and I returned to Olympus before anyone noticed my absence.' Luke drew his new sword. He ran his thumb down the flat of the blade, as if he were hypnotized by its beauty. 'Afterwards, the Lord of the Titans ... h-he punished me with nightmares. I swore not to fail again. Back at Camp Half-Blood, in my dreams, I was told that a second hero would arrive, one who could be tricked into taking the bolt and the helmet the rest of the way – from Ares down to Tartarus.'

'*You* summoned the hellhound, that night in the forest.'

'We had to make Chiron think the camp wasn't safe for

you, so he would start you on your quest. We had to confirm his fears that Hades was after you. And it worked.'

'The flying shoes were cursed,' I said. 'They were supposed to drag me and the backpack into Tartarus.'

'And they would have, if you'd been wearing them. But you gave them to the satyr, which wasn't part of the plan. Grover messes up everything he touches. He even confused the curse.'

Luke looked down at the scorpion, which was now sitting on my thigh. 'You should have died in Tartarus, Percy. But don't worry, I'll leave you with my little friend to set things right.'

'Thalia gave her life to save you,' I said, gritting my teeth. 'And this is how you repay her?'

'Don't speak of Thalia!' he shouted. 'The gods *let* her die! That's one of the many things they will pay for.'

'You're being used, Luke. You and Ares both. Don't listen to Kronos.'

'*I've* been used?' Luke's voice turned shrill. 'Look at yourself. What has your dad ever done for you? Kronos will rise. You've only delayed his plans. He will cast the Olympians into Tartarus and drive humanity back to their caves. All except the strongest – the ones who serve him.'

'Call off the bug,' I said. 'If you're so strong, fight me yourself.'

Luke smiled. 'Nice try, Percy. But I'm not Ares. You can't bait me. My lord is waiting, and he's got plenty of quests for me to undertake.'

'Luke –'

'Goodbye, Percy. There is a new Golden Age coming. You won't be part of it.'

He slashed his sword in an arc and disappeared in a ripple of darkness.

The scorpion lunged.

I swatted it away with my hand and uncapped my sword. The thing jumped at me and I cut it in half in midair.

I was about to congratulate myself until I looked down at my hand. My palm had a huge red welt, oozing and smoking with yellow guck. The thing had got me after all.

My ears pounded. My vision went foggy. The water, I thought. It had healed me before.

I stumbled to the creek and submerged my hand, but nothing seemed to happen. The poison was too strong. My vision was getting dark. I could barely stand up.

Sixty seconds, Luke had told me.

I had to get back to camp. If I collapsed out here, my body would be dinner for a monster. Nobody would ever know what had happened.

My legs felt like lead. My forehead was burning. I stumbled towards the camp, and the nymphs stirred from their trees.

'Help,' I croaked. 'Please . . .'

Two of them took my arms, pulling me along. I remember making it to the clearing, a counsellor shouting for help, a centaur blowing a conch horn.

Then everything went black.

* * *

I woke with a drinking straw in my mouth. I was sipping something that tasted like liquid chocolate-chip cookies. Nectar.

I opened my eyes.

I was propped up in bed in the sickroom of the Big House, my right hand bandaged like a club. Argus stood guard in the corner. Annabeth sat next to me, holding my nectar glass and dabbing a washcloth on my forehead.

'Here we are again,' I said.

'You idiot,' Annabeth said, which is how I knew she was overjoyed to see me conscious. 'You were green and turning grey when we found you. If it weren't for Chiron's healing . . .'

'Now, now,' Chiron's voice said. 'Percy's constitution deserves some of the credit.'

He was sitting near the foot of my bed in human form, which was why I hadn't noticed him yet. His lower half was magically compacted into the wheelchair, his upper half dressed in a coat and tie. He smiled, but his face looked weary and pale, the way it did when he'd been up all night grading Latin papers.

'How are you feeling?' he asked.

'Like my insides have been frozen, then microwaved.'

'Apt, considering that was pit scorpion venom. Now you must tell me, if you can, exactly what happened.'

Between sips of nectar, I told them the story.

The room was quiet for a long time.

'I can't believe that Luke . . .' Annabeth's voice faltered. Her expression turned angry and sad. 'Yes. Yes, I *can* believe it. May the gods curse him . . . He was never the same after his quest.'

'This must be reported to Olympus,' Chiron murmured. 'I will go at once.'

'Luke is out there right now,' I said. 'I have to go after him.'

Chiron shook his head. 'No, Percy. The gods —'

'Won't even *talk* about Kronos,' I snapped. 'Zeus declared the matter closed!'

'Percy, I know this is hard. But you must not rush out for vengeance. You aren't ready.'

I didn't like it, but part of me suspected Chiron was right. One look at my hand, and I knew I wasn't going to be sword fighting any time soon. 'Chiron . . . your prophecy from the Oracle . . . it was about Kronos, wasn't it? Was I in it? And Annabeth?'

Chiron glanced nervously at the ceiling. 'Percy, it isn't my place —'

'You've been ordered not to talk to me about it, haven't you?'

His eyes were sympathetic, but sad. 'You will be a great hero, child. I will do my best to prepare you. But if I'm right about the path ahead of you . . .'

Thunder boomed overhead, rattling the windows.

'All right!' Chiron shouted. 'Fine!'

He sighed in frustration. 'The gods have their reasons, Percy. Knowing too much of your future is never a good thing.'

'We can't just sit back and do nothing,' I said.

'*We* will not sit back,' Chiron promised. 'But *you* must be careful. Kronos wants you to come unravelled. He wants your life disrupted, your thoughts clouded with fear and anger. Do not give him what he wants. Train patiently. Your time will come.'

'Assuming I live that long.'

Chiron put his hand on my ankle. 'You'll have to trust me, Percy. You will live. But first you must decide your path for the coming year. I cannot tell you the right choice . . .' I got the feeling that he had a very definite opinion, and it was taking all his willpower not to advise me. '. . . But you must decide whether to stay at Camp Half-Blood year-round, or return to the mortal world for seventh grade and be a summer camper. Think on that. When I get back from Olympus, you must tell me your decision.'

I wanted to protest. I wanted to ask him more questions. But his expression told me there could be no more discussion; he had said as much as he could.

'I'll be back as soon as I can,' Chiron promised. 'Argus will watch over you.'

He glanced at Annabeth. 'Oh, and, my dear . . . whenever you're ready, they're here.'

'Who's here?' I asked.

Nobody answered.

Chiron rolled himself out of the room. I heard the wheels of his chair clunk carefully down the front steps, two at a time.

Annabeth studied the ice in my drink.

'What's wrong?' I asked her.

'Nothing.' She set the glass on the table. 'I . . . just took your advice about something. You . . . um . . . need anything?'

'Yeah. Help me up. I want to go outside.'

'Percy, that isn't a good idea.'

I slid my legs out of bed. Annabeth caught me before I could crumple to the floor. A wave of nausea rolled over me.

Annabeth said, 'I told you . . .'

'I'm fine,' I insisted. I didn't want to lie in bed like an invalid while Luke was out there planning to destroy the Western world.

I managed a step forward. Then another, still leaning heavily on Annabeth. Argus followed us outside, but he kept his distance.

By the time we reached the porch, my face was beaded with sweat. My stomach had twisted into knots. But I had managed to make it all the way to the railing.

It was dusk. The camp looked completely deserted. The cabins were dark and the volleyball pit silent. No canoes cut the surface of the lake. Beyond the woods and the strawberry fields, the Long Island Sound glittered in the last light of the sun.

'What are you going to do?' Annabeth asked me.

'I don't know.'

I told her I got the feeling Chiron wanted me to stay year-round, to put in more individual training time, but I wasn't sure that's what I wanted. I admitted I'd feel bad about leaving her alone, though, with only Clarisse for company . . .

Annabeth pursed her lips, then said quietly, 'I'm going home for the year, Percy.'

I stared at her. 'You mean, to your dad's?'

She pointed towards the crest of Half-Blood Hill. Next to Thalia's pine tree, at the very edge of the camp's magical boundaries, a family stood silhouetted – two little children, a woman and a tall man with blond hair. They seemed to be waiting. The man was holding a backpack that looked like the one Annabeth had got from Waterland in Denver.

'I wrote him a letter when we got back,' Annabeth said. 'Just like you suggested. I told him . . . I was sorry. I'd come home for the school year if he still wanted me. He wrote back immediately. We decided . . . we'd give it another try.'

'That took guts.'

She pursed her lips. 'You won't try anything stupid during the school year, will you? At least . . . not without sending me an iris-message?'

I managed a smile. 'I won't go looking for trouble. I usually don't have to.'

'When I get back next summer,' she said, 'we'll hunt down Luke. We'll ask for a quest, but if we don't get approval, we'll sneak off and do it anyway. Agreed?'

'Sounds like a plan worthy of Athena.'

She held out her hand. I shook it.

'Take care, Seaweed Brain,' Annabeth told me. 'Keep your eyes open.'

'You too, Wise Girl.'

I watched her walk up the hill and join her family. She gave her father an awkward hug and looked back at the valley one last time. She touched Thalia's pine tree, then allowed herself to be led over the crest and into the mortal world.

For the first time at camp, I felt truly alone. I looked out at Long Island Sound and I remembered my father saying, *The sea does not like to be restrained.*

I made my decision.

I wondered, if Poseidon were watching, would he approve of my choice?

'I'll be back next summer,' I promised him. 'I'll survive until then. After all, I am your son.' I asked Argus to take me down to cabin three, so I could pack my bags for home.

Find out what happens next!

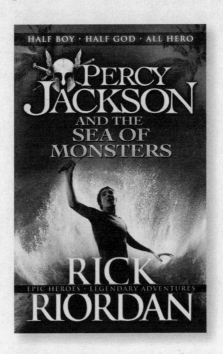

Turn over to read the
thrilling opening of

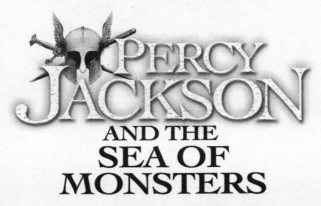

MY BEST FRIEND SHOPS FOR A WEDDING DRESS

My nightmare started like this.

I was standing on a deserted street in some little beach town. It was the middle of the night. A storm was blowing. Wind and rain ripped at the palm trees along the sidewalk. Pink and yellow stucco buildings lined the street, their windows boarded up. A block away, past a line of hibiscus bushes, the ocean churned.

Florida, I thought. Though I wasn't sure how I knew that. I'd never been to Florida.

Then I heard hooves clattering against the pavement. I turned and saw my friend Grover running for his life.

Yeah, I said *hooves*.

Grover is a satyr. From the waist up, he looks like a typical gangly teenager with a peach-fuzz goatee and a bad case of acne. He walks with a strange limp, but unless you happen to catch him without his trousers on (which I don't recommend), you'd never know there was anything un-human about him. Baggy jeans and fake feet hide the fact that he's got furry hindquarters and hooves.

Grover had been my best friend in sixth grade. He'd gone on this adventure with me and a girl named Annabeth to save the world, but I hadn't seen him since last July, when he set off alone on a dangerous quest — a quest no satyr had ever returned from.

Anyway, in my dream, Grover was hauling goat tail, holding his human shoes in his hands the way he does when he needs to move fast. He clopped past the little tourist shops and surfboard rental places. The wind bent the palm trees almost to the ground.

Grover was terrified of something behind him. He must've just come from the beach. Wet sand was caked in his fur. He'd escaped from somewhere. He was trying to get away from . . . something.

A bone-rattling growl cut through the storm. Behind Grover, at the far end of the block, a shadowy figure loomed. It swatted aside a street lamp, which burst in a shower of sparks.

Grover stumbled, whimpering in fear. He muttered to himself, *Have to get away. Have to warn them!*

I couldn't see what was chasing him, but I could hear it muttering and cursing. The ground shook as it got closer. Grover dashed around a street corner and faltered. He'd run into a dead-end courtyard full of shops. No time to back up. The nearest door had been blown open by the storm. The sign above the darkened display window read: ST AUGUSTINE BRIDAL BOUTIQUE.

Grover dashed inside. He dived behind a rack of wedding dresses.

The monster's shadow passed in front of the shop. I could smell the thing – a sickening combination of wet sheep wool and rotten meat and that weird sour body odour only monsters have, like a skunk that's been living off Mexican food.

Grover trembled behind the wedding dresses. The monster's shadow passed on.

Silence except for the rain. Grover took a deep breath. Maybe the thing was gone.

Then lightning flashed. The entire front of the store exploded, and a monstrous voice bellowed, 'MIIIIINE!'

I sat bolt upright, shivering in my bed.

There was no storm. No monster.

Morning sunlight filtered through my bedroom window.

I thought I saw a shadow flicker across the glass – a humanlike shape. But then there was a knock on my bedroom door – my mom called, 'Percy, you're going to be late' – and the shadow at the window disappeared.

It must've been my imagination. A fifth-storey window with a rickety old fire escape . . . there couldn't have been anyone out there.

'Come on, dear,' my mother called again. 'Last day of school. You should be excited! You've almost made it!'

'Coming,' I managed.

I felt under my pillow. My fingers closed reassuringly around the ballpoint pen I always slept with. I brought it out, studied the Ancient Greek writing engraved on the side: *Anaklusmos*. Riptide.

I thought about uncapping it, but something held me back. I hadn't used Riptide for so long . . .

Besides, my mom had made me promise not to use deadly weapons in the apartment after I'd swung a javelin the wrong way and taken out her china cabinet. I put Anaklusmos on my nightstand and dragged myself out of bed.

I got dressed as quickly as I could. I tried not to think

about my nightmare or monsters or the shadow at my window.

Have to get away. Have to warn them!

What had Grover meant?

I made a three-fingered claw over my heart and pushed outwards – an ancient gesture Grover had once taught me for warding off evil.

The dream couldn't have been real.

Last day of school. My mom was right, I should have been excited. For the first time in my life, I'd almost made it an entire year without getting expelled. No weird accidents. No fights in the classroom. No teachers turning into monsters and trying to kill me with poisoned cafeteria food or exploding homework. Tomorrow, I'd be on my way to my favourite place in the world – Camp Half-Blood.

Only one more day to go. Surely even I couldn't mess that up.

As usual, I didn't have a clue how wrong I was.

My mom made blue waffles and blue eggs for breakfast. She's funny that way, celebrating special occasions with blue food. I think it's her way of saying anything is possible. Percy can pass seventh grade. Waffles can be blue. Little miracles like that.

I ate at the kitchen table while my mom washed dishes. She was dressed in her work uniform – a starry blue skirt and a red-and-white striped blouse she wore to sell candy at Sweet on America. Her long brown hair was pulled back in a ponytail.

The waffles tasted great, but I guess I wasn't digging

in like I usually did. My mom looked over and frowned. 'Percy, are you all right?'

'Yeah . . . fine.'

But she could always tell when something was bothering me. She dried her hands and sat down across from me. 'School, or . . .'

She didn't need to finish. I knew what she was asking.

'I think Grover's in trouble,' I said, and I told her about my dream.

She pursed her lips. We didn't talk much about the *other* part of my life. We tried to live as normally as possible, but my mom knew all about Grover.

'I wouldn't be too worried, dear,' she said. 'Grover is a big satyr now. If there were a problem, I'm sure we would've heard from . . . from camp . . .' Her shoulders tensed as she said the word *camp*.

'What is it?' I asked.

'Nothing,' she said. 'I'll tell you what. This afternoon we'll celebrate the end of school. I'll take you and Tyson to Rockefeller Center – to that skateboard shop you like.'

Oh, man, that was tempting. We were always struggling with money. Between my mom's night classes and my private school tuition, we could never afford to do special stuff like shop for a skateboard. But something in her voice bothered me.

'Wait a minute,' I said. 'I thought we were packing me up for camp tonight.'

She twisted her dishcloth. 'Ah, dear, about that . . . I got a message from Chiron last night.'

My heart sank. Chiron was the activities director at Camp Half-Blood. He wouldn't contact us unless something serious was going on. 'What did he say?'

'He thinks . . . it might not be safe for you to come to camp just yet. We might have to postpone.'

'*Postpone?* Mom, how could it not be *safe*? I'm a half-blood! It's like the only safe place on earth for me!'

'Usually, dear. But with the problems they're having –'

'*What* problems?'

'Percy . . . I'm very, very sorry. I was hoping to talk to you about it this afternoon. I can't explain it all now. I'm not even sure Chiron can. Everything happened so suddenly.'

My mind was reeling. How could I *not* go to camp? I wanted to ask a million questions, but just then the kitchen clock chimed the half-hour.

My mom looked almost relieved. 'Seven thirty, dear. You should go. Tyson will be waiting.'

'But –'

'Percy, we'll talk this afternoon. Go on to school.'

That was the last thing I wanted to do, but my mom had this fragile look in her eyes – a kind of warning, like if I pushed her too hard she'd start to cry. Besides, she was right about my friend Tyson. I had to meet him at the subway station on time or he'd get upset. He was scared of travelling underground alone.

I gathered up my stuff, but I stopped in the doorway. 'Mom, this problem at camp. Does it . . . could it have anything to do with my dream about Grover?'

She wouldn't meet my eyes. 'We'll talk this afternoon, dear. I'll explain . . . as much as I can.'

Reluctantly, I told her goodbye. I jogged downstairs to catch the Number Two train.

I didn't know it at the time, but my mom and I would never get to have our afternoon talk.

In fact, I wouldn't be seeing home for a long, long time.

As I stepped outside, I glanced at the brownstone building across the street. Just for a second I saw a dark shape in the morning sunlight – a human silhouette against the brick wall, a shadow that belonged to no one.

Then it rippled and vanished.

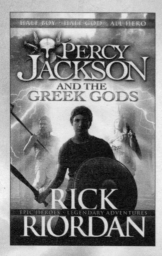

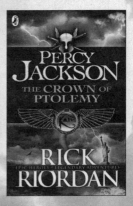

THE ADVENTURE
NEVER STOPS...

THE GREEK GODS ARE ALIVE AND KICKING!

They still fall in love with mortals and bear children with immortal blood in their veins. Those kids who learn the truth about their parentage must travel to Camp Half-Blood – a secret base dedicated to the training of demigods. From there, young heroes like Percy Jackson, the son of Poseidon, embark on dangerous quests to prove their bravery.

The Percy Jackson series:

PERCY JACKSON AND THE LIGHTNING THIEF
PERCY JACKSON AND THE SEA OF MONSTERS
PERCY JACKSON AND THE TITAN'S CURSE
PERCY JACKSON AND THE BATTLE OF THE LABYRINTH
PERCY JACKSON AND THE LAST OLYMPIAN

THE DEMIGOD FILES

PERCY JACKSON AND THE GREEK GODS
PERCY JACKSON AND THE GREEK HEROES

THE GODS OF EGYPT AWAKEN!

When an explosion shatters the ancient Rosetta Stone and unleashes Set, the Egyptian god of chaos, only Carter and Sadie Kane can save the day. Their terrifying quest takes the pair around the globe in search of the truth about their family's magical connection to the gods of Ancient Egypt.

The Kane Chronicles series:

THE RED PYRAMID
THE THRONE OF FIRE
THE SERPENT'S SHADOW

HEROES OF OLYMPUS

PERCY JACKSON IS BACK!

Join Percy and his friends from Camp Half-Blood as they face off against rival Roman demigods of Camp Jupiter, and set out on a deadly new mission: to prevent the all-powerful Earth Mother, Gaia, from awakening from her millennia-long sleep to bring about the end of the world.

The Heroes of Olympus series:

THE LOST HERO
THE SON OF NEPTUNE
THE MARK OF ATHENA
THE HOUSE OF HADES
THE BLOOD OF OLYMPUS

THE DEMIGOD DIARIES

MAGNUS CHASE

THE GODS OF ASGARD ARISE!

Magnus Chase has always run away from trouble, but trouble has a way of finding him. After being killed in battle with a fire giant, Magnus finds himself resurrected in Valhalla as one of the chosen warriors of the Norse god Odin. But now isn't a good time to be joining Odin's army. The gods of Asgard are preparing for Ragnarok – the Norse doomsday – and Magnus has a leading role . . .

The Magnus Chase series:

THE SWORD OF SUMMER

RICK RIORDAN

EPIC HEROES · LEGENDARY ADVENTURES

www.rickriordan.co.uk